It's Not Like It's a Secret

It's Not Like It's a Secret

MISA SUGIURA

HARPER TEEN
An Imprint of HarperCollinsPublishers

HarperTeen is an imprint of HarperCollins Publishers.

It's Not Like It's a Secret
Copyright © 2017 by Misa Sugiura
All rights reserved. Printed in the United States of America.
No part of this book may be used or reproduced in any manner whatsoever
without written permission except in the case of brief quotations embodied
in critical articles and reviews. For information address HarperCollins
Children's Books, a division of HarperCollins Publishers, 195 Broadway,
New York, NY 10007.
www.epicreads.com

Library of Congress Control Number: 2016961849
ISBN 978-0-06-247341-7

Typography by Torborg Davern
17 18 19 20 21   PC/LSCH   10 9 8 7 6 5 4 3 2 1
❖
First Edition

For Joan

1

"SANA, CHOTTO . . . HANASHI GA ARUN-YA-KEDO."

Uh-oh.

Something big is about to go down.

It's Sunday afternoon and we're almost ready to leave the beach at Lake Michigan, where I've begged Mom to take me for my birthday. It's just the two of us because Dad is away on business—he's always away on business—and I'm crouched at the edge of the water, collecting sea glass. I've decided I'm not leaving the beach until I've found sixteen pieces, one for each year. Sweet sixteen and never been kissed, but at least I'll have a handful of magic in my pocket. Sixteen surprises. Sixteen secret treasures I've found in the sand.

And now this: *hanashi ga arun'*.

Mom never asks if I want to "chat" unless she's actually

gearing up for a Serious Discussion. She walks over and stands next to me, but I'm too anxious to look up, so I continue picking through the sand as possible Serious Discussion Topics scroll through my head:

She's pregnant.

She has cancer.

She's making me go to Japan for the summer.

"It's about Dad," she says.

Dad's leaving us.

He's dying.

He—

"Dad got a new job with start-up company in California."

—what?

"It's the company called GoBotX," she says. "They make the robots for hospital surgery."

I don't care what the company makes.

"Did you say *California*?"

When I say Serious Discussion, I suppose I should really say Big Announcement Followed by Brief and Unhelpful Q&A Before Mom Closes Topic:

"How long have you known?"

"Dad applied last month. He signed contract today."

"Why didn't you tell me earlier?"

"No need."

"What do you mean, no need?"

She shrugs. "No need. Not your decision."

"But that's not fair!"

"'Fair' doesn't matter."

"But—"

"Complaining doesn't do any good."

"Are we all moving? When?"

"Dad will go in two weeks, at end of May. He will find a house to live, and we will go at end of June."

She doesn't know the answers to the rest of my questions: Where will we live, where will I go to school, what am I supposed to do all summer all by myself. Then she says, "No more questions. It is decided, so nothing we can do. Clean the sand off your feet before we get in the car."

We don't talk on the way home. Mom's not the type to apologize or ask questions like, "How does that make you feel?" My own unanswered questions swim in circles around the silence like giant schools of fish, chased by the most important question of all—the only one I can't ask.

When we get home, I go to my room to finish some homework. But before I start, I take out a lacquer box that Mom and Dad bought for me when we visited Japan seven years ago. It's a deep, rich orange red, and it has three cherry blossoms painted on it in real gold. Inside, I keep my pearl earrings, a picture of me with my best friend, Trish Campbell, when we were six, all the sea glass I've collected from trips to Lake Michigan, and a slip of paper with a phone number on it.

I pour in my new sea glass, take out the piece of paper, and stare at the numbers. They start with a San Francisco area code. Could this be the real reason we're moving?

The paper is small and narrow, almost like something I might pull out of a fortune cookie. Like if I turn it over, I'll find my fortune—my family's fortune—on the other side: Yes, these numbers are important. No, these numbers are meaningless. But of course the back of the paper is as blank as ever. I bury the phone number under the other things, put the box away, and lie down on my bed to think.

A few minutes later, Mom comes in and frowns when she sees me lying on my bed, staring at the ceiling. Mom is the most practical person I know. She doesn't sugarcoat things, and she doesn't look for a bright side. Which is okay right now, because a fake spiel about exciting new experiences, great weather, and new friends would just piss me off.

"I am sorry that you have to leave your friends," she says, not looking one bit sorry, "but the pouting doesn't make your life better. It just prevents you from doing your homeworks."

Then again, it probably wouldn't kill her to show a *little* sympathy. Also, she's totally off base about what's upsetting me. But since correcting her is out of the question, I just turn and face the wall.

"Jibun no koto bakkari kangaen'no yame-nasai. Chanto henji shina-sai."

I don't think I'm being selfish. But since "AAAGGGGH-HHH! I'M NOT BEING SELFISH!" is probably not the "proper reply" she's looking for, I just say, "I'm not pouting. I'm thinking."

"There is nothing to think about. If you want to think, you

can think of being grateful for a father who works so hard to get the good job."

"It's not that I'm not grateful—"

"Ever since he was teenager," she continues, "Dad dreamed of working for the Silicon Valley start-up. That's why he came to United States."

"But what about me? Don't *my* dreams count?" Okay, maybe now I'm being a little selfish. Especially since the truth is that I don't actually have what might be called dreams. What I have are more like hopes: Straight As. A love life. A crowd of real friends to hang out with. But it's also true that if I did have dreams, they wouldn't count anyway. Not to Mom.

"You are too young for the dream," she says. (See?)

I want to remind her that she just said Dad's start-up job was a teenage dream. But she has a conveniently short memory about things she's just said that contradict other things she's just said, so instead, I switch tracks. "What about *your* dreams?"

"My dream is not important."

"Ugh. Come on, Mom."

She crosses her arms. "My dream is to make the good family. I can do that in Wisconsin or California."

"Mom, why do you say stuff like that? Like, 'Oh, our lives are just going to change forever, no big deal.' It *is* a big deal! It's a *huge* deal!" I can hear myself getting screechy, but I can't help it. Dad changes our lives around without consulting anyone— well, without consulting me—and Mom just . . . lets it happen.

It would make anyone screechy.

"Shikkari shinasai," she snaps.

But I don't know if I'll ever be able to do that: gather myself into a tight little bundle with everything in its place—shikkari—like she wants. I put my head under my pillow.

She's quiet for so long that I begin to wonder if she's left the room. When I peek out from under the pillow, she's waiting for me, her face softer, even a little sad. "Gaman shinasai," she says, and walks away. *Gaman*. Endure. Bear it without complaining.

Her life's motto and my life's bane.

2

I'M UNDER ORDERS TO PACK ALL OF MY belongings into boxes labeled KEEP and THROW AWAY by the end of the week. Which is harder than you'd think, because who knew I had so much stuff? I'm drowning in a sea of books, old papers, and odds and ends that I've spent over a decade smushing into the corners of my closet, cramming into the back of my desk drawers, and piling on the edges of my bookshelf.

It started off easily enough:

My lacquer box: KEEP

Four Super Balls from who knows where or when: THROW AWAY

Collection of poems by Emily Dickinson, my favorite poet: KEEP

Assorted elementary school certificates: Perfect Attendance, Fourth Grade Math Olympiad Participant, etc.: THROW
AWAY

But now it's getting tricky, because some of the things I've
dug out have some messy feelings attached to them, and I'd
rather not go there right now.

Don't think. Just sort. The wedding picture that I found
in the attic last year and that Mom refuses to display because
it's "showing off." KEEP. The Hogwarts robe that I loved so
much, I wore it two Halloweens in a row. I'd meant to be
Hermione but everyone said I was (who else?) Cho Chang.
THROW AWAY. A cheap plastic vase left over from my thir-
teenth birthday party, which three girls skipped to go to the
movies instead. THROW AWAY.

Don't think.

As I toss the vase into the THROW AWAY box, a scrap of
fabric flutters out: a swim team ribbon that I found in the Glen
Lake Country Club parking lot when I was seven. Hmm. Now
that's a feeling I can do something about.

All the best families in Glen Lake belong to the Glen Lake
Country Club, which has a historic redbrick clubhouse, a lush
green golf course, and a lily-white membership. Back in grade
school, when Trish and I spent more time together, she used
to bring me with her to the club all the time during summer
vacation for barbecues and lazy afternoons at the pool. But in
high school, she became suddenly, dazzlingly popular. The
boys and queen bees started swarming, her Instagram filled

up with likes and pictures of people who barely acknowledged me in the halls, and our country club days became a thing of the past.

Don't get me wrong. It's not like she's been mean, or anything. Days might go by without her texting me, but she always answers my texts right away. She's usually too busy to hang out with me, but she's always apologetic. And even though it's painful to sit on the edges of her crowd at lunch, listening to stories about parties I haven't been invited to, it's not like anyone's ever asked me to leave the table.

When we used to see more of each other, Trish was always after me to "open up" and "spill everything." Which, whatever, she's an oversharer. For example, she texted me seconds after Toby Benton, her first boyfriend, put his hand up her shirt in eighth grade. (OMG I just let Toby touch my boob!! Under my shirt!! 😳🔥🔥🔥)

But whenever I thought about telling her anything important, I froze. Even now, when people talk at lunch about who wants to hook up with who, or who hopes their dad gets custody on the weekends because he's totally cool about drinking at the house—I feel relieved that no one's especially interested in me or my life. I don't want anyone poking around and freaking out about what's wrong with my family, what's wrong with me. Like what if I'd answered honestly the first time Trish asked me at the beginning of freshman year, "Sana, who do *you* like?"

"Well actually, Trish, I think I might have a crush on *you*."

Nope. Forget it. Not happening. I'm not even a hundred percent sure it's true, and life is already complicated enough.

But now . . . things have changed. I mean, we leave in three weeks, and I might never see her again. So I'm going to ask her to bring me to the first Glen Lake Country Club barbecue of the summer, for old times' sake. I've got nothing to lose, right? We'll get drunk together for the first and probably last time—I've never been drunk before—and maybe . . . maybe if all goes well, she'll get nostalgic, we'll bond again, and . . . and . . . something good will happen. I don't want to think too hard about what, exactly. But something good.

On Friday, I find Trish in the parking lot after school, sitting with her boyfriend, Daniel, on the hood of his car. Daniel is a big-shot football player, with a face like your favorite love song and a body like fireworks on the Fourth of July; sadly, though, he doesn't have the brains or a personality to match. His biggest claim to fame is that he got a Mustang for his six-teenth birthday—and one week and a six-pack of Milwaukee's Best later, he drove it into a tree and his dad gave him *another Mustang*.

When I ask Trish about the barbecue, it turns out she's already going with Daniel, but she seems excited to have me come, too.

"Oooooh!" she says. "We. Are going. To get. So. Wasted. Together. It'll be so much fun! And Daniel can drive us back to my house afterward." She snuggles up to him. "Right, honey?"

"Sorry, babe, but Drew and Brad are back from college and they're bringing a bottle of Jägermeister tomorrow night." As he says this, a couple of football bros walk by. "Did you hear that?" he shouts at them. "Jäger shots!" The three of them high-five each other and howl together like a pack of teenage werewolves, and for the millionth time, I wonder what Trish sees in him. Beyond the obvious, I mean.

When Daniel sees that Trish—thank goodness—is unmoved, he whines, "Come on, make someone else drive."

Trish rolls her eyes at me. Then she wraps herself around Daniel and says, "I'll make it worth your while," and whispers something to him. She starts nibbling his ear and kissing his neck, and pretty soon they're making out right in front of me, and I have to look away or I'll vomit. If she's using her womanly wiles to get her way, he seems to be falling for it—though from the sound of it she's having as much fun as he is.

But at least he seems to have agreed to drive.

Trish and Daniel arrive to collect me and my overnight bag at six o'clock on Saturday. I've persuaded Mom to let me go by reminding her of all the times I used to tag along with Trish's family to the club when I was younger. "Her parents will be there the whole time," I said, which is true.

The plan is to begin sneaking vodka from flasks during dinner, while the adults are too busy getting drunk themselves to care. Then we'll go to the golf course to finish up. I can hardly wait. All I ever hear about is how much fun it is to get drunk, and I am so ready to try it out and be part of Trish's life again, even if it's just for one night.

We arrive at dusk, and pretty soon Trish and I are on the patio with barbecue on our plates and orange juice (and vodka—shh!) in our cups, surrounded by a hive of popular girls. Minutes into my first drink, my face starts to feel warm, and Trish says, "Sana, are you okay?"

"What?"

"Your face is, like, turning red. Like you have a sunburn."

I rush to the bathroom to check the mirror. I'm flushed and my eyes look puffy, as if I'm having an allergic reaction. I'm about to start trying to remember what I've eaten when I take another look in the mirror and recognize someone: Mom. I look just like Mom when she has a glass of wine with dinner. Dad, too, come to think of it.

I realize it's the alcohol, and I don't dare take another sip. Plus my head is starting to throb, and I have a feeling it will get worse the more I drink. Great. Leave it to my parents to make it genetically impossible for me to fit in—as if my hair and eyes weren't enough to make me stand out in a crowd of white kids, now I can't even get drunk with everyone.

Trish makes sympathetic cooing sounds when I tell her I can't drink, but then something catches her eye, and she squeals. "Ooh, Sana, look—there's Mark Schiller! He told me when we got here that he thinks you look hot! I bet he's looking for you! Come on, let's go dance!"

She grabs my hand and drags me to the dance floor,

collecting members of the hive on the way. In a couple of minutes, the guys wander over as well. Trish vanishes for a moment, then reappears. And suddenly, despite my genetically enforced sobriety, I'm feeling pretty good. Pretty great, actually. I mean, look at me. Here I am dancing, surrounded by the cream of the social crop with Trish by my side and ignoring Daniel for once.

Then it gets even better. The first notes of that old Beach Boys version of "California Girls" start to play, and Trish shouts, "I requested this for you, California girl!" She gives me a hug while the entire hive shrieks, "Sanaaaa!" over the music, and now I feel positively giddy. I wonder if just that little bit of vodka and orange juice was enough to get me drunk, after all.

The Beach Boys begin cataloging the different girls in the United States—the hip East Coast girls and the Southern girls with sexy accents, and when they get to Midwest farmers' daughters, we all raise our arms and scream our Midwestern hearts out. We scream for good old-fashioned Midwestern values and hospitality, for prairies and cornfields, for the Heartland. *No matter what,* I vow, *I will always be a Midwesterner.* Things are pretty good here, really.

Soon, Trish decides it's time to get back to the business of eating and drinking. As we retrieve our plates and cups, Maddie Larssen turns to me and says, "Hey, Sana, you know during 'California Girls' when they were like, 'Midwest farmers' daughters' and you were all, 'Wooo!' like, super loud? That was so *cute!*"

"Well, I'll never get to do that again," I remind her. "I'll look like a freak if I yell for the Midwest when I'm living in California."

"Omigod, Sana, you look like a freak yelling for the Midwest now!" She giggles. Everyone laughs. "I mean, you do *not* look like a Midwest farmer's daughter!" A dense, cold fog blooms in my chest, and all I can do is stare.

"Oh, honey, we're not being mean. It's just so . . . sweet," Trish says. "It's like you forgot that you're like, Asian or whatever. I totally forget, too. But that's good, right? Like it doesn't matter that you're not white, you know? You're like, one of us!"

"I guess," I mumble.

Emily Whittaker puts her arm around me. "You're not mad, are you?"

"Yeah, I mean, it's not like we're being racist or anything," adds Trish. "It's just cute how you forgot. Come on, Sana, we love you!"

And with that, all the girls chime in: "We *love* you, Sana!" What can I do? I swallow my pride and give them a smile. *Gaman*. Hah. Mom would be pleased.

With the racism issue safely behind us, the vodka flows, and Trish drifts toward Daniel. Mark appears at my side to escort me to the golf course.

Oh, right. I'd forgotten about Mark. I study him. He *is* cute, in a golden retriever kind of way. He's a swimmer, so he's tanned and muscular, with chlorine-bleached hair that keeps falling over his big brown eyes. Kissing him might be fun. It would certainly be less complicated than kissing Trish.

We sit in a circle on the grass, and I find myself snuggled up next to Mark, with his arm draped over my shoulder. Daniel wants to play "I Never," where one person says something they've never done, and everyone who's done it has to drink. Even if I were able to drink, I'd have to stop now—I've never done anything. I've never cut class. I've never been high in front of my parents. I've never crashed my car into a tree.

Predictably, the game starts getting dirty. I've never sexted. I've never done it in my parents' bed. I've never done it in a car. "I've never done it outside," someone says, and Trish and Daniel don't drink. The group starts chanting, "Do *it*! Do *it*!" and the two of them grin at each other and stumble off into the darkness to whoops and cheers. The icy fog that's been hovering in my chest congeals into a hard gray ball. *Fine.* I scooch in closer to Mark. When he asks me to take a walk around the course, I agree.

It's a nice night for a first kiss—a star-spangled sky, the silver bangle of a crescent moon suspended above the trees. We sit silently at the edge of a sand trap, so close our legs are touching. Then Mark leans in to kiss me, and in the moment before his lips touch mine, my heart flutters. Maybe this will be magical. Maybe it will sweep me off my feet.

But the moment passes and my first kiss turns out to be just a lot of his tongue in my mouth, and all I can think is *ick*. I put up with it for a couple of minutes in case it gets better.

It doesn't.

His hand strays toward my butt. I push it back. It starts creeping up my shirt. I push it down. Between getting my face sucked off, worrying about where Mark's hand is going to go next, and wondering what I'll do when it gets there, I can't—

"Relax," he says. "Stop fighting."

"I'm not fighting."

"You're all tense. C'mon, just let go. Have fun." He moves in again. "You're so hot," he whispers. And there's his tongue again. And his hand. Hands. Must. Get. Out of here. Think. Think of an excuse.

I push him away, a little harder than I mean to. "Um . . . I feel a little weird kissing you out here. It uh, doesn't feel very private." Which is true.

He nuzzles my neck. "Don't worry. No one cares." Also true, unfortunately.

"Yeah, but . . . maybe another time." I stand up, and Mark stands up with me.

"You sure?" he says, wrapping his arms around me and slobbering on my ear. Ew.

"Uh, yeah. I'm sure. Maybe you can text me." I twist away and try to smile. Mark shoves his hands in his pockets and walks back to the group with me. He doesn't look at me again.

I never should have come to this stupid party.

At two in the morning, I leave Daniel and Mark playing Thumper with their buddies at the fifth hole, and drive Trish and myself back to her house. As I help Trish to bed, she flings her arms around me and slurs, "Omigod, that was so much fun. You're such a good friend," and passes out.

On Sunday morning I get up early. I don't even bother waking Trish. I just change clothes, pack up my stuff, and text her:

> Hope you slept OK. Too bad we didn't get to hang out like
> we planned. See you Monday

Against my better judgment, I add a heart and a smiley face. Her phone chirps, and I pad downstairs. Mrs. Campbell is in the kitchen, nursing a coffee and, from the looks of her wan face, a hangover. "Oh, hi, Sana honey. I'm sorry I'm such a mess—I keep thinking I'm still young enough to handle more than a couple drinks." She winks. "I didn't hear you girls come home last night," she adds, yawning. "Did you have fun?"

"Oh . . . yeah," I lie.

"Trish didn't drink too much, did she?"

"What? Oh. Uh."

"Oh, honey, it's okay. I know she drinks," says Mrs. Campbell with a smile. "I just want her to do it responsibly, you know?"

I nod. I wonder if she knows what else Trish may or may not be doing responsibly, but all I say is, "Oh, she was fine. Maybe she had a *little* too much."

Mrs. Campbell tilts her head and smiles—ruefully? Affectionately? "That girl. Just like her mother." Then, as if seeing me for the first time, her eyes widen in surprise. "You've got your bag. Are you leaving? So early?"

"Yeah, my mom needs me to help her pack today." Another lie.

"I wish you and Trish hung out more." Mrs. Campbell sighs. "You're such a good influence. You study hard, you get good grades, you don't drink . . . such a sweetheart." She sighs again and smiles at me. "We're really going to miss you, Sana."

"I'll miss you, too."

"Grab a cinnamon roll on your way out, honey. They're delicious. I'm so glad I thought to buy them yesterday—I just can't face making breakfast right now." She winks again. Then, as I take a roll and head toward the door, "Do you need a ride home?"

"No, it's just a couple of miles. It's a nice day. I'll walk."

"Really?" Mrs. Campbell puts her coffee cup down and leans forward, as if she's considering getting up. Her mouth purses into a little frown of doubt.

"Yes, it's fine."

"Well, if you're sure," she says. Her face relaxes into a relieved smile, and she sinks back into her chair. "Bye, honey! Oh—try not to slam the door on your way out, okay?"

I thank her and head out, shutting the door behind me as quietly as I can.

3

THE END OF SCHOOL COINCIDES WITH A WEEK of hot humidity and humming cicadas that make the air feel so oppressive, I want to push it out of the way like a too-heavy blanket. But our last night in Wisconsin brings a sudden rush of cool wind, the smell of water, and the splotch-splotch-splotch of the first raindrops on the sidewalk. Mom and I pack the car to the sound of rain pelting the roof of the garage like wild applause for show-stopping flash-boom-bangs of lightning and thunder.

In the morning, the world offers the scent of wet asphalt and earth, the sparkle of rain on bright green grass, and the magic of shape-shifting oil rainbows in puddles. It's dawn, the best time to start a road trip. Mom locks the door for the last time, and we roll through the silent streets of Glen Lake in our packed-to-the-gills white Prius. We grab one last coffee at the Starbucks on Kohler Avenue before heading west on I-94 toward California, toward Dad and his new job, toward a brand-new life.

When I was twelve, Mom, Dad, and I took a weeklong summer trip to Wisconsin Dells, a resort town that grew around the spot where the Wisconsin River has carved its own tiny version of the Grand Canyon—the Dells. It's only a couple of hours west of Glen Lake on I-94, and everyone goes there for weekend trips.

Mom was driving because Dad had returned late the night before from a business trip to California; I sat in the front seat as navigator while Dad slept in the back.

As so often happens when she drives someplace new, Mom took the wrong exit and got lost. But she didn't want to wake Dad up, so I fished his phone out of his jacket pocket for her.

"This would be a lot easier if you'd just let me have a smartphone," I grumbled, entering his password and tapping on the map app.

"I don't need such expensive toy, and you don't need, either. The regular cell phone for communication is enough for twelve-year-old."

"Turn around and go three miles back to the highway."

As I played with the map to get a better picture of our route, a text message popped up at the top of the screen. It was in Japanese, from an area code I didn't recognize.

I'm about as literate as a first-grader in Japanese, despite Mom's best efforts and two miserable years of Saturday

Japanese school in Milwaukee, so I couldn't read most of what the text said. I was about to ask Mom to take a look when another message appeared that I *could* read. It said,

Hearts and lips? Who would send Dad something like that? It had to be a mistake. I tapped the text and discovered that it was part of a long thread between Dad and someone who was apparently a huge fan of emojis—hearts, kissing smiley faces, shoes, and lips being her particular favorites.

I looked out the window at the cornfields. There had to be some explanation. Maybe Dad had a niece or a little girl cousin who loved emojis that he'd never told us about.

Living in the United States. Whose name he hadn't saved in his contacts list. Who'd texted emojis of a bikini, a wineglass, and the ever-present lips exactly two weeks ago, the morning he left for a three-day business trip . . .

"Sana, chotto! Tsugi wa?"

What next, indeed.

I fumbled with the phone. "Um, go west—take this first entrance ramp on the right. For seven miles."

As Mom negotiated the merge, gripping the steering wheel anxiously and casting many a backward glance out the window, irritation crawled up my spine like a snake. She was a terrible driver. For starters, she couldn't—or wouldn't—keep constant pressure on the gas. She alternated between pushing down and easing off the gas pedal, so that we were always either speeding up or slowing down: vrROOoom . . . vrROOoom. On straightaways, she did what people do when they pretend to drive, turning the wheel quickly left and right, left and right, making a thousand unnecessary adjustments as she jiggled the car cautiously down the road.

It was maddening. I could see Dad wanting a break from that.

I looked at Mom and tried to see her as Dad might. She is short—at twelve years old I was already pushing past her. Her hair was true black, not almost-brown like mine, cut in a shoulder-length bob and pulled back on one side—childishly, I thought—with a barrette. She had a classic moon face, a soft oval, with the high nose bridge and long earlobes that I inherited. "Lucky," she told me once, rubbing my ears affectionately, "and high class," stroking the bridge of my nose. She was no fashion model, but she was pretty enough.

I looked back at Dad. Dad, who was always working, who traveled a couple of times a month and always brought back presents for me. Who used to tell me stories, and fling me into the air, and slip me candy when Mom wasn't looking. But that was when I was little. In the past couple of years, he had somehow faded into just a nice guy who drifted in and out of the background of my life.

Who were they to each other? Dad always said they'd known each other all their lives. Baba, Dad's mom, once told me the whole story, and it had sounded so romantic: Dad had gotten very sad and sick while he was in grad school, and Mom had taken care of him, and they'd fallen in love and gotten married. But that was all I knew. It was a long time ago. Did they still love each other? Could they have stopped?

I decided not to say anything about the text. Not talking about it meant that it wasn't a big deal. And if it wasn't a big deal, it might not even be true.

But even if I didn't talk about it, I couldn't forget about it. I checked the number, wrote it down, and later put it in my lacquer box. I Googled it and learned that it had a San Francisco area code. For the next few weeks, every time Dad stayed out late, every night he was on a trip, I thought about the phone number in my box and I gnawed my suspicions to shreds. But I said nothing.

Months went by. Nothing changed between my parents. No one talked about having affairs. No one filed for divorce. My silence paid off. But for some reason, I couldn't bring myself to get rid of the phone number. Maybe I was still suspicious— sometimes I thought I'd call it one day and find out for sure who it belonged to. But I never did, and the phone number slowly disappeared under my growing collection of sea glass.

The number is still tucked safely in my little lacquer box, which in turn is tucked safely in my suitcase next to my Emily Dickinson poems. I watch neighborhoods of cookie-cutter McMansions slip by and give way to miles and miles of corn-fields as Mom and I lurch and jiggle our way across the state, across the country, away from the land of Midwest farmers' daughters and toward the land of the California girl.

4

IT'S BEEN FOUR WEEKS SINCE WE ARRIVED. FOUR weeks, and I've spent the entire time doing nothing, going nowhere, and meeting no one.

Scratch that. Mom and I have spent the entire time unpacking, arranging, and rearranging furniture, going to Ikea, Target, and Costco, and meeting . . . no one. On the other hand, it's not like I had a full social calendar back in Wisconsin. And it's better than going to math day camp, which is how I spent last summer.

Today's list of errands takes us to Bed Bath & Beyond to pick up a bath mat, a step stool, and a duvet cover and new sheets for my bed. When we walk in the door, I do a quick scan-and-count. A Latino couple, a few Asian women, a couple of white men . . . ding-ding-ding! It's majority minority! Mr.

Williams, my world history teacher last year, was always saying how this is happening in America, but I'd never actually seen it until we moved here. I get a kick out of it every time. In Wisconsin, when Mom and Dad spoke Japanese in public, I could feel people not-staring. I couldn't even linger a few feet away and pretend I was with another family—all anyone had to do was look at my face and hair to know who I was with. But here in San Jose, we blend in. In fact, it's beyond blending—here, we are completely inconspicuous. We fade into the background—dark hair, Asian faces, foreign language, and all. I love it.

I'm reveling in our anonymity as we approach the bedding section, which is where life gets difficult. No matter what I choose, Mom points out flaws that, once she's shown me, I can't unsee:

Sky blue with a pattern that looks like dandelion seeds floating across it? "Makes me feel like allergy."

Pale gray with a single cherry blossom branch? "Only good for spring."

Pure white with a bold arabesque print down the middle? "Looks like Raw-shock."

"It's *Ror*shach, Mom."

"Raw-shock."

And then, oh, this one. Powder blue with a deep blue coral plant (or is it an animal?) that grows from the bottom corner and spreads intricate, lacy branches across the fabric. It's perfect.

"How about this?" I ask, patting it lovingly.

Mom runs her own hand over it. "Ahhhn. It makes me feel like sandy, like drippy—"

"Mom! Can't you just let me like something without telling me what's wrong with it? It's my bed! It's my room! This is America, Mom. Let me express myself a little!"

She snorts. "Hah! That's the problem with America. Be different is cool, express yourself is cool, and don't care how the other people feel. It's so selfish."

Right. How could I have forgotten? For Mom, *different* equals *disrespectful*.

"Can I help you? Looks like you're having a little trouble deciding on something."

. . . aaand a stupid, useless store clerk has overheard our stupid, useless argument. Great. Why can't she just leave us alone? Or actually . . . maybe she can stay. She's about my age and height with light brown skin and black hair pulled into a ponytail that spills in waves down her back. Brown eyes, clear and wide, under delicately arched eyebrows. Cupid's bow lips with a slick of rose lip gloss. A dimple on her chin. Shimmery dark green nail polish at the tips of slender fingers. And the way she stands—not clerkish at all. Graceful. Regal, even. Like she's a queen in disguise.

I'm hooked. Who *is* she? I stand up a little straighter. " . . . any normal pattern?" Mom is saying.

"Mom, I really like this one." My voice is reasonable, well modulated, mature. No more petulant whining. Must impress Fascinating Store Girl.

"Yeah, it's great, isn't it?" Fascinating Store Girl says. "It's my favorite, actually." She smiles at me, and my brain goes a little flittery. Fascinating Store Girl and I have the same taste in duvet covers. How cool is that?

"Oh! Yes, I see. It's beautiful!" Mom smiles and nods thoughtfully, and even picks up the plastic-wrapped package, but I know from experience that she's lying through her teeth. I've seen her do the fake smile and nod with tons of store clerks, and besides, hundred-and-eighty-degree changes of heart are not her thing. "Thank you for your helping!" she chirps.

Fascinating Store Girl takes this as her cue to say, "You're welcome. Let me know if you need anything!" and fade discreetly into the background. Much to my disappointment.

Mom picks out a sensible blue-and-white windowpane print while I protest (quietly, this time). "Mom, even the store person liked my choice."

"Hn. She is Mexican."

"What?"

"If she likes it, then it is Mexican taste."

"Mom!"

Mom is genuinely confused. "What?"

"How do you even know she's Mexican? And you say that like it's a bad thing."

"I just guessed. Mexican taste is not Japanese taste," she says simply, as if that explained everything. I can't believe what I'm hearing.

Actually, I can. You'd think that being a member of a racial minority would make her extra sensitive, but Mom has something racist, ignorant, or just plain weird to say about everyone who's not Japanese: Koreans are melodramatic and smell bad; Jewish people like purple; white Americans are selfish, disrespectful, and love guns. And apparently Mexicans have bad taste.

"Mom, that's racist," I say. "Just because she likes it, doesn't mean it's 'Mexican taste.' And even if it was, it shouldn't matter."

"I didn't say it's bad. I just said I don't like it. It's not racism if I don't like Mexican taste."

This is pretty much always how it goes, and at this point I know it's useless to argue. I resign myself to the Mom-approved duvet cover, and fume while Mom finds the other items we came for. There are two lines at checkout, and—oh! There's Fascinating Store Girl at the cash register on the left. I steer Mom in her direction. She's got such a nice smile. She even has pretty ears.

"Did you find everything you need?" She gives Mom and me a quick customer-service-y smile and starts scanning.

Beep.

Notice me. Notice me. Notice me.

Beep.

Look up. Look up. Look up.

Beep.

Oh well.

But when she scans the sheets, she looks up and says, "Oh, so you didn't go with that other set, huh?"

Mom smiles apologetically. "No, we decided this one."

"*I* really liked the other one," I say, suddenly desperate to make a connection. "Just . . . you know." I jerk my head at Mom, who ignores me. Omigod, what. Did I. Just. Do. That wasn't bonding over similar taste in bed linens. That was acting like a spoiled brat. Smooth, Sana. Nice going.

"Aah," says Fascinating Store Girl, and goes back to scanning. But not before she gives me a smile. Wait, what? "That'll be two hundred sixteen dollars and fifty-seven cents. Cash, credit, or debit?"

Or did I imagine it? Or maybe she was smiling at Mom and me both, to be polite? No, it was definitely at me. Maybe we did just have a bonding moment. Did we? Aggh, just stop. Mom finishes paying, Fascinating Store Girl says, "Bye, have a nice day," (Did she smile at me again? I mean, at me specifically? Omigod, stop.) and it's on to Mitsuwa Marketplace, the Japanese grocery store, for *tofu*, Japanese eggplant, and *soba* noodles.

I follow Mom around Mitsuwa and think about Fascinating Store Girl. How cool would it be if I ran into her somewhere? Like maybe at that Starbucks across the street from Bed Bath & Beyond. Maybe I'd be there after another of our endless errands (I could leave Mom at home. This is my fantasy, after all.), and Fascinating Store Girl would be stopping by after work. Maybe we'd start talking, and I would be witty and funny and say all the right things, and we'd become best friends. And then maybe one evening we'd be splashing around in the pool in her backyard (hey, it's a fantasy, remember?), and she'd swim over to me and we'd look into each other's eyes, and . . .

Maybe it's better not to go there.

Mom and I go home to spend another ridiculously beautiful afternoon indoors—Mom fussing over dinner, and me fussing over the details of my fantasy, trying to steer it in a safer direction, trying to think about boys instead. But no matter how handsome the boys are, no matter how ripped their bodies or how green their eyes, those fantasies end up feeling as pale and empty as the California sky.

5

TODAY IS THE FIRST DAY OF SCHOOL, AND AFTER a week of careful deliberation, I've picked an outfit that will look good without standing out too much: a cute jean mini-skirt, a fitted scoop-neck white tee, and gladiator sandals that Mom almost refused to buy. ("Why do you want to look like Roman soldier?") I twist my hair into a loose bun, with a few strands poking out artfully here and there. Putting it up makes room for a silk cord necklace with multicolored glass beads that look good against my skin. I wish I had cool earrings to go with it, but Mom thinks that pierced ears are for barbarians. But whatever, I'm starting to realize that I've spent too much of my time moping and sulking. It's time for a change. New school, new attitude. Let's go.

My new attitude and I walk into the kitchen, where Mom is scrambling eggs.

"Sana, kaminoké naoshi-nasai."

"Mom, there's nothing wrong with my hair. I did it like this on purpose."

"Darashi-nai." She is always telling me that I'm darashi-nai. It means disrespectfully messy, sloppy, or careless—it's what she says when my ponytail is loose or my shirt is untucked or my jeans have holes in them.

"It's fine, Mom. In fact, I think it looks good."

"People don't want to be your friend if you have the messy hair. Teachers think you are disrespectful student. First impression is important for first day of school."

"Mom, I *know.*" Like I'd really leave the house looking like a mess on my very first day at a new school. I'm about to tell her that she's supposed to try to make me feel good about myself, not criticize me, when I catch a glimpse of her face. Her forehead is creased with worry. It dawns on me that she might be just as nervous about my first day as I am. That doesn't exactly inspire confidence, but I guess it's nice to know she cares. Maybe I should forgive her for complaining about my hair.

"You look like porky-pine." *Arrggh!* Forget it. And of course now I'm worried that she's right. I go back to my room and yank my hair into a regular, boring old ponytail.

I walk glumly to school, eyes on the sidewalk. The air is chilly and the sky is gray—sweater weather. But it's an illusion. The clouds are actually fog that always "burns off" by midmorning, as the weather reporters like to say. The neighborhood is full of pale wooden ranch houses just like ours. Concrete driveways serve as walkways to front doors set atop a gray concrete step or two. Faded green lawns stretch down the block, punctuated by the odd rosebush or line of shrubbery—or even odder, a palm tree and a redwood tree next door to each other. There's even a yard full of cacti.

We live three blocks from school, and as I approach the campus, my heart starts tripping over itself. I would be panting if not for the lump in my throat. When kids in movies and TV shows first arrive at a new school, they always look around and take a deep breath before plunging in, but not me. Pausing for even a moment would be like holding up a big sign saying, "Hi, I'm new! Please stare." Not that there's an "in" to plunge into, anyway. The school is basically a collection of long, low, rectangular buildings divided into classrooms and separated by strips of grass and concrete, all sprawled haphazardly around a quasi-central quad. I studied the map over the weekend, but there are so many buildings and so many intersections that I'm sure I'll get turned around at some point.

Okay, stop. This is ridiculous. New school, new attitude, remember? What was that saying—fake it till you make it? Or how about *carpe diem*? Or maybe Just Do It?

So in the spirit of faking it till I make it, seizing the day, and just doing it, in—or actually *around* the first building—I plunge. Without pausing.

Miraculously, I find my way to my first-period class (trigonometry, room 27) a few minutes early. I peek inside. The desks are arranged in classic schoolhouse fashion, in six rows of six, with a table and a whiteboard at the front. The teacher—Mr. Green, according to my schedule—is busy with something at the back of the room. A boy wearing a black T-shirt, torn black jeans, and combat boots—looks like the goth uniform is the same nationwide—lounges at a desk in the middle, picking his fingernails; two girls in cheerleader uniforms sit close to the door, giggling over a phone.

As I falter on the threshold, Mr. Green walks over and greets me. "Hi, there. Who are you?"

"Sana Kiyohara."

"Nice to meet you, Sana," he says, and points to the whiteboard. "I'm assigning seats, so check the board and find your seat." Sure enough, there's my name printed in a box right in the middle of a grid of thirty-five other boxes. "I see you're right over there, in front of Caleb," says Mr. Green. The box below mine is labeled "Caleb Miller." The goth. Caleb glances up when he hears his name, and I see a nose ring and an eyebrow ring. Expressionless, he goes back to his fingernails.

New school, new attitude. Fake it till you make it.

I walk to my desk, sit down, and say, "Hi."

His eyes flick up and back down. "Hi." He continues picking at what I can now see is black nail polish.

"I'm new." Facepalm. I quit. Forget faking it—I can't do this.

But Caleb looks up with real interest now. He considers me for a couple of seconds, leans forward, and whispers, "Run." A joke! I smile. "No, seriously," he says. "Get out while you can. This place is a cesspool."

"Then why are you here?"

"Because my mom'll kick my ass if I ditch the first day of school." He asks me where I'm from, why I moved, and all I have to do is answer. I relax a little. This is easy. As other kids wander into class, Caleb forgets about asking questions and gives me his opinion of each one, starting with the two cheerleaders: "They actually think people give a fuck about them, for some reason." A tall Asian boy with gelled hair: "Andy Chin. President of the junior class. He thinks he's the shit but he's just another dumbass." A gaggle of Asian girls: "You'll probably end up being friends with them. They're nice, but they're all the same, and I don't mean that they look the same—they *are* the same." *What the . . . ?* Did he just say—my shock must show on my face, because Caleb interrupts himself. "No, really. They are."

"Why do you think I'm going to be friends with them?"

He looks at me like I've missed something obvious. "You're Asian. They're Asian. You do the math." *Sounds like your math is racist,* I think, but I say nothing.

"What? Didn't the Asian kids all hang out together at your old school?"

"No."

"How many Asian kids were at your school?"

"Like, three."

"And you weren't friends?"

"No."

He is nonplussed, but steadfast. "Well, wait and see. I'll bet you anything that's who you end up with. People think they're unique, but they're really stereotypes. It's just the way they are. They want to be in a group, and they'll sacrifice their individuality to fit in." This from a guy who probably dresses just like *his* friends. But I don't see the point in arguing with this twenty-first-century Holden Caulfield, and anyway, Mr. Green has started talking.

Mr. Green has everybody pair up and interview each other: name, how we feel about math, one little-known fact about ourselves. Apparently he's one of those math teachers who thinks he's an English teacher. Caleb and I are partners. When it's our turn, I introduce him and then wait while Caleb intones, "This is Sana, she likes math but doesn't love it, and she hates broccoli." As he lowers himself back into his chair, he adds, "Oh—she's new."

He grins at me as he sits down, and I'm so stunned I can't even react. Anderson High School is huge—2,500 students— so I'd hoped I could sneak by anonymously today, but there's no chance of that now. I can feel my cheeks burning as everyone perks up a little and kids all over the classroom practically fall out of their desks trying to get a better look at the new girl. I have never felt so conspicuous, so . . . scrutinized, and I begin to understand what writers mean when they say that a character wishes the ground would open up and swallow them whole. Finally I muster up a feeble smile, shrug my shoulders, and wave my hand at shoulder level, the universal sign for, "Hi, I'm really embarrassed." Andy Chin, class president and alleged dumbass, leans back, flashes a smile, and says with a smarmy wink, "Stick with me, baby. I'll introduce you to all the right people." Groans. He holds his arms out wide, in protest. "What? I was being ironic."

Behind me, Caleb mutters, "No, he wasn't."

Finally, we start doing math, and I take notes dutifully for the remainder of class. When the bell rings, I surreptitiously check my map for my Spanish classroom as I close my notebook, trying to make it look like I'm going over my notes one last time.

"Sana?"

I snap the notebook shut and look up. It's one of the Asian girls. She's tiny, with huge eyes and an open smile.

"Hi. I'm Elaine. And that's Hanh, and that's Reggie." She gestures to two other girls who are waiting at the door. They wave. One of them is tall and thin, with long, straight black hair, wearing coral lip gloss. The other has her hair woven into an elaborate braid, and has a pleasant, round-cheeked face. "We were wondering if you want to have lunch with us after second period. What class do you have next?"

"Oh. Uh, sure, thanks. Um, I have Spanish. Spanish III with . . . Reyes."

"Cool! Same as us! Come on, we can go together!" Elaine's

enormous eyes light up, and she actually claps her hands. I feel like if we were six years old instead of sixteen, she'd offer one of those hands for me to hold, and ask if I wanted to be her best friend.

I finish packing my backpack, and we start threading our way through the desks toward the door. Elaine is already throwing questions around like confetti: What's Wisconsin like? Is it cold? Is it full of white people? Where do I live now? What's my class schedule?

Caleb, just walking out the door, turns and mouths, "I told you," and disappears.

Walking to Spanish is a totally different experience than walking to trig. The fog has burned off, the chill has lifted, and the weather is California-perfect: sunny, warm-but-not-hot, a cloudless and faintly blue sky overhead. I'm feeling a little sheepish because Caleb seems to have been right about the Asian thing, but mostly I'm feeling glad to be part of a group as we stroll to our next class.

Hanh is the tall, thin one, and Reggie is the one with the round cheeks and fancy braid. As we walk, we listen to Elaine talk about Jimmy Tran, who was assigned to sit next to her in trig and is walking several paces ahead of us. "He has the most beautiful eyes. Don't you think he has gorgeous eyes?" she asks me.

"You say that about every guy you ever like," says Hanh, pulling out a mirror to touch up her lip gloss.

"I *so* don't. You're such a— Shhh!"

Jimmy has stopped to talk to someone, and we're coming right up on him.

"Hi, Jimmy!" Hanh trills as we walk by. Jimmy nods at us, confused. Elaine stares straight ahead, and once we've passed him, she starts sissy-hitting Hanh and hissing, "Omigod, I can't believe you!" Hanh just flips her hair, bats her eyelashes, and coos, "Oh, Jimmy, you have such gorgeous eyes!" Reggie smothers a laugh and Elaine flits around Hanh like a squirrel, scolding and shushing and smacking her arm. I'm enjoying the show when I happen to look away for a moment, and something way more interesting catches my eye.

It's Fascinating Store Girl from Bed Bath & Beyond.

6

SHE'S WALKING DOWN THE BREEZEWAY TOWARD us. Her hair is down today. She's wearing skinny jeans and a navy blue T-shirt that says ANDERSON CROSS-COUNTRY on it in sky blue. A sea-star pendant dangles from a silver chain around her neck. Not that I care what she's wearing or what she looks like. She spots a couple of guys beyond us and heads over to meet them, so she doesn't see me. Which is a good thing because I've just realized I'm staring at her. Jeez. Stop.

When I drag my attention back to my new friends, Hanh is still fake-gushing about Jimmy and his eyes and Elaine is still trying to make Hanh shut up. But Reggie looks at me and shakes her head. "These two," she says, like she's their babysitter. "Sometimes I just can't with them."

"Yeah . . . Hey, Reggie, see that girl over there, with the

cross-country T-shirt? Talking to those two guys?"

"You mean that Mexican girl?"

"Uh, I guess. How do you know she's Mexican?"

"I dunno. Most of the Latino kids around here are Mexican. I mean, some of them are like, Nicaraguan or whatever, but mostly they're Mexican—Mexican *American*," she corrects herself. "Though, actually, everyone just says Mexican. Kind of like how we say Asian instead of Asian American. Ethnic pride and all that, right?"

"What's her name?"

"Jamie Ramirez. Why?"

Jamie Ramirez.

"Hey, Sana, why do you want to know?"

I pretend not to hear the question, and Reggie doesn't get a chance to ask a third time because the bell rings and we have to go to class.

Lunch. There are rows of lunch tables in the "multipurpose room," but everything else is outside—the hot-lunch line, the snack bar line, the vending machines, and most of the kids, who are eating their lunches on the ground or at cement picnic tables scattered around the quad. All the school clubs and sports teams have set up tables in the quad as well, to recruit new members. We sit behind the Vietnamese Student Association table, but after gobbling down their lunches, Elaine and Hanh have to go and register new members. Reggie stays and finishes eating with me before leaving to hand out flyers and recruit freshmen for the Volunteer Club.

"Don't worry," she says apologetically, "lunch tomorrow'll be more chill."

It's not so bad being alone with nowhere to sit, though, since half the school seems to be wandering from table to table anyway. I start at the Volunteer Club and make a slow circuit around the quad. Water polo. Dance team. Queer Straight Alliance. Poetry Club. Animé Club. Polynesian Student Union.

"Hey, Sana." It's Caleb the goth. Where the heck did *he* come from?

"Oh, hey."

"Your friends abandon you already?" he asks, falling in step with me.

"No, they all had to work tables for their clubs."

"Oh, right." He scans the quad, taking in the tables and the mobs milling around them. "Ugh. This is so pointless."

"Huh?"

"All these clubs do is meet once a week to organize fundraisers. Or they get together and do the same boring hobbies they do at home. They get a faculty advisor and call it a club, and suddenly their hobby becomes important and they can be president of something and put it on their college applications: President of the Animé Club? Riiight. *That's* significant."

"Mm-hm." This "everyone is a shallow hypocrite but me" act is getting irritating. I wonder if Caleb is just going to follow me around for the rest of lunch period.

"Anyway," he continues, "I was with my friends over

there—" He gestures across the quad toward a group of kids sitting under a tree, all dressed in black. "—and saw you alone, so I thought I'd ask you if you wanted to sit with us for lunch."

"Oh. Um." That was nice. But . . . "You know, I think I'm just going to walk around and check out the rest of the clubs and stuff. I don't mind being alone."

"Ohhh, okay. You don't want me around."

"No, it's not that. I mean—"

"Yeah, yeah, I know when I'm not wanted."

"No, I just really want to see—"

"No, whatever. I see how it is."

That's it. I do want him gone. "'Bye." I wave him off, and his mouth and eyes open wide in mock outrage. I can't help smiling a little. It's kind of nice to joke around with someone, even if it's a dork like Caleb.

I turn back to my circuit and find that I'm approaching the cross-country table. Fascinating Store Girl—I mean, Jamie Ramirez—was wearing a cross-country T-shirt, wasn't she? A sport could be a good thing. Clubs typically meet just once a week, like Caleb said, but I feel like I'll need something to do every day, or I'll die of boredom.

Sports teams practice every day. Hanh and Reggie are on the badminton team, but I am *not* going to play badminton. Especially not after they told me that the entire team is Asian. Plus, how silly would I feel whiffing one of those teeny rackets around? But running is something I could do.

I get to the cross-country table just in time to see Jamie

take off. Darn. I mean, whatever. It's just, she looks so interesting. She's headed toward the Latino Student Union table. Maybe I'll swing over and say hi on my way to see Elaine and Hanh, just to see if she remembers me from—

"Hi, did you want to sign up for cross-country?" It's an Indian girl with possibly the longest ponytail I've ever seen.

"What? Oh. Yes." The girl's name is Priti, and she's the girls' team captain. Priti and Coach Kieran take my name and email, hand me a couple of forms, and tell me to show up after school outside the gym in running clothes as soon as I can get signatures on the parent permission slip and the physician-release form certifying that I won't drop dead of a heart attack during practice.

On my way to the Vietnamese Student Association table, I see that Jamie's still at the Latino Student Union table, in animated conversation with a girl wearing a Niners jersey and lipstick that's about three shades darker than I would have chosen; the kind of dark red that's named after a fancy wine, like Pinot Noir. Maybe the lipstick is making her lips look pouty, but she looks like she's in a very bad mood. I almost change my mind about detouring in their direction.

Almost.

And now here I am, directly in front of Jamie and Pinot Noir, clearing my throat to get their attention, and now they're looking at me like, "Yeah?" Pinot Noir, in particular, looks annoyed at the interruption. Here goes nothing. Fake it till you make it.

I smile at Jamie. "Hi."

"Hey." She looks at me curiously. "You need something?"

"No, I just, um. I just recognized you. From Bed Bath and Beyond. I came in a couple of weeks ago and I was going to get that duvet cover with the blue coral design on it—you said it was your favorite? But my mom ended up making me get something else."

Her head tilts, her forehead wrinkles. . . . Omigod. She doesn't remember.

"Sorry," she says, shaking her head. "We get a ton of customers toward the end of summer. . . ."

"No—no, it's okay. I uh . . . just thought I'd say hi. You know, just in case." Oh, God. I feel like such a loser.

Pinot Noir throws her head back and cackles. "Ha! Like she'd remember you. You're funny." Then she folds her arms, clearly ready to wrap this up and get back to whatever it was she was all upset about before. "All right. Say hi, Jamie." Pinot Noir tilts her head at me.

"Hi," says Jamie. "Nice to meet you—what's your name?"

"Sana."

"I'm Jamie."

Still incredibly awkward, but better. At least she's smiling at me. But Pinot Noir ruins it. "I'm Christina. Did you want to sign up for LSU?"

"LSU?"

"Uh, Latino Student Union?" she says, pointing to the banner hanging from the table next to us.

"Oh. Uh, no."

"Okay, then." She raises her eyebrows at me. *"Bye."*

"Bye."

"Bye," says Jamie, and she's still smiling but I can see the pity in her eyes. How could I have been so thick? Pinot—I mean, Christina—is right. I went into that store *two weeks ago* and I thought Jamie would recognize me? Like I was something special? What was I thinking? Who was I kidding? If I had a wall I'd be banging my head against it right now. Note to self: No more faking it till I make it.

Also: Stay away from Christina. She's mean.

7

"TADAIMA," I CALL AS I WALK IN THE DOOR. I kick my shoes off and arrange them neatly in the shoe cabinet in the foyer.

"Okairi," Mom calls back. I drop my backpack in my room and head to the kitchen for a snack. "How was school?" she asks in Japanese. She's just prepared some green tea, and she pours me a cup to go with the cookies I've pulled out of the cupboard.

"Okay."

"Do you have homework?"

"Yes."

"How much?"

I shrug. "An hour. It's only the first day."

"Did you make any nice friends?"

"A couple of people. They're Asian, actually."

"Japanese?" She perks up a little.

"No. Vietnamese and I think maybe Chinese."

"Hmm," she says, sipping her tea. "Be careful. Chinese people can be untrustworthy."

"Mom!"

"It's true. I know what you think. You always point your finger and say, 'You're wrong. That's a stereotype!' but you don't know the world. If enough people act a certain way, others will name what they see. If those people don't like it, they shouldn't act the way they do."

Time to change the subject. "I'm thinking of joining the cross-country team."

"Crossing country?" she repeats in English.

"Long-distance running."

She frowns. "You aren't a fast runner."

"You don't have to be. It's about endurance. You know, slow and steady wins the race. Anyway, I'm faster than you think." I have no idea if this is true—the fact is, I'm worried that I'm not fast enough, too. But someone has to stand up for me.

"I know how fast you are. I've seen you run."

"Mom. I just want to try. Can't I just try?" I can feel my neck tightening, hear my voice rising to a petulant whine.

Mom heaves a sigh. "There will be girls who are natural runners on that team, not like you. You'll have to work harder than everyone else to keep up."

"I know, Mom. Of course I'll work hard."

She sighs again. "Okay, then. Do your best. Work hard."
She holds her hand out, and I put the permission slip and doctor's form in it. "Maybe it will make your legs more shapely," she muses.

This is too much. "God," I snap. "Would it kill you to be a little supportive?"

"I'm just being honest," she says with a huff. "You and I have the same legs—short and thick-kneed. Not good for running. And I am *very* supportive—I let you join the team, I encouraged you to work hard, and I said that crossing-country will make your legs look good. What else should I say?"

"How about, 'You're going to be great?' That's what an American mom would say."

Mom looks stung. "Too bad for you, then. I am not American. I am Japanese. I don't *know* if you're going to be great—how can I say that? I can *want* all kinds of things for you, but I only *know* that you can do your best. I am teaching you to see the world the way it is, not the way you want it to be. That's my job."

I'm on my bed reading when Dad gets home at nine o'clock. He's working later than ever with this start-up. He walks in the door, and from my room I can hear the evening routine, same as always:

He says, "Tadaima!"

Mom answers, "Okairi!"

He says, "Aaahh, I'm exhausted. I'm going to take a bath."

Mom says, "What about dinner?"

Dad says, "After my bath."

And three . . . two . . . one . . . He sticks his head in my doorway and says, "Oi, Sana-chan."

"Hi, Dad."

"Did you have a good day? First day of school, right?"

"It was okay."

"Lots of homework?"

"Not too much. I finished it before dinner."

"Ah, good girl." He comes in and pats me on the head like a puppy, and walks out. After his bath, he'll eat dinner and work until he goes to bed, probably without saying another word to me except "good night."

It wasn't always this way. When I was little, Dad used to tell me stories at night. His favorite—and mine, even though it was sad—was the story of Yama-sachi, who went to the bottom of the sea and married Toyo-tama-himé, the Dragon King's lovely daughter. The Dragon King gave him two huge jewels—one to bring the tides in, and one to send them out again—and sent him back to live with Toyo-tama-himé on land. They lived happily together in their home by the sea until she gave birth to their son. She told him to let her do it alone, but he peeked in on her, and was horrified to see her in her true form, as a sea dragon. Heartbroken, the dragon princess fled back to her father's kingdom and never returned.

"She should have told him right away, so he wouldn't be

surprised," I said the first time I heard the story.

"I think she was afraid. Maybe she thought he wouldn't love her if he knew."

"Then he shouldn't have peeked."

"No, perhaps not. Sometimes it's better not to know everything about a person."

"But when he found out, she should have stayed! I bet he still loved her."

"Yes, I think he did. But she didn't want him to be ashamed of her."

"If you found out I was a sea dragon, would you still love me?"

"Of course. I would keep you as a pet and feed you lots of seaweed."

"Sea dragons like frozen custard, actually."

"Seaweed flavored?"

"No!" I made a face. "Chocolate!"

The next night, Dad arrived home just before bedtime. "Sana-chan!" he called as he came in the door. "Oidé!" I jumped up from my bed, where I'd been reading, and flew to meet him, knowing this would buy me a sizable chunk of before-bed playtime, and maybe a repeat telling of Yama-sachi and Toyo-tama-himé. Dad had a conspiratorial grin on his face and a white paper bag in his hands. I recognized the logo right away—it was from LeDuc's Frozen Custard, my favorite dessert place of all time. "I went after work with friends," he said, holding the bag up like a prize. "I told them

I had a dragon to feed at home. Do you want some?"

"Yes!" I shrieked, jumping up and down. "Yes! Can I have some now?"

"Jiro-chan!" Mom protested from the kitchen. "It's her bedtime!"

"Eh-yan. It's okay. Let her have some fun," he replied, and led me—skipping and making my best dragon noises—into the kitchen, where I devoured a bowl of cold, creamy, custardy goodness under Mom's disapproving gaze.

When I was twelve, shortly after I discovered the strange text on Dad's phone, Dad brought home a different surprise present: pearl earrings, the ones I keep in my box. "They're like the two Tide Jewels," Dad said when I opened the box, "from the story of Yama-sachi and Toyo-tama-himé." They were beautiful—smooth and white, with a luminous pink sheen. "Everyone—even an ugly oyster—has power and beauty inside. But sometimes they keep it a secret. And sometimes it takes patience to find it."

The best part, though, was that they had posts for pierced ears. I thought this meant that I was going to be allowed to get my ears pierced—like getting a set of keys in a gift box before being led to the new car waiting in the driveway with a big bow on top.

"Akan." Of course Mom would forbid it. Apparently the earrings were not Mom-approved, and no amount of wailing and whining on my part could change her mind. "Not while you live with us."

I thought very seriously about running away. Dad smiled at me. "Mom's right—I should have checked. I know you're angry, but you should remember what I said about the pearls. Your mother, especially, has great strength and beauty inside her." I was not so sure.

"Keep them for when you do get pierced ears," he said to me later. "They are very special pearls, and I want you to wear them one day." So into my lacquer box they went, these beautiful jewels that grew around grains of sand, so powerful they could control the tides, hidden away and waiting for a future free from Mom's old Japanese ways.

8

ELAINE AND HANH MEET ME IN FRONT OF campus before school. While we wait for Reggie to arrive, Hanh fishes a mirror out of her bag and starts applying makeup. Elaine keeps an eye out for Jimmy. We're talking about what clubs I should join, and I'm telling them about cross-country as Reggie walks up to us.

"Holy pain and suffering, Batman," she says. "Why? You get hot and sweaty and tired, and what—your races are going to be much more fun? No, just more hot, sweaty running. Plus no one cares about cross-country—no offense—so you just have to like, toil in obscurity for nothing."

"Yeah, but I can't do any of the other sports. Anyway, I got my mom to let me do it," I say. "But first we had to have this whole argument about whether I was good enough, and how everyone else is probably better than me, so I'm going to have to work extra hard. . . . Not one word of support. She's the worst." The words are barely out of my mouth before I regret saying them. I feel like I've shared an ugly secret.

Hanh puts on the last touches of lip gloss, examines her reflection, and says, "She's not the worst. It's just Asian Mom Syndrome."

"Wha—huh? Is that, like, a thing?"

"What? Yeah, it's a thing! What's wrong with you? Did you think you had a *white* mom?" says Reggie, smiling.

I just stare at her. "No."

"Maybe there weren't any Asian moms where she's from," Elaine offers.

I nod.

"Oh, right. Seriously?"

I nod again.

"God, wow. That is so weird," says Hanh. "Okay, so Asian moms. Ask any Asian with an immigrant mom. They'll tell you. There's like a million videos about it on YouTube."

"Get good grades is better than have friends," says Elaine in an exaggerated Vietnamese accent, shaking her finger.

"No tampon. Tampon makes you lose virginity," says Reggie firmly.

Hanh puts her hand on her hip, scowls, and says, "Why you want boyfriend? No boyfriend until graduate from college."

Wow. Mom's not *that* extreme, but still, it all rings true. I try out something weird Mom said once: "Pair of socks is good Christmas present for teacher," and Reggie high-fives me.

"*Total* Asian mom!" cries Hanh, and then she squawks in that heavy Vietnamese accent, "Cut the toenail at night is bad luck! Don't eat too much, you get fat! Only A minus? Why you not work harder? Teenager wear makeup is for prostitute!"

I look around at Hanh, Reggie, and Elaine, and feel something I've never felt before. I've only just met them, but they get me like none of my Midwestern friends ever did. They don't think I'm weird or feel sorry for me. They make me feel normal. And special at the same time, somehow, like we're all part of an exclusive club with a secret handshake and everything.

I hadn't realized how much of my life—of *myself*—I'd been trying to keep hidden in Wisconsin. In Wisconsin, I was constantly trying to escape the fact that I was Asian, and hoping that people either didn't notice or didn't care. Now, I feel like it's springtime and my new friends have just peeled off a hot, heavy jacket. I can be openly Asian. For the first time in my life, I feel like I belong.

Hanh says, "You're lucky you got your mom to say yes. I wanted to do cross-country when I was a freshman, but my mom wouldn't let me."

I'm a little surprised to hear this from Hanh. I mean, I don't really know her yet, but she doesn't seem the type. The girls who ran cross-country at my old school were typically Plain Janes who didn't mind toiling in obscurity and getting hot and sweaty for nothing, as Reggie puts it. But Hanh is fashion-model pretty, and I get the feeling she knows it, the way she's always flipping her hair and checking out guys. Not only that, but here she is in full makeup. And she doesn't dress like she has an Asian mom, either. Today she has on a spaghetti-strap cami covered up with a cute crocheted shrug.

"Why wouldn't your mom let you do cross-country?" I ask.

"Well, it was actually my grandmother."

"What?"

"Yeah, she didn't want me running around in shorts and a tank top where you could see the bra underneath. She said it was 'immodest.'" Hanh puts air quotes around "immodest" and rolls her eyes. "She was like, 'I'm not going to let you run all over town looking like a prostitute.'"

"Whoa. For real?"

"The old ones are the worst," says Elaine. "They want everything to be like it was when they grew up, so it's like, old-fashioned even for being Asian."

"And she's my dad's mom," says Hanh, "and my mom pretty much just does whatever she says. It sucks."

"Your grandma's the worst, for sure. Even my mom feels sorry for you," Reggie says, shaking her head. "Thank God my grandparents are still in Hong Kong."

I look at Hanh's cute little camisole. "How come you get to wear that, then?"

"She doesn't know I'm wearing it. I give my friend Janet money, and she buys my 'inappropriate' clothes online and brings them to school for me. Then I put a jacket on over stuff like this before I leave my room."

"What about laundry?"

"Hanh just gives me all the clothes that she's not allowed to wear, and I take them home and do them with my laundry," says Elaine. "My mom makes me do my own laundry, so I'm the only other one who knows. Except Reggie and you."

"Genius," I say, impressed.

"You do what you have to," says Hanh, looking down modestly.

Reggie grins. "It's in our sneaky Asian blood."

"Hell, yeah." Hanh and Reggie high-five.

I could get used to being a member of this club.

Anderson High School is on a block schedule, which means that from Monday through Thursday, we have four classes a day for eighty minutes each, and on Fridays we have eight classes for forty minutes each. Mondays and Wednesdays are my big days, with trig, Spanish, Honors American Lit, and psychology. On Tuesdays and Thursdays, I have physics, P.E., a blessed eighty-minute free period—which almost makes up for the exercise in torture that is block-schedule periods of trig—and Honors American History.

Ms. Owen, who I have for Honors American Lit, is my favorite teacher so far. She's probably Mom's age, but much cooler, with a swingy bob haircut, lots of black clothes, and a laid-back attitude. And it doesn't hurt that she's a big Emily Dickinson fan.

"Dickinson might be my favorite—my *favorite*—writer to teach," Ms. Owen says as she goes over the curriculum for the year on the second day of class. (The first day was spent entirely on touchy-feely get-to-know-you activities.) Then she's off on a tangent about poetry in general. "Poetry demands *exploration*. It demands *excavation*. But we just don't have enough time this year to give it the attention it deserves. So I want *you* to take some initiative to discover what *excites* you."

She hands out a bunch of blank notebooks—poetry journals, she calls them—which we're supposed to write in throughout the year. All we have to do is look for cool poems ("Poems that *speak* to you," Ms. Owen says. "Poems that *resonate*."), copy them down, and write about them. We can do literary analysis, write our personal reactions, write about the poet, whatever. Just *explore* and *excavate*. Talk about easy points. And I know just what to start with.

POETRY JOURNAL, HONORS AMERICAN LITERATURE
THURSDAY, AUGUST 20

"I'm Nobody! Who are you?"
by Emily Dickinson

This is the poem that inspired me to get my own book of Emily Dickinson poems. Dickinson is cool (and sometimes frustrating) because her poems seem really short and simple, but they're not.

I sometimes used to feel like I was nobody. Like no one cared about me. In this poem, Dickinson makes being nobody into something cool: "I'm Nobody!" When you capitalize a word, it becomes more important, like a name or a title. Or maybe it's like Truth-with-a-capital-T, like it's the universal concept of Nobody-ness. The exclamation mark makes being Nobody kind of exciting and fun. And she says that she and the reader get to be Nobodies together without telling anyone, like a secret club.

In the next stanza she talks about how "dreary" it would be

to be Somebody, like a frog announcing your name all day long to "an admiring Bog!" It reminds me of popular people who think their group is the center of the universe. Except that being a frog announcing your name over and over in a bog seems lonely, too. So I don't know for sure about that one.

If you're Nobody together with someone, doesn't that make you Somebody? At least to each other? That can't be bad, right?

This is what I mean by Emily Dickinson being more complicated than she seems at first.

9

THE PHYSICIAN'S RELEASE FORM FINALLY arrived yesterday afternoon. I'm wearing a University of Wisconsin Bucky the Badger tank top that Trish's mom gave me as a going-away present, and I'm headed out of the locker room to practice, forms in hand and heart in mouth.

There are only four people stretching when I arrive at the fence between the parking lot and the track, and Jamie is one of them. She's wearing a sleek black tank top over a running bra and she looks great—I'm sorry, but anyone would think so—and I begin to regret wearing my derpy Bucky the Badger tank.

Look at her! At the others! Long, lean, muscular legs. Runner's legs. Not like my short, thick Hobbit legs. Mom was right. Cross-country was a mistake.

It's not too late to change my mind. I make a slow, casual arc so it's not too obvious that I'm chickening out and running away—*ho-hum, just out for a little stroll after school with medical and parent permission forms in my hand*—and I've almost made it all the way around when someone says, "Hey! Bed Bath and Beyond, right?"

Jamie. She's making fun of me. Keep walking. Pretend you didn't hear.

"Hey, wait up!" I hear footsteps, and then there's a hand on my shoulder. "Sana! Aren't you Sana?"

She remembers my name.

"Oh! Hi, sorry. Um, Jamie, right?"

"Mm-hm. You coming out for cross-country?"

"Oh. Uh . . ." *No* means I leave now and avoid risking further humiliation. *Yes* means possibly, possibly . . .

"You should."

"Yes! Yes, I am." Further humiliation and possibly, possibly it is.

"That's Coach Kieran. Come with me and you can give him your forms." Jamie walks me over to Coach Kieran, who's pacing the sidewalk and muttering over a clipboard.

"Hey, Coach. This is Sana . . . what's your last name?"

"Kiyohara."

"Oh, right," he says, taking my paperwork. "You signed up last week. You're a junior, right? No running experience? Okay. You can start with the JV team, then—none of them are here yet. Have you met the captains?" He calls the other kids over:

Priti and two Indian boys. "You've met Priti already," says Coach, nodding at her. "This is Jagwinder, the boys' captain—we call him Jag—and this is Arjun." And with that, he returns his focus to his clipboard and wanders off.

Jag and Arjun are tall, lanky, and handsome. Jag leans over and shakes my hand, and asks, "Have you run cross-country before?" I shake my head. "You're gonna love it," he says. "Best sport ever."

Jag looks to Arjun, who says, "Speak for yourself, bruh—I only do it so I can stay in good enough shape to run away from all the ladies when they get to be too much. They just can't get enough of all this"—he gestures to himself—"spicy Indian hotness. It's exhausting, know what I mean? They're relent-less." He nods and waggles his eyebrows at Priti, Jamie, and me. "Amiright, ladies?"

Jamie rolls her eyes and shows Arjun her palm. Priti starts coughing, "Loser! Loser!" Then she adds, turning to me but really talking to the guys, "They're delusional. Especially Arjun. Don't listen to anything he says. Everyone knows he's a virgin."

"Bruhhhh!" Jag cackles, while Jamie and Priti high-five each other. Arjun just shrugs good-naturedly and assures us that he is a skilled but very discreet lover.

Other kids start showing up, and soon there are about forty of us milling around. There's Jimmy, that guy that Elaine has a crush on. There's Janet Lee, from my physics class, the one who buys clothes for Hanh. She's a short, sturdy-looking girl with decidedly Asian features, except for the hazel eyes and light brown hair.

Eventually, Coach Kieran calls for our attention. "Okay, three-mile loop, everyone. Varsity, do an extra half mile out and back. Janet, you stick with Sana today and help with the route, okay? Make sure she doesn't get lost." Three miles? But that's so . . . far. A knot of anxiety starts to form in my stomach.

The JV girls immediately start whining, except for Janet, who does a mini-victory dance.

"No fair!"

"Why just Janet?"

"Why can't we *all* stick with Sana?"

"C'mon, Coach, we're tired. Pleeeeease?"

Great. They all think I'm slow. The knot in my stomach tightens and my cheeks start to burn as I stare at my feet.

"Aw, shut up, JV. You're such babies. Sana'll probably kick your ass. Right, Sana?" It's Jamie, and she's smiling at me. Right at me. I don't want to disappoint her, but I know in my bones that I'll be lucky to get out of this alive, so I sort of half shrug, half shake my head no. Jamie folds her arms. "Don't say no. You haven't even tried yet." Oh, God. And now she thinks I'm a wimp.

Coach breaks in and says, "Okay, runners, enough chit-chat. Go. See you back here in thirty minutes."

With that, the guys take off, a jumbled pack of skinny arms and legs that stretches out as they make their way through the parking lot and down the street. The varsity girls are close behind, ponytails bouncing and swinging, and then it's our turn to head out.

My stomach still hurts and my heart is pounding as if I've already run a thousand miles, but now I have no choice. We're on the move. I fall in at the back of the pack with Janet at my side. "Start off slower than you think you need to," she advises me as we turn onto the sidewalk. "Save a little for the second half." I nod—no need to remind me.

We run through the neighborhood to West San Carlos Avenue, the main commercial street, then past a Korean grocery store before looping back through another neighborhood. We're past halfway, and I'm feeling pretty good about myself because we've left a few of the JV runners behind us.

But I also feel like my lungs are going to burst. Why am I doing this, again? Oh, right. I'm chasing the slim, slim chance that Jamie might notice me. That is, if my legs don't collapse beneath me first. Maybe there's another, less painful way to get to know her.

Janet asks me, "Are you okay? Do you want to walk for a bit?" I don't even have enough oxygen to answer. I just nod my head gratefully and start walking.

"Hey!" We look up, and it's Jamie, running toward us on her extra half mile out and back, presumably. Only we're still a mile away from school, instead of half a mile, which means she's run extra, extra far to reach us. And she still looks great. "I'll take over," she says to Janet when she reaches us. "You can run back."

"Gee, thanks, Jamie, you're a pal," says Janet, but she smiles and doesn't hesitate. "Great job, Sana! See you back at school!" She waves and takes off so fast that I feel guilty for having held her back with me.

Then Jamie turns to me and says, "Why are you walking? You can run."

"I don't think I can."

"C'mon, don't wuss out on me. You can do it," she insists. "Just go slow. We'll walk ten more steps, and then we'll run all the way back to school. I'll help you through it." I'm not so sure anyone can help me, but I'm sure as heck not going to wuss out in front of Jamie.

"Okay."

We pick up the pace, and in a quarter mile, I feel like I'm going to fall apart. Literally. My arms will drop off first, then my legs, then as my body hits the ground, my head will snap off and roll away. Jamie, who is loping easily alongside me, says, "Keep going. We'll take it down a notch, but keep going." I'm panting. I'm so desperate for rest, I think I might cry. I glance at her. *Please, let me stop.* "You can do it," she insists. "Control your breathing." I try. "You look like you're about to cry. Relax your face." Well, I *am* about to cry. But I fix my face, and oddly, I feel a teeny, tiny bit better. "Come on, you can do it."

And finally, I do. I drag myself into the parking lot thinking, *I never want to do that again.* But Jamie pats me on the back and says, "Way to tough it out, Sana. I'm impressed." I'm bent over double, hands on my knees, gasping, but I feel a tiny fizz of energy inside because Jamie is impressed. And frankly, so am I.

I raise my head to look at her. "I thought I was going to have a heart attack."

"Yeah, I kinda did, too." She grins at me. "But you're tough. You'll get used to it."

"'You'll get used to it?' Not, 'It gets easier'?"

"No, it does get easier. But it also gets harder—you know, like school. The better you get, the harder you have to work. Coach always says you gotta have something special to run cross-country."

"A death wish?"

Jamie laughs and gives me a push. Yes. She thinks I'm funny.

"I like you," she says. "C'mon, let's get a drink." She leads me to the water station, and we're smiling at each other as we walk. "So what classes are you in?"

"Uh . . . trig, Spanish Three, Honors American Lit, Honors American History, physics, psychology." The same list sounded normal when I told Reggie, Elaine, and Hanh, but now it suddenly sounds like I'm showing off about how smart I am, and I wish I hadn't rattled it off so quickly.

But Jamie says, "Yeah, me too! How come we're not in anything together? Who do you have for trig?"

"Green." And now I'm embarrassed that I assumed she wasn't in any classes with me. Should I say something?

But Jamie just keeps going. "Lucky. I have The Bird. She's

like, epically bad. And she's a bitch." Ohhkay, that seems a little harsh. I'm probably a prude, but it just seems wrong to use swear words about teachers. Though I've actually already heard of Mrs. Byrd, and she does seem to be a bit of a legend in the—in that category. Jamie launches into a long list of The Bird's many and varied punishments for crimes real and imagined—mostly tardies, talking, and late homework. "Everyone's terrified of her," says Jamie. It's hard for me to imagine Jamie being terrified of anyone.

Coach calls everyone back, and I don't get another chance to talk to Jamie for the rest of practice. Oh well. Hopefully I'll get a chance tomorrow.

On the way home, I indulge in a little fantasy about being best friends with Jamie. We're in all the same classes, basically, so she could come over after school and we could do our homework together. And then I'd say, "Wanna stay over?" and she'd say, "Sure," and we'd curl up under a blanket together and share a pint of Ben & Jerry's, and eat popcorn and watch movies together, and she could sleep in my bed, and we'd stay up all night talking. It wouldn't be like with Trish. Jamie's much nicer, I can tell. So if I ever felt like, say . . . oh, I don't know . . . kissing her, let's say, I'd feel totally comfortable telling her. And I bet she'd probably be open to it. Just for fun. Okay, maybe that's going a little too far.

Still. Cross-country was definitely the right decision.

10

CALEB, THE GOTH FROM TRIG, CALLED IT THAT first day. I've become one of the Asian girls. It wasn't like I had much of a choice—they kind of snapped me right up—but it's fine. So we're all Asian. Who cares?

I've noticed that a lot of kids at school tend to hang out with kids with the same ethnic background: the Filipino kids all seem to know each other, groups of turbaned Sikh boys hang out in pods, and the Samoan kids have a couple of lunch tables all to themselves.

I see Jamie during lunch every day, but she's all the way across the quad. I wish I could walk up and say hi to her, but her friends make me nervous. For one thing, they don't seem very welcoming. Christina is . . . mean. JJ, one of the guys, is in psychology with me, and he just sits there all through class with his arms folded and his legs stretched out in front of him, and he never knows any answers. I bet they'd think I'm a sheltered little Asian nerd. Technically they're not wrong, but I'm not eager to go over and test that theory.

Next week is a special week where the whole school will be participating in some kind of anti-drug campaign. Greg Nakamura, the student body president, got on the P.A. during first period and read a short anti-drug blurb and a long list of all the Special Activities meant to remind us that it's fun not to do drugs.

In addition to the activities, we're supposed to come dressed according to a different theme each day: Mexican on Macarena Monday (Dance Away Drugs!), boots on Tuesday (Give Drugs the Boot!), etc. Student government representatives will go around during first period and count the number of people in each classroom who are dressed for the theme. The classroom with the most thematically dressed people in one week wins a pizza party. Groans from everyone, everywhere.

Well, almost everyone. The cheerleaders, Stacy and Rochelle, are pleading, "Come on, you guys! It'll be fun!" Andy Chin, in his role as junior class president, is going, "Show some spirit! Help fight drugs! Come on, we could win a pizza party!"

Caleb says, loudly enough for Andy to hear, "Don't do drugs. Because pizza."

Andy just grins and shrugs.

Caleb leans over and whispers, "He's such a hypocrite. He gets high every weekend."

I've heard that Andy is kind of a party animal, but really? I have a hard time believing it after all the confirmation I've had about other Asian parents being as strict as—or stricter than—mine.

"How do you know?"

"We have the same . . . source. If you know what I mean."

My mouth drops open. Nice. Way to reveal what a nerd I am.

"What? It's not a big deal."

"I know it's not a big deal," I say defensively.

Caleb mimics me in a prim falsetto, "I know it's not a big deal."

Mr. Green is at the front of the room saying, "Time to talk about cosines," which gives me a good excuse to turn around and ignore Caleb.

When class ends, Caleb continues our conversation. "C'mon, don't get all shocked on me," he says. And then, jerking his chin at Andy, "All the *cool* kids do it."

"Well, how does *he*?"

"I heard his parents are like, these high-powered people who travel all the time. He gets the house to himself a couple weekends a month, apparently."

"Huh." I can't imagine my parents leaving me alone in the house for an evening, let alone a whole weekend.

"Not your parents, huh?"

"Never."

"Hey, have lunch with us," he says, in a bizarre change of

subject. "My mom made, like, a hundred chocolate chip cookies and I brought them for us all." When I hesitate, he says, "What—you so in with your Asian friends that you're too good to hang out with anyone else?"

What the—?

"Fine," I hear myself say. "But those cookies better be *really* good."

Thankfully, Elaine and Hanh have a VSA meeting today, so I don't have to explain anything to them. When I tell Reggie that I'm eating lunch with the goths, she says, a little incredulously, "What? Why?" I explain that Caleb won't leave me alone, and that he's promised me cookies, and I offer to save some for her. She gives me a skeptical, raised-eyebrow stare— one of her specialties, I've noticed—and shoos me off.

I sidle up to the goth tree, where Caleb and his friends are already dipping into a huge Tupperware container full of cookies. They all look up, and Caleb makes room for me next to him and introduces me: Ginny, Thom, Brett, Andrew, Luisa. Ginny, the girl sitting next to Caleb, scoots over, and I sit down between them.

"We're talking about that ridiculous anti-drug stuff next week."

I help myself to a cookie and roll my eyes, as I'm sure they're expecting me to. "Right?"

"Like any of that's going to keep people from doing drugs. All anyone cares about is winning pizza anyway."

A guy named Thom shakes his head and says, "Seriously.

Macarena Monday? What the fuck does the Macarena have to do with drugs? I don't even think it's really Mexican."

"Knowing Lowell, she's probably trying to get the Mexican kids involved," says Luisa. "She probably thinks we'll get all excited and want to do the Macarena."

"Who's Lowell?" I ask.

"Mrs. Lowell. She's activities director and student government advisor."

"How 'bout, you have to be high to want to do the Macarena," Caleb offers.

"They should call it Marijuana Monday," Thom says. "Dress up in a Mexican costume and dance away drugs to a song that's not from Mexico because no one who dances does drugs. God, it's so fucked up on so many levels, it makes me want to puke."

About halfway through lunch, I realize that I haven't hung out with white kids since I left Wisconsin. How's that for weird? The bell rings and we start gathering up our things. I say good-bye and head off to English, but Caleb tags along after me for a few steps. "Hey. That wasn't so bad, was it?"

I shake my head. "Your friends are nice."

Caleb looks at me, as if he's making up his mind about something. Then he says, "So, uh, we're all probably gonna just chill at my house on Saturday. That's usually what we do."

"Huh?"

"My mom's going to be around, too, if your mom is hung up about stuff like that." Oh. He's inviting me over to his house.

Okay. It suddenly occurs to me that Caleb might like me—like, *like* me-like me.

"Um . . . I think I have to stay home to help my mom with some stuff."

"Oh. Sure, okay, no problem. See ya." He raises his hand in a half wave and turns and walks off. Maybe he's just being friendly?

"See ya."

He's just being friendly. Yeah, that's probably what it is. It has to be.

11

OMIGOD, SOMEONE PINCH ME. JAMIE—JAMIE!—IS walking home with me. Right now. I know. My fantasy is coming true.

Ten minutes ago, we were all straggling out of the locker room after practice, hair still damp from the showers, hauling our hundred-pound backpacks and saying good-bye to each other as kids piled into cars or headed to the bus stop. I was starting off on my walk home when I heard Jamie complaining to Priti. "My brother spilled soda all over the laptop last night, so now I won't be able to finish that online assessment for tomorrow."

An idea sprang to life in my head. "Hey, wanna come over to my house?"

"Huh?" Jamie turned to look at me.

"I mean, uh. I live just a couple of blocks from here. You could use my computer. You know, to do your homework. Or whatever. And catch a later bus home. If you want." Her eyebrows shot up. She took a quick look around her, then pointed to herself—*Me?* "Or . . . not. No big deal, I just, you know. Just thought I'd—"

"No, that would be great." She hesitated. "You sure it's okay?"

"Oh, totally. No problem."

"Sweet. Thanks." She smiled at me and I smiled back and after a couple seconds of smiling at each other I started to feel silly, so I looked away. But I've been smiling all the way home.

After a brief, mortifying, and very Japanese introduction to Mom (*Hello, I'm sorry my daughter is such a loser, it's so kind of you to be nice to her, I really owe you one*), we escape to my room, and Jamie checks out my bookshelf while I run to the kitchen for some snacks.

"Emily Dickinson?" she says when I return laden with Diet Cokes, a bag of kettle corn, and a bowl of rice crackers.

Oh, no. "Yeah. I know, I'm a nerd."

"No, that's cool. We had to read a poem by her in eighth grade: 'I'm Nobody! Who are you?' I liked it."

"That's the poem that made me want to get that book!"

"But I don't get her sometimes—she's a little weird for me, you know? This shy white lady shut up in her house all day writing poems. All those white writer ladies ever did was sit around and write and sew—Charlotte Brontë, Emily Dickinson, the *Little Women* chick . . ."

"No, they did other things. Like knit lace and drink tea." I giggle, and she laughs with me, which feels kind of magical for some reason.

"Louisa May Alcott," Jamie says next.

"Oh, right."

She adds, "You should read Sandra Cisneros. She wrote this poem called 'Loose Woman' that's like the opposite of 'I'm Nobody.' She says whatever she wants, she does whatever she wants, and she doesn't give a shit about what people say. No sitting around inside and sewing."

Note to self: Google "Loose Woman" by Sandra Cisneros. But I have to defend Emily.

"I don't think she cared what people said. I mean, she didn't mind people thinking she was weird or whatever. I thought that was kind of the point of 'I'm Nobody.'"

Jamie chews her lip. "Huh. Yeah, I guess you're right." She smiles. "You need to read 'Loose Woman,' though. It's pretty great." *Oh, I will.* She moves on. "Ooh, this is pretty," she says, taking down my red lacquer box.

"Oh. That's—"

"Huh?" She opens it.

—*private.* "Oh, nothing. I was just going to say my parents gave it to me."

She admires the pearl earrings. "Wow. Are these real?"

"Yeah."

"Best friend?" She holds up the photo of Trish and me.

"Meh. Used to be."

She holds up the phone number.

"Someone my dad knows. I don't know why it's in there."

Now she's playing with bits of sea glass in her palm. "Where'd you get these? They're so pretty."

"I know, right? I used to like to collect them whenever we went to the beach—Lake Michigan. When I was little, I'd pretend they were like, magic stones from an underwater kingdom and I was actually the long-lost princess . . . kinda silly, I know."

"No." Jamie looks up and smiles. "It's not silly. I was thinking the same thing. Like, they're pieces of your soul that got lost or something. Like who you really are, like the princess. Or like people who make it through a tough time—you know, like you start off sharp and broken, and then over time you become smooth and beautiful and like, your own piece." If I didn't have a crush on her before, I definitely do now. A girl-crush, I mean. "You're laughing at me. You think I'm a total nerd. I can tell from your face," she says.

"No! No, I think you're . . . cool."

"Oh, right. I heard you hesitate there. You totally think I'm a nerd." She smiles. "That's okay. We can be nerds together. Poetry nerds."

"You saying *I'm* a nerd, then?"

She looks at me and raises an eyebrow. "Your own personal volume of Emily Dickinson?"

"Oh, okay, fine. You win. Nerds together."

I lie on the bed and Jamie sits on the floor as we do our trig homework. She finishes ahead of me. Out of the corner of my eye, I watch her stretch, shut her textbook, and slide it into her backpack. So unfair. I turn back to working out how deep I would have to dig to reach a bed of coal that is tilted at twelve degrees and comes to the surface six kilometers from my property. Right. Like that would ever happen in real life. I struggle to put together an equation involving opposite and adjacent sides, angles and tangents. Or maybe cosines. Algebra and geometry were easy, but I just can't put the pieces of trigonometry together in a way that makes sense to me. I don't even really understand what some of the pieces are.

I look up to see Jamie watching me. Ack. Please let me not have been doing something embarrassing without realizing it, like making a funny face or picking a zit or something. I don't *think* I was.

"What?"

"Oh! Nothing," she says, looking away. "I was just, you know. Nothing."

Omigod. Is it my imagination, or is she blushing? I feel my own cheeks grow warm, and I pretend to play with my hair so I can cover my face. Could it be? Maybe. But I could be wrong. Slow down. Make some space. Redirect. "God. I can*not* do this trig homework. How is it so easy for you?"

"Seriously?"

"Seriously."

"It's not hard."

"It is for me."

She groans dramatically and climbs onto my bed. "Scoot over. I'll help you."

Both of us on the bed. Okay. I scoot over as directed, and I'm still lying down and she's sitting, but my bed isn't that big, so there's a pretty significant stretch of my body that's touching hers. She didn't have to get on the bed and sit this close, but she did. She's so close I can feel her thigh on my ribs. But she's just helping me with my math homework. Still, there's the way she was looking at me before—she wasn't just staring off into space and I happened to be in her line of sight. She was gazing at me—at *me*—I know she was. Well, I think she was. Was she?

"Hey, pay attention!" She nudges me with her knee.

"Sorry. It's just so . . . boring and confusing." *And thinking about you is just as confusing, but so much more interesting.*

"It's not. Just listen." I make a superhuman effort to focus on trigonometry. Tangent, sine, cosine. All too soon, it's six thirty, time for Jamie to go back to school and catch her bus. As she packs up to go, she holds out the Emily Dickinson. "Can I borrow this?"

"Sure. Nerd."

"Thanks. Nerd."

We walk to the bus stop together, and lean against the little bus shelter, so close we're almost touching. We gaze down the street in silence. The bus appears, and as Jamie stands up and hoists her backpack, it throws her off balance and she stumbles sideways a little.

"Whoa! Sorry," she says, catching herself on my arm. A shivery little *zing!* shoots up my spine. A good zing. A great zing. I try to catch her eye, but she's already headed toward the curb. She climbs onto the bus while I stand there with my heart bang-bang-booming like a bass drum, and she waves good-bye as the door closes behind her. My hand waves back, but my mind seems to have left the premises. I turn and walk home, alternately feeling like I'm going to levitate and float away on a pink cotton candy cloud, and feeling like I'm teetering on the edge of a huge cliff, looking down into a wild and windy abyss.

I like her. Like, *like* her-like her. No doubt. Even more than I liked Trish. She's smart, she's beautiful, she's real, she's romantic. She thinks pieces of sea glass are like pieces of a lost soul, for crying out loud. I like her so much I can hardly even breathe.

But I so don't need this. After a lifetime of feeling different and out of place, I finally fit in. I'm finally comfortable. I can finally work on the subtler points of being uniquely me, instead of having to explain the obvious Asian flag that everyone can see. I don't want to fly a new freak flag. I really, really don't.

When I get back, Mom is using her little wooden pestle to grind sesame seeds in a special ceramic bowl. She's making broiled mackerel for dinner—my favorite—with sides of vinegar-sugar cucumber salad, boiled spinach with ground sesame seeds and sea salt, and, of course, rice and miso soup. I wonder if I should have asked Jamie to stay for dinner, but then decide that the mackerel would probably have grossed her out. Broiled mackerel is served with its head and tail on, and you basically pull the meat off the bones in little chunks until there's just a skeleton and a fish head left. You're pretty much face-to-face— literally—with the fact that you're eating a dead fish.

"Did you finish your homeworks?" asks Mom.

"I have a little Spanish left to do, and a couple of chapters to read for English."

"Dinner is in twenty minutes. You can do some more homeworks or set the table."

Not a word about Jamie. Which is a little strange because she often has something to say about the few friends that I've ever brought home—usually that they're prettier, taller, smarter, or more polite than me. But still. I'm curious.

When we sit down to eat, and after I serve myself some mackerel, I hand it to Mom and ask, "So what do you think about Jamie?"

Mom pokes her chopsticks into the fish and tears out a piece. "She wears lot of makeups."

"So?"

"Too much." She tears off another hunk.

In Mom's eyes, any amount of makeup is too much, so I'm not surprised. "I think she looks pretty."

"Too much makeups is not pretty. Girl should look like girlish, not like trying to be grown-up."

"She's not trying to be grown-up. She just wears makeup. Lots of girls do."

An image of Christina's Pinot Noir lips flashes in my mind, along with a flicker of doubt. Why does her makeup bug me, but not Jamie's?

"Hn." My mom digs the mackerel's eye out of its socket—it's her favorite part—and pops it into her mouth. "She doesn't look like good student." The pronouncement of death. My mom will never approve of anyone who is not a good student. Not that I need her approval.

"Mom, she's in all the same classes as me."

"Affirmative action."

"Mom!"

"She's a Mexican, isn't she? Schools just want to say they have multiculture in advanced classes."

"Just because she's Mexican *American* doesn't mean she's a bad student."

But Mom's not having it. She picks a stray fishbone out of her mouth and says, "The Mexicans are lazy, and not so smart—look how long they live in America, and they still need the Spanish language on everything—even for driver's license and voting! That is lazy. I only live here for seventeen years and I had to learn English for driver's license, reading newspaper, and everything. I didn't ask for everything to be in Japanese."

"Mom. Jamie's not lazy. Mexicans aren't lazy. It's way more complicated than that."

"I didn't say Jamie is lazy! I said Mexican is lazy. Japanese started with poor, and no English, and discriminated. But Japanese are successful now. San Jose airport is named after the Japanese person. The Mexicans are still just the gardeners and kitchen workers."

She's never going to get it, so I give up trying to explain and go back to defending Jamie. "Well, Jamie aced her last trig test." So there.

"Well, maybe Jamie is good student." Mom looks sternly at me. "But she's the exception." I shake my head. There really are no words. No, wait. Mom has a few left. "And she *looks* like bad student. That's her fault if I think so. If you want people to think she is good student, tell her to stop wearing so much makeups."

I pour a trickle of soy sauce on my sesame spinach and take a bite. When I was little, I used to pester Mom to make Hamburger Helper like Trish's mom. Or just order pizza. Trish's mom was a good cook, but she said she liked to take a break and relax sometimes. She didn't want to waste energy worrying all the time about what Trish ate, or who she hung out with, or where she went on the weekends. Mom, on the other hand, refused to relax. "Being a mother is my job. You say relax, but relaxed worker is just lazy. How can I be a good mother for you if I cook lazy food? If I let you do whatever you want, if I let you be friends with bad people or let you wear sloppy clothes, I am being the lazy mother who doesn't care enough to be strict." Typical. I guess it's nice that she cares enough to look out for me, even though she's totally wrong. But sometimes I wish she cared enough to listen, as well.

"Hey, Sana! C'mere a sec!"

I adjust my course and angle over toward Jamie and three of her friends, who hang out not far from where I meet Elaine and Hanh before school. It's a cold morning, and they're all slouched in oversize black hoodies. Christina is leaning against one of the boys, and they're all staring at me impassively, except for Jamie, who's smiling.

"These are my friends," she says. "That's Arturo and Christina—you remember Christina," nodding at the couple, "and this is JJ."

Arturo looks like he could be twenty—he's short, but he has a muscular build, broad shoulders, and thick, straight eyebrows over serious brown eyes. JJ, from psych class, looks like he wants to be twenty. He's taller than Arturo, with bright eyes and a ridiculous, scraggly little mustache. He's shifting back and forth like he's either freezing or just has too much energy to stand still. He's twirling a Darth Vader key chain on his finger.

"'Sup." Arturo tips his chin at me and JJ flashes me an impish smile.

"You're in psych with me," JJ says. "You're one of the smart ones."

I *think* that's a compliment. But Christina gives me a slow once-over that makes me doubt she sees it that way.

"Hi," I say. Christina briefly turns the corners of her mouth up into something resembling a smile, but her eyes remain cold.

"I just wanted to give you your book back," Jamie says, handing over Emily Dickinson.

"Oh, right. Thanks."

"You were right. She's more complex than she seems at first."

"*Pffff*, you two are like homework buddies *and* poetry buddies?" Christina sniggers when she sees the title. "You competing for Nerd of the Year?"

"Shut up," Jamie retorts as I busy myself cramming the book into my backpack, wishing I could climb in after it.

"Aww, I'm just playin'," says Christina. "Hey, Sana, you don't have to look so embarrassed! It's okay." Except it's not okay, because she's clearly enjoying my embarrassment. I smile weakly. I'm not sure what's going on exactly, but if her goal is to make me feel small, it's working.

Arturo asks, "You smart, like JJ says?"

"'Course she's smart! All Asians are smart, right, Sana?" Christina's voice is friendly, and maybe it's because I'm so sick of that stereotype, but it's not clear whether she's laughing *at* me or *with* me.

"Isn't that kinda racist?" asks JJ.

"It isn't racist if it's nice," says Christina. "I'm just being nice."

"It's still racist," says Jamie. "Anyway, *I* helped *Sana* with her trig homework, right?"

"Jamie's the smart one," I agree.

"*She* helped *you*?" asks Arturo. "I know she's smart, but aren't Asians supposed to be good at math?" He's joking. He has to be.

"Not this Asian."

"That's for sure." Jamie grins at me.

"Yeeeah," says JJ. "I suck at math." He puts his fist out for me to bump, and as I put out my own fist, I feel a thrill of solidarity—which is ruined when I see Christina rolling her eyes. But Jamie and Arturo are rolling their eyes, too.

Arturo says, "Failing math isn't funny, bruh. If you fail out this year, I'm gonna fucking kill you." JJ waves him off.

Then Jamie starts in, too. "How many times do we have to tell you? You gotta go to college if you want to get anywhere in life."

JJ groans wearily. "I know, I know. Just chill the fuck out, okay? What are you, my mom? Maybe I don't *want* to get anywhere in life. What's that even supposed to mean, anyway? What if I end up becoming . . . becoming a movie star? Diego Luna didn't go to college. That Ironman dude didn't go to college."

Christina groans. "Seriously? You're going with movie star?"

Jamie adds, "Yeah, and I bet most movie stars did go to college. Anyway, you can't bet your future on something like 'I wanna be a movie star.'"

"Okay, fine. How about being a plumber? Or like, a store

manager? Your mom works the desk at Kaiser. What's wrong with that? Why you gotta be such a hater?"

"No one's being a hater," Arturo says. "We're just saying there's more opportunities."

"As long as white and Asian people don't take them all," says Christina, and for a moment, I forget to breathe.

"Hey, babe, back off," says Arturo. "Be nice. Sana, don't listen to her. She doesn't mean it personally. She's just pissed because Lowell made her get three references to work in the student store, and she only makes the Asian and white kids get one."

I look at Jamie, who nods. "It's true."

"Oh. That sucks."

"Yep," Christina replies grimly. I can't say that I blame Mrs. Lowell for being reluctant to hire Christina though. She doesn't seem like she'd be very friendly to customers.

"Well, see you at practice," I say to Jamie.

"'Bye," say Christina, Arturo, and JJ together. Arturo and JJ turn their attention back to the group. But Christina wraps herself in Arturo's arms and watches me leave. I can feel her eyes boring holes into my back as I walk away.

"What were you doing with those guys?" asks Reggie when I reach my friends. They're peeking over their shoulders at Jamie and her friends.

"Yeah, since when do you hang out with the Mexican kids?" says Elaine.

"Oh. Uh, Jamie was just returning a book she borrowed

from me after practice yesterday. For um, English."

"Oh, right. She's in a bunch of my classes. She's cool."

"Yeah, but her friends hate me, I think. Especially that girl, Christina."

Hanh glances over. "Yeah, I know her. She was in my P.E. class last year. She's a bitch."

"She's pissed because Lowell made her get three references to work in the school store. She says Lowell's racist."

"She *should* have to get extra references. She was tardy to P.E. all the time. Plus, I heard she got suspended in middle school for fighting," says Hanh.

The five-minute bell rings, and we start walking to class. "You shouldn't have to get extra references for screwing up in *middle* school," Reggie protests. "And I heard that fight was about JJ, before he got tall. Like some bigger dude was picking on him."

"Where'd you hear that?"

"I sat next to JJ's cousin in chorus freshman year."

"Well, I don't care. That's no excuse. And anyway, I told you she was tardy a lot. Like literally every day."

"Janet works at the store, and she's late a lot," Elaine says. "She only had to have one reference."

"Everyone knows Lowell totally lets kids off the hook if they suck up to her," says Reggie. "I bet she said something about the tardies to that Christina girl and Christina wouldn't play, and now Lowell's punishing her for it."

"That doesn't seem fair, though," says Elaine doubtfully.

Hanh shakes her head. "It doesn't matter. If she had a lot of tardies and a bad discipline record, she *should've* sucked up to Lowell. She knows the rules. It's her own fault if she doesn't want to play by them. All those Mexican kids come in with this attitude like people are so racist and Asian kids are such suck-ups. Well, then, suck the fuck up! Stop complaining."

I can't decide who's right. On the one hand, it's true that school is a big game, and it's not that hard to play along. Still. It seems like Hanh's being pretty harsh. Because it's also true that the game isn't always fair.

I'm still thinking about this when we reach my locker. There's a tiny corner of paper sticking out of the vent, and when I open the door, I see a folded note inside. I tuck it into my backpack before the girls see it. When I open it during Mr. Green's homework review, my breath catches in my throat, and trig class melts away. It's a handwritten copy of a poem: "My Garden—like the Beach—" by Emily Dickinson. It's signed, "Your nerdy friend, Jamie."

She must've put it there before I even saw her with her friends. Okay. Calm down. Maybe I'm reading too much into this. Maybe it's just a reference to the sea glass and pearls in my lacquer box. Purely surface. No metaphor. Maybe she's just saying she wants to be friends.

Or maybe it's something else.

I spend the rest of the day pulling the poem out and reading it whenever I can. When I get home, I take the photo of Trish out of my red lacquer box, and replace it with Jamie's note. After I do my poetry journal entry about "My Garden—like the Beach—," I copy it, plus "I'm Nobody! Who are you?" into another, brand-new notebook. Then I scour the internet for a good poem for Jamie.

"In the Morning in Morocco" by Mary K. Stillwell is perfect. It's about waking up in an exotic, dreamy place (Morocco) after having traveled from Omaha. In the beginning of the poem, the speaker seems to think she's still in Omaha, just as she's waking up. The light is coming in through the cracks of her window shade, and it's like the dream is seeping into reality, or maybe it's the other way around.

So. Page One of the new notebook: "I'm Nobody! Who are you?"

Page Two: "My Garden—like the Beach—"

Page Three: "In the Morning in Morocco"

I'm going to give the notebook to Jamie after practice tomorrow afternoon. I hope she likes it. I hope she makes a Page Four.

POETRY JOURNAL, HONORS AMERICAN LITERATURE
THURSDAY, SEPTEMBER 10

"My Garden-like the Beach-"
by Emily Dickinson

A friend of mine gave me this poem today. I'm not sure
what it's really about, or what it means. There's some kind
of comparison between a garden, the beach, the sea, and
summer. Maybe having a garden and going to the beach
are both associated with summer? Maybe the beach and
summertime are both times/places where you can be free? The
beach is wild nature and the garden is tamed nature?

The last part is my favorite: "the Pearls / She fetches-such
as Me." Maybe since pearls are a treasure, the speaker, "Me,"
is also a treasure. Maybe the speaker is offering herself like a
pearl, to be someone's treasure.

12

I GET HOME AFTER PRACTICE ON FRIDAY AND
wolf down a snack. Reggie, Hanh, and Elaine are coming to
pick me up in ten minutes so we can go to Valley Fair Mall.
Mom has agreed to let me go, since it's Friday and I have all
weekend to do my homework.

Reggie drives up to my house in her mom's Honda
Odyssey with Elaine riding shotgun and Hanh in the back.
I buckle up as Reggie inches back out into the street and
Hanh applies a little extra eye shadow. With maybe the strict-
est of all our Asian parents, Hanh hardly ever gets to go out
unchaperoned—not even with girlfriends during the day.
Reggie got Hanh's mom to let her come by telling her that
Mrs. Lin, Reggie's mom, would be with us. Which is sort of
true. Reggie's cousin Sharon just got engaged, and she's going

shopping for a mother-of-the-bride dress at the mall with *her* mom and Mrs. Lin. They're going in Sharon's car, an hour from now, but that's not important. The point is *they'll* be at the mall, and *we'll* be at the mall. Hanh's mom doesn't need to know that we don't plan to cross paths.

"I just wish my parents would trust me," grouses Hanh.

"They do trust you. They trust that you're with my mom. And they're wrong. So you can't blame them for not trusting you," says Reggie, not unreasonably, I guess. But I still feel sorry for Hanh.

Valley Fair is an endless maze of atriums and walkways, and I follow the others' lead, glad they know where they're going. At Forever 21, Reggie examines a cute pink long-sleeved tee trimmed with sequins and says, "Hey, Janet wants to go to karaoke after homecoming. Her sister's at Santa Clara University, and she said she'd help us reserve a party room and bring some alcohol. Wanna go?"

"Yeah, right," says Hanh. "Last time I checked, both of my parents were Asian. Janet's so lucky her mom's white. She gets to do everything." She pauses, then adds, "Try that top in charcoal."

"No, I talked to Sharon," says Reggie, holding up the charcoal top. "She'll tell your parents that we're having a sleepover at her apartment and that she'll be there. It won't be a lie, 'cause I'll just drive us there after karaoke."

"Reg, you're a genius!" I say, and Reggie takes a bow.

We call our parents, give them Sharon's phone number,

and set up next weekend. I can hardly believe it. Never was I ever invited to go out drinking in Wisconsin, unless you count the country club, which I don't because I invited myself. Even if I'd ever been invited, I had no one to lie to my parents for me. But it seems so natural now, so easy, like in movies where teenagers go to parties all the time.

Reggie buys the charcoal top to wear to the party, and we all decide to buy something, too. The rest of the afternoon is a flurry of "Is this too see-through?" "Does this make me look fat?" "Can I borrow your pink flats to go with this?" and "Do you think Jimmy will be at karaoke?"

All the while, despite the girl bonding, my mind keeps going to Jamie. When I try on a top, I wonder if she'd like me in it. I wonder if she's going to homecoming, and if I should invite her to karaoke with us. And what that would mean. I mean, Elaine isn't about to invite Jimmy, but Jimmy isn't her friend, not really. Jamie and I, on the other hand, are friends. Reggie invited me, and she's *my* friend, right? But what if Jamie wants *her* friends to come? Like Christina, who hates me? And before I know it, I'm asking a question.

"Hey, if you're like, kinda friends with someone, and like, you're kinda interested in them, but you think their best friend might not like you, so you don't really want to hang out with their friends, is it cool to say that to the person you're interested in, or should you wait until you're like, dating or whatever?"

And even though Elaine has just found the cutest top *ever*, no one seems to care about it anymore.

"What? Who? Who's your friend?"

"She said she's *kinda* friends with them. Not real friends, right?"

"Girl or boy?"

"Boy, duh. She said she wants to date them. Right? I mean, you're not gay, are you?"

"Of course she isn't, she's way too normal to be gay!"

"Who is it, Sana?"

"Is it that guy, that goth—Caleb? Didn't you eat lunch with him and his friends the other day? Omigod! Is it him?"

They're fluttering and cooing like pigeons around popcorn. I should have known this would happen. "Stop!" I say. "Jeez, I'm sorry I said anything. It's not important. It doesn't matter." But it does to Elaine, Hanh, and Reggie, and without my help, they decide that it has to be a guy—who likes me. But who? They proceed to guess the names of a hundred different guys, and they only back off when I promise to tell them who it is later.

"Like, how much later?"

"As soon as I know what's up."

"What if you don't know what's up for like, months? It happens, you know."

"I'll tell you in a month, no matter what." Oops. Where did that come from?

"Swear?"

"I swear."

"Jeez, you're so secretive."

"Inscrutable Asian."

Why can't I keep my big mouth shut?

I'm sitting in the food court saving a table while the others go and get a ton of food to share when I get a text from Caleb.

What are you doing?

At the mall with Elaine, Hanh, and Reggie

AZN grl

Whatever

I'm just finishing up when Reggie arrives with her tray of food.

"Who's that?"

"Oh, that guy, Caleb."

"I knew it! Is he the 'friend' you were talking about before?"

"No!"

She raises her eyebrow at me. Elaine and Hanh are now sitting down and arranging their trays and food. "I *thought* he was flirting with you during trig!" exclaims Elaine, clapping her hands.

"He's a little weird, but he's cute! Do you think she should go for him?"

"Oh. My. God. It is *not* like that, I do *not* like him that way."

"It's *totally* like that, and you should give him a chance. He's nicer than he seems at first." Elaine is really excited about this, for some reason.

"How would you know?"

"I sat next to him last year in Algebra Two, and we had to

be partners all the time. He was always all 'Everything sucks.'"

"I know!"

"Right? But he's kidding. Plus he's smart. And kind of funny."

"Then why don't *you* go for him?"

"Jimmy, duh."

After dinner, we walk across the street and get an out-door table at this fancy place called Straits Café, and sip six-dollar lemonades for the next forty-five minutes, much to our waiter's irritation. Hanh and Reggie try to order a cock-tail, and he doesn't even bother to ask for ID—just stares at them, shakes his head, and walks away. "Asshole," grumbles Hanh. The night crowd is starting to come out now, and I feel so grown-up, surrounded by adults. The place is flooded with Asians—mostly techies, judging by the snippets of con-versation we can hear, and Hanh starts to get nervous that she might be seen by someone who knows her family, so we pay up and leave.

When they drop me off at home, I'm about to get out of the car with my Hollister shopping bag when Elaine grabs me. "Stop! You can't take that in the house! Are you crazy?"

"Why?"

"What the hell are you going to tell your mom when she sees what you got?" says Hanh. "Do you think she'd let you keep it?"

"Good point."

"Right? Pack it with your overnight stuff next week, leave

the house in something else, and we'll all change at school. Here—" She takes my super-cute, fifty-percent-off, scarlet, low-backed halter top out of the Hollister bag, grabs my purse, and stuffs the top inside. "That's better."

"Hanh Le, master of deception," intones Reggie.

Hanh shrugs and grins. "Learn from the best."

13

WE'RE FINISHING UP *THE SCARLET LETTER* FOR
English. It would be a cool book if it weren't such a depressing
slog to read. I mean, a Puritan girl named Hester gets married
to an ugly old man and has a love child with her hot Puritan
minister while her husband is away, and then the ugly old husband comes back in disguise to get revenge—sounds fun, right?
Except that most of the book is written in horrible, torturously
long sentences about how horrible and tortured everyone feels.
Because no one knows it's the minister's child, Hester is the
only one who gets punished, and she has to go around wearing
a big red A for Adultery on her chest while the minister gets off
scot-free. Except he's supposedly suffering silently and being
eaten away by guilt on the inside, which I think is a load of BS,
and he should just man up and tell everyone he loves her.

Actually, I was a little like Hester when I lived in Wisconsin. I got labeled just like her: A for Asian. Except I couldn't help being Asian, while Hester could have prevented herself from cheating. I say this to Reggie, Elaine, and Hanh at lunch a few days after our shopping spree.

"A for Asian?" says Reggie. "That's awesome."

"A for Awesome Asians," quips Elaine. "We should get T-shirts!"

"Yeah—it would be like when Hester put gold thread on her A, like she didn't care about what people thought, you know?"

"Yeah, like she was proud of it, like she refused to feel ashamed! Just like us, right?" Elaine is getting excited. "Maybe if there was a group of girls like Hester, like with As on their chests, maybe if they all stuck together, maybe they could have changed things. You know, friends, community, power!"

I love California. I love my new friends.

"Yeah, or maybe they all would have been burned at the stake for being witches," says Jamie.

A week later, Jamie and I are sitting on the floor in my bedroom after practice, drafting analytical essays on *The Scarlet Letter*. Jamie's been coming over to do homework regularly, pretty much every day except Thursdays, when we have meets.

"Anyway, Hester put gold thread on the A to make herself feel worse, not better. She was just as fucked up as the rest of them," says Jamie.

"Aw, don't say that. You just ruined it."

"A for Asian. You think being in a group changes what people think about you? Try wearing an M for Mexican. *That's* like Hester. It doesn't give you more power. It doesn't change people's minds. It just makes people judge all of you together. They stop seeing you as an individual."

"That's not true." I think about how much more *myself* I feel with my Asian friends than with my white friends.

"It is. Think about Christina. Eight kids applied to work at the school store, three white, four Asian, and one Mexican. How come only Christina had to get extra letters of rec? She gets good grades. It's not like she's a criminal. It's because she's wearing an M for Mexican."

"Yeah . . ." It's plausible. But how can anyone really know for sure? I remember what Hanh said a while back. "What about . . . I mean, I heard that Lowell likes kids to brownnose. Maybe Christina . . . I mean, I'm sure she's nice and everything. But like that day with the Emily Dickinson book. She comes off kind of . . ."

"Bitchy?"

Well, yes. But I'm not going to say that, am I? "Maybe. Kind of."

Jamie grimaces. "I know. I mean, that day. It was . . . well. She's had a hard year and she was worried about getting the job. And when she's worried it sometimes comes out as anger, you know? Like kind of a defense mechanism. It's not personal."

I doubt that. It felt *very* personal. And about as defensive as a punch in the nose.

"But I bet you're right," Jamie continues. "She probably got upset with Lowell because she was worried about not getting a spot. But I know for a fact that no one else got asked for extra letters. Not Janet, and Christina says she's late all the time. Not even Jason Cole, and he's an asshole, even to teachers."

"Yeah, but Jason's like, the smartest kid in our class."

"It shouldn't matter. If Lowell was being fair, she should've made him and Janet get extra references, too. But she didn't. Christina might've been a bitch to Lowell, but mostly she got screwed because she's Mexican, and she didn't want to play Lowell's game. Because she's part of a group that Lowell doesn't trust."

When she puts it that way, I guess it makes sense. "Okay, you're right. I get it. But I still think that having friends who are like you is better than being the only one. It's better than being alone."

"Yeah, maybe." Jamie wraps her arms around her knees and rests her chin on top. "So was that what it was like for you in Wisconsin? Did you feel alone?"

"Yeah."

"But not anymore, huh."

"It's different here. I have friends who get where I'm coming from, you know? And I have you." Oops. Too far? I look away, because somehow it feels like looking somewhere else will separate me from what I just said.

But Jamie seems pleased. "Aww, really? Thanks."

"Even if you are a nerd."

She laughs and says, "Actually I'm glad I got you, too. I mean, I got my friends and everything, but . . ." She nudges me with her shoulder. "I feel like I can really be myself around you. I can relax."

"Oh. Yeah, me too." Which isn't a hundred percent true. Like right now. My senses are on high alert. I can smell the citrus shampoo she uses in her hair. The spot where her shoulder touched mine is practically tingling. The whole situation is making me nervous. "But what about Christina and them?" I say, just to say something.

"Well, yeah, of course I'm myself around them. But like, I dunno. Like I've always wanted to go to Stanford and be a doctor, right? So they're totally supportive and they totally think I'm gonna go and like, find the cure for cancer or something. But sometimes it just feels like a lot of pressure, you know? And . . . they have a thing about honors kids, like you guys are a bunch of snobs, and why would I want to hang out with you. I mean, it's true, I don't fit in, but that doesn't mean I don't want to, sometimes. So that's hard.

"And teachers treat me like I'm this special snowflake just because I'm Mexican, like I should be doing average at best, or getting pregnant or something. They'll pat me on the back and bend over backward for me even if I don't get As. And I know there's kids who think the teachers are going easy on me because I'm Mexican, which is bullshit—but sometimes I think, what if that's true? What if I fail? My mom and everyone would be so disappointed. And the haters would be all, 'I knew she couldn't do it.' So I have to work extra hard to make sure none of that happens."

She heaves a sigh, and we sit in silence for a while, the weight of her burden heavy between us. Her knees are still tucked up under her chin. She starts picking at a stray thread on the cuff of her jeans and says, "That's one reason I like running. I can just leave all that behind for a while, you know? I can just be me, and run." Now she leans into me. "That's kind of how I feel when I'm with you. The pressure's off. I don't have to be anyone but me."

I nod. We're just sitting there, arms touching, looking at each other, then not looking. After a few seconds, I don't think I can take it anymore. I'm in a movie where the boy and girl are moments away from kissing, and I realize with a start that that's exactly what I want to happen. Not just a hopeless and confused daydreamy wondering how it might feel, like with Trish. Not just a momentary flutter, like with Mark. This is for real. I want us to kiss. I want us to kiss now. I think Jamie might want the same thing. I turn to her, my heart pounding, and say:

"So. The significance of light and dark imagery in *The Scarlet Letter*. How many examples are we supposed to include?" And we're back in the safety of Hester's illicit love affair.

After Jamie gets on the bus, I wonder how Hester and Dimmesdale first kissed. In the woods—the dark, romantic, uncivilized woods, where anything goes. I imagine the time before they kissed, both of them wanting it but unsure if they should go for it. I wonder if they were happy when it finally happened. Probably not—the whole novel is so depressing.

But me, I'm happy. I know something, for once. I know what I want. I want to kiss Jamie, and I also want to spend days at the beach with her, spend winter vacation and Valentine's Day with her, read poetry with her, go to prom with her. I want it all. Actually, I guess I've kind of wanted all of that since the beginning, but the difference now is that I'm not scared of wanting it anymore. I'm not scared of what it means. I don't know if Jamie wants the same thing. That's what scares me now. But if she *does* want what I want, then oh. Oh, how amazing that would be.

For the rest of the evening, it's Jamie-land in my head. Jamie loves poetry. Jamie wants to be a doctor. Jamie's talented and smart and tough and scared and she's fighting her way toward a real goal—I don't even know what I want to do next year, let alone with the rest of my life, except be with her. Jamie said she can be her true self when she's with me. Jamie's arm touching mine. Jamie's face, so close to mine. Jamie.

So I guess I can be excused for bringing up the topic of gay relationships with Mom after dinner, while she relaxes with a cup of tea. It's like when Rapunzel spaces out and asks why the prince is so much lighter than the witch, even though the witch is smaller—and the witch realizes that the prince has been climbing up to see Rapunzel. Maybe not quite so airheaded. Just a little reckless.

"Mom, do you know anyone who's gay?"

She wrinkles her nose and gives me a funny look. "Nandé?"

"It uh . . . came up at school. In history," I lie. "How uh . . . social attitudes toward different minority groups change over time."

Mom blows on her tea and shakes her head. "Just your math teacher from sixth grade. Mr. Freiberg?" I nod. Mr. Freiberg was a walking stereotype. "You know," she continues thoughtfully, "Shizuka-obasan married a gay." Mom's baby sister? I know she was divorced once, when I was a baby—is this why?

"You mean a gay *person*?"

"Yes, that's what I mean. She married a gay," she repeats, thinking that I am expressing shock, rather than correcting her language. "That's why she's divorce and no children. So I know about the gay people." She looks at me across her cup of tea. "I'm not as innocent as you think."

"Naïve, Mom. Innocent means you didn't *do* it. Naïve means you didn't *know* it." Suddenly I am sure that her look means that she *does* know it—about me. Quelling my panic, I return to the subject of my former uncle. "How did she know he was gay?"

"It was arrange-marriage," she says, as if that explains everything.

"So?"

"So after they got married, he didn't want to have a sex. So she figured out."

"But why didn't she figure it out earlier? Like while they

were engaged or something?"

She draws herself up and says haughtily, "Japanese people have moral. They don't have a sex all the time before marriage, like Americans."

I happen to know that this is wrong, because in Health Ed last year we had to research attitudes toward premarital sex in different countries, and the teacher gave me an article about the huge popularity of Japanese "love hotels" that rent rooms by the hour to unmarried couples. "What about love hotels?" I say.

Mom turns up her nose and sniffs. "Only the loose-moral people in the city go to love hotels." Of course that's what she thinks. But as always, there's no point in trying to change her mind.

So I just ask, "Why did he even marry her in the first place?"

She shrugs and sips her tea. "He wanted to get married like the respectable person."

"So then why did he tell her after he married her?"

"He didn't tell her. I told you, she figured out."

"Huh?"

She sighs with exasperation and puts the cup down. "Only the gay man doesn't want to have a sex with the new bride." Oh. Well. She sighs again, deeper this time, and gazes into the cup between her hands as she continues, "She just told everyone that they couldn't get along, so he didn't have to tell that he was a gay. It was very nice of her, so he and his family didn't have to be ashame. In Japan it's not good to be a gay, you know.

It makes the other people upset. Many of the gay get married so they don't make their families ashame."

"But that's ridiculous," I blurt. "There's no shame in being gay."

"Ha!" she snorts. "Here, all the gay just think they should tell everyone. They say oh, be yourself is the best way, no shame, and everyone else should accept. It's selfish." This is one of Mom's favorite complaints about America and Americans. Selfish. Disrespectful. Inconsiderate. Women were happy before feminism—until those selfish feminists had to go mess everything up and demand equal treatment. Same with Black people. Forget individual freedoms and differences—it's all about making the majority feel comfortable.

On the other hand, if her big complaint about gay-rights activists is that they're selfish—well, it could be worse. Maybe the ice isn't as thin as I thought.

"Asking for acceptance and equal rights isn't selfish. It wouldn't be an issue at all if other people accepted them instead of thinking of them as freaks."

"They *are* the freaks. That's *why* it's selfish to make a big protest. They should accept the society because they are living in it."

"But that's wrong. That's unfair."

She drains the last drop of tea from her cup and stands up. "That is the life. No one can have perfect life without suffering. People have to accept."

"But you can try to make it better, at least."

Mom puts the teapot and cup in the sink, and turns to face me. "You are young, so you think everybody should get everything they want. But one day, you will see. Life is not so simple."

"How would you know?"

"Ha! I know."

And suddenly, I get the feeling that she's not talking about social justice anymore.

"What? What do you know?"

"I am grown-up. So I know."

"Know what?"

"I don't need to tell you. It's just life."

She turns her back and starts washing the dishes. Conversation over. Though to be honest, I'm not sure I want to hear what she's not telling me, anyway. So I say, "Hmph," so she knows I'm not conceding, and get up from the table.

"Chotto. Tetsudai-nasai."

I go to the sink to help her. We wash the dishes, put away the leftovers, rinse the sink, and wipe down the counters. When we're done, the kitchen is neat and clean and shiny. Meanwhile, our secrets whirl around us and obscure us from each other like a cloud of dust.

POETRY JOURNAL, HONORS AMERICAN LITERATURE
TUESDAY, SEPTEMBER 16

"Loose Woman"
by Sandra Cisneros

I'm not really comfortable with swear words in poetry. But I can
see why Sandra Cisneros used them in hers—just the b-word,
actually.

"Loose Woman" is sort of like the bold, loudmouthed version
of "I'm Nobody! Who are you?" Instead of being Nobody, the
speaker is a "b****" and a "beast." But she's proud of it. Most
of the poem is the speaker boasting about who she is and what
she does, though, so maybe she's like the Somebody who says
his name all day in Dickinson's poem.

This part toward the end is probably my favorite:

> I'm an aim-well,
> shoot-sharp,
> sharp-tongued,
> sharp-thinking,

fast-speaking,
foot-loose,
loose-tongued,
let-loose,
woman-on-the-loose,
loose woman.
Beware, honey.

There's a lot of stuff about talking: sharp-tongued, fast-speaking, loose-tongued. But it's a different kind of talking than a frog repeating its name all day long. It's speaking your mind, not just your name. Each line is short, one after another. Maybe it's supposed to be like a stream of bullets (because of "aim-well / shoot-sharp")??? Maybe it's like words are her weapons? So that would make her dangerous? ("Beware, honey.") Who is she threatening? Her oppressors? Society in general? Is she angry, or is she kind of joking a little?

But she also says she's an outlaw, and that she breaks things, and generally makes people uncomfortable. So all of that would make her like Emily Dickinson's Nobody. Except I feel like that kind of person is a Somebody.

I'm not sure I would like this person if I knew her, but I admire her strength. Because she's the opposite of me and I tend not to rock the boat, even though I sometimes wish I could.

14

I'M AT THE STARTING LINE FOR OUR MEET against Cupertino High School. I've been in four meets so far, and every time, I get so nervous I think I might be sick. My insides tie themselves in knots and I wish I could hit the bathroom just one more time before the race. Janet keeps telling me, "Don't worry. What's the worst that could happen? You get tired and slow down? You don't win? So what?"

I know in my head that she's right—it's just one race, and really there's nothing at stake except for a few points—but my body doesn't care. My mouth still goes dry and my heart still thuds away like something terrible is about to happen. "Find your stride. Find a good pace and stick with it," Coach Kieran keeps saying.

The gun goes off, and I start running. It's a three-mile race today, so I have to stay loose in the beginning, which is difficult, what with the adrenaline coursing through my veins and everything. At least I've improved enough over the weeks so that I know that I can keep Janet in sight for most of the race without flaming out at the end.

I cross the finish line and barely make it off to the side, I'm so exhausted. Bent over double and heaving, I feel Janet's hand on my back, and Coach Kieran's, too. Someone shoves a water bottle in my face, and I stand up to take a sip.

"Great race, Sana," says Coach. "Way to finish strong! That's what I'm talkin' about—reaching down deep. Great job. Go warm down." He gives me another pat on the back and is off looking for the next runner.

"Way to go, Sana!" It's Caleb. What's he doing here? His friend Ginny is at his side, waving. Thom is on the other side looking bored, but he gives me a thumbs-up. I wave back.

"Omigod, that's Caleb Miller! And Ginny and that Thom guy. What're they doing here?" asks Janet, staring.

"I dunno," I say. "I'll ask them later."

"You know them?"

"Well, yeah. Caleb sits behind me in trig. I have lunch with them sometimes."

"Really." Janet looks at me curiously. "Are they as weird as they look?"

"No—yes. Well, kind of."

We focus our attention back on the finish line and cheer as Melinda Tsai crosses, then Sruthi Agrawala. When I turn around to see what Caleb, Thom, and Ginny are doing, they're gone. Janet sees me looking and muses, "I've never seen any of them at a meet before. . . . And the only person they cheered for was you." She narrows her eyes at me. "I think he *likes* you."

"No."

"Why else would he come? Is he a cross-country fan?" I can't answer that one.

"Aww, that's so cute! He totally came to see you!" I scowl at her. I have a feeling she's right but I shake my head no. "Totally! Hey, Melinda! Sruthi! You guys! Come here!" Four red-faced girls trot over and Janet gives them her opinion and her evidence.

Melinda immediately starts singing, "Sana has a *boy*-friend! Sana has a *boy*-friend!"

"Seriously, Melinda. What are we, second-graders?" Janet says.

"Thank you, Janet," I say. "God, Melinda. Grow up." Then I turn to Janet so we can share an *amirite?* moment, but Janet has started reciting that old Justin Bieber song, "Boyfriend."

If I was your boyfriend I'd never let you go
I can take you places you ain't never been befo'. . . .

Man, did I misjudge her. "Omigod." I stalk off with as much dignity as I can muster, but Janet comes with me, spouting more Justin. In fact, she seems determined to prove to the world that she's memorized the entire song, and by the time we reach the team tent, where the varsity runners are lounging, she's reached the part about how I should just spend a week with Justin and he'd be calling me his girlfriend.

The varsity runners look up. "What up, Biebs?" says Jag.

"Sana has a boyfriend," Melinda announces to the tent, looking extremely pleased with herself.

Jamie looks at me.

"NO! No boyfriend!" I splutter.

But it's lost in a chorus of "Caleb Miller came to watch her run! He was totally cheering for her! He left right after she finished!"

"Do you *like* him?" Arjun bats his eyes at me.

"No, not at all! Never!"

Jamie is watching me closely and my cheeks start to tingle. Melinda yelps, "Oh, Sana, you're blushing! Look at you! You *do* like him!"

I'm surrounded by the team ooh-ing and ahh-ing at me and all I can do is cover my face and say, "No, no, no!"

"Why are you blushing then?" asks Janet pointedly.

"Yeah, why are you blushing?"

"I don't know! Jeez, leave me alone!"

"Why are you blushing?"

"Why are you blushing?"

"Why are you blushing?"

I'm about to give up when I see Jamie, still watching me. I can't let her think I'm interested in Caleb. "I like someone else," I blurt, looking right at Jamie. And she turns her head away, but not before her cheeks flush and a smile spreads across her face, not a big, laughing, public smile, but a small, shy, private one just for me.

And now Arjun is preening and telling me he's sorry to have to break my heart but he really only likes me as a friend, and everyone else is clamoring to know who I *really* like, and I don't even care because Jamie Ramirez smiled and blushed when I (kind of) said I liked her.

When I get home, Dad's car is in the driveway. He's home for a quick bite and a shower before he goes back to work. Apparently there's some big presentation with a venture capital firm tomorrow, and the robots still have a glitch or two that need cleaning up.

"They could give us fifty million dollars," Dad says between slurps of his udon noodles.

"Usō!" says Mom incredulously. I can hardly believe him, either.

Mom's busy making onigiri, one of my favorite snacks, for Dad to take back with him tonight. She presses some salmon into a handful of salted rice and starts pressing the rice into a ball around the salmon. As it comes together, she turns it once, then presses again. Turn, press. Turn, press.

"Honma," replies Dad, nodding, so I know he's not kidding. Fifty million dollars hanging on one meeting. I guess that would make it worth going back to work after dinner.

"What time do you think you'll come home?" I ask.

"Very late—probably past midnight."

"See how hard Dad works?" Mom says, looking at me as if somehow I've been slacking off my whole life, and my laziness has caused the robots to glitch. "You should work just as hard."

"I *do* work hard," I grumble as I head back to my room to do my homework. I hate it when she does this—it's like she's speaking in code. Does she think she's being encouraging? Is she making excuses for Dad not ever being home? Or does she really just think I'm lazy? As I pass through the living room, Dad's cell pings from the pocket of his jacket, which is slung over a chair by the front door. "Hey, Dad," I say, reaching into his jacket for the phone. I glance at it as I walk back to the kitchen. Then I stop.

The phone number from my lacquer box is flashing at the top of the screen.

Quickly, I type in Dad's passcode.

Jiro-chan! 金曜日 7時ね。

Jiro is my dad's name. "Chan" is something you add onto someone's name when you're close to them. No one calls Dad "Jiro-chan" except Mom, and my grandmother, who lives in Japan and doesn't own a cell phone. I'm not very literate in Japanese, but I know what "7:00 on Friday" looks like. And I don't need to be able to read to know what the emojis mean.

"Oi, Sana. Nan'ya?"

"Oh, um. Nothing, never mind." I put the phone back in

Dad's jacket and go to my room. Please don't let this be what it looks like. I could ignore it four years ago, but now I don't know if I can.

I try to put it out of my head and focus on trig.

Solve $\sin(x) + 2 = 3$ for $0° < x < 360°$

Who is sending those texts?

Solve $2\cos^2(x) - \text{sqrt}[3]\cos(x) = 0$ on $0° < x < 360°$

Is this why we moved out here?

Solve $\tan2(x) + 3 = 0$ for $0° < x < 360°$

What am I supposed to do?

My head is spinning. I can't do any of these. I give up.

15

THERE IS A SEMI-AWKWARD MOMENT WITH
Caleb in trig this morning. I thank him for coming to the meet,
and he says, "Oh, my cousin is on the cross-country team at
Cupertino High, so that's why I was there."

And I'm blushing again, furious at myself for being so foolish (though also a little relieved that he wasn't there for me).
"Oh! I wondered. I mean I thought you hated school sports and
school spirit and stuff."

"I do."

Caleb doesn't say anything else, but Elaine, Hanh, and
Reggie attack me at lunch and Hanh says, "You were totally
blushing when you were talking to Caleb during trig! Janet

says he came to your meet yesterday to cheer for you—is that true? Do you like him?"

"God! No! Why do people keep asking me? It's so annoying!"

"Okay, okay! Jeez-us Christ! Don't get so offended!" Hanh raises her hands up protectively.

"Sorry. I didn't mean to yell."

We eat in silence for a few seconds before Reggie asks, "Hey, are you okay? You seem a little out of it today."

The truth is, I've been worrying about Dad's mysterious text almost nonstop since last night. But it's not like I can just come right out and accuse him of having an affair. Or make a big announcement at breakfast. Why couldn't yesterday evening not have happened? Until dinnertime, I got to daydream about Jamie, and about how she smiled at me when I said I liked someone who wasn't Caleb. Then Dad and his stupid texter had to go ruin it all by having a rendezvous with lips and wine tonight.

For a moment I'm tempted to tell them everything— about Dad's text and how it was from the same number as the one I saw four years ago, about how I convinced myself back then it wasn't what I thought it was, and how now I'm afraid that the real reason we moved out here wasn't just another job, but another woman. But I can't. It's too humiliating. And somehow, just like last time, I feel like if I keep quiet, if I keep it a secret, it's still a question. Telling will turn it into an answer.

Señor Reyes catches me off guard twice during class, which never happens. I can feel Reggie looking at me, and I actually catch her and Elaine exchanging worried glances. I don't care. This is my problem to solve, and it's none of their business anyway.

After practice, I go straight home without taking a shower. I just want to be alone. Or with Jamie, I guess, but she had to head right home, too, to babysit her niece. Besides, now that I'm in a place where, when I'm near her, all I can think about is kissing her, it's confusing to also be worried about Dad. One thing at a time. After a long shower during which I come up with zero ideas about what to do about Dad, I ask Mom, "Is Dad working late again tonight?"

She nods over the chicken she's dredging in potato starch. "Probably. VC presentation went well, so maybe they will celebrate." Yeah, I'll bet he's celebrating. With Emoji Woman. Mom slides a few pieces of chicken into a wok full of oil, and as they bubble and spatter she turns and looks closely at me. "Sana, kibun warui?"

Well, yes, actually, I feel terrible. I'm worried that Dad is having an affair.

"Yeah, I'm fine. I'm just tired, I guess."

"Hmm." Mom turns back to the stove, this time to lift the lid on a pot of kabocha simmering in sweetened soy broth. Then she turns again and comes to me, her face concerned. "Just tired, Honma-ni?" She puts her hand on my forehead.

"Yes, really." I'm annoyed that she has no idea, annoyed

that I can't tell her without potentially ruining everything, but I submit to her touch. It feels nice to be babied a little.

"Go lie down," she says. "I'll call you when dinner is ready."

So I do, and while I'm on the couch, I make up my mind. I get out my phone and text Dad.

> Hi, Dad. Heard the presentation went well. When are you coming home?

The phone makes a whooshing sound as the message is sent, and I sit and stare at the screen, willing Dad to respond. It's six thirty. I wait two minutes. Nothing. Jeez. The least he could do is answer. Even if he's lying. I'm his daughter, for crying out loud. Then a car door slams outside, and a few seconds later, Dad walks in the door looking tired and pale.

"Jiro-chan mo shindoi no?" says Mom, wiping her hands on her apron as she comes out of the kitchen.

"Mmm. Chotto . . ." Dad shakes his head a little. "I'm feeling a little sick," he says, and heads toward the bedroom. "I'm just going to lie down."

Mom scoops the last of the chicken out of the oil, and the pumpkin out of its broth, and spends the next twenty minutes fussing over Dad. It turns out that Dad and his colleagues went out for sushi right after the presentation, and Dad didn't even make it to the end of dinner. Bad sea urchin, he jokes weakly. I'm relieved that he's home, and comforted to see how tenderly Mom takes care of him, and how he thanks her. Maybe I was wrong after all. Maybe they do love each other. Maybe things are okay.

But I can't ignore the feeling that they're not. It was easy to convince myself that things were okay when I was twelve. Not anymore.

On Saturday Dad is too sick to get out of bed, too sick to do anything but sleep. Mom makes him rice porridge, and brews a concoction of pickled plums, green tea, ginger, and soy sauce. I wonder if this will remind them of how they fell in love. By Sunday evening, Dad is feeling well enough to sit on the couch in the living room, and we all eat ice cream and watch *My Neighbor Totoro*. It makes me long to have a family like the one in the movie: the handsome, devoted father; the sweet, understanding mother; and two carefree girls, all looked after by magical forest creatures. We could have that. We could. Well, just one carefree girl. And maybe without the magical forest creatures, though that would be nice.

"It's been a long time since we've had an evening like this," observes Mom.

"Mmm," Dad says, nodding his head. "We should do this more often." He ruffles my hair and gives it a tug and says, "I'll have to try to spend more time at home. I've been working too hard. What do you think?"

"Yes!!" I practically shout. This is great. Dad home more often. I can keep track of him. Maybe we can have a family like the one in the movie, after all. It occurs to me that this means that I'll have to stay home, too, but that's a small price to pay if it means Dad isn't having an affair. Dad stretches and goes to take a bath. Mom sits down with her laptop and starts catching up on her email. It's almost as sweet and cozy as the family in *Totoro*. Please, please let this be enough. Please let things stay this way. "Good night, Mom."

"Oyasumi," she says, and smiles at me.

I'm headed down the hallway to my room when I hear the familiar ping of Dad's text alert. I pause. Dad probably can't hear it over the water running into the bath. It's probably a colleague texting to check on him or ask if he's well enough to get some report done. Probably nothing. I turn to go into my room. The phone pings again. Hmm. It won't hurt to check— I'm sure it's nothing. Dad's in the bath, the phone's charging on his bedside table. He wouldn't just leave it lying around if there were private texts coming in. Unless he didn't expect them.

I rush in and snatch up the phone.

Jiro-chan, 元気？ 木曜日! 🍷 🍴 🍮 💙

Thursday. She's having dinner with him on Thursday.

16

THE KNOWLEDGE THAT DAD HAS A DATE tomorrow night has been digging into me all week like a pebble in my shoe. What's worse, Jamie hasn't been coming over after practice. Her sister Sarah has the same flu that Dad had over the weekend, which means that Jamie has to go straight home every day and babysit her niece, Ariella. Sarah's a teacher, so even though her husband can drop Ariella off at daycare, someone still has to pick her up and take care of her in the afternoon. Dad has been coming home early every night—still not in time for dinner, but early enough to check my math homework and watch the news. We've even planned a family day for Saturday: go out for pancakes, maybe drive to the beach, and come back and watch a movie at home together. But he's supposed to meet Emoji Woman tomorrow night.

The girls and I walk into trig just as the first-period bell rings; Caleb walks in right after us. "Hey, you got another meet tomorrow?" he asks, and Reggie, Elaine, and Hanh exchange significant glances.

"Yeah, she does. Are you going to be there?" says Hanh, with a voice like silk.

"He was only there last week to watch his cousin," I remind her with a glare.

"Yeah." Caleb shrugs. "I dunno, it's kind of fun hanging out at the park, you know? And seeing all these weirdos running by. It's entertaining. God, why do you do it? Why put yourself through that on purpose?"

Reggie nods. "Right? Exactly."

"It's fun. It feels good."

Caleb shakes his head. "Suit yourself. Where's your meet tomorrow, anyway?" He threads his way to his seat, and I shoot a glare at Hahn, Reggie, and Elaine as they huddle up and begin whispering.

"Silver Creek. You'd have to drive or take the bus there."

Caleb nods thoughtfully. "Thom's dad's house is in Silver Creek. I drive him down there sometimes. Maybe we'll stop by."

I'm about to tell him not to bother, when something he said hits me, and I get an idea. "You have a car?"

"Yeah. It's a piece of shit, but it works."

Okay. Here goes nothing. "Do you think you could do me a huge favor? Like, huge?"

Caleb leans back and eyes me skeptically. "I don't know. What's it worth to you?"

"What? I—" *This is ridiculous.* "No, forget it. It's a bad idea." *Bad and risky and . . . just bad.*

"No, what? Now I'm curious. Just tell me. You won't owe me anything."

"No," I insist. "Really. Just forget it."

"All right, class, good morning! Let's get started." It's Mr. Green, thank goodness. I'm off the hook. I shrug my shoulders at Caleb and he scowls at me, but then presses and cajoles at every opportunity, of which there are many, because as luck would have it, it's a partner-work day and we're partners.

We finish figuring out the width of a south-flowing river being measured by surveyors across the river from a tree, and finally I give in. Partly because I owe Caleb for doing most of the work on the problem, partly because I'm sick of the pestering, and partly—okay, mostly—because I just can't help it, I *have* to know what Dad is up to.

"I need a ride to my—to this company after my meet tomorrow. And then, um, I need you to wait with me outside and uh, follow someone when they leave." Once the words are out of my mouth, I realize how kooky they sound. "Actually, no. I just heard myself and I sound . . . yeah. So, yeah, just—"

"No, no, no!" Caleb cuts in. "That sounds sick! Like a stakeout, right? I'm totally down for that. Who're you following? What are you trying to find out? Let's do it. It sounds fun."

"No, no, it's stupid."

"No, it's gonna be fun. We can, like, eat sandwiches and drink Red Bull, you know? I'll bring binoculars—"

"No! No binoculars!" I don't need him figuring out who it is we're tailing.

"What? Come on! We need binoculars if we're gonna be like real detect—"

"We're not real detectives. I know what his car looks like. That's all we need."

Caleb slumps in his chair and pouts. "Okay, fine. But it sounds like you're going for it. Right? We're on for tomorrow, right?"

"Ugh. Fine. Meet me in the parking lot at six." Then I remember that *I'm* the one who asked *him* to do this. "Thank you."

"No problem."

Thursday passes as if the whole school is underwater. Everything moves slowly. Nothing anyone says penetrates or makes any sense. I feel like I can't breathe properly, like my lungs are bursting and I just need to get *out, out, out* of there. Elaine, Hanh, and Reggie keep giving me funny looks during lunch and asking if I'm okay, but I just shake my head and look away. "I'm fine," is all I can manage, because if I say any more, my worries about Dad will come tumbling out. Worse, I might start crying right out there in front of everyone, and there's nothing more attention-grabbing than a teary-eyed drama queen at lunch. And attention is the last thing I want right now.

The meet lifts the heaviness a little. I can feel my adrenaline pick up even as I get on the bus with my teammates. Seeing Jamie always helps, of course. And during the race I get to run, breathe, and feel pain that I can define and understand. I get to talk—oh, let's be honest, I'm flirting—with Jamie, gossip a little with Janet, and focus on something besides Dad and the dumb thing I'm about to do.

As we gather our things and head to the bus back to school, Jamie trots up to me and says, "Hey, my mom said she'd take Ariella tonight. Wanna chill for a while after we get back? I'll take the six forty-five bus back home instead of the six fifteen—I can say the meet ran late."

Come. On. All week I've been missing Jamie, and now that I finally get a chance to be alone with her, I have to tell her that I'm going to spend the next two or three hours alone in a car with Caleb?

We climb onto the bus and I pick a seat at the front, away from everyone else. Jamie sits next to me. We sit with our backpacks on our laps, our arms draped over them and touching a little at the elbows.

"So?" says Jamie.

"Um, so this is gonna sound weird, but I have to . . . Caleb Miller is picking me up after we get back. We have this . . . project we have to do."

"Oh." Jamie straightens up and shifts away from me. "What project? I thought you said you only had trig with him. Trig doesn't have projects."

Cringing inside, I say, "I know. It's for something else."

"Something else like a date?" She's smiling, but only with her mouth. Her voice is light, but brittle.

"No! It's not like that."

"I thought you said you liked someone else."

"I do."

"Then what—"

I have no choice if I want her to believe me. I have to tell the truth. "My dad's having an affair," I mumble.

"Your—what?"

"I mean, I *think* my dad's having an affair, and Caleb has a car, so he's driving me to my dad's office to spy on him because I think he's going to meet her this evening after work."

"Holy shit."

"I know." My throat starts to close up at the thought, and I have to stop and clear it. "So anyway," I continue, trying to sound casual, "I'm not into Caleb. I'm just. I'm worried about my dad." My voice breaks, and it's as if the words have cracked something inside me on their way out, and one tear rolls down my cheek, followed by another, and I'm staring hard out the window, hoping no one notices me wiping away tear after tear after tear, thinking, *Please no one see me, please stop, please stop.*

"I'm sorry." Jamie moves back toward me. "Hey, I'm sorry," she repeats. "That sucks."

I'm sniffling and wiping my eyes like mad, and the tears keep coming.

"It's okay. I'm fine," I whisper.

"Hey, Sana, what's wrong?" Janet asks from three seats back, and suddenly I'm in a sea of concerned faces all saying, "Sana, are you okay? What's wrong?"

"Her cousin died. She just found out," says Jamie, without missing a beat. Then she adds, "Back off for a minute. Give her some space."

She follows her own advice and leaves me alone for a while.

Coach Kieran gets on the bus and takes attendance, and the bus lurches out of the parking lot and heads back to school. Once we get on the highway, traffic is crawling due to an accident somewhere, and finally I stop crying. I take a few steadying breaths and turn to Jamie. "Thanks."

"You okay? I mean, considering."

"Yeah, I think so." We sit in silence for a minute as the bus trundles along the road with a thousand other cars, a thousand other lives. I look out the window at them and wonder if any of the people in those cars are having affairs.

"My dad left us when I was eight," says Jamie quietly, "for another woman."

"Oh. God." I imagine Jamie at eight, with sweet ringlets and big brown eyes, abandoned by her cheating father.

A horrified expression crosses Jamie's face and she gasps. "Oh, shit. I didn't mean that *your* dad was going to leave you and your mom. Crap, I'm sorry." She leans forward onto her backpack and buries her head in her arms. "Sorry. Me and my big mouth. You probably hate me right now."

"No, I don't hate you. It's okay."

Jamie peeks at me with one eye. "Really?" She looks so contrite like that, so hopeful.

"Really."

"I guess I meant to say that I know how it feels, you know?"

"I know."

She sits back up and smiles at me. That secret just-for-you smile that's been keeping me up at night, that gives me goose bumps and makes me forget about everything else. Then I feel her hand clasp my hand, and her fingers intertwine with mine, and just like that, we're holding hands, and for the rest of the ride home, that's all that matters.

When we get off the bus, Janet and the other girls take turns hugging me and saying, "I'm so sorry," and "Call me if you need to talk," and even Jimmy gives me a few awkward pats on the back. Jamie hovers in the background, and then as the crowd disperses, she comes over and puts her arms around me. I can feel her breath in my hair, feel her cheek next to mine.

"I'm feeling a little bit bad about the cousin thing," she whispers.

"Yeah."

"Do you even have any cousins?"

"No." I start to giggle, and she does, too, her arms still wrapped around me.

"Can we hang out next week?" she asks, and I nod. I wish we could stay like this forever. But Jamie lets go and says, "Your boyfriend's here. Sweet ride." She points, and I see Caleb leaning on a battered, dark gray Honda hatchback in the parking lot. He does the chin-up nod then puts his head down and starts playing with his phone.

"Oooh, Sana, is that your ride home?" says Janet in a stage whisper. "I thought you said you weren't into him." Suddenly, all the girls are waving at Caleb and calling, "Hi!"

"Omigod, stop! We're. Just. Friends," I say, wishing I had told Caleb to meet me at six thirty instead of six. What was I thinking? On the other hand, maybe this is easier than the entire cross-country team knowing I'm into Jamie. "We have to finish a project," I say.

"Does this project involve . . . *kissing*?" says Janet.

"Shut up."

I pick up my stuff and charge grimly out into the parking lot to a rousing chorus of good-byes and "good luck on your *project!*"

"Nice friends," says Caleb as I approach the car.

"They *are* nice," I retort, feeling a little defensive, never mind the fact that I was wishing them all evil just a few seconds ago. I get in and sit down gingerly—the passenger seat looks like it has definitely seen better days, what with its fraying cover and what I hope is an old coffee stain right in the front.

"So your mom's okay with this?" he says.

"I told her that I had this last-minute Spanish project to do that involved recording stuff around town, and that I'd finish the rest of my homework at the house where we're going to edit the video." A derisive snort escapes Caleb as he starts the car and backs out of the parking space. "Well, it's kind of true," I say.

"Yeah. Kinda."

"Oh, yeah. And I, um, kinda gave her your cell number and said it was my Spanish classmate's home phone."

"And you want me to, what, pretend I'm your friend's dad? You're asking me to lie for you, is that it?"

I shrug. "Please?" Jeez, he's not making this easy.

But then he flashes me a half grin and says in a deep voice, "Yes, Sana's right here. She and Caleb are working very hard on their Spanish project. Would you like to speak with her?" He adds, "Hey, which way? Where are we going?" I pull up the address on my phone. He regards the map for a few seconds, then nods and pulls into traffic. His iPod is playing on a set of speakers he's attached to the dashboard—some song about how everybody wants to live how they wanna live, and everybody wants to be closer to free. It's a catchy tune, kind of bouncy and fun.

"Who is this? Doesn't sound like a goth song."

"What, you were expecting Slipknot? Don't stereotype. It's the BoDeans. *You* should know them—they're from Wisconsin."

"Never heard of them."

"It's an old song, from like, the nineties."

We listen to the BoDeans a while, and then Caleb asks, "So, really. Like this is kinda cool and all, but seriously, what's going on? Are you like a private eye in your free time or something?

Who are we stalking and why?"

"I'm not a private eye and we're not stalking anyone."

"Waiting outside someone's work and then following them around is stalking." He has a point. I look out the window and say nothing. I don't want to tell him the truth. But what I can say that won't make me sound like an actual stalker? "Is this guy a criminal?"

"No."

"An undercover secret agent?"

"Yeah, right."

"Some older dude you're into?"

"No! God, Caleb, yuck!"

"Okay, okay!" He pauses. "An older chick?"

"Omigod. No."

"Well, who is it? I'm driving, and I have a right to know." I stare out the window some more, as if the discount furniture stores and Vietnamese phô restaurants we're passing will have a good answer posted in their windows. "If you don't tell me, I'll just drive you right home."

"No, no. Okay. I just. Just, it's stupid and crazy and I don't want you to like, think . . . I don't know. Think badly of me, or like I'm some kind of freak, or—plus it's kind of private. I don't want people to know."

"Okay." We wait through three cycles at an intersection at Winchester Avenue and I-280 and Caleb swears under his breath at the traffic. I begin to feel bad that I'm making him do this.

"I'll probably tell you at some point. Just not yet," I offer.

"You know, I would never think badly of you," he replies. "That's one of my best qualities—I don't judge people."

"Hah!" Now *this* I can talk about. "That's *all* you do— judge people! Student government kids are tools. Animé Club kids are hopeless nerds. Everyone but you and your friends are mindless robots. The heck you don't judge people."

"Yeah, well—"

"Yeah, whatever." I give him the hand. "You *so* judge people."

We've finally made it onto the freeway, and Caleb sets his jaw a little and lapses into silence.

"Well, they judge me," he says finally.

"I don't think they do."

"Oh, they do. When you have a single mom who's only seventeen years older than you, and you live in a shitty little apartment and you have to go to school with holes in your shoes and eat the crappy free lunch that the state gives you, and in seventh grade you wear a T-shirt that your mom got for you at Salvation Army and it turns out it used to belong to Andy Chin's brother and he tells everyone at school? Trust me, Sana. They judge you."

My heart drops. Nice one, Sana. Now I feel like a jerk. "Oh," I say, "I'm sorry."

He shakes his head and drums his fingers on the steering wheel. "No, it's okay. I'm sorry I laid all my shit on you like that. That wasn't cool."

"'S'alright."

He's quiet for a while, and then says, "Anyway, it's not so bad now. My mom graduated from nursing school the same year I graduated eighth grade, so she has a decent job, plus she's not paying for school anymore."

"That's good."

"I just get pissed at all the kids who, like, think they're cooler than everybody else because of shit they own, or sports they play, you know? And it's always the rich kids and the jocks."

"Not cross-country runners."

"Well, duh. No one gives a shit about cross-country." His face is serious, but after a moment I can see his mouth twitch.

"Omigod. Whatever." We fall back into silence for a minute, then I say, "It's my dad."

"What? Where?"

"No, dummy. My dad is the guy we're going to follow."

He digests this for a moment. "Okay. Um, why?" I tell him the story of Dad's late nights at work and the suspicious texts, and how it sounds like he's supposed to meet this woman this evening. "Does your mom know?"

"No. I told her I'm working on a Spanish project, remember?"

"I mean, does she know about your dad? Like, don't you think she'd have seen some of these texts herself?"

"I don't see why. I mean, if she knew, why would she stay married to him?" But even as I ask the question, I know the answer: because she's Japanese, and she wouldn't want the shame of having to divorce her husband because he was cheating on her. Forget changing her life for the better, or taking a stand. Because she's all about *gaman*. You can't change things. Just do your best. I've heard her grouse about American women and their high divorce rate: "Americans say, 'I am unhappy, so I get divorce.' Getting divorce to be happy is so selfish thing to do. Marriage is not about one person's happiness; it's about doing right thing for your family."

But Caleb, who doesn't know my mom and her Japanese countryside ways, nods. "Good point," he says.

But really. Maybe Mom does know. Caleb is right—it seems like she'd have had plenty of opportunities to find out, the way Emoji Woman keeps texting Dad. On the other hand, I've only seen three texts in the last four years. I've never seen Mom with Dad's phone—she's got her own. And they don't fight or anything. She never complains about him staying out late, or about anything except how he doesn't brush his teeth properly or take his blood pressure meds when he's supposed to. You'd think that if she knew, she'd be at least a little bit grumpy about it.

I turn these thoughts over and over in my mind until we reach the exit and turn right onto Stevens Creek Boulevard. We grab a couple of slices of pizza and some soda at a place called Gumba's, and five minutes later we're parked on the street across from GoBotX, eating dinner.

"This is sick," says Caleb through a mouthful of pepperoni

pizza. "We shoulda got, like, donuts and chips and Red Bull, like in the movies."

"We don't need caffeine. It's not like it's the middle of the night."

"Why you gotta be such a wet blanket? I was just saying. It would make this even cooler."

"There's nothing cool about waiting around to find out who my dad is cheating on my mom with."

"Yeah, you're right. Sorry." He looks abashed.

"Actually, maybe it's a little bit cool." In fact, it is kind of exciting, sitting in a car waiting to track someone. I'm not sure what we'll do when we see where he goes. I figure I can decide later—I don't want to think about it now, and luckily, Caleb hasn't asked.

The next two hours pass quietly, with Caleb and me taking turns doing homework and keeping watch. They also pass very . . . very . . . slowly. Especially when it's my turn to be lookout. I keep checking my phone to see how many minutes have passed, and it's always only seven or eight. At eight thirty I call Mom from Caleb's phone and tell her we're hard at work, but the editing process is taking longer than we expected.

"When will you be finished?" she asks.

"Um, it's hard to say."

"No later than nine thirty. Even if it's not finished," she says in Japanese. "I will come and pick you up. What is the address?"

"No! No, no, Mom, um, Caleb's um, Caleb's dad is going to drive us all home, so it's okay," I say in a rush.

I hear her sigh, and I can see her face, impatient and irritated.

"I promise, it's fine, Mom."

"Hmph. Be home at nine thirty," she says, and hangs up.

Argh. What now? I put the phone down and groan.

"What?" says Caleb.

"My mom doesn't trust me."

"With good reason."

I glare at Caleb. He sounds just like Reggie. "She's going to call you and demand an address if I'm not home by nine thirty."

Caleb shrugs. "I'm sure your dad'll leave soon. Don't worry. Then we'll follow him and go home. By nine thirty. Easy."

I'm about to say he can't make predictions like that when I see Dad's silver Avalon pull out of the driveway.

17

I PRACTICALLY SCREAM AT CALEB, "THAT'S HIM! That's him! Hurry, start the car!"

Caleb shoves his laptop at me and turns the key. The engine starts to turn over, groaning and coughing for what seems like an eternity. Caleb releases the key.

"What—don't tell me the car is broken!"

"No, it just does this sometimes. It always starts up eventually, though."

"We don't have time for 'eventually'! Why didn't you tell me this before? Why didn't you just keep the car running if you knew it wasn't going to start?" Oh-god-oh-god-oh-god. Dad is getting away.

"Jeez, just shut up for a sec! I'm doing you a favor, remember? Lemme try again." The engine complains for a few more excruciating seconds, during which I stare daggers at the steering wheel as if somehow that will help. Thankfully, the car comes to life this time, and I let out the breath I didn't realize I was holding.

"Okay, go, go, go!"

After carefully checking over his shoulder for oncoming traffic (*aagh, really?*), Caleb pulls into the street and heads in the direction Dad took, toward Stevens Creek Boulevard. The intersection comes into sight two blocks down just as Dad turns right.

"See? You didn't have to scream at me. We haven't lost him," Caleb grumbles, but he speeds up and makes it onto Stevens Creek about four cars behind Dad. Not yet, I think. I keep my eyes on Dad's car. I'm almost afraid to blink, lest he vanish into some magical cheating husbands' portal. Luckily, at eight thirty the traffic is pretty light and Caleb is able to maneuver our car to just two cars back from Dad. We follow Dad over Highway 85, then south on I-280, back toward San Jose. My initial panic has subsided, and I relax a little.

"Sorry I freaked out at you," I say to Caleb.

"Whatever. It's okay."

"Thanks for doing this for me. There's not a lot of people I trust like this."

"Anything for you, doll."

"What?" I look at him and he's laughing. "Whatever, weirdo."

Then he says with studied casualness, "Hey, we're doing an

anti-homecoming thing next weekend. Just having pizza and watching movies and shit. If you're not going out with your Asian girl squad, you can come over if you want."

Wow. Out of nowhere. "Oh. Um, actually I *am* going out with my Asian girl squad, so, yeah," I tell him. "Sorry." And I really am. He's turned out to be a lot of fun to hang out with.

"'S'okay. Just thought I'd ask."

Dad exits the freeway and Caleb and I follow him onto Winchester, then Alta Loma, and I wonder why Dad would agree to meet this woman so close to where we live. Caleb must be thinking the same thing, because he says, "Pretty ballsy. He must really think he's not going to get caught." But the farther we go, the clearer it becomes that Dad is going . . . home. He pulls into the driveway, and Caleb continues past the house about halfway down the block before doing a U-turn. I don't know whether to feel relieved or disappointed. "Well?" Caleb looks at me.

"I don't know. I'm confused. I swear the text said Thursday for dinner."

"Maybe she canceled on him."

"Maybe."

"Maybe he's not having an affair."

"Maybe." Suddenly I'm bone-tired. I don't want to talk to anyone, don't want to think about anything. I just want to get inside and go to bed. I guess I'll get up early in the morning to finish my homework.

"Hey, it's okay. I mean, I had fun, anyway." I take a good

look at Caleb. He's actually really cute. Strong jaw, nice cheek-bones, kind eyes. And he's a good person. I wonder why he doesn't have a girlfriend. If I weren't so crazy about Jamie, I could see being into him. I'm not a huggy person (blame my no-physical-contact parents) but I'm suddenly overcome with gratitude for this guy who, for no reason, just wasted an evening driving me on a wild-goose chase, and is nice enough to say he had fun. So I reach over and give him a hug.

"Thanks. Really."

His look of surprise melts into a big smile.

"Anytime, doll. See you in trig."

I roll my eyes, shut the door, and head inside to face my (probably maybe) cheating dad and (impossible but it seems that way) unsuspecting mom.

18

ON FRIDAY, JAMIE COMES OVER. HOMEWORK ON a Friday afternoon is too much, so we're just in my room, me sprawled on my bed, Jamie pushing herself around the room on my rolling desk chair. "So, what do you think?" I ask her. I've told her on the way home from school about last night's escapade, chasing Dad from work right back home.

"I think Caleb has a crush on you." She spins herself (it's a spinny chair, too).

"Why does everyone keep saying that? I meant what do you think about my dad? Do you think he canceled dinner?"

"Everyone keeps saying that because it's true. I mean, it's obvious. And you said your dad had a date and then he didn't go, so yeah—I think he canceled dinner. That's obvious, too."

Oh. She stops spinning, chews her lip for a second, and

asks, "You sure you're not into him?"

Caleb? How much clearer can I make this? "Yes. I'm sure." I look right at her so she knows I'm telling the truth. "Okay?"

"Okay."

Is she jealous? As exciting as this possibility is, I still can't let go of my worries about Dad. "But why do you think he canceled?"

"I dunno. He's trying to be a good husband? He's bored? He wasn't feeling it last night? Could be anything. It's no use guessing."

"Yeah . . ." I roll over on my boring blue-and-white duvet cover and look at the ceiling. "I just don't want him to be the guy who cheats on his wife. I don't want to believe that about him. I don't want him to leave us. I just want him to quit."

"Yeah, I get it." Jamie pushes the chair over to the bed, next to me. "You know, though." She hesitates a moment and then says slowly, "My dad—he never stopped cheating, no matter what happened, no matter what he told my mom." She looks at me, chewing her lip again.

"She knew about it?"

"Yeah, and when she found out, she threatened to leave, but then she believed him when he said he'd stop. And he was good for a while, but then he went back to his old ways. She never had the courage to walk out, and finally one day *he* did. He just said he was going to LA with the woman he was seeing, and we never heard from him again."

"God. That sucks."

"Yeah . . . I dunno. I just don't know why she trusted him. Or why she never left him—I'm pretty sure she stopped trusting him after a while."

Jamie shakes her head and looks at her hands. "The thing is, I admire her, kind of. For her loyalty. Is that messed up, or what?"

I don't know how to answer that, so I just say, "It must have been awful."

"Yeah, well. It was shitty but it worked out for the best. He was an asshole, anyway. I mean, life was hard when he left, but it was hard when he was with us, too, you know? I mean, he didn't hit us or anything, but . . . so, yeah . . ."

"God. I'm sorry."

"No, it's fine. I mean, it wasn't fine for a long time. I never would have made it through if it wasn't for Christina and JJ and Arturo. I ate at their houses all the time when my mom didn't have enough money to buy food, and we even lived with Christina for a few months when I was ten and my mom lost her job and couldn't make the rent. They still help us out a little every now and then." Oh. Jamie continues, "Christina's been kind of protective of me ever since. She says I'm just like my mom."

"What do you mean?"

"She thinks that when I fall for someone, I let them walk all over me. I mean, it only happened the one time—the one time I dated someone—so . . ."

"Oh. Did you have a—a boyfriend or something that broke up with you?"

"Kinda . . ." Jamie looks up at the ceiling for a second, like she's remembering . . . what? "Anyway, so I was a fool, but sometimes love makes you foolish, right? But it doesn't have to make you poor. So that's where Christina's wrong. I'm not like my mom, because maybe I can't stop someone leaving me, but I'm sure as hell not gonna let 'em leave me broke. I don't ever want to go through what she went through."

"Yeah."

"And your mom shouldn't have to go through it, either. Or you. I mean, not like *your* dad's gonna leave you broke. He's probably a better man than that."

"Yeah." A little shakier this time. Because he might be a better man than *that*, but he's not better enough to be faithful. I close my eyes against the ugly possibilities. I reach inside for something solid to anchor myself. *Gaman.* Jamie puts a steadying hand on my shoulder, and that almost pushes me right over the edge into tears, but I concentrate on the warmth of her palm, and I manage to pull myself together. I sit up, open my eyes, and smile.

"You okay?"

I nod. Then she pats my knee briskly and says, "Hey—you wanna do something this weekend? I have church and then I have to babysit Ariella on Sunday, but I'm free tomorrow."

Yes! Oh. No. "My dad and I are supposed to hang out tomorrow because I told him I wanted to do family time on the weekend. I can't really back out."

"Oh. Yeah, you probably shouldn't . . . You're going to

homecoming, though, right?"

"Well, yeah."

"Perfect. We'll see each other there. Promise to look for me?"

"Promise."

"Good."

"Hey." I reach across to hug her. "Thanks."

She hugs me back, and as we break apart, she pats my knee again, gently this time, and then her hand lingers for a moment. And then another moment. For a couple of seconds we sit still like that, looking at each other. My body is urging me to *kiss her, kiss her, kiss her,* but my terrified little brain won't cooperate and move the requisite parts. What if I kiss her and it turns out she doesn't want me to?

Yes?

No.

Yes?

No.

Yes?

Jamie clears her throat, pulls her hand away, and says, "Um. I should um. Probably get going."

No. Damn.

Fifteen minutes later, Jamie's climbing onto the bus, waving good-bye. I go back to my room, flop onto my bed, and imagine what would have happened if I'd stopped thinking so much and just kissed her. Of course, in my imagination, she wants to kiss me back, and we end up entangled in a passionate embrace. And the more I think about it, the more I'm sure she really does want to kiss me back. She has to. Okay. The next chance I get, I'm not going to overthink it. I'm going to act. I'm going to take charge. I'm going to kiss her.

Dad comes home from work early—right after I get home from the bus stop, in fact. "Sana-chan, I'm really sorry, but I have to go into the office tomorrow to get some extra work done. Can we watch a movie tonight?"

"Dad, I just canceled plans with a friend because of tomorrow!"

"I'm sorry. Things didn't go as I planned today. I have to finish this presentation before I leave for the East Coast on Sunday. Can you still play with your friend?"

First of all, I don't "play" with my friends anymore. Second of all, why do *you* get to cancel, just like that? But third, yay! I have to call Jamie ASAP. I open my mouth to say okay, I'll call my friend, when it hits me. He's probably planning a day with Emoji Woman, since he canceled on Thursday.

Over my dead body. "No, it's okay. But can I please come into the office with you?"

He pulls his chin back and a crease appears between his eyebrows. "Why?"

"I haven't seen it since I first got here—you can show me around so much better now! And I have tons of homework to do, so I'll just sit at a desk and work the whole time, like you." Hah. Take that.

"You'll be bored. I may be there all day."

"If I get bored, I'll drive home. And then I can come pick you up later when you're done."

Dad laughs. "Like school! I will be the student and you can be the parent who picks me up!" He tousles my hair and says, "Okay. And can you buy me some ice cream after school, too?" I didn't expect it to be this easy. But ice cream with Dad sounds good, even if it means a boring day at the office. Especially if it means I know where Dad is all day.

"Okay."

Saturday is boorrrring. Dad either canceled plans with Emoji Woman or he was telling the truth about having hours of work to do. But I don't want to leave him, really, so after I finish my homework, I spend my time surfing the web and texting everyone I know. Maybe Jamie was wrong. Maybe Dad really is reforming. Maybe Emoji Woman is out of the picture.

But then again, on Sunday, Dad is leaving on a twelve-day trip to Boston, New York, and Washington, DC.

Or so he says.

19

HOMECOMING WEEK IS LIKE BEING AT SUMMER camp. I mean apart from having classes, of course. Every day, there's a spirit competition in the quad. Monday, all four classes gather in the quad and shout at each other; Tuesday, it's sack races; Wednesday is tug-of-war; Thursday is races to fill buckets of water with tiny Dixie cups; Friday is the pep rally. Then on Friday night, the game, the dance, the party.

When we're not yelling our brains out for the junior class, Reggie, Elaine, Hanh, and I spend most of our lunches planning the logistics of going to the karaoke club and then to Reggie's cousin's house after the dance. As usual, Hanh's parents won't let her go to the football game (because boys) or have Reggie pick her up at home after the game (they might go somewhere besides straight to Sharon's house).

So Hanh proposes a plan. Reggie will go and wait at Sharon's apartment after the game, pretending to get ready for a night in with Sharon. Hanh's parents will drop her off there, and then Reggie and Hanh will join us at the dance.

"Don't even say it, Reg," says Hanh when Reggie looks doubtful. "I'm sick of you telling me I should feel guilty about going behind their backs. It's not like I've ever done anything worse than they did when they were teenagers. If they can't handle it, that's their problem."

So the schedule for the evening looks like this:

5:00–6:30 Football game (except for Hanh)
6:30 Reggie goes back to Sharon's house
7:00 Hanh gets dropped off at Sharon's house
7:30–9:30 Dance
9:30–?? Party at PopStar Karaoke Club!!!

Jimmy and his friends are planning to go to karaoke, too, so Elaine is completely out of her head with excitement. Hanh and Reggie are excited about the college guys that Janet's sister has promised to bring in addition to the alcohol. I'm just glad to be going out with friends, and enjoying all of this secret planning we're having to do. This is going to be so much fun.

Homecoming madness extends into the evenings. Mom lets me participate because I tell her it's for school, and because teachers will be chaperoning everything. On Monday night, I help decorate the Junior Hall—or what would be the hall if it had a ceiling—and on Tuesday, Wednesday, and Thursday, I go to Janet's house to help work on the class float. Apparently her mom was homecoming queen at Anderson like thirty years ago, and she's still totally into it. It's another week where I can't hang out with Jamie, but at least I can look forward to seeing her at the dance.

I've decided that short of flying to the East Coast, the best I can do to prevent Dad from cheating is to text and call him constantly, to remind him of his family. He'll probably be suspicious, since we've never been very communicative. But I try to do it in moderation—a couple of texts in the afternoon to ask about a trig problem, and in the evening a photo of the sunset, maybe, or what Mom has made for dinner.

Thursday evening I text him and Mom a selfie of me at Janet's house in front of the junior class homecoming float. "Hecka smart!" exclaims Elaine. "Build their trust—let them see that you are where you say you are." Which is kind of ironic, considering the only reason I'm sending it is because I don't trust Dad to be where *he* says he is. Elaine and Reggie take photos of each other and send them to their parents. Hanh doesn't need to—she's at home because her parents won't let her go out on weeknights, even for school stuff. Then Elaine has a brainstorm. "We should do a picture inside the house and send it on Saturday night from karaoke at like, ten o'clock, and say we're at Sharon's house. Our parents will never know the difference—they'll just think we took it at Sharon's!"

"Yeah, except I won't be wearing this butt-ugly thing to homecoming," I say, gesturing to the grubby paint-stained T-shirt I threw on so I could help paint a giant pirate on the side of our class float.

"Borrow one of Janet's tops. Then bring it home with you and wear it when you go to the game on Friday. That way your parents will see you looking like the picture you send them. And you can just change into your cute little halter top in the bathroom at the dance. Oooh, I am a *genius* sometimes!" says Elaine, holding her hand up for a high five. It does sound like a good plan. So we find Janet and she takes us to her room and pulls out a few things.

Janet has a thing for body-conscious, tight-fitting tops, and Reggie suddenly balks at taking the photo because she's all worried that she's too fat. "Look at these rolls!" she wails.

"You look fine. Besides, you're not actually going to wear it to the party," Janet reminds her.

Eventually we coax her into posing with us for a few photos in the hallway. Then we stuff our borrowed shirts into our bags and head out to put the finishing touches on the float.

The homecoming parade on Saturday afternoon is mildly disappointing. Andy Chin is homecoming king, and Jimmy and Janet are part of the court. They get all dressed up in gowns and rented tuxes and ride down Alta Loma Street on a special float for the homecoming court. Plenty of neighbors turn out to see the parade, but in the end it feels like hours of work on a float that no one saw.

The game is a close one, and even though I know nothing about football and could care even less, it's hard not to get caught up in the excitement. The score is tied with two minutes to go, and I spend those minutes alternately clutching Elaine and Reggie until Isaia Fualema runs twenty-seven yards for a touchdown and I scream and jump up and down and pump my fist, like everyone around me. I have a brief flashback of the Beach Boys debacle at the country club with Maddie Larssen and Trish. I wish they could see me now. *See? What's more American than screaming for your team at a homecoming football game?* And—I take a quick look around—probably two-thirds of the people in the stands have parents or grandparents from Asia, Central America, and the Pacific Islands. Take that, Glen Lake.

After the game, Elaine and I go to my house to eat a little dinner and shower and change before we head back for the dance. Reggie goes to her cousin Sharon's house so that she can be there when Hanh's parents drop her off.

"You have Sharon's phone number, right?" I ask Mom as Elaine and I eat dinner.

"Yes."

"I'll text you tonight, maybe around ten o'clock, from Sharon's house," I say.

"Good idea," Mom says, and nods. Then she smiles at me, her eyes tender. "I am proud of you, Sana. You're very responsible." Elaine and I exchange glances. A little worm of guilt bores through the back of my neck and starts creeping around, prickling and tickling. Mom hardly ever praises me, and now that she's doing it, I don't even deserve it. I put a piece of ginger pork in my mouth and shrug.

"Um-hmm," I say around the pork. If I look uncomfortable, maybe she'll just figure it's because my mouth is full.

"Don't take such big bites," she says, and I feel a teeny bit better. "See what a good manner Elaine has?"

"Um-hmm."

"You look like cow, chewing so much."

I swallow the pork and the guilt goes right down with it.

After dinner, I change into my-slash-Janet's black T-shirt with fluttery cap sleeves and hide the red halter in my bag. Elaine and I parade in front of Mom to show off our outfits and to make sure she'll recognize them when I text the fake photo later. Then I pull an Anderson XC fleece on top.

It's ridiculous how cool it gets at night here. Sunny and seventy-five degrees all day and suddenly fifty-five at night. Totally unreasonable. There's no point in wearing anything nice if you don't want to freeze to death, I think, and then I laugh. Since when is fifty-five degrees on an October night freezing? I've turned into a real California girl.

At seven twenty, Elaine and I head out the door and I say, "Itte-kimasu!" It's essentially a promise to come back: "I go and I will return."

"Itte-rasshai," replies Mom. "Go and then return." Same

thing. It's a send-off, but also an expectation: "You'll go, then come back, and I'll be waiting to welcome you home."

I think about Mom sitting at home alone, waiting to welcome a man who lies to her and a daughter who (kind of) lies to her about what they're doing when they leave the house. The guilt reappears and starts to turn circles in my chest this time, like it's getting ready to lie down and settle in for the night.

"No," I say aloud, startling myself and Elaine.

"Huh?"

"Oh, uh. Nothing."

I set a brisk pace, to clear my head and hopefully leave the guilt behind. Elaine totters along beside me in cute but clearly uncomfortable high-heeled sandals, complaining about how fast we're going and how much her feet already hurt. I wonder if Jamie's there yet. I think about the sexy top stashed in my bag and shiver a little. I can't wait for her to see me in it.

Right after the ID check, we have to stand in line before we're allowed into the gym. "The D and A line," explains Elaine. "For like, flasks and joints and stuff." We scan the crowd while we wait, and Elaine asks me about sixteen thousand times if I see Jimmy anywhere. "Do you think he'll like my outfit?" comes in a close second. I can't tell her, but I know just how she feels. Finally we reach the front of the line. Mr. Van Horne, the vice principal who everyone calls Mr. Van Horny behind his back, greets us with a toothy grin.

"Well, good evening, ladies! Don't we look lovely tonight?"

he booms. "Time to check our purses!" And he holds out a pair of hands like grizzly bear paws. There's a paper bag on the table behind him, full of what I assume is confiscated contraband. "I know I don't have to worry about you Asian girls," he chuckles, "but I have to check anyway. Rules are rules." Elaine hands her bag over and he sticks an enormous paw in and stirs it around. "Oh, ho!" he cries. "What have we here?" And he starts to pull out Elaine's new top.

"That's in case I have to change," Elaine says, flipping her hair. "You know, like if someone spills something on me?"

"Don't change, you're perfect just the way you are," replies Van Horne with a smarmy wink and gun hands. Blech. "You're always so well prepared. Well, all done. Let's have ourselves a fun but safe evening, ladies!"

"Asshole," Elaine mouths at me as Van Horny addresses the next kids in line. Once we're out of earshot, she says, "It pays to be Asian, but still." And also, just yuck.

Elaine and I hustle into the bathroom to change. Off comes Janet's T-shirt, on goes my red halter top. Janet's borrowed T-shirt fits into my bag, but there's nowhere to put my cross-country fleece. Tying it around my waist looks dorky, wearing it defeats the purpose of the halter top, and leaving it somewhere is just asking to get it stolen. "Wait 'til Reggie gets here, then put it in her van," suggests Elaine. "Hey, you can take my shirt, too. And our bags." We survey the edges of the gym for a table where Reggie can find us. Which gives us a good excuse to crowd-scan for Jimmy. And Jamie.

It doesn't take long. Jimmy is hanging out on the opposite side of the gym in a group that includes Janet and Andy. "C'mon!" Elaine grabs my hand and we take off on a very uneven journey across the gym floor. Elaine alternates between a wobbly saunter and a mincing trot in her strappy heels, with her desire to appear sexy, cool, and collected clearly battling her desire to sprint right over to be near Jimmy. As we saunter-wobble-mince our way across the floor, I catch a glimpse of Jamie, already dancing with a clutch of her friends. Darn. They probably don't want me there. Why does she always have to be with them? Her hair is out of its usual ponytail and cascading down her back. She's got on black skinny jeans, flats, and a peach-colored Y-back camisole top with a plunging neckline. She looks gorgeous.

I would stop and stare at her but a) I have to look where I'm going, b) I don't want anyone to get suspicious, and c) Elaine is tugging on my hand and urging me toward Jimmy and the others. So I keep going and sneak peeks in Jamie's direction whenever I can, pretending that I'm just looking around to see who else is here. We finally reach the group and after a round of hugs and "Omigod, look at you, sexy/hottie/cutie!" we settle in. Pretty soon, Reggie and Hanh arrive, spot us, and hurry over. "Holy shit, you would not *believe* how hard it was to get my mom out of Sharon's apartment!" complains Hanh, and she and Reggie launch into The Saga of Getting Rid of Hanh's Mom. I smile and nod along, but I'm only half paying attention because now that I have a little time, I'm watching

Jamie more closely. Wow. She's a great dancer. I mean, she can move. How am I going to get over there? Maybe I can lead everyone onto the floor and we can dance in a group near Jamie's friends. At least I'd be closer to her then. I watch her as she shakes her hips in a way that makes me want to walk right over and—

"Sana! Yoo-hoo! Earth to Sana!" I come back to the conversation with a jolt. Reggie is waving her hands in front of my eyes and calling to me, and the whole table is laughing. "Who are you looking at?" asks Reggie, staring in Jamie's direction.

"Oh. No one, really," I reply, shrugging, but Reggie raises her eyebrow at me.

"Are you sure?"

"Yes! Who's there to look at? It's just Jamie and her, um—"

"Punk-ass gangster friends," interrupts Hanh. "C'mon, you guys, let's dance!"

"Jamie's friends are gangsters?" That makes me a little nervous.

Reggie shoots Hanh a sharp glance and says, "No."

"C'mon, I was just kidding," says Hanh. "Besides, I'm allowed, cause I'm half-G."

Reggie and Elaine roll their eyes and drop their stuff on a chair, motioning me to do the same.

Some of the guys hang back, talking to each other, and Hanh shouts at them, "Watch our stuff!" As I follow Hanh out onto the floor I wonder if her comment about Jamie's friends being gangsters is worse than Christina's about all Asians being smart. And half-G? What does that even mean?

It's only a couple of songs before Elaine grabs my arm and drags me and Reggie protesting back to the table, where Jimmy is babysitting our bags and my fleece. "Reggie, can Sana borrow your key and put our stuff in your van?" she shouts over the music, and then, as if she's just noticed him, she does a double take and her Bambi eyes get even bigger. "Jimmy! What are you doing sitting here? Come and dance with us!"

Jimmy gets up and follows Elaine back to the group, and Reggie hands her key over to me, rolling her eyes. "Omigod, I can't even. It hurts to watch her throw herself at him like that. But she's always been that way. It's like she can't help it." We watch Elaine twisting and posing in front of Jimmy, who's doing the boy-shuffle dance and looking amused and a little uncomfortable.

"She's terrible."

"Yeah."

"At least she's up front."

"You can say that again. All up front."

"How does she do it? I mean, where does that come from?"

"It's probably easier if you're little and cute like her. She never has to worry about what she looks like, you know? Same with Hanh. Look at her—she's so skinny and pretty."

We watch Hanh, who looks like a fashion model, flipping her hair like mad and stealing glances at everyone to see if they're looking at her.

"What was that thing she said about being half-G?"

"Hanh? It's because her dad used to be a gangster."

"Shut up."

"No, I'm serious. Her dad was in one of those Vietnamese gangs, and her mom . . . I don't know. Had bad judgment. Don't tell her I told you, but her parents got pregnant with her by accident. It's probably why they got married."

"No."

"Yeah. They eventually got their shit together, but her mom didn't finish college. She came here when she was in middle school and couldn't speak a word of English, and by high school she was in all AP classes and she was going to be an engineer, but she's just a lab tech now. And Hanh's dad went to junior college and ended up in IT support. I mean, it's a good job, but it's not a master's degree and start-up stock options like his mom wanted. I think that's why they're extra strict, 'cause they don't want her to screw up like they did, you know? And her grandmother blames her mom for getting pregnant—how messed up is that? No wonder Hanh hates her. I would."

"Wow." So would I.

"Right? I bet that's why she acts the way she does, with the makeup and the clothes and everything—to piss off her grandma."

"I guess you can't blame her," I say.

"Right? I'd probably do the same thing. They better watch out, though, because one day she's gonna go too far, I know she will." Reggie continues, "My parents met in college here, so I have it easy, relatively. As long as I get decent grades, they let me do a lot more than some other parents. . . . Anyway, enough family drama. Here, take my stuff, too, okay? Thanks."

I walk out of the gym with my arms full of purses and my fleece. After being in the gym even for half an hour, the night feels refreshing rather than cold, and it feels good to breathe air that doesn't smell like sweat and floor wax. I think about Hanh's parents and their mistakes—this whole other life that happened before she even existed, and now Hanh has to pay for it. It's so unfair. I wonder if Hanh really will go too far and get herself into some kind of trouble one day, and it occurs to me that maybe this is why Reggie seems to have appointed herself to be Hanh's über-conscience.

A few kids are smoking weed in a dark corner of the parking lot, but otherwise the lot is empty. No reason to be nervous, but I'd rather not be out here all alone in the dark, so I hurry over to the van and climb in quickly. I figure the safest place to stash our stuff is in the back—if anyone breaks into the van, they're not going to waste time fumbling around under the backseat.

Which is what I'm doing when someone knocks on the side of the van and says, "Hey!" I whirl in terror. But even as my momentum sends me stumbling backward, the initial jolt has dissipated enough for me to place the voice, and by the time I've fallen on my butt I know it's Jamie.

"Jeez, Jamie! You scared me to death!"

"Sorry," she says, peeking into the van. "I didn't mean to. I saw you come out here and I just wanted to see what you were doing."

"I'm putting some stuff away so we don't have to deal with it in the gym." I get up and finish shoving everything under the seats.

"Nice ass, by the way."

"Shut up." I twist back around to face her, embarrassed. But also, I have to admit, feeling a little like *Yes!*

"Hey, can I come in?"

"Sure."

I take a seat in the way back and she climbs in and sits down next to me. I steal a glance at her and I'm overcome by how perfect she is—her brain, her poetic soul, her grit, her too-trusting heart . . . her hair . . . her eyes . . . her skin . . . that clingy . . . low-cut . . . camisole top . . . draped over the swell of her breasts. . . . *And* she likes my ass. And now here we are, alone.

Oh, God. Okay. Just be cool.

For a few seconds we just sit there, perfectly still, in the dark. But while the outside of me is sitting stiffly on the seat, my insides are going haywire. My mouth is dry. My stomach feels like all its little stomach molecules have come apart, and I think I can actually feel the individual atoms quivering against each other. My heart is pounding so hard, I'm worried that Jamie might see it beating through my shirt.

"So," she says.

"So."

"So . . ." Jamie takes a big breath, holds it, then lets it out. "Hey, remember when I was at your house last Friday?" I nod. Now my lungs have jumped on the bandwagon and I can barely breathe. "Right? Well. I feel like. Like we were . . . on the verge of something. You know?" She pushes a stray lock of hair away from my face and looks at me with those liquid brown eyes, and my heart picks up even more speed. I nod, yes, I know what she means. Do I ever. "So I was wondering if maybe we could . . . see what happens next."

The world narrows down to just us, just her in front of me, just her face, the dimple on her chin, the tiny mole on her left cheek, her eyes, her lips. I'm already leaning toward her, my hand is already on her knee, my face is already so close to hers, our noses are almost touching, but I whisper, I whisper as if I don't know the answer, "What happens next?"

"This."

And then her lips are on mine and they're soft and sweet and they taste like apricots, and then she stops and we look at each other and all I want is more, so I kiss her back and she kisses me back and it's quiet and soft and electric and spar-kling all at once, and Jamie opens her mouth a little, and I open mine, and our tongues are touching, our teeth are click-ing against each other, and then her hand is on my waist, and then on my hips, and my thigh, and I can feel her breath on my ear, her lips on my neck, and I want to be closer, closer, closer to her, so I lean toward her and she pulls me down with her and then my whole body is pressed against her whole body and it feels like she's fulfilling a wish I've had all my life and I want this to keep going forever and ever and ever and ever.

Finally, I lift my head for a moment to look at her, and she smiles at me, and I smile back. In fact, I can't stop smiling.

"Wow," she says.

"I know."

"I'm so glad this is happening."

"Me, too."

And then we're kissing again. And it's amazing. We spend a little longer making out, hands in each other's hair, stroking each other's skin, hips, shoulders, arms, legs. I swear, it's the best feeling I've ever had. Ever.

But I've only just come out here to stash my fleece and our purses, and the van door is still wide open for anyone to peek in and get a free show, so eventually we have to stop. I fix my hair and Jamie wipes the traces of her lipstick off my lips, cheeks, and neck, making sure to nip my earlobe while she's at it. Then she reapplies her lipstick and lip gloss, shakes her hair out, and lifts my hair up and plants one final kiss at the nape of my neck, which makes me shiver up and down.

We lock the van and float back to the gym together. No one will suspect anything because we're already friends from cross-country. But as we walk through the parking lot and past Mr. Van Horne and Mrs. Lowell ("What were you two up to out there?" "I just had to put my bag and stuff in the car." "Oh, right. Well, you two are good girls. Go on back in."), and as we head into the gym and onto the dance floor, I feel as if it must be obvious to anyone who sees us that we're now much more than just friends. As if the energy between Jamie and me is lighting up the space around us, sparkling and shimmering. As if Jamie's kisses are glowing under the black light like silver on my skin, every imprint of her lips as clear as if she had left the lipstick on. I must look different. I certainly feel different. Light. Ethereal. Sexy.

Then Jamie bumps up against me and puts her arm around my waist and an icy wave of self-consciousness splashes over me. The sparkles and shimmers vanish and I'm suddenly aware that we're back in the real world of high school. "Come dance with me," she whispers, sneaking a kiss behind my ear. My stomach lurches. What if someone sees her?

"Uh . . ."

"Hey, Sana! Where have you been?" Reggie comes rushing up out of the dark. She sees Jamie at my side and a look of confusion crosses her face. "Oh. Uh, hi, Jamie."

I take a little step away from Jamie and say, "Hey, what's up? I stashed all our stuff." *La-la-la, easy-breezy, I wasn't just making out with a girl in the backseat of your minivan.*

"Sana, I was starting to get worried. Didn't you get my text?"

Text? I start to go for my pocket but then realize that I've left my phone in my bag. Which might explain why I didn't see the text. That and the fact that I was busy having an epic make-out session with Jamie, which no one must ever know.

I take another step away from Jamie and pretend to check my pockets.

"Oh, shoot. Sorry. My phone's still in my bag."

Jamie breaks in abruptly. "Hey, I gotta go. I'll uh, text you later, 'kay?" she says, and waves and plunges into the crowd. As I watch her walk away, I swing back and forth between wanting to leap back into her arms and kiss her again, and thinking, *Whew, she's gone.*

Reggie watches her, too, then cocks her head and asks, "What took you so long out there, anyway?"

"Nothing!" I say, maybe a bit too emphatically, because Reggie's eyebrow shoots up. "I—I put the stuff away and on my way back I ran into Jamie and we just hung out and talked for a while because it's so freaking hot and smelly in here."

"Talked," she repeats, giving me some serious side-eye.

"Yes!"

"Hmm."

"What?"

Reggie shrugs, still looking at me sideways. "Nothing, forget it. Well, come on—we need to find Elaine and do an intervention. I've tried to drop a few hints, but she won't listen. She's like a leech. Plus she thinks she's Beyoncé, and she's so, *so* not, and I just can't watch it anymore." Reggie gestures toward Elaine, who is now whipping her hair around in circles and thrusting her tiny hips back and forth like a maniac for Jimmy's benefit.

"Yikes." Happy to do anything that takes Reggie's sharp

eye off me, I add, "She's a mess."

"Right? Holy whiplash, Batman," agrees Reggie.

But just before we head off to try to mitigate the disaster that is Elaine, Reggie points her finger at me and says, "I'm not done with you. We. Are talking. Later."

"Pshhh. Whatever." Not if I can help it.

We snag Hanh on the way to Elaine's one-person carnival, and the three of us successfully extract her from the Dancing Hole of Doom she's digging for herself by telling her that we want some girl time. Jimmy wanders away and sits down with the guys, but there's no stopping Elaine, who is pretty much the living embodiment of "dance like no one's watching," so Hanh, Reggie, and I form a human shield and let her go for it. I actually envy her, in a way. I wish I could throw myself into the moment like she does. Though maybe with a little more grace.

Over the next hour, I find myself glancing over at Jamie constantly, and I know she's watching me, too, because I catch her at it five times (yes, I'm counting). Each time our eyes meet, I'm filled with that same shimmering energy that I felt when we were next to each other, and even though I still have to be sneaky about looking at her, it's kind of exhilarating to know it's *our* secret now, not just mine. At nine thirty, we leave the dance and head to PopStar. I've never been out to karaoke, and with the exception of the Glen Lake Country Club disaster, never out with friends this late. And definitely never after having just made out with the most beautiful, amazing, perfect girl at school. I tune in and out of the conversation in the van, and I close my eyes and smile to think that just a while ago I was stretched out on this very seat with Jamie. The memory gives me goose bumps. This is the best night ever.

20

JANET, JIMMY, AND A FEW OTHERS MEET US in the parking lot in front of PopStar, which is located in a random Korean strip mall in Santa Clara. Janet's sister Debbie is there with three of her SCU friends and a backpack full of vodka. After a quick round of introductions, we head in, with Hanh keeping a firm hand on Elaine's arm so she won't rush over and start hanging on Jimmy.

The host, a bored-looking older lady, confirms Debbie's reservation and leads the way through a warren of narrow fluorescent-lit hallways to our room. The room itself is about the size of my bedroom—which is to say you could squeeze a full-size bed, a dresser, and a desk into it with a little room left in the middle to walk around. In the corner across from the door, there's a raised platform with a mic stand and a teleprompter-looking thing. On the wall behind the stage is a large plasma screen, and a tiny disco ball hangs from the ceiling. The other walls are lined with benches. A remote control for the karaoke machine sits on top of a stack of binders full of song titles in five different languages: Mandarin, Korean, Japanese, Vietnamese, and English.

We file in, and Elaine rushes for the binders, picks one, and starts flipping through it. She's got a great voice, so I'm sure she wants to get herself in the queue early and show off a little for Jimmy. "Hey, lemme see," says Jimmy, and he beckons Elaine over to sit beside him. In a flash, she's practically in his lap as they pore over the selections together. Reggie shrugs at me.

"Who knew that throwing yourself at someone could work?" she mutters. "It's so unfair."

"What's unfair? It's not like you ever do *anything* to let guys know you're interested," says Hanh. "Though actually, it is unfair. It's not supposed to work that way."

"It's because she's a tiny, adorable little kitten." Reggie looks down at herself and shakes her head.

"Shut up," I say. "Give me a break. You're just fine."

"My mom says I look like a water buffalo," says Reggie.

"Fuck your mom," says Hanh. "*My* mom says I'm fat. Well, my grandmother does. Asian moms live to say shit like that. It's what they do. You should know better than to listen. And you should also know better than to think you have to be skinny to be pretty. Anyone who cares what size you are is an asshole. Come on, let's go get some snacks."

Hanh collects cash from everyone, and in a couple of minutes, Hanh, Reggie, and I are standing at the vending machine in the lobby, evaluating the selection. If you had by some miracle missed the K-Pop posters on the wall and the little ceramic cat waving good-bye on the front desk, you'd know who this place catered to by looking at the vending machine. Rice crackers. Shrimp chips. Squid jerky. Pocky. Pretz. All Asian brands except for a row of Pringles and kettle chips at the bottom.

We decide on ten boxes of Pocky, one of my favorite snacks and the least disgusting of our options, though I do love shrimp chips. Pocky are cracker sticks—actual thin little sticks of cracker—dipped in chocolate. They're delicious, and they have a ton of different flavors: regular chocolate, milk chocolate dipped in almonds, white chocolate, dark chocolate, maple, cheesecake, strawberry, green tea. Nom.

Hanh and I are feeding dollar bills into the machine when I hear the door open behind us and a group of customers walks in, jabbering in Japanese. Suddenly, my ears prick up. I could swear I hear Dad's voice in the mix. But that's impossible. He's not due back in town for four more days.

"Hello, I hab resa-bation fo Kiyohara. Pahty obe six." I freeze. Now there's no mistaking it. It's his voice, loud and clear and drunk—his accent gets extra heavy when he's been drinking. Reggie looks at me warily.

"My dad!" I mouth at her. I don't know which is worse: feeling humiliated that he sounds like such a loser, or feeling terrified that he'll see me.

Reggie enters the numbers for the Pocky and raises her eyebrows. "Are you sure?"

I nod.

"Fuck," whispers Hanh.

Ka-thunk. Ka-thunk. Ka-thunk. Three boxes of Pocky fall out of their cubbyhole. Someone in the group behind us says something that's funny, apparently, because they all laugh, my dad loudest of all. I crouch down, pull my hair to the side to hide my face, and reach in to grab the Pocky boxes, and Hanh chooses this moment to pull out her phone and take a selfie. I can feel her doing her fashion model pose.

Omigod-omigod-omigod, she's going to get me killed. I stay in my crouch and try to scoot behind Reggie's legs. Please don't let him look over here and see me.

"What the hell are you doing?" Reggie hisses at me.

"Reg, take one with me!" says Hahn.

"What—no!" protests Reggie. "Hanh, stop it!" But Hanh gives Reggie's arm a yank, and Reggie gives in, to prevent her from drawing any more attention our way. "Oh, okay, fine."

I smash myself right up against the machine and stick my hand in the opening at the bottom, scrabbling around at nothing, hoping it looks like I'm just trying to reach that one last box and praying Dad doesn't decide to come over to buy some Pocky, himself.

But no one comes over. They follow the receptionist down the hallway to their party room, and I stand up and start breathing again. "So he said your last name, but was that really your dad?" Hanh asks, her voice low.

"I don't know. I was afraid to look. It sure sounded like him."

Reggie appears from around the corner and waves frantically. "They've gone in. Quick, hurry before they send someone out for snacks!"

I start to run, but Hanh grabs my arm. "Walk! Running draws attention! Here, pretend you're looking at this. Then no one can see your face." She shoves her phone in my hands and the three of us speed-walk back to our room, me with my head bent over Hanh's phone, just in case. Once in the room, Hanh and Reggie shove Elaine and Jimmy off the bench next to the door, and I sink onto it, shaking.

"What?" demands Elaine. "You just took our spot!"

"Sana thinks her dad's out there," explains Reggie. "She needs to sit where no one can see her through the door."

The whole room erupts.

"Oh, shit!"

"You're in troublllllle!"

"Move farther into the corner!"

Hanh sits down next to me and takes back her phone. "Here." She opens up her photo gallery. "Wanna see the photo I just took?"

"Ugh, you and your stupid selfies! No, I don't want to see it. I already know what you look like."

"No, you idiot. God! Look."

Sighing, I look. "Oh." It's not a selfie. Clever Hanh just took a picture of the group in the lobby over her shoulder. With my dad, red-faced and bleary-eyed, right in the middle. Which is awful. But it's not the worst part.

"Is he in there?" I nod. "Jeezus, what a close call! We're so lucky he didn't see you. Which one is he?" Numbly, I point. "That guy? Huh. But who's—" Hanh stops abruptly. She clears her throat. "Who's that?" She points.

I shake my head. It's not just that I don't know the answer. It's that I don't know anything—what to feel, what to think, what to say. Because Hanh is pointing to a beautiful Japanese woman hanging all over Dad's shoulder.

21

IT'S NOT EVEN LIKE THE WOMAN IS DOING an Elaine-the-Leech move and he's just patiently waiting until she detaches herself. Or like they're good friends just chilling. Dad's old-school, countryside Japanese. He doesn't touch people if he can help it. The most PDA I've seen between him and Mom is probably a pat on the back. But now he's got his arm snaked around this strange woman, and their laughing faces are inches apart. I can't ignore it, can't make up excuses, like I did with the texts. There are witnesses. Photographic evidence.

I stare at the picture on Hanh's phone and shake my head, as if this will make the image disappear. For the second time tonight, my heart is racing, my mouth has dried up, and I can't breathe. For a fleeting moment I wonder why my body can't tell the difference between being about to kiss Jamie, and finding out for sure that Dad is cheating on Mom. I feel a hand on my arm. From somewhere far away, I hear Reggie's voice asking, "Sana, are you okay?"

I manage a nod, but to my horror, the picture clouds up and a tear splashes onto the phone. Frantically, I wipe my eyes and then the phone, hoping no one saw what just happened. I can't cry in front of all these people—they'll want to know what's wrong, and then what will I say? I look up to see Reggie and Hanh gazing anxiously at me. "I'm fine, I'm fine," I choke, and wave them off. They look unconvinced.

"Wanna talk about it?"

No. I shrug and wipe away another stupid tear. "It's fine. I'm fine."

"Sana, come on. You're not fine."

Hanh's right, of course. I'm so not fine. But I'm in no shape to talk about it. I'm having a hard enough time just existing, just being in the world with the fact of my father and that woman together. And anyway, I'm not going to chat about my family's awful secrets like I'm on some dumb reality TV show. Why can't they just leave me alone? "I said I'm fine, okay?" I snap. "Just—just let it go. I don't want to talk about it."

The next couple of hours go by in an excruciating slow-motion blur. At first, Reggie and Hanh keep looking at me when they think I'm not looking, and then looking at each other. But I refuse to look at them, and eventually they give up and move on. It turns out that Reggie has an amazing voice, too, and she and Elaine sing hit after pop hit to wild applause. At some point, Jimmy's arm finds its way around Elaine's shoulders.

I try to look like I care about what's going on. But it's difficult, because the sentence "Dad is cheating" keeps repeating itself in my head like some kind of horrible mantra: *Dad is cheating. Dad is cheating. Dad is cheating.* Each time the truth declares itself, it feels heavier, and I have to concentrate hard to keep a smile on my face, to look like I'm floating effortlessly along with everyone in the giddiness of the karaoke room.

Finally, finally, it's time to leave. Jimmy has apparently asked Elaine to go to the movies with him next weekend and she's whipped herself into a whirlwind of thoughts and feelings, which she unleashes in the van on the way to Sharon's apartment: "Omigod, he's so cute! And so sweet! Do you think he really likes me? Do you think I should go? What should I wear? What if my parents find out?" I let Reggie and Hanh handle Elaine and thank God for Jimmy for providing a distraction. Hopefully this will keep everyone occupied for the rest of the night, and they'll leave me alone about Dad. I close my eyes and let the girl talk wash over me, and try try try to push away the stomach-churning image of Dad and That Woman.

And then, thank God again, I get a text from Jamie.

Hey, you

Hey

I miss u! ;-)

:-) I miss u too

I'm at a party but it's hella boring. U?

Karaoke . . . My dad showed up w his gf

WTF! Holy shit! Did he see u?

No

Wanna talk?

Nah. Maybe tomorrow

U sure?

Ya

I'm so sorry about your dad

But I'm so happy about us.

Can't stop thinking about u.

. . .

ttyl . . .

I close my eyes, and it's hard work but I hold the text in my mind, and slowly I start to re-feel Jamie's lips on mine, remember how her body felt, how her hair smelled. I remember her eyes, how I felt like I could see into her soul, and the tenderness I saw there. By the time we arrive at the apartment, I'm almost smiling. When Hanh shakes me gently and says, "Wake up, Sana, we're here," I play along, figuring it will give me a good excuse to burrow right under the covers once we're inside, and escape any inconvenient turns in conversation.

"So, Sana, we have to talk about last night."

Damn. Shoulda known. "What?"

Reggie and I are at the Starbucks around the corner from Sharon's apartment, picking up coffee and pastries to take back for everyone. Sharon, being on a ridiculous diet to get even super-skinnier for her wedding, has nothing but kale and lemons in her fridge, and nasty protein bars in her cupboards.

"Well, let's just start with the dance," she says. I head for the door, but Reggie plants herself at a table and stares at me until I go back and sit down next to her.

"Okay, what?"

"So . . ." Reggie stirs her pumpkin-spice latte and regards it with intense interest, like maybe she thinks she sees the face of Elvis in the foam.

"What?"

Reggie snaps the top back on, takes a fortifying sip, and says, "So did you know that there've been rumors going around about Jamie? That she's a lesbian?"

"Oh. Um, no, I hadn't heard." I start examining my own latte for Elvis's face.

"Yeah. Janet says that she heard from her cousin in Palo Alto (*What's with people and their freaking cousins all over the place?*) that Jamie hooked up with some girl at this Stanford track-and-field camp she went to last summer. Like, Janet's cousin was at the camp, too, and she says that Jamie had a roommate and they like, ended up being more than roommates. If you know what I mean."

Oh. Yes, I suppose I do.

"Why are you telling me this?"

Reggie looks away, then directly at me. She sort of gathers herself and says, "So Janet says that you and Jamie are all, like, buddy-buddy all the time. Like you sit together on the bus, and she hangs out at your house after practice. Which is like, you know, totally whatever, right? Except then you like, kept staring at Jamie last night, you know?" I work on balancing the tiny bags of scones and muffins on top of Elaine's and Hanh's drinks so I don't have to look at Reggie. "And then you went MIA for like, half an hour and you came back with Jamie all giggly and stuff, and, well . . ." She shrugs helplessly. "It just . . . it just seems like you might be, you know . . ."

"I might be what?" Which is a stupid thing to say, but some part of me is still desperately clinging to the hope that maybe she'll say something I can truthfully deny, like, ". . . an alien."

" . . . a lesbian," Reggie says. "You know, like, with Jamie."

Ka-pow.

"What—no! I—I mean, it's not like—aaack!" My coffee-scone-muffin tower topples, and as I grab for the pastries, I knock over my own drink and the table is flooded by a grande-size deluge of nonfat vanilla latte. As I scramble for napkins, I'm grateful that the next couple of minutes will be devoted to cleaning up my mess and not discussing my love life. Or Dad's, for that matter.

"It's totally cool if you are, you know."

Man, this girl does not give up. I don't know what to do. Admit the truth? Flat-out lie? Something in between?

The best I can come up with is, "If I said I wasn't, would you believe me?" Ugh.

Reggie smiles. "Probably not."

We toss the soggy napkins in the trash, apologize repeatedly to the poor guy who's left mopping the rest up, and make our way out of Starbucks and back around the corner to the apartment complex in silence.

We turn left down the walkway to the building and Reggie reaches into her bag for the keys, then stops dead and demands, "So? Are you and Jamie a thing?" I think about kissing Jamie last night, how magical it felt, and how I can't wait to see her again. I can't help it. I smile. "I *knew* it!" cries Reggie triumphantly. I mean, she's practically bursting with triumph. It's coming out her ears. How long has she suspected? "Sana, this is epic! I'm so happy for you!" And she throws her arms around me, almost spilling the rest of the coffee in the process.

Wow. "Epic" was not the reaction I was expecting. I could cry with relief—in fact, I have to struggle not to. Reggie releases me and unlocks the door, and on our way up the stairs to the apartment, she says, "We have to tell Elaine and Hanh." I don't want to, but she is firm. "No point putting it off," she says. "It's best to be honest, especially about love—you have to have someone to talk to about it, right? Anyway, you're one of us now. No secrets."

Elaine and Hanh are slightly less prepared for the news than Reggie. Both of their mouths actually fall open and they sit there gaping like two beanbag-toss targets for a few seconds that feel like an eternity. Elaine is the first to speak.

"But you can't be a lesbian. You're Asian. Asian girls aren't lesbians!"

I'm not sure what to make of this. But Reggie and Hanh laugh.

"Are you kidding? What does that even mean?" Reggie says.

"Well, do *you* know any Asian lesbians? I mean, besides Sana," Elaine shoots back, crossing her arms.

"Margaret Cho. Jenny Shimizu," says Reggie. She knows the most random things.

"Who?"

"Margaret Cho is a comedian. And Jenny Shimizu is like, this fashion model who used to go out with Angelina Jolie and Madonna."

"Angelina Jolie and Madonna are gay?!" Crumbs of Petite Vanilla Scone fall out of Hanh's mouth as she says this, and she puts them on her plate absently.

"I think they're bi. So's Margaret Cho."

"Wow."

Elaine and Hanh are impressed. I am, too.

But Elaine still wants more. "But I meant someone you don't have to Google. Someone young. Someone like us."

Reggie shrugs and grins. "I guess Sana's the first."

I haven't said a word this whole time because I'm putting most of my energy into keeping my body from shaking itself into a heap of rubble. Which is weird, because coming out to my friends could not be going better. After the initial surprise, no drama. No freaking out. No awkwardness. Nothing I expected. Like, the next thing Elaine says is this:

"You're so lucky."

What?

"Yeah, right?" says Hanh. "Think of how much easier it's going to be for you to get into a good college."

"What?!"

"Oh, come on. Asian lesbian? You can get in anywhere you want! It's so unfair."

"Oh, I know!" Elaine chimes in. "I mean, practically no one can write that on their college app. You're a total shoo-in. *And* you get to have a girlfriend and your parents won't even care if you go on a date because they won't know it's a date."

"Yeah. You can go in your room and shut the door, but Elaine's going to have to do it in the backseat of Jimmy's car," says Hanh, ducking a punch from Elaine.

Somewhere back in a corner of my mind I'm annoyed that they're talking about my being gay as nothing more than bonus points on college admissions and secret dating possibilities, but mostly I'm relieved they're taking it so well. "So you guys are fine? Like, with me?"

"Omigod, Sana!" Elaine says. "We're totally fine! I mean, we're surprised. But you're one of us no matter what."

"Yeah, come on. It's the twenty-first century. This is Silicon Valley," adds Hanh. "Nobody cares. Not even most old people."

"You're not in Kansas anymore," Reggie says.

"I'm not from Kansas, I'm from Wisconsin."

Reggie groans. "I know that. It's a figure of speech. Like from a movie. *The Wizard of*— forget it."

"Can we tell people?" asks Hanh.

"Um. Not yet."

"Because, seriously, no one cares. I mean, they care, like, it's news, but they don't *care*, you know?"

"I have a gay friend," says Elaine dreamily. "How cool is that?"

"Okay, Elaine cares." Hanh turns to her and says, "Elaine, *everybody* has a gay friend. Jonathan Luckhurst is gay. Danny Nguyen is gay. Chimere Hackney is gay. And that's just in our class. Besides, she's not a trophy. You don't get points. God, I just can't with you sometimes." Hanh shakes her head. Reggie does, too.

"Well, she's my first *good* friend who's gay." Elaine glares at both of them.

"Yeah, I don't want to be everyone's new gay friend. Just keep it quiet, okay?"

"Okay." They all nod.

"But thanks for trusting us. It's good to talk about it, isn't it?" Reggie says.

Yeah. It is.

There's one thing we don't talk about, though, and that's Dad. I thought I'd spent the night awake and fretting about Dad, with brief commercial breaks to think about Jamie, but it seems that I fell asleep at some point, and that's when Hanh and Reggie told Elaine about Dad. The three of them start to press me to talk about the karaoke disaster.

"I'm not ready to talk about it yet," I tell them, which is true. If I even think about that photo, my stomach lurches like the floor has dropped out from under me, and I start feeling light-headed.

And yet I need to have it. I need to examine it. So I ask Hanh to text me the photo she took, which she is only too happy to do, so that she can then erase it from her own phone. Her paranoid parents check her phone periodically to make sure she's not doing anything she's not supposed to.

"Well," Reggie points out—as she always does, "it's not like they'd be wrong."

22

MOM COMES TO PICK ME UP FROM THE APARTMENT
at eleven o'clock. I go right to bed and take a nap. When I wake
up, there's a series of texts from Jamie.

> Hey
>
> Sana?
>
> Just txtng to say I shouldn't have put my arm around u at the
> gym wo asking. Sry. Got a lil carried away, I guess 😌 😍
>
> Tmb

Aww. So I text her back:

> > Hey, s'ok. Just took me by surprise. I think I'd have
> > been jumpy even if u were a guy. I guess I'm kinda
> > shy about that stuff in public, sry
>
> No problem
>
> xoxox
>
> xoxox

I spend most of the rest of the day in my room, finishing my homework, texting with Jamie, daydreaming about Jamie, and fretting about Dad's whereabouts.

By five o'clock, I can't take it anymore, so I text Dad:

How's New York?

Fifteen minutes pass and there's no reply.

I can't sit still, I can't look at the picture anymore, I can't focus on my homework, and I definitely can't talk to Mom. I pace around my room like an animal at the zoo and finally change into shorts and a T-shirt and tell Mom I'm going for a little run.

Once outside, I take off down the street. Good long stride. Get your heels up. Breathe. I can feel my head starting to clear already. I run faster, breathe harder, feel my ponytail brushing against my back, feel my feet on the ground, the muscles in my quads, my heart and lungs pumping blood and oxygen, just run, just run, just run.

I don't know how long I go like this, just running, feeling glad to be away from my brain, from my ridiculous life for a while.

Which is why I practically jump out of my skin when a car horn honks at me and someone yells, "Hey, doll!"

Caleb slows down and pulls over and I walk to the curb to yell at him. My heart, already working hard from my run, is now hammering a hole in my chest.

"God, Caleb, don't *do* that!"

"Sorry," he says, but he's working hard not to smile, I can tell. That jerk. "No, seriously. I didn't mean to scare you. Just wanted to say hi."

"Okay, well, hi."

"How'd the karaoke caper go last night?"

Great. And here I thought I'd escaped it for a while. "Oh, fine," I say, but I can't look him in the eye.

"Fine?" He's leaning across the front seat, peering intently at me. Suspiciously.

And then I hear myself saying, "Yeah, pretty much. Except for the part when my dad showed up with his girlfriend." It's meant to sound flippant and ironic but my throat closes like a fist on the word "girlfriend" and it comes out as a squeak and suddenly I'm crying *again*. Godammit. In public. Out on the sidewalk. And here comes an old couple walking their dog. "Can I get in?"

"Sure."

Once I'm safely inside the car, I start crying for real. Not horrible wracking sobs, thank goodness—I've still got a little pride—but definitely a steady stream of tears, and some pathetic sniffly, weepy little hiccups every now and then for good measure. It's embarrassing, making Caleb sit there and watch me dissolve in a puddle of tears when all he did was ask how last night went. But I'm too tired to care very much. Eventually I dry out and tell him the whole ugly story of seeing Dad with That Woman at PopStar last night.

"That sucks," he says. I shrug. "What are you going to do?" I shrug again.

"Would you mind driving me home?"

Caleb obliges and we stop a couple of driveways down from my house. On a sudden impulse, I reach for his hand.

"Thanks."

"Anytime, doll," he says, and winks.

"Stop calling me *doll*! And don't do the wink. It's not a good thing." He winks again. Ugh. I get out of the car, wave good-bye, and jog home. When I get back, my phone has a message on it from Dad:

> NYC is good! Very exciting. How was the homecoming?

Liar! I want to type. *Where are you* really? But I don't. I can't. I don't know what I'll do if he texts me back another bald-faced lie. I think of the dance, of kissing Jamie, of how everything should have turned out. How Dad and his girlfriend ruined what should have been a perfect evening. I type,

> Homecoming was fun
>
> Mom misses you, tho. You should call her

There. How's "NYC" now, you evening-ruining cheater? For a moment, I feel sort of vengefully happy for hopefully ruining *his* evening.

But as I reread my text, the righteous anger fades, the truth of what I've just typed comes through, and all I feel is sad.

23

OH. MY. GOD.

Jamie's left the poetry notebook in my locker, with a new poem: "Wild Nights—Wild Nights!" by Emily Dickinson. And a note:

> This makes me think of you. Not just because of the wild nights part (haha), but also because you're like my harbor in a wild ocean.
>
> Love, J

I reread the last part of the poem:

Rowing in Eden
Ah, the Sea!
Might I but moor—Tonight—
In Thee!

I'm her harbor. My heart is melting. Other parts of me are heating up, too, but in a different way. Wild Nights. Wow.

I don't think I can put this one in Ms. Owen's journal.

The poem that Jamie left for me in my locker has me moving through the day in my own personal bubble of happiness. I want to hug myself and spin around every time I think about Jamie, about the way she looked at me, about the poem. And if I did spin around, tiny sparkling stars would come streaming out of my pockets. Everything is ice-cream sundaes and rainbows and Christmas all rolled into one, and most of the time it's enough to make me forget about Dad and That Woman. When that memory threatens to burst my bubble, I take a peek inside the poetry notebook and immediately feel better. Until one time it occurs to me that the poem could refer to Dad and That Woman, too. Ick. I shove that thought out of my head, out of my bubble. Just concentrate on Jamie's signature and how it says "Love, J."

There, that's better.

After cross-country practice, it's difficult not to hold Jamie's hand on the way to my house. It's really difficult not to fall right onto my bed and start making out the moment my door is shut. Well, let's be honest. It's impossible. We spent all of Sunday apart after our first kiss(es) on Saturday—what do you expect?

Eventually—reluctantly—we take a break and get our books out. When I've managed to concentrate on my trig homework for almost forty minutes, I reward myself by looking up at Jamie, who is lying on the bed scribbling notes in the margins of *The Awakening*—another fun nineteenth-century book about adultery. It's about a woman named Edna who feels trapped in her marriage, and she falls in love with a man who's not her husband. In the end, she can't bring herself to subject her family to the scandal it would cause if she were to run away with her lover—but she also can't bring herself to go back to life the way it used to be. So . . . she drowns herself in the ocean. Cheery stuff. I feel sorry for poor Edna, trapped in a time when women had no choice but to become housewives and have lots of babies. Though I'm mad that she killed herself. I wish she'd fought back. Then I think about what's okay to do in society today, and what's still scandalous.

I remember how Jamie started to put her arm around me at the dance.

"Do your friends know? I mean, about. You know."

Jamie puts her book down. "About you? Or about me?"

"You, I guess."

"I came out to a few of them this past summer—you know, Christina, Arturo, JJ. A couple others. I was with this girl, Kelsey, from Stanford track camp. But we weren't together for very long, and I dunno. I didn't post anything anywhere. I don't think a lot of other people know. But as long as they don't give me a hard time about it, I guess I don't really care who knows."

"Was Kelsey the one who . . . walked all over you?"

"Yeah. I . . . she was the first girl I ever . . . you know. And she was so, like, experienced. I guess I fell pretty hard, and then she basically punted me when camp was over. She was just playing me the whole time. And I kinda lost it. I was so pathetic, like, 'Why? What did I do? How can I change?' Texting, calling . . . ugh." She shudders. "Christina was so mad at me."

Christina again. "I don't think she likes me."

Jamie exhales slowly. "I know. I wish you guys could get to know each other better. She's been there for me through everything, and she's just afraid I'll get hurt again. I told her it's not like that with you, but you know." She shrugs, then takes my hand. "You wouldn't do that to me, right? You wouldn't just leave me like that."

"Never."

"Promise?"

"Promise."

"Good." She leans over and kisses me once, twice, three times.

Time for a study break.

After a few minutes, I start worrying about the pile of homework still waiting to be done. I know. I'm so messed up. Feeling guilty about homework makes me think of Mom, and thinking of Mom makes me worried she'll walk in on us, so I pull away and ask Jamie, "Does your mom know?"

Jamie shakes her head. "Are you kidding me? She would freak if she knew. She's like old-school Catholic. She's all 'strong Latina' this and 'independent woman' that, but I think that underneath she's pretty old school. Like, she made me promise not to have sex until after I become a doctor and get married." She giggles. "She'll probably get that part of her wish even after I get married—*if* I get married . . . and if you define 'having sex' as 'putting a dick in your you-know-what.'"

I don't know why, but that makes me blush.

Jamie laughs again, then says, "Maybe I *should* tell my mom about us. At least she'd stop worrying about me getting pregnant." She sighs. "Do *your* parents know?"

"*I* didn't even know for sure until you."

"Really?"

"Uh-huh."

"Hm. And what do you think so far?"

I guess homework can wait a little longer.

A couple of study breaks later, Jamie asks if Mom knows about Dad's affair. I don't have a good answer. "I don't know—it's not like they're acting different or anything. They've never seemed really close. But I mean, people in Japan don't like, hug and kiss or say 'I love you' to each other, really."

"That's messed up," says Jamie. "I didn't know Japan was so, like, weird."

Suddenly I feel a bit defensive. "It's not like that so much anymore. Plus they're from the countryside from like, super-traditional families."

"Huh. Well, anyway. I think you should tell your mom, just in case. Show her that picture. She deserves to know the truth."

"Yeah, maybe. But she'll kill me for being out at karaoke."

"So tell her your friends went out, took the picture, showed it to you, and you recognized your dad."

"Then she'll think they're bad kids and she'll never let me go out with them again."

"So hang out with me and my friends."

"Yeah . . . maybe. I dunno. I don't want to ditch my friends."

"Hanging out with my friends doesn't mean you're ditching yours."

"I know, I just—whatever, that's not the point. The point is I don't want to tell my mom about my dad. It'll mess everything up."

"Like things aren't gonna get messed up anyway?"

"I know . . . but maybe they won't. I—it's been going on for years, now. How am I gonna tell her that? Maybe . . . maybe she'll figure things out on her own. I mean, it's her marriage, right?"

"But it's your family. I know it's hard, but she's your *mom*. You have to stick together. Someone has to tell her, and it's not gonna be him. She deserves to know. She deserves to have a choice."

"Yeah, I know she does, but I just . . . I wish I didn't feel like it was up to me."

"I know." Jamie puts her arm around me, and we sit like that, with my head resting on her shoulder, for a long time. It feels even better than everything we've done together so far.

After I see Jamie off at the bus stop, I come home almost ready to have a talk with Mom. But not quite. Because how can you ever be ready to tell your mom that your dad is having sex with another woman? I don't know.

Tonight's dinner is special, for o-tsukimi, the harvest moon festival. Everything is round, like the full moon. Mom's making tsukimi-soba—buckwheat noodles with a raw egg cracked on top—chicken meatballs, kabocha with sweet-salty sauce, and daikon, carrots, and taro root boiled in fish broth. She's even found some fu—tiny starch dumplings to go in the miso soup—that have pictures of rabbits on them, because in Japan, instead of the man in the moon, there's a rabbit. Mom's a good cook, and she's proud of the meal she's made. I take a photo and text it to Dad, to spite him:

Nom nom! You should be here!

I poke a hole in the egg yolk with my chopsticks and stir the yolk into the noodle broth a little. It makes a rich, silky contrast to the salty broth and chewy soba noodles. Dad *should* be here. And it's not like he couldn't. He's somewhere in town, after all.

The more I eat—the sweet pumpkin, the daikon seasoned and cooked to melt-in-your-mouth tender perfection—the more resentful I feel about Dad's absence, and by the time Mom and I are carrying the dishes back to the sink, I'm ready to tell her. Jamie's right. She deserves to know the truth.

"Mom," I begin, "do you ever wish that Dad didn't work so much? Or go away so much?"

Mom is sorting through her Tupperware, eyeing what's left in the serving dishes and figuring out which containers to use. "No point," she says, selecting four containers. "He has to work hard and go on business trip no matter what."

"Yeah, but do you ever wish it was different?"

She starts scooping the pumpkin into a round container. "What difference does it make? Wishing does not change the life."

"But is that what you want?"

She stops scooping and looks at me, exasperated. "What I want does not matter. It is the life." She resumes scooping and shakes her head. "An'ta ni wa wakarahen."

No, I don't. I don't understand at all. And anyway, we're getting off track. I fill another container with carrots, daikon, and taro root.

"But what if . . ." *What if what? What if he's sleeping around? What if he cheats on you?* How can I say this to my own mother?

"*What if* does not change the life, either."

Arggh. Am I going to be reduced to the "I have a 'friend' with a problem" ploy? Then I have an idea. "But like, in this book we read for class, *The Scarlet Letter*. The wife cheats on the husband. When he's like, traveling or whatever."

"Cheat? Dou iu imi?"

"Cheating. It means . . ." *Keep it clean.* "It's like falling in love with someone else. Or like, kissing someone else who's not your husband or wife." Even with this G-rated version, I have to hide behind the refrigerator door with my head in the fridge, pretending to rearrange things so I can fit the Tupperware in.

Silence. The sound of water running as Mom prepares to rinse the dinner dishes. I don't dare come out from behind the door.

Then, "Ah!" She laughs and I can hear incredulous delight in her voice as she says, "You think I am cheating Dad? Aho-rashii."

Well, of course, *that's* ridiculous.

"How can I do such a thing?" She laughs again.

I guess it wasn't the best example. Beautiful young wife has affair while ugly old husband travels? No wonder she misinterpreted. I try again. "Okay, well, what about Dad? What if he . . . What if, while he's on his business trips he . . . you know."

I watch Mom's back stiffen as she leans over the sink, swirling hot water around in a serving bowl. Without straightening up, without turning around, she says, "If Dad does cheating, what can I do? I am his wife." She stops rinsing and motions me over to open the dishwasher. Then with an air of finality, she says, "Aho-rashii hanashi yame-nasai."

"But—"

"Yame-nasai." And that's the end of that. No more foolish talk.

She hands me dish after dish and I load them into the dishwasher without a word, like she wants, the same way we stow away our secrets in this family, shutting the door on them and locking them away from sight until we come up with a version clean and respectable enough for all to see.

In the same way that being with Jamie is like carrying a star in my pocket wherever I go, knowing about Dad's affair is like walking around with a backpack full of rocks. Talking to Mom last night only made it heavier.

"Why don't you tell your dad you saw him?" asks Caleb at lunch. It's Tuesday and I've pulled him away from his friends, and I thought I saw his cheeks go a little pink, but I had other things to think about. I have to talk to someone, and I'm still too embarrassed to pull Jamie away from her friends. And since our spying misadventure the other week and my little breakdown on Sunday, Caleb is the only person besides Jamie who I feel comfortable talking to about Dad.

"Are you out of your mind? What am I going to say, 'Hi, Dad, I was out at PopStar—where, by the way, I wasn't supposed to be—and I saw you and your mistress . . . canoodling'?"

"I wouldn't say *canoodling*, but yeah. Something like that. Anyway, it's not like he could get you in trouble. He was doing something way worse."

"No. I'm not doing it."

"Why not?"

"Oh, come on. How awkward would that be? Would you

tell your dad you saw him cheating?"

"I don't have a dad."

"Fine. Your mom's boyfriend. Would you tell him?"

"Hell, yeah. I'd kick his ass."

"Well, your mom's boyfriend is not my dad, and I'm not you, and anyway, I can't kick my dad's ass."

"Fine. Suit yourself. But I think you should say something. I think people should always be honest with each other."

He gives me a look so serious that suddenly I'm sure he's talking about Jamie. He takes a breath like he's going to spill some really big news. Does he know? Did Elaine go blabbing it to someone? I try to look innocent. Then, thank God, he lets his breath out, and I can see him change his mind. "If your dad can't be honest with you, then you have to step up and be honest with him. It sucks, but I really think it's what you have to do."

My own sigh is one part aggravation with all this harping about honesty and three parts relief that he isn't talking about me and Jamie. "Fine. Okay. I'll think about it."

But I know I won't do it.

Poetry Journal, Honors American Literature
Wednesday, October 7

"Wellfleet, Midsummer"
by Kimiko Hahn

It's kind of a long poem, but it's easy to read. It's almost not even poetry—each stanza is just a sentence or two about the speaker's life at a rented cottage on a beach somewhere— Wellfleet, I guess. Her mother is dead, her boyfriend is there, and it's hot and humid and sad. She has a daughter and an ex-husband, too, but they aren't at the cottage. Maybe the daughter is at her dad's house for the weekend.

Here is one of my favorite stanzas:

> Loneliness is the habit of this house: even with two
> box turtles in a box
> on the porch I wonder what home may be.

It's sad to think of loneliness being the habit of a house, like you can't escape it. Probably the speaker misses her mom, but maybe she misses her daughter, or even her ex-husband, even though she says she doesn't. I don't even know what box turtles are, but it seems like having two of them in a box on the front porch is like making a home for husband and wife turtles. Maybe the box is like a symbol of the cozy home that she wants. But it isn't enough. Maybe the box turtles still look lonely. Maybe they look trapped.

24

I'M STAYING OVER AT JAMIE'S TONIGHT; I'VE taken the bus half an hour across town to where she lives. She greets me with a shy hug at the bus stop, and we walk together toward the apartment she shares with her mom and brother.

The houses are smaller and older here than where I live, but the paint is bright, and all the lawns are neat and tidy. A couple of garage doors are open, revealing people lounging on chairs, eating chips, and watching the world go by. Some of them are wearing Giants T-shirts; I guess there's a game tonight. I try not to look around too much, try not to let on how different this is from my neighborhood, where the garage doors are closed and the lounging happens in the backyard. Why do I care, though? There's nothing wrong with me being curious about a new place . . . is there?

Two little girls and a boy are kicking a soccer ball around the concrete driveway of a blocky, beige stucco apartment house. Another girl is riding a pink bicycle up and down the sidewalk in front. They wave at Jamie and me as we walk past them to the back of the building and climb the stairs to the second floor.

"Ta-daa!" she sings as she ushers me in. "You can put your stuff here in the corner for now. We'll pull out the couch later, or we can sleep on the floor." Jamie and her mom share a bedroom, and her brother Tommy has the other one—a less than satisfactory situation, to say the least, when you're spending the night with your girlfriend. But Jamie has promised that her mom will be asleep by eleven o'clock, and Tommy's working the night shift in his new job as a security guard.

The apartment is immaculate, though it's crammed with stuff. There are framed photos on every surface—Jamie as a baby; Jamie in a kindergarten graduation cap and gown; Jamie in a lacy white dress and gloves ("my First Communion," she says); Jamie wearing various soccer uniforms; Jamie in her eighth grade graduation cap and gown; Jamie in her Anderson cross-country uniform. There are photos of her sister, Sarah, wearing all the same outfits, plus high school graduation, college graduation, wedding, and family photos with her husband and baby. There are even more photos of Tommy. There are photos of everyone together. There are photos of what must be cousins, uncles, aunts, grandparents.

The only photo my family displays is a small black-and-white one of Jiji, Dad's dad, who died when I was a baby—and that one's shut up inside a little black altar in the corner of our living room.

Mrs. Ramirez is tiny—shorter than Mom, even. She has curly hair like Jamie's, but it's shoulder-length. She's in the kitchen, stirring a pot of something that smells sweet. Her face lights up when she sees me, and I notice that she has the same dimple on her chin that Jamie does. "Chocolate pudding," she says, nodding at the pot. "For your dessert."

Jamie puts her arm around her mother's shoulders and kisses her on the cheek. "She makes the best chocolate pudding in the world," she says, smiling at Mrs. Ramirez.

"Ay, mijita, basta. Enough." But she looks pleased. She dips a spoon in, blows on it to cool it, and holds it out for me to taste. "I haven't put the chocolate in yet," Mrs. Ramirez says, "but it's already delicious—sweet and creamy. You like it?" I nod.

A guy with spiky black hair and eyes just like Jamie's appears from the hallway—Tommy, I guess. The guy who broke the computer and made it so that Jamie could hang out at my house after school. I should thank him. He glances at me as he pushes past Jamie into the kitchen. "You Jamie's Asian friend?"

That throws me off balance, because a) duh, and b) why does he have to go pointing it out like that? Is he making fun of me, somehow? Or Jamie? Or is he just that bad at conversation? I'm too confused to put together a real response, so I just nod.

"Who's paying you to hang out with her?"

Jamie punches him on the arm. "Shut up, Tommy." To me she says, "Just try to pretend he's not here." Tommy pulls a spoon out of a drawer and starts to dip it into the pudding, but Mrs. Ramirez slaps his hand away.

"¡Ay! No toques!" Then she reaches her arm out. "Ven aca. Dame un beso, mijo." Tommy rolls his eyes and bends down to kiss Mrs. Ramirez. "¡Ya vete! Go!" She shoves him away and waves her spoon at him. "¡Ándale! ¡Vas a llegar tarde a trabajo!"

Tommy heads out, shouting, "Bye!" and slams the door behind him.

"Terminalo," Mrs. Ramirez says, handing Jamie the spoon and gesturing at the pot. Sarah's having date night with her husband, so Mrs. Ramirez has to get ready to go and babysit Ariella.

As I watch Jamie stir the pudding, I hear the rattle-rumble of an old engine, the squeak of breaks, and then three doors slamming—*bam! bam! bam!*—emphatic as exclamation marks. A minute later, Arturo, Christina, and JJ troop inside without even knocking. "Buenas noches, Señora," all three of them say to Mrs. Ramirez, who's back in the kitchen, checking on the pudding one last time. Christina is carrying two Tupperware containers, which she plunks on the kitchen counter. "These are from Mami and me, to say thank you for driving her to work last week."

"Ay, no tenias que hacer eso, mijita. Ya estas bastantes

ocupada," says Mrs. Ramirez, frowning at Christina as she accepts the containers.

"No fue molestia. You're busier than anyone, anyway."

Mrs. Ramirez peeks inside the top container. "¡Mira, estas galletas! ¡Que deliciosas!" She pulls out a cookie, takes a bite, and winks at Christina. "Pero tu mami no las hizo."

"No, I made them," Christina admits, turning pink.

Mrs. Ramirez takes another bite of the cookie and lifts the lid of the bottom container. "Y tu pollo especial. Gracias, mijita. Que buena niña eres." She gives Christina a warm hug and a kiss.

Christina smiles, and her expression softens into something warm and shy and almost sweet.

Mrs. Ramirez lets her go and asks, "¿Cómo está tu papi?"

Christina shrugs, her face still soft and now tired, too, and I can't tear my eyes away—it's so strange to see her like this. But then she looks up and catches me staring, and her face hardens back to its usual iciness. Guiltily, I look away. I get the feeling that I've just witnessed something she didn't want me to see.

The boys have made themselves comfortable on the couch, and Jamie's mom leans over and kisses them, too, before calling, "Buen provecho, mijitos. ¡Adiós!" and rushing out the door.

We settle in and eat Christina's special chicken, and I don't even have to lie when I tell Christina how delicious it is. She looks genuinely pleased, and says with a hint of pride in her voice, "My dad taught me how to make it, but I changed a few ingredients. And added a couple steps." I relax a little. Maybe we're making progress.

"Christina's going to be a famous chef someday," says Jamie. "She's going to own her own restaurant."

"Oh! You could go to, like, that cooking school up in Napa Valley. The CIA. It stands for Culinary Institute of America." Mom showed me an article about it when we were back in Wisconsin trying to learn about what was out here.

There's an awkward pause before Jamie says, "Yeah, maybe you could!" a little too cheerfully.

Christina eyes me and says drily, "I know what CIA stands for." And the conversation sinks like a brick in a well, taking my heart along with it. It doesn't seem fair. I was only trying to be encouraging.

Maybe it's the sauce, or maybe it's just how things work, but as the mound of chicken dwindles, the atmosphere lightens again and talk resumes. Having learned my lesson, I keep quiet and watch, impressed, as the others gnaw every last sliver of meat off the chicken bones: fat, gristle—JJ even crunches on the cartilage at the ends.

I don't like the chewy, slimy bits, so I'm nowhere near as thorough, and when I push away my plateful of bones, Christina says, "What—you done?"

"Uh, yeah. It was really, really good." It can't hurt to say it again.

"You gotta pick the bones clean," explains JJ, licking his fingers.

"Don't trip, though, not everyone does it," says Arturo. "It's like old-fashioned manners or something. Like from when everyone was poor and they hardly ever got to eat meat."

"No shit, really?" says JJ.

"You dumbass, what'd you think it was from?" Arturo snorts.

"I just thought . . . I don't know. I never thought about it."

"Ughhh," Christina groans through her teeth. "You drive me crazy. You never think about anything. How do you go through life like that?" And I'm so relieved not to be the target for once that I laugh. Big mistake. Christina looks at me and asks, "What's so funny?"

I turn my laughter into an awkward cough. "Nothing."

"Enough of this," says Arturo, giving Christina a shove. "Get me some of them cookies."

"Fuck you. I'm your girlfriend, not your slave. Get them yourself."

"Yeah, you know where the plates are," adds Jamie. "And while you're up, get us some of that chocolate pudding."

Arturo refuses, and after some bickering back and forth, it's agreed that everyone should serve themselves. As we dig into the chocolate pudding ("Not too much, though," says Jamie. "My mom'll kill us if we finish it."), and some of Christina's (delicious, ugh) cookies, we channel surf and make jokes about everything that comes on. Actually that's not entirely accurate. They make jokes, I sit in awkward silence.

Like when a commercial comes on featuring a young

Black man in a hoodie. This sparks a debate that could be entitled, "Hoodies: Freedom of Expression, Tempting Fate, or It Doesn't Matter What You Wear, You're Still Screwed?" All four of them have strong opinions, but I have nothing to add. And I feel nervous about participating, anyway. I'm afraid that if I say, "Yes, wear whatever you want," someone will tell me I don't get it; if I say, "No, people might think you're up to no good," someone will wonder if that's what *I* think. I guess I can't blame them. I mean, what do I know? I feel . . . like an impostor. It's like being back in Wisconsin when I couldn't find my way into the Midwest Farmers' Daughters' Club.

You'd think that as a Person of Color, I would feel some kinship here, some bond. But I don't, not exactly. Why is that? Is it really race or ethnicity or whatever, that's making me feel like I'm not in the club, or am I making it all up and it's just a personal thing? Or something else entirely? If I don't think it's about race does that make me a racist? If I do think it's about race does that make me a racist?

"I'm bored," JJ complains, eventually. "Let's do something else. Let's get some chips or something. Let's go to the 7-Eleven on South Bascom. I just got a new ID and I wanna break it in. I heard they don't have one of those scanner things to check IDs yet."

"Nuh-uh," says Christina. "I'm not gonna get in trouble just because you want to try out your new little fake ID— which no one is gonna fall for, by the way, 'cause you look like a twelve-year-old. And if Jamie gets in trouble, I'll tell her mom it was your fault."

"Chill, Christina. It's fine," Jamie says.

"No, it's not. I'm not gonna let fuckin' JJ fuck everything up for you—for all of us—just 'cause he wants to be a big man and buy some beer."

"Oh, look who's talking." JJ jeers. "Who got drunk just last weekend?"

"Yeah, at someone's *house*. Where it's safe and no one's gonna call the cops."

"Nothin's gonna happen. No one's gonna get arrested. Stop being such a whiny little—"

"Don't you say it," Christina warns him.

We end up getting into Arturo's car and heading over to the 7-Eleven, but only after JJ promises not to try his new ID. The spots closest to the store are all taken, so we park in a corner of the lot, go in, and load up with chips and soda. On our way out, JJ holds his hand out to Arturo.

"Gimme my Funyuns," he says.

"What Funyuns?"

"What the fuck, bruh? I told you to get me some Funyuns 'cause I didn't have enough cash and you owe me twenty bucks!"

"The fuck you talking about? You never said that."

"I did, too, you—" JJ stops and shakes his head. "Fine. Whatever. But you owe me, so just give me the money and I'll go get 'em myself."

Arturo grimaces and pulls a twenty-dollar bill from his pocket. "Sometimes I don't know why we keep you," he mutters as he hands it to JJ, who takes it, raises his middle finger at Arturo, and trots happily back into the store for his Funyuns. "Idiot."

We go back to the car and break into the chips while we wait for JJ. Jamie and I sit on the hood of the car, sharing a can of Pringles. She scoots over so that our legs are touching, and rests her hand on my knee. I have a girlfriend. She's got her hand on my knee. In public. No big deal.

But it is kind of a big deal. I'm split between feeling giddy with excitement and jittery with self-consciousness. I might as well post a photo on Instagram: "@entireworld, here's me making out with my girlfriend! #lookatme #getaroom." I glance at Christina and Arturo to gauge their reaction, but they're starring in their very own Instagram couples' moment—he's leaning against the car and she's leaning back against him, her head resting in the little hollow between his shoulder and his neck. It would be kind of romantic, except for the ginormous bag of Cheetos that Arturo is snarfing down in between whatever cheesy nothings he's whispering in her ear.

So, okay. I'll try to relax and enjoy being with Jamie. That's what couples do, right? But as Jamie's fingers start tracing a series of loops from my knee up to my thigh, I'm afraid it will become as distracting to the others as it is to me. I put my hand over hers as a gentle hint to stop, but she misinterprets and pulls my hand around her back as she turns to me and plants a salty kiss next to my mouth.

I can't help it this time. I stiffen and sit straight up. "What?" says Jamie.

"Oh. Nothing, really, it's just—"

"Are you embarrassed? About us?" I can't read her expression. She's kind of smiling, kind of not. Hurt? Confused? Amused?

"No, I—well, kind of. Sort of. But not about us because of . . . you know. It's more like . . ." I can't explain it without sounding like a total prude. I almost want to say that I don't want people knowing what we do in private, but that's not it, either. It's not like it's a secret what couples do behind closed doors.

"You don't have to be embarrassed. Look at them." Jamie nods in the direction of Christina and Arturo, who are now staring deep into each other's eyes and licking Cheeto dust off each other's fingers.

How can I explain? "I'm just, I'm not that comfortable with—stuff like that. In public," I say. "It just seems—" I clamp my mouth shut before the word "immodest" escapes, and I realize that Mom has taken over my brain. I cast about for a better word, but all I can come up with is "inappropriate," "indiscreet," and "unseemly." "I'm sorry, it's just. It's an Asian thing, I guess. It's my mom and dad. I've never even seen them hug each other, and forget about kissing. It just feels too private to show other people." Wow, does that sound weak. Jamie considers this for a moment, and then nods and lets go of my hand. "Sorry. Maybe I'll get more comfortable later. You know, like with time."

"No, it's okay." She makes puppy-dog eyes at me. "But can you just give me one little kiss? To tide me over?"

"Oh, all right." I kiss the corner of her jaw, where it meets her neck—chaste and seductive at the same time, I figure, and then we spend a few seconds smiling besottedly at each other. That, I can handle. Soon, with Arturo and Christina safely enveloped in a haze of lust and Cheeto dust, Jamie and I drift into a warm, hand-holding, dreamy discussion of possibilities for romantic dates in the future.

JJ bursts out of the store and storms over to us, holding a six-pack of Dr Pepper. No beer. He dumps the soda on the roof of the car ("Watch it!" yelps Arturo) and starts griping. "He swore this ID would work here. Robert's such a liar."

"Omigod, JJ, you better not—" Christina says, but JJ is already making his way toward an older couple, holding out what remains of his cash and saying, "Hey, could you do me a huge favor?"

Christina looks like she's going to go after him, but Arturo pulls her back. "Don't trip. He'll give up in a few minutes, and then we can go." She settles back irritably into his arms.

Five minutes and three failed attempts later, JJ throws up his hands and turns back to the car yelling, "I quit!"

"It's about fuckin' time!" Arturo calls back. We're all laughing as JJ swaggers toward us shouting abuse and trading insults with Arturo when a cop car pulls into the lot.

"Aw, shit," breathes Arturo. JJ morphs visibly. He hunches his shoulders, sticks his hands in his pockets, and drops the swagger in favor of a sort of shamble.

Even here at the car, there's a change. Jamie moves the tiniest bit away from me, and although Arturo and Christina don't change their posture, their attention has clearly shifted away from each other. "I bet that store guy called them," says Christina. "I knew this was gonna happen."

"No one gets in trouble for trying to buy beer," I say.

Everyone looks at me like I've just asked where I can find the switch to turn off the moon. Jamie says, "If the cop's in a bad mood you can get arrested." I think back to all the drinking stories I used to hear in Wisconsin, but of all the failed attempts to buy alcohol that I can remember, I've never heard of anyone being arrested or getting in trouble. People got turned down and that was that. It never seemed like a big deal.

JJ has almost reached us when the squad car door opens and a police officer gets out and saunters over to our corner of the lot. "Shit," says Arturo again. "Be chill." Then he shoves Christina off him, wipes his orange fingers on his jeans, and walks out past JJ with his hand extended to greet the cop. "Good evening, officer. Can we help you?" he says brightly.

The cop, a tall man with a paunch, too-tight trousers, and a name tag that reads D. BARLOWE, ignores Arturo and surveys the scene: me and Jamie on the hood of the car, Christina leaning against the rear door, clutching the Cheetos bag and licking her fingers, and JJ slouching by the rearview mirror.

"Looks like a party," he says.

"We're just hanging out with friends, you know, just snacking on junk food and soda," offers Arturo. He points at the Dr Pepper on the roof of the car.

"Good. Wouldn't want to have to take you in for anything shady." Officer Barlowe looks pointedly at JJ.

"Oh, no, sir."

"Seriously," Jamie breaks in, "we were just sitting here. Eating." She holds up the Pringles can.

"I'll decide whether you're breaking the law. Let's see your ID, amigo."

Arturo pulls his driver's license out. "See? I just turned seventeen. Had my license for thirteen months now. No tickets, no nothing."

I turn to Jamie, confused. She whispers, "You're not allowed to drive other teenagers until you've had your license for a full year. He just wants a reason to nail us."

After scrutinizing Arturo's license, Officer Barlowe returns it with a glare. Then he sniffs the air, to check if we've been smoking, I guess. Not getting anything, he looks around at us again, and this time his gaze lights on me. "Well, look at this— one of these things is not like the others. What's your name, young lady?"

"Sana," I croak.

"Nice name. What is that, Korean?"

"Japanese."

"Huh." He nods. "My brother was stationed in Yokohama

for a coupla years. Right near Tokyo, right? What a great city."
I've never been to Yokohama or Tokyo, but I nod. "No crime,
real clean, people are real polite and friendly . . . Not like here."
He chuckles. I give him what I hope is a polite and friendly
smile. "Japanese food, too. Love that stuff. Even sushi. Ma-*goo*-
roh. That's tuna, right?"

"Uh-huh."

"You ever been to Gombei in Japantown?"

Behind Officer Barlowe's back, JJ is mouthing the words,
"What the *fuck*?" which are my sentiments exactly, but I just
shake my head.

"What? A Japanese girl and you've never been to Gombei?
Now, *that's* a crime. It's very authentic. One of the original restaurants in Japantown. They even have tatami mats for you to
sit on—gotta take off your shoes and everything."

"Oh."

"So, Sana." The cop looks closely at my face. "You look like
a good kid. You get good grades?"

Wait—what? I nod.

"Straight As, I bet?"

"Um, mostly. I'm getting a B in trig." B minus, actually, but
I figure it's best to round up.

"So what are you doing here with this bunch? You don't
look like you belong with them. They your friends?" My
mouth opens and closes. And opens and closes again.

"She's my girlfriend," Jamie announces, and puts her arm
around my shoulder. Oh, no.

Now Officer Barlowe laughs. "Ohhhh, I see how it is." He addresses me again. "Do your parents know what kind of, ah, girl you're dating?" I nod. It's not exactly a lie. Mom knows Jamie, right?

"Do they know where you are?"

"They know I'm with her right now." Which is also not a lie, so please, please, please don't let him call Mom and Dad.

Now he nods slowly, as if making up his mind. "I'm gonna let you and your friends go because you look like a good kid and I don't want you to get in trouble. But you need to find yourself a new . . ." He grins and winks at me. ". . . *girlfriend*, young lady. You keep hanging out with these kids, they'll drag you down, and I won't let you off so easy next time. But there's not gonna be a next time, right?"

I shake my head. "No."

"You gonna get yourself a new girlfriend? And a better crowd to hang out with?"

What am I going to say—No? And openly defy a police officer? But I can't exactly say yes in front of Jamie and everyone, can I? I look at my feet as the gears spin wildly in my head.

Finally, Officer Barlowe rescues me. "Ah, you don't need to answer, I'm just givin' you a hard time. Making sure you're more careful in the future. Making sure *all* of you are more careful in the future." He looks hard at JJ, Arturo, Christina, and Jamie.

Christina stares back blankly (she's good at that), and JJ shrugs and looks away, but Arturo nods and says, "Yes, sir, officer. Thank you." He sticks out his hand to shake once more.

Officer Barlowe narrows his eyes and shakes Arturo's hand. "Adios, primo."

As he walks away, Arturo mutters, "I'm not your primo."

Christina lets out a nervous giggle and says, "Ave Maria Madre Purissima, I thought we were dead!" Then she turns to JJ and says, "I told you not to try that fake ID. I told you we'd get in trouble."

JJ laughs and says, "Jeezus, calm down! No one got in trouble. Let it go! Why you gotta be such an old lady all the time?"

Christina clicks her tongue—*tsk*—and fixes JJ with that icy stare that I've come to know so well. "You've got nothing on the line, but I've got a job, Arturo's got a job, Jamie's got her whole future. You could've flushed her whole fucking *future* down the toilet, JJ, and you don't even care. So shut up and think about someone besides yourself for once."

JJ scowls at her but doesn't say anything—just gets in the back seat of the car and slams the door shut.

Arturo whistles, long and low. "Well, okay then," he says, and gets in the driver's seat, leaving Jamie, me, and Christina standing outside the car.

In the silence Jamie says, "Christina, I don't need you to protect me."

"Yeah, well. Someone has to," she replies, and for the briefest of moments, her eyes meet mine and I get the feeling I've failed some kind of test.

Jamie must feel it, too, because she glances at me before saying, "No, they don't. And there's no guarantee I'm gonna get in, anyway, so just—"

"Other people might not understand what it means to you, but I do." Another significant look at me. Then she ducks into the passenger seat and slams the door, hard.

Jamie looks at me apologetically. I don't know what to do—Christina's such tricky territory—so I say, "It's okay," even though it's not really.

After a couple minutes of awkward silence in the car, JJ says to no one in particular, "Just because we're Mexican, bruh. That's it. Just because I'm wearing a hoodie and I got brown skin. That's fucked up."

"You don't think the clerk called the cop because of your ID?" I venture.

"Nah. As far as he knows, we left right afterward." JJ has a point. And that cop didn't even pull into the lot until after JJ had given up asking other people. "Anyways," he continues, "remember the time that security guard questioned me, and all I was doing was buying diapers for Mateo? And I was wearing my nice button-down shirt 'cause it was after church, so you can't blame it on a hoodie, either. It's who I am, not what I'm wearing or what I'm doing."

"We all know why he came over," says Arturo. "Just be glad it ended okay."

"Yeah, good thing Sana came along," Christina says. "It could've been worse if you weren't with us, with your sushi and your Tokyo and all that. Did you see how nice he was to you?"

"She's our Asian good-luck charm," Arturo quips. "You gotta come out with us more often." I smile weakly. No, thanks. No way I'm risking getting stopped by cops again.

"She's not *that* lucky, bruh. I didn't get my beer," says JJ.

"Shut up, JJ. No one bought you beer because you look like a thirteen-year-old with that sad little mustache," Christina snickers.

They go back and forth like this until we turn off Bowers Avenue and into the neighborhood, and Jamie asks Arturo to drop us off at home.

Arturo says with a grin, "Yeah, I see how it is. You two need some"—he puts up air quotes—"alone time."

"Shut up," says Jamie, but she's smiling.

I, of course, say nothing.

When we get back into the apartment, Jamie wraps her arms around me and presses her forehead against mine. "I'm sorry," she says. "I was kinda hoping it would be a little different with them tonight. I mean, we don't usually get harassed by asshole cops."

"It was . . . an adventure," I say.

Jamie lifts her shoulders and shakes her head. Then she says, "It was going okay until then, though, right? Did you like hanging out with everyone? Aren't JJ and Christina a trip?"

If anything, tonight's experience has left me feeling even more uncomfortable than before, and not just because of the cop. But Jamie looks so hopeful, and I know how much she wants me and Christina to like each other, so I say, "Yeah. I did."

Apparently I'm not very convincing, because she looks carefully at my face. "You sure?"

"Hey, let's not talk about this anymore." I kiss her. "Everything's fine." I kiss her again. "I promise." And again.

Success. We don't talk about it again for the rest of the time I'm at her house.

25

BEFORE SCHOOL, I TELL HANH, REGGIE, AND Elaine about my night out with Jamie and her friends. "But that can't be true, right?" I ask, about Officer Barlowe with a brother who was stationed in Yokohama. "He didn't let us off just because I'm Asian, did he?"

"Holy blinders, Batman. Yes, he did," says Reggie.

"Totally," agrees Elaine. "Why do you think he asked you about your grades?" Ugh. I'd been hoping I was wrong about that.

"He couldn't have arrested us anyway. We weren't doing anything illegal."

"JJ was," Elaine points out.

"But the cop didn't know that. Anyways, cops don't arrest kids for trying to buy alcohol. They have better things to do," says Hanh.

"See? That's exactly my point. There was no need to worry."

"On the other hand, you think he woulda come over if it was us in the parking lot?" she asks.

"Anyway, Sana, are you sure it's a good idea to keep hanging out with Jamie's friends?" asks Reggie. "I've been meaning to say something, but I wanted to give them a chance. Because like, I don't know. Stuff like Friday night. You could get in trouble. Plus, I hear that JJ smokes a lot of weed."

"He can't possibly smoke more than Andy Chin," says Hanh.

"It's not the same thing," says Reggie.

"It's exactly the same thing," retorts Hanh, but I get what Reggie means. Except I'm not sure why it's not the same thing.

"What I mean is . . ." Reggie starts to explain, but she just trails off. She can't seem to explain it, either. Could we be wrong?

"I've been thinking we should try smoking, actually," says Hanh, off on a new tack.

"Oh, right," says Reggie. "You wouldn't even know where to get it."

"Elaine!" I can't believe it.

"What? Everybody smokes."

"You mean Jimmy smokes," says Reggie.

"Sometimes. So? There's nothing wrong with it."

Reggie rolls her eyes, and Elaine crosses her arms and scowls. "Stop being so judgy."

"I'm not being judgy. You two just sound like a health class movie." Reggie turns to me. "But seriously, Sana, what do you have in common with those guys? Like what do you even talk about?"

I consider asking her what she really means, but I don't ask because what if she's literally talking about common interests? How will I look then? So I say, "Arturo and JJ are really nice."

The five-minute bell rings, and as we head to class, Janet shows up and asks Elaine how her date at the movies with Jimmy went. As Elaine gives Janet the details, it occurs to me that everyone involved in her story is Asian, and I get a wave of that good feeling of being part of a club. Maybe Reggie's right. Maybe I just don't have anything in common with Jamie's friends. We don't listen to the same music. We don't wear the same clothes. We don't take the same classes or have the same plans for our futures, except for Jamie.

But should that even matter? Is it even true? Or am I just making excuses? I think of how I felt like I couldn't keep up with everyone the other night, how I wished Jamie was friends with Luisa Campos. Is it really just because Luisa is nicer? But what else could it be? And what does that even mean? Am I trying hard enough? Are they? Should they? Jamie and I are totally comfortable with each other. Why can't I feel that way with her friends?

It's Thursday, and I've just gotten home from a cross-country meet in Santa Clara. Mom's been in a bad mood all week, and now she's on my case because apparently I've been spending too much time with my friends. By which I'm sure she means Jamie's friends, even though I've told her they aren't really my friends.

I think it's because I showed her a picture of Arturo, JJ, Jamie, and me at Jamie's house with Mrs. Ramirez in the background, to prove that we had a chaperone all night. That was probably a mistake. One look was all it took to trigger a barrage of classic Mom commentary: See how those boys are sitting? Sloppy. They look like the bad students and criminal. Maybe Mrs. Ramirez is nice lady, but how can she let her daughter have those boys for friend? Those boys look like gangster. I don't trust them." Translation: "I don't trust you."

Which is totally unfair, considering the most untrustworthy person in this house—the one who's going out and getting drunk and secretly kissing other women—is Dad. Okay, so there are two of us secretly kissing women. But the point is, Dad's the one who's doing wrong, not me. Dad's the one who's betraying Mom. And I'm the one who's getting in trouble.

I'm studying for my physics test tomorrow and Mom's busy with dinner in the kitchen when Dad gets home early from work. "Tadaima," he calls, and rushes to his bathroom and turns on the shower. That's weird. Usually he takes a bath when he gets home. Something's up.

I sneak into his room to go through his pockets while he's in the shower—if Mom isn't going to do it, then someone has to. I don't know what I think I'll find, or even if I think I'll find something. Phone: Locked, with a new passcode. Damn. Wallet: Nothing. Five twenty-dollar bills, a bunch of credit cards, a receipt from Gumba's Pizza for $8.99.

But wait. What's this? In the inside breast pocket, there's a little box, wrapped in silver paper. Hands shaking, I undo the wrapping paper at one end, tug the box out, and open it.

It's a pair of pearl earrings. For pierced ears. Which means they can't be for Mom or me. Which means that they have to be for That Woman. Which means they're evidence.

Which means that I sneak out of the room with the earrings and the wrapping paper under my shirt, go into my room, rewrap the present, and hide it in my lacquer box.

I'm so freaked out about what I've just done, and so mad at Dad, that I can't come out of my room until well after he's gone off to dinner "with clients." I wish I hadn't gone through his pockets, after all—I realize now that I really didn't want to find anything. Why do I keep looking for stuff? And why do I have to keep finding it?

I can't concentrate on studying for physics. I can't even sit down—I just walk in circles in my room until Mom calls me for dinner. I consider showing her the box, but I just can't bring myself to do it. Besides, I'm too busy arguing with her about Jamie's friends.

When Dad gets home, he isn't drunk, as I've been dreading, but he is in a foul mood. Dad doesn't yell or anything when he's mad. He just won't talk to anyone. Not a word. When he walks in the door, he doesn't even say "Tadaima" to announce himself. Ha. Serves him right.

"Dō yatta? Umaku itta?" Mom asks him. Silence. Dad stalks to his room without telling Mom how it went (not well, obviously) and without looking at me. I hear him opening and closing drawers; dropping his change, his keys, and his phone on the dresser as he goes through his jacket pockets; opening and closing the closet door. "Nan'ka nakush'tan?" Mom calls from the kitchen.

As if he'd tell her what he's lost. I imagine coming out of my room with the box in my hand and asking innocently, "Is this what you're looking for?" and then, "Is it a present for Mom?" But the only possible outcome would be a huge confrontation, a lot of tears, and the humiliating collapse of our family. So instead I say nothing and stay awake all night wondering what to do.

Mom and I had an argument at breakfast about whether I could go and get a pedicure this afternoon with Reggie and Janet, which ended in her threatening to ground me for the whole weekend, including today, Friday, which shouldn't count—more evidence that she's in a bad mood, because she never grounds me. I wonder if she knows about the earrings.

The varsity team is running in the Stanford Invitational tomorrow, and the rest of us, including Reggie, Hanh, and Elaine, were all going to drive up to meet them and hang out in downtown Palo Alto afterward, so that's another missed opportunity to be with Jamie. On top of it all, I didn't sleep last night because of the earring thing, so I totally bombed my physics test.

And now, I'm having an uneasy lunch with Jamie, Arturo, JJ, and Christina, in case I can't hang out with them—well, with Jamie—tomorrow.

"School doesn't care about me," JJ is saying. "Why should I care about school? Teachers all just think I'm a lazy Mexican, anyways, so why should I do shit for them?"

"They think you're a lazy Mexican *because* you don't do shit, bruh. That's what lazy *is*," Arturo says, laughing.

Jamie adds, "You can't just walk in and expect teachers to care about you. You want them to give a shit, *you* gotta give a shit . . . *two* shits."

"Forget two shits. If you're Mexican you gotta shit gold," says Arturo.

"Naw, doesn't matter how much I try. They're gonna be racist anyway," insists JJ. "They look at me and they think 'dropout.' 'Cholo.' They don't want to get to know me as a person."

"Well, duh," says Jamie impatiently. "But you can let them believe the stereotype or you can work against it."

"I shouldn't have to work against it, that's my point. It's bullshit."

Suddenly, I'm filled with impatience for this boy who could be so much more than he is if he would just stop blaming others for his problems in school. I hear myself saying, "Aren't you listening? Teachers don't assume anything about you. You have to take some responsibility for getting their respect." There's a pause just long enough for me to realize I've said something wrong.

"Um, actually . . ." says Jamie slowly, "actually, they do assume things about you."

"No, they don't."

"Are you kidding me?" says Christina. "Were you not there with us at the 7-Eleven last week?"

"Okay, yeah. But it's not true at school. All you have to do is work hard."

Christina gapes at me, then appears to collect herself. "Some Asian nerd-boy misses a few assignments, and the teacher's all, 'why aren't you doing your homework, is everything okay at home, here's a chance to make it up.' A Mexican kid doesn't do his homework, and that's that. The teacher doesn't say shit. Just lets him fail."

"Maybe that's because so many Mexican kids don't do their homework." Oh, no. I can't believe that just came out of my mouth. It's true, though. I mean, it's probably true. Besides, Jamie said not to take any crap from her.

"Oh, now you've got a Mexican girlfriend, so you know all about Mexican kids. How do you know we don't do our homework?"

"Well, I don't see how you could get bad grades if you were working hard," I say. I'm keenly aware that I'm screwing up, and scared of where this argument is going, but I don't know how to fix it, and it's too late anyway.

"You guys," says Jamie, frowning.

But Christina's fired up. "You think we don't work hard. You think we're lazy."

"No. I don't think you're lazy. I just. I just think you could work harder if you really wanted to."

"*You* think *I* could work harder?" Christina's voice swings up, incredulous. When she speaks again, it's low and steely. "I know I'm not the sweetest person and all, so you probably won't believe this, but I've been trying to be friends with you. I've been trying to be nice. But you keep judging me, even though you don't know anything about me. You cooking your family's meals? You helping to pay the rent? You been working thirty-two hours a week bagging groceries at Safeway 'cause your dad started chemo the day before school started and had to stop working?"

I swallow. That would explain why she was so upset the first day of school. "No."

"Did you know I'm getting straight A's right now?"

"No."

JJ's giving me some curious side-eye. Jamie's just standing there with her arms crossed, looking uncomfortable. I've obviously just dug myself a hole, but I can't see how it happened. I mean, I can, but how was I supposed to know about Christina's dad? And I never said Christina was stupid. Everyone knows that the Mexican kids get bad grades. Stuff like that is always in the news, so it had to be true, right? And a third of the students at Anderson are Mexican American, but Jamie's the only one in any of my Honors classes. They can't all be working thirty-two hours a week.

Something inside me squirms uneasily, poking and jabbing, but I squash it down. Surely if I can just explain myself, everything will be better. But to my horror, the very accusations I hate hearing from Mom come streaming out of my own mouth. "Okay, so you don't have as much time to spend on your homework. And you're getting good grades. But—but it's not just about how much work you do, anyway. It's about attitude. People *don't* just judge you on your grades. It's how you act. It's how you dress."

You know how if a drowning person can't swim, the best thing they can do is stop trying to swim, and just float? But instead they panic and flail, and the more they flail the worse it gets, and the worse it gets the more they flail? Right now, that's me. Flailing. Thrashing. And making things worse. "If you dress like a thug and act all hard," I continue, "what are people going to think? No wonder teachers assume you won't work hard. No wonder you get followed around in stores. No wonder my mom and my friends don't want me to hang out with you guys. You *look* like thugs, you *act* like thugs, so how can you blame people for thinking that you are?"

Silence.

No, wait. If I listen closely, I can hear the sound of nails being pounded into my coffin.

"I look like a thug?" Christina says finally. "I act like a thug?"

See? This is why I keep my mouth shut—things never come out the way I mean them. I hear how messed up my words are, how horrible I sound, but it's like I can't stop them. The words just keep coming, like ants out of a flooded anthill. "I didn't say that you *are* a criminal, I didn't say it was okay for people to judge you! I just said—"

"Yeah, I know," says Christina, "I heard you. You said no *wonder* your mom doesn't want you to hang out with us, because we act like *thugs*. Fine. Leave. I'm done with you. Get out of my sight before I punch your face in."

Wisely, I decide it's best not to point out to Christina the deep irony of her last sentence. Then I realize that I'm shaking. I look at Jamie for help, but she just takes my hand and leads me away.

Once we're out of earshot, Jamie turns to me. "What the fuck was that?"

I stare at her, confused. "Huh?"

"What. The fuck. Was that. What's wrong with you?"

Then it sinks in. She thinks that mess we just left is my fault. And that pisses me off. "What's wrong with me? *They're* the ones who attacked *me*. All I did was back you up. Didn't you just tell JJ that he had to act against stereotype? Didn't Arturo just call him lazy? Just because I said it and not you, just because I'm Asian and not Mexican. Like I haven't experienced racism. Like they're not racist. Where does Christina get off calling me a loser nerd just because I'm Asian? She never liked me." Which is true. "And it's because I'm Asian." Which might be true.

Jamie looks back at Christina, then at me. "She didn't trust you at first because she didn't want me to get hurt. But now, yeah. It's about more than that. Why *should* she trust you?" You don't trust her. You're . . . biased. Because you think she's too 'Mexican'—no, it's true. Admit it."

"She just said she was going to punch me in the face."

"She was being ironic."

"It didn't sound that way to me."

"That's because you're afraid of her. And for no good reason."

"I'm not afraid of her." Okay, I might be, a little bit. But is that because she's Mexican, or is it because she puts me down all the time? I'm not racist, am I? How do I untangle all these threads? "Anyway, how come it's okay for you and Arturo to say that JJ needs to work harder, but not okay for me to say it? That's messed up."

Jamie's jaw tightens and she gazes at me and says, "Because Arturo and I have been friends with JJ since kindergarten. We know that he's a good person and a sweet big brother. We know that he loves *Star Wars* and that he used to love school. We know that he got picked out of the audience to do some acting thing this one time at an assembly in elementary school, and people gave him a standing ovation. Not just to be nice, but because he was so good. But his parents won't pay for classes or let him take theater at school because they don't want him to be an actor. We know all of that. So we get to say whatever we want. You're not allowed because you've known him for a couple of months and you think he's a lazy Mexican. You think he's a loser. You basically said he's a criminal."

"I did not."

"You said he looks and acts like a thug. Same thing."

"I didn't mean it like that. It's just—how can your friends expect people to treat them like individuals if they dress like stereotypes?"

"The same reason you expect to be treated like an individual even though you look like a stereotype."

"I don't look like a stereotype."

"No makeup. No jewelry. No nail polish. Conservative clothes. Big heavy backpack. You're a total stereotype."

This takes me aback a little, but I'm not giving up. "Yeah, and Christina treats me like one."

"She calls *me* a loser nerd, too, you know."

"I know. But with me, it was different. She was totally talking about me being Asian."

Jamie looks like she's going to argue, but she stops herself. "Yeah, I know. I never said it was right."

"Your friends think I'm not good enough for them."

She doesn't say anything. Just starts walking again.

Then she stops and says, "No. You think *they're* not good enough for *you*."

"That's not true."

"You know, Christina's as smart as anyone in the Honors program. The only reason she's not in it is because she missed the application deadline in eighth grade. I missed it, too, but I got lucky because my mom went to the office and fought for me."

"School has nothing to do with it."

"I bet if she was in Honors classes you'd have given her a chance."

"Yeah, and if I wasn't in Honors classes, or if I was Mexican, she'd have given me a chance. I mean, JJ's failing math, and we get along. Anyway, my point is they don't want you to hang out with me."

"*My* point is, maybe that's because *you* don't want to hang out with *them*. And don't forget your friends don't want you to hang out with them, either."

"Yeah, but I still am. I'm still trying."

"I know. But they are, too. Christina is. She really is." She lets out a long breath and looks back at JJ, Arturo, and Christina. "Maybe we shouldn't hang out this weekend, after all. I'll just go home with them after school today, and I'll spend some, like, quality time with them over the weekend after the invitational, and I'll talk to them, and it'll be all good next week. I promise. 'Kay?"

"Um. Okay." What else can I say? But there's still a part of me that feels like things aren't quite fair. "I just wish I could explain that I didn't mean what I said in a racist way."

A shadow passes over Jamie's face. "I'll tell them you didn't mean it. But . . . maybe you could think about it from their point of view. 'Cause it's—it's kind of my point of view, too."

That knocks the wind out of me a bit. I hadn't thought

about it that way. I don't know why.

"Can you just try? For me?"

"Yeah. I'm sorry."

"Thanks." She takes my hand and laces her fingers through mine.

A warm glow flickers somewhere inside me and radiates through my body, and I can feel a sort of bashful, lovestruck smile spread across my face.

Jamie's got the same smile on her face, and it looks like she's really hoping I'll kiss her, and I really want to, and think I might be able to screw up the courage to do it, but at that moment Caleb and his friends come clomping around the corner in their big boots. So I drop Jamie's hand and back up a step instead. "So, okay," I say, "we'll hang out next week."

26

MOM'S BAD MOOD FLARED RIGHT BACK UP when I got home on Friday afternoon and asked her if I could please go out with Janet and Reggie to get a pedicure, and she grounded me for the whole weekend, as promised. I got to send them one text saying I couldn't make it, and then I had to surrender my phone as well. I would blame it on her finally clueing in to Dad's affair, but she's just as attentive as ever toward him. It doesn't make sense.

When she returned my phone this morning on my way out the door, there were five messages. Three are from Jamie, who missed me and sent kisses on Friday, and hearted and kissed me on Saturday afternoon and hearted and thumbed-up me on Sunday. The sweet rush of "hearts from Jamie!" is sideswiped by the jittery question of how successfully she managed to control the damage I did with Christina. And that's replaced by panic over the possibility of Mom having seen these incriminating texts, and I spend a nervous minute trying to recall the exact expression on Mom's face when she handed me the phone. But nothing comes to mind, and I figure Jamie wouldn't text me hearts and thumbs-up if things had gone badly, so I allow my panic to subside, and bask in the glow of Jamie's virtual kisses.

There are also two texts from Reggie:

Hey, do you have ur phone back? Tmb asap

U there? Just checking. Tmb!

I send hearts and kisses back to Jamie and then shoot Reggie a text (Got my phone, finally! What's up?) but this time she just says, Tell u at school, hurry!

I practically run the rest of the way to school.

"What? What is it?" I shout when I see Reggie and Hanh in our usual spot. "I ran all the way here, so it better be good."

"Heeyyy!" says Reggie with an enormous smile. "How are you?" She opens her arms and gives me a big hug.

"Hey, girl!" says Hanh, who gives me a hug after Reggie releases me.

After a whole weekend without any communication, I'm so glad to see them—it really feels like I've been let out of jail—but this seems a little excessive. I look around.

"Where's Elaine?"

Hanh nods in the direction of the opposite side of the quad. "With her boyfriend. Probably making out somewhere."

"Shut. Up."

"It's true." Hanh looks at Reggie, who nods her confirmation.

"Omigod!" I'm so excited, I make a noise that almost rivals a classic Elaine squeal.

"Is that what you wanted to tell me? Did it happen this weekend? When? Where?" Elaine pined over Jimmy much harder than I did over Jamie. And not just a few weeks, like me. Since sophomore year, I've heard. I'm so happy for her. I wish I'd been able to have a girl-talk session on the weekend. It would have made life so much more bearable.

The details are these: After the pedicure field trip that I should have been a part of, Janet and Reggie picked Elaine and Hanh up (having made up another elaborate story for Hanh's parents) and the four of them drove all the way up to Stanford to meet Jimmy, who's on the boys' varsity team and ran in the invitational, so they could hang out in Palo Alto afterward. I feel a twinge of jealousy, which probably shows, because a flicker of guilt crosses Reggie's face, and she breaks from her story to say, "I wish your mom would've let you come. We totally missed you."

I shrug and say, "Just tell me the rest."

The Palo Alto part was meh, Reggie says, and not worth talking about except that Elaine and Jimmy held hands the whole time. The good part was the end of the afternoon, when Elaine got in Jimmy's car instead of Reggie's and he took her home and kissed her good-bye.

"Look at what she texted me," Reggie says, showing me her

phone. She scrolls through the thread and stops where it says,

OMG! Jimmy kissed me!!!!!!!!!!!!!!!!!!

Then there's a whole other text that's nothing but about a hundred exclamation marks. And another of a hundred faces with hearts for eyes. And another of a hundred super-happy faces.

"So I guess she's kind of excited," I say.

"Kinda."

Good for Elaine. I'll bet *she* won't be afraid to kiss her boyfriend in public. This train of thought leads, of course, to my girlfriend. "So, um, did you see Jamie there?"

Reggie and Hanh exchange looks. "Yeah, so . . ." says Reggie, shifting on her feet.

"That's kinda what we wanted to talk to you about," finishes Hanh.

"Jamie?" I ask. "She was going to maybe hang out with Arturo and them afterward."

"Oh, they were there," says Hanh. She and Reggie look at each other again.

"So, what? Just tell me."

"Yeah, so . . ." says Reggie again. "We were with Janet's cousin Amy, you know, the one who goes to Palo Alto High School? And we saw Jamie right after the meet, and— Actually, forget it. It's no big—"

"She was with this redheaded chick, and Amy says that's the one who got together with Jamie at camp this summer," interrupts Hanh.

I look at Reggie. "I'm sure it was nothing," she says. "I'm sure they're just friends." For a very long moment, it's like the data is buffering—everything just stops except for the spinning wheel of death, which turns . . . turns . . . turns . . .

"I have to say, though, she was pretty hot," says Hanh helpfully.

"Hanh!" Reggie glares at her.

"*And* I was going to *say*," says Hanh, glaring right back at Reggie, "*but* she looks like a total slut."

Reggie rolls her eyes. "God, Hanh! That is *so* not appropriate! You can't say that about girls just because they dress a certain way!" She turns to me and says, "It's not like they were doing anything. Really, I don't even know why we brought it up."

"Reg! We brought it up because Amy says that the red-headed chick—Kelsey? Chelsea?—was talking about trying to get back together with her hot ex-girlfriend after the invitational, so, you know." Hanh turns to me and shrugs. "Two plus two."

"Wow," I say. I nod slowly, hoping this makes me look thoughtful instead of suddenly cast off into deep space, which is how I really feel. No air, no anchor, nothing to keep me from hurtling off into the void. They're watching me closely, so I have to work extra hard to keep it together.

"'Wow'? That's it? Aren't you upset?" asks Hanh.

"There's nothing to be upset about!" says Reggie.

"I'm— Reggie's right. I'm sure it's nothing. I'll be okay."

The five-minute bell rings and we head toward class. Reg-gie and Hanh begin bickering about whether or not Hanh should have told me that Kelsey looked hot. ("I *also* said that she looked like a *slut!*" Hanh keeps saying, as if somehow that makes things better—to which Reggie keeps replying with increasing impatience, "Stop. Saying that. It's not okay.")

As we reach the classroom, Elaine and Jimmy appear from the opposite direction, arms slung around each other. When she sees us, Elaine glances anxiously at Reggie and Hanh, and then at me. "Just calm down already," I want to say. Though to whom, I'm not sure.

Meanwhile, the download meter in my brain is still inch-ing toward a hundred percent. I have a little video playing in my head now: Jamie and hot Kelsey, walking down the streets of Palo Alto together. I try out a sentence in my head: Jamie was with Kelsey. It's not too bad. Nothing tragic. So she was with her ex-girlfriend. So she didn't tell me about it. That's okay, right? She's under no obligation to reveal her every move to me. No need to panic. If it hadn't been for Mom and that awful argument on Friday with Christina, it would have been me walking down the streets of Palo Alto with Jamie.

Right?

As I make my way to my seat, my brain finally kicks in and I start generating a list of questions I want to ask Reggie and Hanh as soon as class is over: Did they see you? Did you say hi? Did they look friendly, or like, *friendly*? Why did Kelsey look "slutty"? What does that even mean? Did Jamie look guilty? Did she look happy? What were her friends doing?

Then I remember how much Christina supposedly hated Kelsey. If Jamie's hanging out with her, does that mean Christina approves of Kelsey more than me? Did I screw up that badly? Have I been voted out and replaced by committee?

Under all of these questions is another one that keeps bubbling up: Why didn't she tell me?

I'm staring out the window going over my questions when the bell rings and Caleb slides into his seat behind me.

"Hey, distracted much?"

"Huh?"

"Dis-tract-ed much?" he repeats.

"Oh. Sorry. Hey."

"Hey," he says, smiling, pleased with the success of his little joke. "Hey, guess what," he continues, "I think your cross-country friend Jamie is a lesbian. I heard someone saw her like, kissing another girl this weekend. My cousin was at this meet at Stanford and she said her teammate saw a Mexican girl from Anderson and some runner from Palo Alto totally kissing. A girl runner, I mean. Obviously."

"Kissing?"

"Uh-huh."

"Are you sure?"

"That's what my cousin said."

"Caleb and Sana. Is there something you'd like to share with the class?" Caleb shakes his head and leaves me to spend the rest of trig playing a new endless loop in my head of Jamie and hot Kelsey totally kissing, over and over and over.

On the walk from trig to Spanish, I ask Reggie and Hanh if Caleb's rumor is true (Elaine, uninhibited and with no need to consider how people will react to her being straight, has left us to be part of Jimmy-and-Elaine). They can't confirm it, but Hanh thinks that Jamie and Kelsey were acting friendlier than just friends. She can't explain it. "Just, you know, body language" is the best she can do.

I spend the next eighty minutes worrying about Jamie instead of doing Spanish, followed by ten minutes of worrying about Jamie instead of listening to the announcements, which, let's face it, no one really listens to anyway. The rest of the day passes the same way—everything that happens, everything anyone says, gets pushed out by Jamie and Kelsey, Kelsey, not me, Kelsey.

At practice, I avoid Jamie. Everything I do or say around her feels like a lame cover-up for my worries about her and Kelsey, and I'm afraid she'll see right through me. Though why I don't want her to know I'm upset is beyond me. And is it my imagination, or is Jamie acting a little distant, too?

By the time we're walking back to my house, I'm a tangle of nerves. I want to hear the truth, I don't want to hear the truth. I don't want her to know I'm upset, I do want her to know I'm upset. We never hold hands on our walk home, but usually we walk close enough to touch each other every once in a while. Today—is it me, or is it her?—there's no touching.

We reach the house; even Mom notices that something's not quite right. Ever since I showed her Jamie's perfect scores on a couple of trig and physics tests, she's found it in her heart to ignore Jamie's makeup and welcome her in. And since I've been doing better on my tests as well, Mom is happy to leave us alone to "study." And in true Mom fashion, she often seems more concerned about Jamie's well-being than my own.

As I put a bowl of chips and two cans of Diet Coke on a tray, she asks, "Jamie, are you feeling bad? You're very quiet today."

"Oh, no, I'm fine. Just a little tired from practice," Jamie says. Except that practice wasn't that hard today.

Then we're alone in my room with the usual snacks, but without the usual easy conversation. She has to feel the tension—we've been apart all weekend and we haven't so much as pecked each other on the cheek. But I don't acknowledge it and neither does she.

Instead, I sit on the floor and dive right into my homework. We're supposed to be rereading this part in *The Awakening* where Edna tells her husband that she's going to move into her own little house down the block, and he arranges to have their entire actual house redecorated so it looks like that's why Edna has moved out.

I can't get into it. I can't get Kelsey out of my head. She's replaced Christina as my number one worry when it comes to Jamie. Eventually Jamie looks up from her book and says, "So, uh. I haven't told you about the weekend."

"Oh, right. How was it?" I put on an inquisitive smile.

"Yeah, actually. There's something I have to tell you." The smile slides off my face. She chews her lip, then says, "I kind of spent some time with Kelsey after the meet. I wanted to tell you before anyone else did, so you wouldn't get the wrong—"

"Reggie and Hanh already told me, actually. And Caleb. I guess a lot of people saw you together." I mean to sound neutral, like I'm just reporting the news, but it comes out resentful and sulky. I suppose that's better than scared and pathetic, which is how I really feel.

"Oh, no. What did they tell you?"

"I heard you were kissing each other. Is that true?" She's not denying it. I feel like the ground is suddenly tilting, like my life is tipping over. "Is that why you didn't want me to come? Because you knew she was going to be there?"

"No! Yes. I mean. I knew she was going to be there, but I didn't know we were going to hang out. You not coming to Palo Alto—that was about Arturo and JJ and Christina, not about Kelsey."

"Then what—why did you kiss her?"

"I didn't. She kissed me."

"Did you kiss her back?"

"No. I mean, well, not really. Kind of." She pushes her hands through her hair. "She kissed me and I guess I kinda let her." I lean against my bed and hug myself so I don't split in half. "I should explain." What can I do but let her?

"So when Kelsey and I got together last summer, it was. I don't know. My first time with a girl, and I guess it was pretty intense because we were at camp. Like, we got to sleep in the same room like, every . . ." She trails off, thank goodness. Though I can't tell if it's because she's suddenly realized how shitty it is for me to have to hear this, or if she's just lost in the memory of all those hot summer nights she and Kelsey spent in the same room. I pull my knees up to my chest. Grit my teeth. Try to decide whether I should beg her to stay or yell at her to get out. "And I dunno, she was fun and pretty and it turns out her parents have like a boatload of money, so we got to do fun things on the weekends like go sailing—I mean, like, she has her own freaking *horse*—and I guess I kinda got caught up in all of that."

Nice. I lost Trish to a rich white boy with a Mustang, and now I'm losing Jamie to a rich white girl with an *actual horse*.

"And then it was weird because we didn't actually—she just kinda left the whole thing as, we'd keep in touch, right?"

"You never broke up?" Worse and worse.

"No, but we were never even together, really. I mean, *I* thought we were, but Kelsey basically dropped me as soon as camp ended, so. That kinda blindsided me. I told you how I lost it. Christina says I shoulda seen it coming. She said she never trusted Kelsey. She was not pleased to see her at the meet, believe me." At least Christina's an equal opportunity hater. "So, Kelsey came up and said she wanted to hang out after the meet, right? Like no big deal, just friends. And then she said she wanted to get back together, and then she kissed me, and that's probably what people saw."

"But you kissed her back."

Jamie sighs. "I kissed her back for like, . . . I dunno, a second. But then I stopped. Your friends probably didn't see that part. Or else they're not telling you."

"Do you—are you going to get back together with her?" I say to the wall.

"No."

"So you're not breaking up with me?"

"No! I told her I was with you now." A wave of relief washes over me. "But . . . I am going out to dinner with her and her parents in a couple of weeks. I have to!" she protests when I put my face into my knees. "Kelsey's dad's like, this big shot at Stanford, and she said that if I get to know him he could write me a letter of recommendation for my application next fall! What was I supposed to say? I can't turn down an opportunity like that!"

The question is, what am _I_ supposed to say? I don't believe Kelsey for a second. But if I tell Jamie to turn this down, I'm not being supportive of her dream. If I say I think Kelsey's lying, well—what if her dad _could_ write an ace letter of rec? What do _I_ know, really?

We sit in silence for a while.

"Nothing's going to happen, I promise. This has nothing to do with her. Her dad's the reason I said yes, don't you get it? I need him to help me get into Stanford." I pick at the rug, unconvinced. "Please trust me," she says. "I know it's probably a long shot—and I dunno, maybe Kelsey's full of shit. But I have to try, just in case. I can't pass this up." Jamie takes my hand in hers. "You're the best thing that's ever happened to me," she says. "I would never mess with what we have by lying to you."

I look up and see it all written on her face. Her dreams, her confidence, her grit—everything I admire about her. And maybe Kelsey's a liar, but Jamie isn't. She's the best thing that's ever happened to me, too, if I'm being honest. Who else in my life do I trust the way I trust her? My friends know about Jamie and me, Caleb knows about Dad, but Jamie knows about everything. She heard me say terrible things about her friends and she gave me a second chance. She gives me poems that make my brain buzz and my heart sing. We belong to each other. I have to trust her on this.

"Please," she says.

"All right."

27

HANH, REGGIE, AND ELAINE ARE MORE WORRIED about Jamie and Kelsey than I am. Elaine, especially, is trying to get me to break up with Jamie, and I can't tell if it has more to do with me being gay or with me being with Jamie. Especially since she's started getting more serious with Jimmy, it's like she wants everyone to have the exact same amazing adventure that she's having. And for her, I guess that includes being straight. She just can't understand being a girl and not wanting to kiss a boy.

"You should try it, Sana! I mean, Jamie's totally cheating on you, so you may as well," she says at lunch. "Janet asked her cousin, and her cousin said Jamie and Kelsey were kissing, like, for *real*. Like on the *lips*. In *public*. You don't do that unless you're like, committed."

"Like you and Jimmy?" asks Reggie, raising her eyebrow.

Elaine blushes but remains otherwise unfazed. "I can't help it. It's so much fun!" Then she turns to me and makes her plug again. "Come on, Sana, just try. It's way better than kissing girls, I know it is."

"What do you know about kissing girls? And what's wrong with me wanting to? I don't want to kiss a guy, because I actually did once, and it was disgusting. There aren't any guys who want to kiss me anyway—not that I would kiss them. Because I don't. Like. Guys." Naturally, this is the moment that Caleb chooses to text me:

What r u doing Friday?

Want to go bowling?

I glance at my phone and try to shove it back into my bag before anyone can see who it's from, but Hanh is too quick. "Ooooh, *someone* wants to kiss you!" she says. She holds the phone out for all to see and is rewarded with a squeal from Elaine.

"He is *totally* into you. You should go out with *him*!" she says.

"Yeah, he's cute," says Hanh. "So what if he's a little weird?"

Elaine pokes Hanh on the arm. "He's not weird. He just dresses weird."

I look at Reggie, but she just shrugs. "I guess you should be with who you want to be with. Must be nice to be you, though. Boys *and* girls like you."

"Please, Sana, just try!" begs Elaine. "I mean, what if you're straight—or bi—and you just got a bad one that time? I mean, how do you *know* you only like girls?"

"How do *you* know that you only like guys?"

Elaine rolls her eyes. "Okay, fine. But I like the guy I'm with, right? So maybe you just haven't met the right one."

"I have met the right one, and she's a girl. She's who *I'm* with. That's my *point*. And what ever happened to you being totally cool with me being gay? What happened to being happy for me?"

"I am cool with it. But she's *cheating* on you, Sana. We *saw* her. You deserve to be with someone who knows they want to be with you. And Caleb's so nice—you even said. You'd be such a great couple. I bet he wouldn't cheat on you. And I've seen you flirting with him in trig, and you're so cute together."

"I don't recall ever saying he was nice. And I definitely haven't been flirting with him."

At this, Hanh snorts and Reggie lets out a loud "ha!"

"What? I haven't!" Have I?

"Whatever. But you do think he's nice, right?"

"Well, yeah, but—"

"Come on. He's totally asking you out right now. Just go out with him. Just once. What do you have to lose?"

"Uh, Jamie?"

Elaine heaves a melodramatic sigh. "If it turns out Jamie's cheating on you, then. Then you'll try. Because it's not cheating if she's cheating, too." I'm not even sure she cares about Caleb or me or gay or straight anymore—she just wants to win. She's not a tiny, adorable little kitten, like Reggie says.

She's a tiny, adorable little pit bull and she's clearly not going to let go until I give in.

"Fine. *If* it turns out Jamie's cheating, which she's not—*and* Caleb tries to kiss me, which he won't—I will try it. Jeez. Are you happy?" Everyone cheers wildly, and Elaine actually throws her arms around me.

"You're going to love it!" she says, squeezing me tight.

Elaine's campaign to get me to go straight is more funny than annoying when I tell Jamie about it. I've told Jamie that Caleb invited me to go bowling with him and his friends on Friday, and that Elaine wants me to kiss him. It's kind of nice to have him in the background, actually, because it turns out that Jamie's going to dinner with Kelsey and her parents on Friday, too. Though it's not like I'm worried about Kelsey. Or that Jamie might end up falling for her again. Not at all.

The thing is, since Jamie and I cleared the air about Kelsey, our afternoons together have been even better than before. It's such a relief to have everything out in the open between us. I feel like we've cleared a hurdle—we had a hard talk, and we got through it, and we're stronger for it. Also, there's nothing more thrilling than hearing your girlfriend say that you're the best thing that's ever happened to her. And *maybe* just a teeny, *tiny* bit because, in an effort to make Jamie forget whatever intensity she had with Kelsey this summer, well . . . let's just say I know a lot more about Jamie's body than Elaine knows about Jimmy's, unless she's holding out on us. But Elaine has apparently never had an experience that she didn't want to share, so I'm pretty confident on that point. Just a few months ago, I would have been shocked at myself. Now, I'm just happy and excited.

The only glitch is the Dad problem. The more I look at that silver-wrapped box, the angrier I get. He's uprooted Mom and me, and turned both our lives upside down for That Woman. And now he's got the nerve to give her *pearls*? The pearl earrings were supposed to be our thing. They were a reminder of the story of Yama-sachi and Toyo-tama-himé—Dad's promise to me that I was his treasure no matter what, his reassurance that he saw what was precious and powerful in me. Not only does he not love Mom anymore, it feels like he doesn't love me anymore, either.

I'm mad at Mom, too, for letting him do this to us. She has to know—how could she not? I'm sure she'd tell me, "Gaman." She'd say, "Divorce is selfish." But if you ask me, it's Dad who's being selfish, and her having gaman isn't being strong. It's just something she's telling herself so that she feels better about hanging on to a sham of a marriage because she's too weak and embarrassed to stand up for herself and make him stop.

Jamie keeps telling me to just tell Mom straight out, even if she doesn't want to hear it: "That way they can at least talk about it. Like we talked, you know?"

The difference, of course, being that Dad was cheating and Jamie wasn't. And that Dad could end up leaving, but Jamie won't.

Of course she won't.

28

KELSEY AND HER PARENTS ARE PICKING JAMIE UP directly after practice to take her out to dinner and back home, so Jamie's changed into an outfit that seems a little too cute for meeting someone's dad so he can write a letter of rec, and she's taking a little more time with her makeup than I think she needs to. She seems a little more nervous than I think is appropriate, too, but she says she needs to make a good impression on Mr. Bowman.

Normally I'd walk right home, but today I end up hanging out with the kids who are waiting for their parents or their buses. I'm not gonna lie—I'm dying to see what Kelsey looks like. While I wait, I indulge in a little daydream where Jamie pulls me out of the crowd and introduces me to the Bowmans as her girlfriend. Of course, that would also mean coming out to the cross-country team, so I don't *really* want that to happen. But it sure would be nice to watch Kelsey go skulking home, defeated. Or at least skulking defeatedly off to dinner with Jamie and her parents.

When a black BMW sedan pulls into the parking lot at five thirty, the only person in it is Kelsey. She parks the car, gets out, and struts over in all her tall, hot glory. She looks like an Abercrombie & Fitch model. She's wearing super-skinny jeans, and a mostly sheer off-the-shoulder white peasant blouse that would give Mom a heart attack. And is her hair salon-highlighted, or is it just naturally a rich auburn with reddish-gold streaks? And then there's her delicate fairy princess nose, pool-blue eyes, rose petal lips (though that could be her lip gloss), and a complexion that could only be described as sun-kissed. The works. I mean, seriously. Come on.

She surveys us and flashes a dazzling smile, and I feel dark and frumpy with my short, Hobbity legs, my non-see-through top, and boring black ponytail. "Hi! I'm looking for Jamie Ramirez."

Janet points toward the girls' locker room door. It seems I'm not the only one who's lost the power of speech.

"Okay," says Kelsey, tossing her disgusting salon-perfect, auburn-golden locks and pulling out her phone. "I'll just wait here for her."

"Dude, is that the new iPhone?" asks Arjun.

"It is." She smiles at him.

"Can I see?"

"Sure."

In a flash, Arjun—and three other guys—are at Kelsey's side, huddled over the phone and grilling her about its cool new features. And clearly flirting with her. "Give it up!" I want to shout at them. "She's a lesbian!"

Janet elbows me and I'm about to whisper a mean-spirited comment about Kelsey's fancy car and her perfect hair, but at that moment, Jamie bursts through the locker room doors.

"Hey, sweetie! Omigod you are on *fleek!*" Kelsey abandons the boys, wraps Jamie in a hug, and steps back to admire her outfit, which also includes a peasant blouse, just not sheer and white. I look sideways at Janet and I'm gratified to see her looking back at me.

"Hey, you too. Nice shirt."

"I know, right?" Kelsey laughs and slips her arm around Jamie's waist. "Twinsies! Omigod, do you remember when . . . ?"

"Oh, that's right . . . yeah, totally!" says Jamie, and the two of them share a sparkly eyed, just-between-us look that twists my heart right out of my chest. Kelsey starts off toward the car with her arm still around Jamie's waist, and says, "So okay, I'm so sorry, but it turns out my parents have this thing tonight, so they can't make it, but . . ." and then they're too far away for me to hear any more. I watch them as they cross the parking lot, hair bouncing, hips swaying and bumping together as they walk. Kelsey says something that makes Jamie throw her head back and laugh. They get into the car, slam the doors, and peel out of the lot, dragging my twisted-out heart behind them.

Janet's still standing next to me, and I can feel her looking at me. "Ho-ly shit," she says. "Who says *on fleek?*"

She doesn't know about me and Jamie, I remind myself. She doesn't know. But I feel like I'm broadcasting my dismay in big silent waves, like those pictures of radio antennas, so that everyone around me is receiving the signal and knows exactly what's going on in my head. Stop it. Stop it or people will figure everything out. I will myself to shut down the radio signal, look Janet in the eye, and plaster a grin on my face. "Right? Oh. Mygod."

"That car, though," she says, but before she can get going, I interrupt her.

"Actually, I gotta get home. I'll text you later, 'kay?" And I head off with a spring in my step and a stone in my stomach.

I take an extra lap around the block, to make sure I'm not too much on edge when I enter the house. Reggie's coming in half an hour to take me to Bowl-O-Ramen, this cool bowling alley-slash-ramen shop where we're meeting Caleb and his friends.

Mom may not like Jamie's friends, but she's now a hundred percent okay with Reggie and Elaine, whose moms she met randomly at 99 Ranch Market, the Asian superstore, the other day. "Reggie is good girl," she said approvingly, when I asked yesterday if I could go out bowling with her tonight. "And Elaine is top piano player." Which surprised me. I knew that Elaine was taking piano lessons. I had no idea that she was actually good at it, though it kind of makes sense, now that I know how determined she can be when she wants something.

As I head out the door ("Ittekimasu!") I have to squash a little pang of guilt at leaving Mom home alone, waiting for Dad to return from a night out with That Woman. But once the guilt is gone, it's replaced with irritation at Mom for not doing something about Dad. The irritation is sharper than the guilt—pricklier—and it's still sputtering at the base of my skull when I get in the car.

I go to open the passenger-side door and I'm surprised to see Elaine riding shotgun already. "Jimmy's having a boys' night," she explains, "so I got my parents to let me go with you."

"Cool."

I get in the back and settle in, and while I'm buckling my seat belt, Reggie says, "So, Janet texted us. Kelsey came by herself, huh?" Wow. She did not waste time. Can nothing be kept private? My irritation threatens to expand to Elaine and Reggie but I manage to rein it in. It's not their fault that Kelsey is a beautiful, rich, conniving snake.

"We're so sorry!" Elaine says. "She's a total bitch. I could tell just by looking at her."

"Really, it's no big deal. I'm fine with it," I lie. "Jamie's totally over her, remember?"

"Well, I wouldn't be fine with it," says Elaine. "I mean, did Jamie even introduce you, or like, say good-bye or anything? Janet said she just took off."

"It would be weird if she only said good-bye to me. We're not really out to everyone yet," I remind her.

"That doesn't matter. Has she texted you?"

I check my phone for the hundredth time since Jamie drove off with Kelsey in the BMW. "No."

"See? I mean, don't you think she would've texted at least *once*? Just to let you know things are chill?" Another good point. "Plus, you know, they have *history*," she says, as if this is the clincher. "Couples in movies get back together all the time because of history."

"Elaine, shut up." Reggie says exactly what I'm thinking. "You don't have to make it worse."

"I'll just text her right now," I say, and I type, Hey, girlfriend! How's it going? That's good. Light. Not jealous. Just a casual check-in. A subtle reminder to leave history in the past, where it belongs. I show it to Elaine and Reggie and send it.

It's a struggle, but as the evening goes by, there are longer and longer stretches where I forget about Jamie and Kelsey entirely. The sound system at Bowl-O-Ramen is blasting cheery oldies music, Caleb and his friends are friendly and funny, the ramen is yummy, and we all get along great. There's no undercurrent of suspicion, no worries about saying something racist, no need to prove anything to anyone.

I think Caleb's friend Thom might be interested in Reggie. He certainly seems to be paying a lot of attention to her, and there's a lot of playful pushing and shoving going on. Reggie looks so happy. I hope something happens between them.

Meanwhile, Caleb is paying an awful lot of attention to me. He teases me about ordering extra seaweed in my ramen. He gives me tips on my abysmal bowling technique (he's bizarrely, scarily good at bowling). He somehow ends up sitting next to me every time I sit down, with his arm slung casually over the back of my seat. Elaine keeps nodding and widening her eyes significantly at me. Ever the master of subtlety, she even gives me the thumbs-up at one point. It could be about Reggie and Thom. But it's probably not. And even though I'm not into guys, not even nice ones like Caleb, it's kind of nice to feel like he likes me. In fact—even though I'm not into guys—if I weren't with Jamie, I might even consider him. Just to see.

At eight o'clock, I check my phone for a text from Jamie. It's been two hours, a bowl of ramen, and three rounds of bowling, and only one text from her: Hey, sorry about earlier. All good now. ttyl ♥ Not that I'm counting. Not that I'm worried. I trust her. She couldn't help it if Kelsey's parents didn't show up, and she's got every right to a private evening with her ex.

I know I'm just torturing myself, but I open my Instagram and do a search for Kelsey Bowman. Sure enough, there's a picture of the two of them—taken tonight, judging from their outfits and the fact that it was posted about thirty minutes ago. Squeezed together to fit into the frame, arms around each other, both looking beautiful and perfect and happy together in a darkened restaurant. Underneath, it says,

hot date! 🔥 #lafondue #rambo #flomobabes

It's already got a bunch of likes, and a couple of comments:

omg yum!

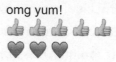

#flomobabes forever! LOL

Jamie said she'd never mess with what we have. But what did she and Kelsey have? I look at the unintelligible hashtags under the photo. I think about the private smile they shared right in front of me. History. Is it enough to bring them back together, like Elaine says? I'm wondering what else Jamie and Kelsey's history might include when some super-old oldies singer starts crooning, "Re-mem-ber whennn you held me ti-ight? And you kissed me all through the night?" It's a catchy tune and I might even think it was cute if it weren't so close to home. Probably they *did* kiss each other all through the night. Four solid weeks of kissing, money, movie-star looks, and inside jokes.

And suddenly I'm thinking about history again—my own history. I remember Trish, and how I clung to her even though she'd moved out of my league, even though she was never going to be into me. How I saw that first text to Dad when I was twelve and just pretended I hadn't seen it. How it's so obvious that Dad's having an affair, that my parents' marriage is a sham, and how I'm just letting it happen. And now, how Kelsey and Jamie are on a date at this fancy restaurant reliving their hot, historic summer together while I just sit around doing nothing, telling myself that Jamie wouldn't just walk out on me.

Elaine said I should be with someone who knows they want to be with me. I thought that someone was Jamie. She promised me she wasn't into Kelsey anymore, but I was invisible to her when Kelsey was around. She said I was the best thing that ever happened to her, but here she is on a "hot date." Jamie fell apart when Kelsey dropped her. "Breaking up is hard to do," the song keeps saying. What if Jamie's not as over Kelsey as she thought? Maybe Elaine is right. Maybe Jamie doesn't really know if she wants to be with me, after all.

29

AT NINE THIRTY, IT'S TIME FOR ME TO GO HOME, Jamie still hasn't texted me, and Kelsey has posted another Instagram pic—this time, it's her pushing a chocolate-dipped strawberry into Jamie's open mouth. The anxiety that's been coursing through my veins all evening is starting to thicken into a sludgy, resentful sort of acceptance. Caleb offers to drive me home instead of Reggie, who wants to hang out a little longer with Thom. Why not, I say. Sure. Fine.

All the way home, Caleb pesters me with questions about Reggie and hints about Thom, all of which I respond to a beat or two late because all I can think about is Jamie and Kelsey and the possibility that Jamie doesn't know if she wants to be with me.

"You're in a weird mood."

"Huh?"

"Exactly."

"Sorry."

We've reached my block, and Caleb has stopped the car. He's turned it off, in fact. I unbuckle my seat belt and open the door. "Hey, that was fun. Thanks for the ride," I say, and climb out.

"Lemme walk you to your house."

I'm about to protest that there's no need, it's just down the block, but he's already out of the car and on his way around the front. The temperature has dropped low enough for me to shiver in my light cotton cardigan, providing a convenient excuse ("Cold?" "A little.") for Caleb to put his arm around me to warm me up.

When he does, I have a moment of clarity.

He wants to kiss me.

Duh. Because come on, I knew this all along, didn't I. I just didn't want it to be true. Like with everything else, I've just been hiding from it, trying not to deal with it. That's why we all went to Bowl-O-Ramen. That's why he drove me home. He's been working the whole night to build up to this moment, this one-block walk home under the autumn moon and stars.

Just before we reach the house, Caleb stops. Which means I have to stop, too, since his arm is basically hugging me to him. Actually, it feels pretty good. He's bigger and stronger than Jamie, which makes me feel small and protected. It's a surprise, and a nice one. Why didn't I feel this way with Mark Schiller way back on the Glen Lake Country Club golf course? Maybe Elaine is right again. Maybe there *is* something between Caleb and me.

"Sana."

Suddenly I'm a little afraid of what might happen if look at him, so I just play with one of the zippers on his leather jacket. "Yeah?"

Now his hand is brushing a stray lock of hair off my face and I'm reminded of how Jamie did the same thing to me in the back of Reggie's van only a few weeks ago. But Jamie's out at this very moment with Kelsey, doing who knows what. A wave of hurt breaks over me, and I have another moment of clarity. I've always been the one who endures, who waits, the one who suffers silently while other people have fun doing stuff they shouldn't. *Gaman.* I'm sick of gaman. But I don't have to stand still as life splashes and churns around me, the way I used to. I don't have to be the rocks and the sand on the beach—I can be the wave. It's time to face the truth. It's time to stop enduring and start acting. It's time to move toward someone who wants me instead of clinging to someone who doesn't.

I turn my face up as Caleb leans down, and I put my hand on his cheek, then around the back of his neck, and I kiss him.

It's nothing like kissing Mark. It's quite nice, in fact. So nice that I don't have to pretend to enjoy it—oh my God, maybe Elaine *is* right. So nice that when it's over, I actually say, "That was nice."

"You don't need to act so surprised."

I look up and Caleb is smiling down at me with such tenderness that I have to look away. He's looking at me the way Jamie looked at me the first time we kissed, the way I looked at her. And as sweet as he is, as nice as that kiss was, I don't have it in me to look at Caleb that way. Elaine was wrong. I like Caleb. It was pleasant, kissing him. He'd be a good boyfriend. But that's not what I want. A black, heavy kind of understanding settles on my shoulders: kissing him was a big mistake.

"Sorry. It's just—" I have to tell him the truth. That's the right thing to do. But instead I hear myself saying, "The last guy I kissed was a terrible kisser. I guess. I mean, I didn't realize it until just now." Well, it *is* true, anyway.

"I guess I owe him one for setting the bar so low," he says. "Now you think I'm a good kisser."

"You are." *Also true! Not lying!* And he kisses me again, and I let him.

"You know, I thought for a while that you might be a lesbian," he says next.

"Oh. Um." *Now. Tell him now.* I take a steadying breath. Ready . . . Set . . . But it's too late. He mistakes my hesitation for offense.

"Sorry, don't be mad! But you know that time when I saw you with your friend Jamie during lunch? You were, like, holding hands, I think. I could have sworn she was about to kiss you."

"Oh, right. Well, actually—"

"But then my cousin saw her with that other girl, so I

figured, you know." Yes, I do. "Then Elaine told me tonight that you might—this is so seventh grade, but she said that you said you'd kiss me back if I kissed you."

Leave it to Elaine. "I'm going to kill her."

"Don't be mad at her. I was kinda hoping to, anyway. And besides, *you* kissed *me*, so I think it all turned out pretty well." No, it didn't turn out well at all. And now he's gazing at me with such open adoration that I don't know what to say. I don't know what to do. I can't talk to him. I can't look at him. I can't hurt him when he's looking at me like that. So—and I know this makes me a terrible, terrible person—in a sort of wild desperation, I kiss him again.

30

Thom asked me to go to the movies tomorrow!

Can u come too?

Pls pls pls?

Yay Reg!

What time? Can Jimmy come too?

Did he kiss u?

No! Jeez

I wish, tho, lol

Lol, I'll ask my parents.

Should be OK tho

Sana, can you come?

T says Caleb will be there.

Maybe. Hafta check

Did Caleb kiss u??

He was totally into u!

Elaine, did u tell him what I said about if he kissed me, I'd kiss him back?

No!

He said u did

Elaine!!!

Oh

Yeah I might have said something

Sorry.

So . . . ????? 💋 😵

OMG ttyl

10:15 p.m. Caleb and me:

Hey, doll (haha)

I had fun tonite

Yeah, me too

Wanna go see a movie tomorrow w Thom and Reggie?

1:30 at AMC Mercado

Reggie said she'd drive you

Thom and I can meet you there

Um lemme check

Parents in bed, I'll have to tyt

I hope u can come

I really had fun w you tonight

This is me: 😍

Just sayin

> Hey, I'm pretty tired.

> I think I'm just gonna go to sleep

OK fine, I can take a hint

I'll just shut up now

Night

> Night

10:30 p.m. Elaine and me:

Hey, Jimmy, Janet, etc. are coming

U have to come too!

Caleb will be there!

xoxoxo

> Idk

Don't u like him?

He is TOTES into u

U should go

> I know, just . . .

> Thinking about Jamie

> You know?

She basically broke up w u, right?

She went out with that slutty chick from Palo Alto and she

didn't text u back all night

You should be w someone who appreciates you

Like Caleb (hint, hint)

I know . . .

11:30 p.m. Jamie and me:

Hey, u awake?

Hey

Yeah

Can u talk?

No, not really

K. Just wanted to say hi

Can't believe that bs that Kelsey pulled with her parents.

Didn't want you to worry, I know I didn't txt you all night.

Anyway, it's 100% over. Talk tomorrow, K?

K

I have to babysit tomorrow, but wanna try to get together

Sunday?

Um . . . yes!

ok ttyt

31

I WAKE UP TO A TEXT FROM JAMIE:

> Good morning, gf. Lemme know when u can talk. I want to
> tell u about last night

I text back, Let's talk about it tomorrow. I want to hear it in person. Because if we start talking about what happened with Kelsey last night, she's bound to eventually ask how bowling was, and what would I say? "I'm so glad that you ended things with Kelsey, and I'm so glad we're still together, and oh, by the way, I cheated on you last night and kissed Caleb. Twice." Yeah . . . no.

Of course, now that I've put that awkward conversation off till tomorrow, I'm dreading tomorrow more than I've ever dreaded anything in my life. Part of me is even hoping I can get away without telling her at all. I mean, why upset her, now that I know everything's okay between us? What if I manage to end things with Caleb before then. Is it okay to pretend it never happened?

Seconds after I send that text to Jamie, Caleb texts to ask me again about the movies, and then Elaine and Reggie join in and beg me to go, too. It doesn't take long for me to cave. I have nothing else to do except for sit around the house and feel guilty. Maybe I'll get a chance to hit reset with Caleb.

Reggie, Elaine, and I are meeting the others at the AMC Mercado complex at twelve thirty for pizza, Jamba Juice, and a movie. We arrive first, and sit down to wait for everyone on a bench outside Jamba Juice. Elaine is atwitter with plans for future triple dates, what with all the boyfriend-girlfriend action going on, but for obvious reasons, I can't share her enthusiasm. Reggie's anxious, too, for other reasons. "I'm not actually going out with Thom yet," she protests. "Don't jinx it!"

"Oh, fine, whatever." Elaine turns to me. "Okay, Sana, your turn for girl talk. What happened with you and Caleb after bowling last night?"

I don't mind girl talk with Elaine, as long as I'm not doing the talking. Why would I share the intimate romantic details of my relationships with anyone? Especially when those details are things I wish I could take back. At best, it'll make them pressure me to break up with Jamie. At worst, they'll think I'm a horrible, slutty lesbian—or bisexual—which, who knows, maybe I am. Bi, that is, not slutty. (Though to be perfectly honest, I think I'm pretty firmly pro-girl. And just because I sort of accidentally on purpose kissed a very nice boy when I was upset about a perfect-for-me girl doesn't make me a slut, does it? That doesn't seem right.) Agh, too much. Brain about to explode.

Elaine is fidgeting impatiently and going, "Well? What happened? Come on, spill it!"

I'm not about to open my mouth and unleash the chaos in my head, so I track back to my original thought and say, "That's none of your business."

"He kissed you!" she shrieks. "He totally did! Oh, Sana, I'm so happy for you!"

You'd think I'd be smart enough to know that *none of your business* is just another way of saying *guilty as charged*. You'd be wrong.

"So, was I right? Is he a good kisser? Was it like sooo much better than that other guy? Are you two like, a thing now?"

Elaine's enthusiasm about my mistake pushes me right over the edge, and I snap, "God, Elaine, why do you have to be so nosy? Just shut up and leave me alone!" She looks so hurt that I immediately feel bad. After all, it's not her fault that I'm a cheater and a hypocrite. "I'm sorry," I say. "It's just, stuff is kind of complicated because . . . you know. I mean . . ."

"Ohhh, *Jamie*." Elaine nods, immediately subdued and sympathetic. "Yeah, okay. I'm sorry. Are you gonna wait 'til you break up with her?"

I look at Elaine, who's trying so hard to be on my side, however misguidedly, and suddenly I'm seized by the notion that if I can just get up the nerve to tell Elaine and Reggie what I did, maybe they can help me out of this mess. Of course. Now. Now is when I confess.

"Uh, yeah. Speaking of which . . ."

"Hang on a sec." Elaine looks at her phone, which has just chirped, and announces, "Jimmy's here! They just parked, and they're walking over. . . ." She cranes her neck and starts peering across the parking lot.

Reggie elbows her. "Hey! Sana was in the middle of something."

"What? Oh, right, I'm sorry! Okay, go ahead." She looks at me expectantly.

"Okay, right. Uh . . ." This is harder than I thought it would be. Maybe it's not such a good idea, after all.

"You were about to tell us about breaking up with Jamie?" prompts Reggie.

Breaking up with Jamie? I blink.

"Or—oh!" Reggie gasps. "Did Jamie break up with you? Oh, Sana, that's what happened, isn't it." She gives me a hug. "Was it this morning? Why didn't you say something earlier?"

"Uh."

"Don't worry, Sana. You'll get over it," says Elaine, patting my arm. "You're too good for her anyway. Plus, now you can be with Caleb. He's so sweet. He'll make you forget all about her."

"Um." If only that were true.

Jimmy and his friends Michael and Bao are within shouting distance now, and I get a text from Caleb telling me that he and Thom have arrived as well, and I'm just not feelin' it anymore, so to speak. "It's okay . . . it's not that big of a deal. We can talk about it later," I say, and even Reggie shrugs it off after a perfunctory "You sure?" I think she's a little distracted because of Thom.

Somehow, I manage to make it through the next three hours without crumbling under the weight of all the truth I'm not telling. Caleb is as smitten as a guy can be. He pays for my movie ticket. He offers his jacket when I shiver in the arctic chill of the movie theater. And he keeps looking at me like I'm this amazing prize he's just won, like he can't believe his good luck.

I feel like a jerk for allowing it to continue, but I can't break up with him the day after our first kiss, not when he's so happy. Especially not in public, in front of all his friends. To make up for lying, I allow him to hold my hand and put his arm around me—and I am not blind to the irony of lying to make up for lying here, but it's all I have to offer. At least he'll be happy today, right?

The problem is, I don't believe it, not really. Because scraping its claws at the edges of every interaction we have is the fact that no matter how I justify it, this day is a lie. Even if Caleb's happy now, I'm just setting him up to feel worse in the end. But in the moment, when he reaches for my hand, it feels cruel not to let him take it. And so I do, and I hide my sharp, scratchy guilt with a smile. I promise myself that I'll find a way to end this without hurting him.

Meanwhile, Elaine and Jimmy look like, I don't know, koala bears or something. Totally blissed out on each other, with their arms permanently wrapped around each other's waists. And Reggie and Thom are now tentatively holding hands, pretending like it's no big deal, but when I catch her eye, Reggie smiles at me and blushes. Janet is there, too, and some of the rest of our particular branch of the Asian crowd. There's Andy Chin, with his arm around a white girl.

It occurs to me that this is what I used to wish for—to be unquestionably, undeniably part of a crowd, and to have places to go, things to do, and people to do them with on the weekend. To have someone's arm around my shoulders. Everyone is goofing around, taking pictures and group selfies left and right, and generally having a great time together. Because despite his Angry Goth look and his occasionally judgmental attitude, Caleb's basically a nice guy who likes people, so people like him back. And it helps that Thom is less spiky, is hilarious, and is clearly into Reggie, whom everybody loves. I was so close—everything looks the way it's supposed to, all the pieces are in the right places. But it feels completely wrong. Because Caleb isn't Jamie.

Jamie texts a couple of times, but I don't reply. I feel bad enough just being here with everyone, and I'd feel worse pretending to her that I'm not. After her third text, the movie starts, and I put the phone on mute, stick it in my bag, and forget about it.

When it's time for Caleb to drive me home, it's clear that

we've all reached a new normal—one where our little Asian girl squad, as Caleb calls it, now includes a couple of white dudes. He's feeling so proud of himself for having broken in that I don't have the heart to tell him I have to kick him out. And so for the second day in a row, I end up kissing him good-bye and then looking guiltily away when he tries to catch my eye afterward, because I don't feel what he feels, and Jamie is the one I want.

I walk in the house at four thirty to find Dad getting ready to walk out. He's putting his shoes on, and he's got a little carry-on suitcase next to him.

"Where are you going?" I ask.

Dad glances up as he struggles with his left shoe. "One of the clients in LA had problem with the hardware interface on a product. It's my specialty project, so I have to go to meet."

Yeah, right. "They contacted you on a Saturday afternoon?"

"Yes! Terrible."

"And you expect to fix this problem . . . tonight?"

"I think it's possible. Maybe I have to stay another day just in case. I may come back on Monday instead of Sunday." He's not meeting my eye, fiddling with the handle of his carry-on.

"What if you'd been, I dunno, on vacation or something? Or at the beach?" Though I actually can't think of anything Dad would be doing on a Saturday afternoon that would be so much fun that he'd forget to check his phone.

"Yeah, you're right! Good thing I'm not!" Dad smiles.

"Hmm."

"I'm sorry I have to go," he says, grabbing his carry-on and clapping me on the shoulder on his way out. "Be a good girl!"

Mom, who's been hovering in the background, calls, "Itter-asshai!"

"Ittekimasu!" replies Dad, already getting into the car. Already on the way to some secret rendezvous with That Woman. Mom stays in the open doorway, waving until Dad is out of sight. As he turns the corner and disappears, she sighs and closes the door.

I can't watch this anymore. Against my better judgment I venture, "Do you think he's telling the truth? I mean, do you think he's really going to LA to fix some dumb robot?"

"Sana!" Mom's voice is harsh. She switches to Japanese. "Didn't I tell you not to talk about that again?"

"Yeah, but—"

"Daman-nasai." Her solution to everything. Silence.

Which brings me to Jamie's texts from earlier today, the ones I ignored. I can feel my insides start to shrivel up as I read them:

12:20 p.m.

　　Hey, girlfriend

12:22 p.m.

　　Just checking about tomorrow

　　Can't wait to talk to u

　　can't wait to see u

1:00 p.m.

Hey there

Txtd earlier—wondering what's up . . . ???

Tmb!

3:00 p.m.

Hey. everything ok?

3:30 p.m.

OK now I'm worried. What's going on? Tmb

Damn. I should have just sent her a quick text right away. Just said I was at the movies with Elaine and Reggie and Hanh, instead of stressing over hiding the fact that I was there with Caleb. But I didn't, and now she's worried. Maybe even suspicious. All this dishonesty is clouding my judgment.

On the other hand, Jamie didn't exactly post regular bulletins about her activities last night. What was *she* hiding?

On the *other* other hand, she did tell me where she was going, and who she was going with. It wasn't her fault that Kelsey probably planned all along to show up without her parents.

But Jamie could just have refused to go—didn't she say that Kelsey's dad was the main reason she agreed to dinner in the first place? If she'd refused, maybe I wouldn't have felt like she was going to leave me. Maybe I wouldn't have wondered if I should be with Caleb instead. And it wasn't like I *planned* to kiss Caleb. *He* was planning to kiss *me*—he said it himself. Like Elaine said, it's not cheating if (you think) the other person is cheating, too. Right? So none of it was my fault, exactly.

Right?

I'm still locked in a heated debate with myself when my phone rings.

Jamie. Shit. I consider my options.

1. Answer the phone.

2. Ignore the phone.

Answering the phone leaves me with only two options:

a) Tell the truth.

b) Lie.

Whereas ignoring the phone gives me time to:

a) Figure out how to tell the truth.

b) Figure out a plausible lie.

c) Put off dealing with this altogether.

Looks like I'm going to ignore it. I put the phone next to me on the bed and wait for it to stop ringing. When it chimes to tell me that Jamie's left me a voicemail, I pick it up and listen.

Hey, Sana, where are you? You haven't been answering your texts, and I've been thinking a lot this afternoon, and I'm kinda . . . well. I dunno. Anyway. We really need to talk. I mean, I . . . I really need to talk to you. It's important. So, yeah, um . . . call me, okay? Or text. Or whatever. Okay, um . . . bye.

Alarm bells start ringing in the back of my head. Why would she "really need" to talk to me? What's so important? Maybe it's my conscience talking, but suddenly I'm worried that she knows about me and Caleb, somehow. Or she suspects something. The more I think about it, the more sense it makes.

Mercado was mobbed with people this afternoon. It would have been easy for someone who knew Jamie to have seen us and told her about it. Or . . . I think back to all the phones and all the photos, all the Instagrams and Snapchats, and my heart sinks. I'm done for.

What am I going to do?

For now, I text Jamie:

> Hi, sorry I didn't get back to u—phone totally glitched out today. I can't talk right now—have to help mom w dinner
>
> We're talking tomorrow, anyway, right?

Seconds later, she replies.

> OK. It's kinda big so prolly best in person anyway.
>
> Can we hang out at your house, maybe, like after lunch?

Kinda big. Best in person. Please let her not know about me and Caleb. Please let her not have decided she's better off with Kelsey after all.

> I'll meet u at the bus stop
>
> Miss u

I add three hearts, delete them because they look pathetic (*See how much I love you? Please don't break up with me!*), then add them again and tap Send before I can change my mind.

Seconds later, she replies.

> OK, see you tomorrow 💜 💜 💜

And even though my own hearts said, "Please don't break up with me," her hearts seem to say, "You're a liar."

I don't think I can handle talking or texting with anyone else today, so I put my phone in airplane mode and waste an hour wishing I had something like those magic jewels from the tale of Toyo-tama-himé, the ones that control the tide. Except they'd control time. Then I could go back and not kiss Caleb. Or at the very least, keep tomorrow from coming.

32

TOMORROW'S HERE. I WAKE UP NERVOUS. DAD'S probably waking up with That Woman. Mom's probably waking up knowing it. Caleb and Jamie are both waking up thinking I'm their girlfriend, and Jamie's also probably waking up knowing I cheated on her.

What a disaster.

I really need to break things off with Caleb. And Jamie is probably getting ready to come over and break things off with me. The prospect of all of the awful things that have to happen today would keep me pinned to the bed all morning, but shortly after 8:00 a.m., Mom makes me get up because she can't stand the thought of anyone wasting a single minute of a perfectly serviceable Sunday morning by sleeping in. Mom actually seems a little down—who wouldn't be, knowing their husband was spending the morning with his mistress?—so after breakfast, to make us both feel better, I suggest we make an apple tart, one of her favorite fall sweets. She smiles, surprised. "Nandé?"

"Oh, I don't know. Because it's apple season."

She makes the crust while I peel the apples. I let her correct me. "Hold like *this*, oya-yubi *koko*," she says, and places my thumb *here*, in front of the edge of the blade, so I can scooch the knife toward it, spiral around the apple, and cut the peel off in one long strip. I don't even argue when she grouses, "Every Japanese knows how to peel apple correctly. American schools should teach it. It's the basic skill."

By the time the tart is in the oven and everything's been washed and put away, it's nearly noon, and Mom's talking about taking a short break before getting lunch ready. Perfect. Just enough room in my schedule for an awkward, painful conversation with Caleb. Come on, just do it. I go to my room and rehearse a speech: *Caleb-you're-the-best-friend-a-girl-could-ever-have-and-I-really-really-like-you-but-I-don't-think-I'm-the-right-one-for-you-as-a-girlfriend-I'm-so-sorry*. Ugh. It's awful. But I don't know what else to say.

I type, Hey, can you talk? and send it.

No response. Two minutes go by. Five. Ten. Finally, the phone chimes.

Sorry, we're having Family Time. 😶 No calls. Ttyl?

Well, I tried. I type, OK, maybe tonight and let relief seep into my body; but it's expelled and replaced with dread on my very next breath. I put the phone down and wish again for those magic jewels, and that it were tomorrow, already. I wish there was a better way.

After lunch, Mom wants to make tonjiru for dinner, a pork stew with carrots, taro root, daikon, burdock root, ginger, and miso—perfect for fall, and really labor intensive what with all those veggies to peel and chop, so I offer to help. It calms me to think of nothing but chopping vegetables and skimming broth, and after working next to Mom for a while, making something delicious that we'll both enjoy later, I think I understand a little bit about why she spends so much time cooking.

And then it's time to meet Jamie at the bus stop.

Jamie gets off the bus, and despite my nervousness I feel a rush of joy. It feels like it's been forever since I've seen her, somehow. I step forward to hug her, then stop, in case maybe she's mad and doesn't want to hug me back. I feel like a gorilla, with my arms just hanging at my sides, and I wish I had something to hold, some excuse for not reaching out for her. Jamie seems nervous, too, and we walk in silence back to the house.

By the time we're in my room, we haven't spoken a word except *hey* when she got off the bus, and the silence has been coiling itself around us like a snake. When I sit down on the bed and she chooses to lean on my dresser, I think I might choke.

"So, I told you we need to talk," she says finally.

"Yeah," is all I say. Inside my head, though, it's *I didn't mean to kiss him, it was a mistake, I'm sorry, please don't leave me.*

"Okay."

Jamie takes a deep breath and lets it out slowly with her eyes closed, and then rolls her head and shrugs her shoulders a couple of times, like she does when she's getting ready for a race. I half expect her to shake her legs out and start pacing.

She opens her eyes and says, "You didn't want to talk yesterday, and you didn't answer any of my texts. I really don't think you were telling the truth about your phone glitching. I bet your phone was just fine. I think you just didn't want to talk to me." Here it comes. My chest starts to contract. "I owe you an apology." My mouth almost drops open. *What?*

"I'm sorry. I didn't know that Kelsey was going to show up alone like that, and it kinda took me by surprise. I should've just told her to go home right then, probably. I don't know, I just got . . . I wasn't thinking clearly, I guess." Jamie looks down and chews her lip. I don't say anything. I'm still trying to catch up from "I owe you an apology." She continues, "And I should've answered your texts, but I didn't know what to say and she, like, wouldn't let me out of her sight, anyway. She kept telling me that we'd go talk to her dad later, you know?" Okay. This time I manage a nod. "It's just. She just seemed so sincere. And I—I really, *really* wanted to meet her dad and get him to write me that letter, so that kinda got in the way of me figuring it out. Like after a while I kinda knew she was lying, but I just couldn't stop hoping she wasn't." I nod again. Where's the part where she grills me about the Instagram with me and Caleb in it? Or where she says someone saw us together at Mercado? "When you didn't want to talk, I realized how upset you must be, and I don't blame you. My mom always says that I think so much about the future that I don't appreciate what I have now. I hate it when she says that, but this time she's right. It was wrong to make you go through all that just because I got carried away about Stanford—like one dinner with Kelsey's dad would make a difference. So, yeah . . . I'm sorry."

She looks at me. "Please don't be mad. I think we have something good, you know? Like really good. And I don't want to screw it up. All I could think about all day yesterday was you. I just want to be with you."

I stare back at her, dumbfounded. A wave of relief flows through me, followed by a wave of gratitude to the powers that be for getting me off the hook, and another wave of pure adoration and admiration for beautiful, honest Jamie. Who thinks we have something really good, who doesn't suspect me of cheating, and who really, truly wants to be with me— with *me*. I can hardly believe my luck.

I take Jamie's hand and smile, and she smiles back. As I pull her to me and we melt into each other, a needle of guilt pricks at me, but there's so much to celebrate right now that I ignore it. It can wait.

After Jamie leaves, it's time to call Caleb and break the news. But I hate to kill the high I'm on right now, and then Dad calls and kills it anyway. He says he can't make it home tonight—surprise, surprise—and now I'm sad about Mom being played. So I text Caleb to tell him that I can't talk after all, and I spend the evening on the couch watching a funny movie with Mom. And by the time the movie's over, it's time for bed. I feel terrible when Caleb and Jamie text me goodnight practically at the same time, but it's too late at night to talk to Caleb about something as big as breaking up, and besides, it's only been two days, so it's not like we're actually, officially together, and—

Oh, all right. Let's face it: I'm afraid to tell him the truth. I can't escape the fact that he deserves to know, and soon. But when I picture telling him, I want to crawl into a cave. Because no matter what happens, I'll feel like a total jerk for lying to him and leading him on, and he'll probably hate me, and I'll lose one of my best friends. How will I ever face him again?

I need time. Just a little bit—just a day or two to come up with something good, some way of getting out of this gracefully. There has to be a way. There has to be.

Poetry Journal, Honors American Literature
Sunday, October 24

"Tell all the Truth but tell it slant—"
by Emily Dickinson

I'm not sure exactly what kind of truth Emily Dickinson is talking
about here, but it's clear to me that she thinks that people
aren't always ready to hear the pure, straight-out truth. She
talks about Truth as if it's something light—it's something
"bright" that will "dazzle" and "blind" people, like lightning. So it's
probably something good, but dangerous. Like sometimes it's
best to let people know things slowly, a little at a time, so as not
to hurt them too much. I definitely agree.

33

WHEN ELAINE, REGGIE, HANH, AND I GET TO trig the next morning, Jamie's waiting for me in front of the classroom door. Her eyes light up when she sees me. My own excitement at seeing her is only a little bit overshadowed by my anxiety about what will happen if Caleb shows up.

"What's she doing here?" Elaine asks me. "And why does she look so happy to see you? I thought you guys broke up."

"We'll give you guys some privacy," whispers Hanh, showing some discretion for once. I slow down while my friends slink behind me into the classroom. I can't see them, but I'm sure they're eavesdropping as hard as they can.

"Hey," says Jamie. "I brought you something." And the excitement stages a comeback. She hands me a little box wrapped in blue paper. "It came in the mail on Saturday, but

I was afraid to bring it over yesterday, in case you hated me."

I unwrap the paper and open the box. Inside is a piece of blue sea glass, wrapped in silver wire and strung on a thin silver chain.

"Do you like it?"

"I love it."

"I was going to wait 'til after school, but when I got here, I couldn't wait." She starts drawing a heart on the concrete with her foot.

It takes everything I have not to throw my arms around her and kiss her right on the lips, right there, right in front of everybody. I settle for just throwing my arms around her and sneaking a kiss on her ear as I whisper, "Thanks. It's perfect."

When I finally let go, Jamie's eyes are shining, and I risk a Meaningful Gaze into them. Just for a moment. But as we're gazing meaningfully into each other's eyes, I see her focus shift, and a split second later, a pair of leather-clad arms wraps themselves around me and a pair of lips kisses me on the cheek. Oh, my God. Oh, no. Oh-no-oh-no-oh-no-oh-no.

"Hey," says Caleb, kissing me again.

Jamie's Meaningful Gaze has turned into a Blank Stare.

My senses, which seem to have fled when Caleb appeared, come rushing back, and I wriggle myself awkwardly out of his embrace.

"Ha-ha! Hey, what'd you do that for?" I squeak.

"What, I can't kiss my own girlfriend?" He drapes his arm over my shoulder and smiles down at me.

"Your girlfriend? Are you two like, . . . together?" Jamie's eyes are wide.

"No, no, not really," I stammer.

"Yeah," says Caleb at the same time, with a quick, confused glance at me. "We are 'like, together.'"

The world starts closing in on me like it did when Jamie and I first kissed, only this time it's a bad closing in. My head starts to pound. I'm dimly aware of other kids filing past us, glancing over their shoulders and sticking around to see the action.

"Since when?" Jamie's shock is morphing into anger with alarming speed; her wide eyes are narrowing and her voice has taken on a steely edge.

"Since Friday," Caleb says. "Not that it's any of your business."

"Actually, it is my business."

Oh, God. I have to stop this. I have to stop this now. "Um. Can't we do this another time? Like somewhere more private?"

"No," says Jamie, "I don't think we can. I think we're going to do this now—it shouldn't take long."

"Sana, what the fuck is going on?"

"Yeah, Sana. Please explain."

How can I explain? How can I make them see that it's all just a horrible mistake? "Okay, it's not—it's not what you think. It's not what it looks like." I'm scrambling for words, searching, searching, but I can't find anything that sounds right. "I, I—"

"She was with me before she was with you. *While* she was

with you, in fact." Jamie looks at me. "Right?"

I look at Caleb, who's staring at me, his eyes wide with disbelief, and nod miserably. "But it's more complicated than that! I mean, it wasn't cheating, exactly—" Jamie scoffs. "No, Jamie, for real. It happened when you were out with Kelsey. You even said! You even said you shouldn't have, you said it was wrong and that she totally wanted to hook up with you. I mean, that was obvious—ask anyone! And then, so . . . I thought you were going to break up with me. I thought—you didn't answer my texts—you said you should have, right? I just—I wasn't sure if you wanted to be with me anymore. I thought maybe you were getting back together with Kelsey. And then Caleb—" I turn to him. "Caleb, I don't know what happened. I mean, my friends were all—they wanted you and me to get together, and I thought that Jamie was breaking up with me . . . and you were so nice—*are* so nice—and you're cute, and I meant what I said about you being a good kisser, and I'd totally be into you if I were straight—"

Oh, my God, what am I saying? All this stuff that no one needs to know, and I can't shut up—it's like that awful racial profiling argument with Christina. Like someone turned a faucet on full blast and the handle fell off. "I feel terrible . . . I didn't tell you because I didn't want to hurt your feelings because, well, I could tell you liked me, like, a lot—and I didn't tell you, Jamie, because I meant to—I was *going* to—but then I thought I'd break it off with Caleb right away and it wouldn't matter. Like it doesn't matter to me that—I mean *if*—you kissed Kelsey, because you said you wanted to be with me in the end, and that's how I feel about you. *You're* the one I want to be with, I knew it the moment I kissed Caleb—oh, God, Caleb, that's not what I meant!" Caleb has gone pale. He shakes his head, as if to clear it of all the crap I just poured into it. Jamie, on the other hand, has gone red and is staring off across the quad.

"So let me get this straight," says Caleb in a low voice. "You're a lesbian. You thought your girlfriend was going to break up with you, so you got together with me because— what, your friends told you to? Because I was better than nothing? And then it turned out she wasn't breaking up with you after all, so you've been getting ready to dump me and get back together with her this whole time? And it doesn't matter? And you feel *sorry* for me? Because you can tell that I like you a *lot*?"

Ouch. "You make it sound like I used you, like I don't even care about what I did."

Caleb considers this for a second. "That's about right."

"But you make it sound like I'm this horrible, self-centered bitch."

"Not a bitch. Just horrible and self-centered. And conceited."

I look at Jamie. Caleb was totally innocent, but Jamie had a part in all of this. Plus I just told her that she's the one I want to be with. Maybe . . . but she shakes her head.

"I was honest with you. I told you everything. And you

totally played me. You cheated on me, you lied to me—why would you do that, Sana? How could you act like that?"

"Jamie—"

"I liked you so much, Sana. I trusted you."

"Jamie, please—"

"I gotta go to class." And she walks away.

"Fuck." Caleb exhales and says quietly, "You know, I thought you were different. I thought you were honest about who you were, not like all the other girls. What a load of bullshit. I'm so fucking stupid." He turns and wades his way through groups of kids standing in aimless, eavesdropping clumps, drops into his chair, and stares dully ahead.

I stand there, frozen. This can't be happening.

The bell rings, and Mr. Green appears and starts herding everyone toward their seats. They fan out across the classroom, murmuring to each other and stealing glances at Caleb, and at me. Reggie, Hanh, and Elaine are the only ones looking directly at me. They look stricken—Reggie actually has her hand over her mouth.

Mr. Green is leaning over Caleb, his face etched with concern. Caleb appears to be ignoring him. When Mr. Green looks up at me, it dawns on me that I'm still rooted to the spot where Jamie and Caleb left me. I'm going to have to walk all the way across the classroom, through a thicket of stares and whispers, and sit for the next eighty minutes right in front of a guy who hates me.

I can't do it. I turn and walk away.

My throat feels like someone's punched it. My eyes are burning. "Sana!" Mr. Green is at the classroom door, calling me. I keep going. If I turn around, I'll cave and go back. Or start to cry. Or both. Don't cry. Don't cry. Don't cry. "Sana!" He tries one more time, then gives up. He's probably calling security.

I have to hide before I fall apart. Before someone finds me and drags me back to class. I duck into the girls' bathroom and shut myself in a stall. I squeeze my eyes shut against the tears. Don't cry. But they come anyway, a torrent of them, along with ragged gasps and whimpers that I'm terrified someone outside will hear, but it's like those awful words that came pouring out of me earlier, I can't control it, they just come, and I can feel my mouth making that grotesque crying-face frown, and the tears and gasps keep coming, and my shoulders keep shaking, and I wish I were home in my bed instead of this ugly, smelly, little stall, I wish I were anywhere but here, doing anything but this, remembering anything but the last horrible, humiliating minutes of my horrible, humiliating life.

How did I end up here? Why, why, why didn't I just trust Jamie? Why did I have to go and kiss Caleb? Why did I have to say all those things I said? In front of all those people? Stupid, stupid, *stupid* me. And now everyone thinks I'm a slutty, lying, lesbo bitch. Oh, no—a slutty, lying, *conceited* lesbo bitch. And it's only October.

Eventually, thank God, the tears slow down, my breath

comes easier, and I regain enough presence of mind to rip some toilet paper off the roll and blow my nose. I try a couple of calming breaths, blowing the air out slowly. My face feels numb and my teeth are tingling. But I'm okay. And no one heard me crying. I check my phone and realize that the last miserable hour of my life has actually only taken a few minutes. There's still over an hour left before the end of first period, but I can't go back to class, not after what just happened. *Don't think about what just happened.* I don't want to start crying again. I stay in the stall for a few more minutes, breathing and not thinking, waiting for my eyes to un-puff and my nose to un-redden before I go to the nurse's office—sanctuary of the sick and the cowardly.

The rest of the day, predictably, sucks. Mrs. Hernandez, the nurse, says I'm not sick enough to go home, so I go to Spanish, where half the class has witnessed my humiliation and the other half gets the news via under-the-desk text messages by the end of the period. I don't know what I'm going to say to Reggie, Elaine, and Hanh, so while everyone is getting started on their homework at the end of class, I go up to Señor Reyes and say weakly, "I don't feel well. Can I go to the nurse's office?" When I show up, Mrs. Hernandez gives me an exasperated look but lets me lie down, since there's only ten minutes left in the period. Halfway through lunch, I decide a little friendship might be nice, after all, so I head out to the quad. But my friends are sitting with Caleb and Thom. So much for friendship. I go back to the nurse's office. Practice is terrible. Jamie stays far away from me, and most of the other girls won't even look at me. Are they mad at me? Afraid of me? The boys, on the other hand, stare at me like I'm a new animal at the zoo, except for Arjun, who comes over and whispers, "Hey, I heard you got outed this morning!" and puts his fist out for me to bump.

When I get home, Mom is furious with me because the school office has already called home and told her that I have to schedule a detention for skipping class—looks like Mr. Green told them what actually happened. "Why did you skip the class?" she keeps asking, but of course I can't tell her. Dad comes home early, for once, and looks at me with grave disappointment—as if *he's* a shining example of ethical behavior.

I can't eat dinner. I can't do my homework. When I give up and go to bed, I can't sleep. All I can do is what I've been doing all day: relive that awful scene, re-see Jamie's face, re-see Caleb's face, and feel my heart slowly breaking into a million pieces.

POETRY JOURNAL, HONORS AMERICAN LITERATURE
MONDAY, OCTOBER 25

"One Art"
by Elizabeth Bishop

This poem is about losing someone. I wonder who Elizabeth Bishop lost? The poem's kind of singsongy, so if you don't listen to the words, it almost sounds happy. Except that practically every other line ends in the word "disaster." I thought at first it was going to be funny, because Bishop talks about misplacing things as an art, which is kind of funny—losing things on purpose, for practice. But she goes from misplacing keys, or wasting an hour, to bigger stuff—her mother's watch, houses, cities, and even a continent—"losing farther, losing faster" and "vaster." Then she talks about "losing you (the joking voice, a gesture / I love)." Since it's after all the other stuff, it makes losing the person worse than losing everything else, even cities and continents. She didn't misplace the person. It was a real loss, like maybe someone left her, or someone died. And then she says it looks "like (Write it!) like disaster." Like she's making herself say something hard, like she's trying to pretend that losing that person isn't a disaster, even though it is.

This poem makes me really sad.

34

MY PHONE WAKES ME AT SIX THIRTY, AND FOR THE
sleepy second that it takes me to turn off the alarm, I think it's
just a regular day. Then I remember what happened yesterday
and a heavy fog gathers itself around me. I squeeze my eyes
shut under the covers, as if that will somehow magically make
it all go away. I wish I could stay down here forever. I wish
I didn't have to go to school; in fact, I wish I hadn't gone to
school yesterday, because I don't know how else I could have
avoided that debacle. Where did I screw up? Or more to the
point, where did I *first* screw up?

There are a ton of texts from Elaine, Reggie, and Hanh
that I don't even bother to read because I can't face their questions or their judgment. None from Jamie or Caleb. Well, what
did I expect?

It's a testament to Mom's good parenting, I suppose, that I drag myself out of bed and get myself to school. Either that, or the fact that the only way she'll believe I'm sick enough to stay home from school is if I have a fever, or if she witnesses me throwing up.

The fog follows me to school. Reggie, Elaine, and Hanh are waiting for me, as usual. Minus any guys, thank God. I can see them watching me as I make my way up the sidewalk, and the horror of yesterday's humiliation sinks in anew and the chill around me deepens. Each step is an effort, a battle against my desire to turn around and run home. They were all rooting so hard for Caleb + Sana. They're probably mad at me for screwing things up.

Finally, Elaine steps forward, impatient. Here it comes. To my surprise, she opens her arms and hugs me. "I feel awful," she says. "I never should've told you to go out with Caleb. I just wanted you to be happy." Reggie and Elaine take their turns hugging me and gazing intently into my face as if I'm an injured baby bird they've found on the sidewalk.

The fog around me clears just a little, and I almost start to cry again out of sheer gratitude. But I've had enough drama queen scenes to last me a long time, so I brush away the tears and turn up the corners of my mouth to simulate a smile. "I'll be okay."

"Poor Caleb," says Reggie, shaking her head. "He's been a total wreck." The fog settles back down again.

"Don't remind me. I feel horrible."

"Hey, Reg," says Hanh, "sisters before misters."

"I know, I know. Sorry. It's just. He was miserable yesterday at lunch and after school."

"But think about Sana. She got broken up with twice in the same day!"

"I know. I'm sorry, Sana."

I shrug, muster up another smile, and start walking to class. The fog, heavy with the weight of Jamie and Caleb, is pressing down on me so hard it's all I can do to stay upright.

I zombie my way through physics and P.E. The morning fog burns off, but I can't ditch the one that's settled around me. It hovers over my head and shoulders and goes with me everywhere, cold, gray, and wet. It drains my energy. It makes everything pointless. A girl from the Anderson Queer Straight Alliance comes over to me in the locker room after P.E. and slips a card into my hand, printed with the club's URL and meeting times—Tuesdays during lunch, how convenient. I wonder what they'll be talking about today. How not to lose your girlfriend by cheating on her with a boy? How not to screw up a friendship with a guy by kissing him even though you already have a girlfriend?

I walk by Jamie's table at lunch, knowing it's hopeless, but hoping nonetheless. It seems I'm just desperate like that. I hope that maybe something miraculous will happen and I'll have the words to apologize and explain without making things worse—that Jamie will even want to listen. But once I'm there, it's clear I've made a bad call. She won't even look up from her food. Christina, however, looks at me like she wants to kick me. As if I haven't been kicking myself for the last twenty-four hours.

I spend a long, lonely free period pretending to do homework in a corner of the library. Then history class drags by. Then another awful practice. It should be festive—it's the last week of practice before league championships next week—but the fog around me filters out all the color, fun, and excitement that everyone else seems to be enjoying. Finally the day is over and I trudge home so I can finally be wretched in peace. It's the happiest I've felt all day.

The week passes, somehow, and then the weekend. I've been grounded because of ditching trig, so I don't have to explain to everyone why I don't want to hang out. I spend every free moment obsessively checking Jamie's social media pages. On Sunday, she posts a short poem called "Still Start" by Kay Ryan. It's basically about how impossible it seems that a heart could go on beating after it's been broken. A few people have posted comments. I consider posting one, too, but what would I say? I close the window.

On Monday, I walk to trig with Reggie, Elaine, and Hanh. Exactly like we did a week ago. Funny how life can look like everything's normal when really it's a huge mess. But when we reach the classroom door, I see Caleb at his desk, head resting on his folded arms.

"He's been like that since last week," says Reggie, as if I

hadn't been in class since last Monday and seen it for myself. She glances at me. "What are you going to do?"

I shake my head. I don't know.

"You could try apologizing," she says. Right. Okay. Better than nothing.

I walk over to my desk, sit down, and turn to face Caleb. "Caleb?" I say, my voice quavering. *Please talk to me.*

All I get is a muffled, "Fuck off."

"Caleb, I just wanted to say I'm sorry. About last week."

"I said fuck off."

I look over at Reggie, who shrugs, and at Elaine and Hanh, who smile mournfully: *You tried.*

The league finals come and go. I don't cheer for Jamie because I'm afraid she'll hate me for it—and I don't hear her voice when I go to the starting line. I have a great race, with a final half mile that is the most painful I've ever run, but somehow I manage to hang on to the end. *Gaman,* Mom would say.

Gaman. I've fought my whole life against it, but looking back, it's all I know how to do. I used gaman when I saw that first text to Dad when I was twelve. I used gaman with Trish when she got popular and made all those new, popular friends. I used gaman when I had a crush on her. I thought I'd changed when we moved to California and I finally made real friends, finally kissed Jamie, finally started to live a little. I thought I was done with gaman.

But I was wrong.

I tried to do something about Dad, and I failed. I tried to tell

Mom the truth about me, and I chickened out. I tried to take action when I thought Jamie might leave me, and I screwed up. So I've resigned myself to my fate like a good Japanese girl, and I'm doing my best to pull myself together, squelch the complaints, and endure, endure, endure. Gaman. This is what Mom has been training me for since I was born, and it's clearly what I'm best at.

The days pass. I become like a boulder on the beach in a time-lapse video. The sun and moon and stars cross the sky again and again, shadows lengthen and shrink, the tide rushes in and out. The sea heaves in the background, crabs and sea-birds flicker in and out of view. Meanwhile, the boulder sits there, stolid, unmoving, all alone, as life whizzes past. Dad continues to disappear on weekends. Mom continues to pretend it's not happening. Elaine and Jimmy earn themselves a nickname: Jimaine. Reggie splits her time at lunch between Caleb and Thom's group, and our group.

When it gets too painful, I start sneaking my lunch in the library. It's not so bad. It's quiet. It's peaceful. In the beginning, the girls ask me how I am, if I'm okay. They ask me if I've talked to Jamie at all, as if she'd ever want to hear from me. Reggie mentions a couple of times that Caleb has been bummed out, as if I need reminding what a terrible person I am. But eventually they stop asking. The sun slides across the sky, the moon waxes and wanes, and I endure. I survive.

POETRY JOURNAL, HONORS AMERICAN LITERATURE
MONDAY, NOVEMBER 23

"Elliptical"
by Harryette Mullen

This is one weird poem—just a paragraph of a lot of unfinished sentences about "them," like, "They just can't seem to ..." and "They never ..." and "Certainly we can't forget that they ..." connected by ellipses. It doesn't look like any other poem I've ever seen, but I found it on a poetry website, so I guess it's a poem.

Either way, it says a lot to me. Someone's talking about regrets, I guess. The speaker is trying not to blame "them" outright, but it's pretty clear that "they" are guilty somehow. Maybe "they" were in a relationship and people are gossiping about them. Or maybe the speaker is saying "they" instead of "he" or "she" and it's really about one person and what that person did (or didn't do).

To me, the ellipses represent the unknown and the undone, as if there were a lot of things "they" could have done differently, but we don't know what they are, exactly. Like, after reading the phrase, "They ought to be more . . ." you could finish it with, ". . . honest" or ". . . forgiving" or ". . . trusting." But we don't know for sure what would have worked best.

I think this poem is about guilt and misunderstanding and confusion. Confusion, especially, because of all the unfinished sentences, like the speaker doesn't know what to say.

35

ANDY CHIN'S PARENTS ARE LEAVING TOWN for two weeks, and he's having a party this weekend. The girls are staging an intervention and trying to get me to go.

"It's not healthy to stay at home and obsess by yourself," says Reggie. "Thom and his friends already have plans, so you don't have to worry about Caleb."

"You have to start trying to have fun again," says Elaine.

"Don't be a loser," says Hanh. We're gathered around Reggie's locker, and Elaine and Hanh are pushing for a repeat of the homecoming plan.

"Jimmy wants me to be there," Elaine whines. "We have to go!"

"Talk to your cousin! See if she'll let us crash after the party," suggests Hanh, adding hopefully, "maybe the boys can come over." She means Jimmy and his friend Bao, who she's been texting with a lot lately. But Reggie is worried about what will happen to the apartment with all of those drunk and drug-addled teenagers around, and what if someone calls the cops? Or worse, a parent?

"We could get in a ton of trouble. My parents are pretty chill, but they would kill me if they found out we had boys over unsupervised. Not to mention drunk."

"Mine, too. But who says we're going to get caught? Janet says her sister had a couple of parties at her apartment last summer and it was totally fine. No one called the cops, no one got in trouble," says Hanh.

"That was at college," Reggie points out. "This is at Sharon's. Totally different."

"It'll be fine."

"It's so unfair that Andy gets to have a whole house to himself and we have to go sneaking around," Reggie grumbles. "I wish we were boys. Or that our parents were white. It would make things so much easier."

"C'mon, Reg. Asian pride! You don't want to be like one of those slutty white girls," quips Hanh.

"Ha-ha. It's so messed up. I know my parents used to party when they were younger, back in Hong Kong. I heard my mom saying once how she used to bribe the maid not to tell her parents when she snuck out."

"That makes both our moms," Hanh says drily. "Except

my mom didn't have a maid."

Hanh and Elaine start planning what they will wear to Andy's party, and I start hoping that everyone will forget about me and I won't have to go. I manage to hold them off for the entire week, and even all day Saturday. But they are relentless. By Saturday night, I'm receiving a text every five minutes— they must have figured out a schedule between themselves, or maybe even set up a texting bot. All the texts say Sana, come with us! At nine thirty I decide whatever, I'll just go for a little bit. Maybe they're right. Maybe I need this. Besides, I'll never hear the end of it on Monday if I don't go. I text Reggie:

> Fine

> Lemme see if my mom will let you pick me up

"Hey, Mom? Reggie just texted—she wants to go to the movies. Can I go?"

Mom glances at the clock and frowns. She hates spur-of-the-moment social plans, and the fact that this one is coming from me, at nine thirty on a Saturday night, has clearly triggered the suspicion-meter in her head.

"No. It's too late."

"Mom!"

"You should plan better." And that's it. No amount of complaining on my part is going to change her mind. She gets up off the couch and heads to her room to get ready for bed. And somehow, just because she said no, it becomes imperative that I get to that party. I devise a three-phase plan and have a quick text conversation with Reggie:

Hey, Mom says no. I'm still going tho

Yay! We'll wait for u on Apricot Ave btwn Steinbeck
and Cabrillo, and we all can go to Andy's together

That's not where Andy lives

Trust me

K fine. Be there around 10:30

This is my plan:

Phase One: Tell Mom I'm going to sleep, wait until ten o'clock, arrange pillows and blankets to look like me under the covers, and sneak out through the window, leaving it open a crack so I can get back in later.

Phase Two: Walk to Andy's neighborhood, which is barely a mile away, and meet the others at Reggie's van.

Phase Three: Hang out at the party for a little while, walk home, and be back in bed by midnight.

Mom will never miss me.

Phase One goes smoothly, except for one harrowing moment when I can't get the screen to pop out, and then when I do it slips out of my fingers and clatters around loudly in the window frame. But I freeze and grit my teeth for five agonizing minutes, and when Mom doesn't appear, I climb out the window and into the night.

Andy's neighborhood is a little fancier than mine, and his house is one of those two-story, fake Italian villas with four bedrooms, a study, a "great room," a living room, and a gourmet kitchen, squeezed onto a square of land that used to be home to a modest bungalow like the one next door. The street is evenly split between the dowdy old houses and the garish new ones. I can't decide which ones look more out of place. There are cars parked up and down the entire street, and all the lights in Andy's house are on, and I begin to understand why Reggie wanted to meet two blocks away. When I reach the car, the door opens, and Elaine beckons me in.

I'm still not feeling up to the squeals and hugs that erupt, but I deal with it.

"Okay. Here, Sana. Take two of these." Hanh shakes two pills out of a little plastic bottle and holds them out. Elaine hands me a water bottle.

"What? What is that?" I did not take Hanh—or anyone here—for a pill popper. This is weird.

"Pepcid AC. It's for Asian flush."

"Pepcid AC? For Asian what?"

"Asian flush!" Hanh wrinkles her nose in distaste and Elaine grins. "You know, how Asians get all red when we drink alcohol?"

Oh, right. That. I wince, remembering my reflection in the mirror at Glen Lake Country Club. Come to think of it, that night at PopStar featured a lot of red-faced Asians, too, Dad and That Woman included.

"I read online that if you take two Extra-Strength Pepcid AC before you drink, you won't get it. At least, not as bad," Reggie explains.

I'm not feeling up to getting drunk for the first time to-night, especially since I don't plan to stay long, but it can't hurt to take precautions. If Mom were to catch me sneaking back in, that would be bad enough. Sneaking back in with Asian flush? I don't even want to think about it. I take the pills and the water, and we're ready to go.

We walk into a high-ceilinged, marble-floored front hall, complete with elaborate chandelier. It opens onto a white-carpeted living room with old bedsheets spread over the furniture and signs posted that say, STAY THE FUCK OUT OF THIS ROOM, MOTHAFUCKAS!

"Uptight much?" whispers Elaine.

Reggie rolls her eyes and says, "Poser." Fake gangsta talk is one of her biggest pet peeves.

Most of the action is in the back of the house, where the alcohol is. There's a few white kids because Andy is a student government guy, and a lot of those kids are white, but most people here are a flavor of Asian: Filipino, Indian, Vietnam-ese, Korean, Taiwanese, Chinese, Japanese. I've gotten used to a mostly Asian crowd in the past few months, but a mostly Asian party still feels odd. I mean, talk about making yourself conspicuously different. Even though I'm technically one of them, I suddenly feel like I don't belong. Like this isn't really my scene.

So I tell Elaine, "Practically everyone here is Asian."

"So?"

"Do you think that's weird?"

"Uh . . . no? What's weird about it?"

It seems I'm destined to feel like an outsider no matter who I hang out with. I also notice that either the Pepcid AC trick doesn't work, or not many people know about it, because red faces abound. Elaine points this out to me, as well, a little nervously. "Tell me if my face gets red, okay?" she says.

"Trust me, you'll know."

"Not if I'm drunk. Did you *see* those pictures of me from karaoke?"

We squeeze through the hallway into the kitchen, where cans of Bud Light vie for counter space with bottles of vodka, rum, and tequila, and two-liter bottles of assorted sodas. Stacks of red Solo cups teeter next to a case of Red Bull. Costco-size bags of chips, pretzels, and popcorn spill their contents across the swirls of marble on the island in the middle of the kitchen.

I pour myself a rum and Coke, and I'm taking an experimental sip, hoping to heck that the Pepcid AC will do its job, when I notice that the party isn't all Asian, after all. There's Thom, and there's Caleb right behind him. I turn my back before they can see me—the advantage of having hair the same color as everyone else around me is that it's easy to blend into a crowd—and search for Reggie.

I find her with Janet and Hanh around the corner in the dining room. "Reggie! You told me that it would be just us!" She looks uncomfortable. And guilty. As she should.

"I know, I know. But I knew you wouldn't come if you

knew Caleb was going to be here. Can't you just, you know, try to patch things up with him? You could go for a walk or something if the party isn't private enough."

"Caleb doesn't want to talk to me."

"He says he's mad, but I think he's starting to get over it. I want us all to be friends. Please? For me?"

"I don't know—"

"Oh—shh! Here they come. Just act normal. I'll get Thom out of the way, and you can apologize to Caleb. Be yourself. Be nice." Panic grips me and I open my eyes wide and shake my head as discreetly as I can, the universal sign for No! No! No! but it's too late. She's waving at them. In the few seconds it takes for them to make their way over, just as I'm about to slide into despair, I feel a spark of hope. Maybe Reggie's right. Maybe Caleb's not as mad as he seems. Maybe I can make things right.

"*Hi*, Caleb! I'm so glad you came! Sana's here, too!" Reggie has put on a mega-watt smile and her voice is high and loud and extra-friendly.

Okay. Go for it. I try for a funny opening—he likes funny. "Hey, stranger."

For a second Caleb stares stonily, stubbornly at some invisible thing in the air above Reggie's head, his hands jammed in his pockets. Then he kicks at something invisible on the ground and mutters, without looking at me, "Hey."

Complete and utter fail.

"Um, I have to go to the bathroom," I mumble, and as

Reggie reaches for my arm, I duck away and hightail it out of the dining room, through the kitchen, down the hall, under the chandelier, and out the door. I walk around the neighborhood for almost an hour, trying to escape the fog of despair that's reappeared and is now hunting me down. I've just about given up when the phone rings.

It's Mom.

36

OH, NO.

Has she been in my room? She has to know I escaped, or she wouldn't be calling me. Maybe I should ignore her. Pretend my phone was on mute or something. Wait to deal with her until I get home. But what if she calls the police next? I answer. "Hello?"

"Sana! Where are you?"

"Nowhere, Mom. I'm just out for a walk."

"You're supposed to be in bed! Why are you on a walk?"

"Don't worry, Mom. I'm just a few blocks—"

"Hayaku kaen-nasai."

"I *am.*"

But I don't hurry home. Who would? Still, I can't take too

long, or she'll be even angrier at me. Eventually I reach my block. The porch light is on. And Dad's car is in the driveway.

Great. This should be fun.

No point sneaking back in through the window—hopefully Mom didn't notice it, or the screen. (Why didn't I hide it under the bed?) Hopefully she believes my story about just going for a walk. I open the door and brace myself. Mom and Dad are waiting for me on the couch, Mom in her robe and slippers, Dad in his work clothes. I don't dare look at them in the face.

"Tadaima."

"Okairi," says Dad. But Mom says nothing. I lean down to take my shoes off, and her silence pools around me like water. I hazard a furtive glance at Mom's face, and what I see surprises me. She doesn't look angry. She looks sad.

"Where were you?" It's Dad again, sounding stern, which disorients me. Why should *he* be angry? Since when did he become the bad cop?

"I told Mom—"

"Mom found the screen in your room. Where did you really go?"

If they planned this Dad As Bad Cop routine to throw me off my game, it's working. I'm confused—I'm pissed at Dad and I feel bad for Mom. I'm not about to tell them where I was, but it's a tough call about what attitude to take. Should I be contrite and retreat, or should I be sullen and push back? To buy time, I heave a sigh that could go either way.

"Chanto henji shina sai." That's Mom's line, but once again, it's Dad who says it. That liar wants *me* to give *him* a proper answer? Fine. Sullen pushback it is.

"Nowhere bad—it's not a big deal. I'm back, aren't I?" I scowl and cross my arms for good measure.

"Sana! Tell me where you were!" I can see a vein bulging on the side of his neck, and his face darkens with anger. I feel my own anger rise and I push back harder.

"No. Why should I? *You're* never at home when *you're* supposed to be. It's not like *you* don't go out to who-knows-where on the weekends. Huh? Where do *you* go?"

"Sana," Mom says sharply, "irankoto iwahen-no." But to me, there's nothing unnecessary about what I'm saying. So I say it again.

"Where do you go, Dad?"

There's a long silence before he says, "That has nothing to do with you."

Suddenly, I'm done pretending. I'm done with Mom avoiding the subject. I'm done with Dad lying. Because where he goes has everything to do with me. And I realize that *gaman*— what I thought was *gaman*—can't be what I've been doing. I haven't been facing a bad situation and enduring. I've been hiding from a bad situation and allowing it to get worse. And I can't allow it anymore.

I run to my room and snatch my lacquer box from its place on the bookshelf. On my way back to the living room, I crash right into Dad, who's coming around the corner into the hallway after me, and the box and its contents fly out of my hands—my pearl earrings, the sea glass, That Woman's little gift box, the phone number, Jamie's poem—all of my treasures and secrets—clatter and bounce like hail, flutter to the floor like dying moths.

I drop to my knees and grab for the poem, which is none of my parents' business. Then the phone number, then my earrings, which have rolled down the hallway. I pick up my beautiful red box and put the earrings, poem, and phone number back in. Then the gift box. Finally, I gather up the sea glass and put it away.

Only after I've put everything safely back in the box do I realize that Dad hasn't moved, and that Mom has joined him in the hallway. I stand up, and he turns and walks slowly, heavily back to the living room, and sits down.

Heart pounding, I follow him. "Gomen," he says as I enter the room, and I'm not sure if he's apologizing for knocking into me, or for something else.

I take a breath and get ready to tell him off, because I'm still so mad, I'm shaking. But once the air fills my lungs, I can't form the words to express what I'm feeling. "I know where you've been, I know what you've been doing," I want to say. "How could you? How could you have an affair? How could you lie like that for so long?" But the words stick in my mouth, and the air remains in my lungs. The space that separates me, Mom, and Dad seems to widen and stretch, soundless and empty.

I realize that I'm terrified that if I say the words, if I demand the truth, there's no going back. He'll have words of his own, an answer that will fill the space between us, then fall and shatter like glass. And the fragile threads that bind us to each other—the memories of my childhood games with him, the stories, the stunted conversations we have now—will be severed by the sharp edges of the truth, and he'll be gone. We'll have no relationship at all, and we'll be separated forever, driven further and further apart by the different currents of our lives.

I look at Mom, sitting silently next to Dad. Waiting. Motionless. I'm filled with a fresh anger, this time at her. How could she hide herself from the truth all these years? How could she have allowed him to treat her this way—to treat *me* this way? How could she have let him continue to lie to us?

Then it strikes me. If I continue to say nothing, if I continue to do nothing, then maybe nothing will happen. Or maybe Dad will leave us anyway. The truth could split us apart. But it's better than drowning with the weight of a secret. Better than waiting for the fraying threads to be worn through one at a time by a lie. The truth will be there, no matter what, no matter how many words we say or don't say. I take the lid off my box and pull out the crumpled slip of paper and the gift box with That Woman's pearl earrings inside.

I put them down on the table in front of Dad and say, "I know where you've been and who you've been with. You don't have to hide anything anymore."

I walk back to my room and close the door.

The light wakes me up in the morning, and last night comes flooding back. Once I got into my room, I pulled out my phone, which was bursting with texts from Elaine, Reggie, and Hanh asking where I was and if I was okay. I answered them (I came home. Mom awake. I'm in big trouble) and put the phone in airplane mode. Then I spent a long time alternately congratulating myself for being honest, worrying about whether I'd ruined my family, and trying to eavesdrop on Mom and Dad, who were still talking in the living room. Finally, I gave up and lay down. The last thing I remember is wondering how I was ever going to fall asleep.

I'm still in my clothes, sprawled on top of my covers, but someone has spread a fleece blanket over me. I look at my phone: ten o'clock. Mom must be feeling bad for me—she's never let me sleep in past eight unless I've been sick. I get up, change into my pajamas, and crawl back into bed. I'm afraid to leave my room, afraid to find out what consequences my actions last night might have had. I wish I could stay here for the rest of my life. Then I'd never have to deal with Dad, with Jamie, or with Caleb. Mom could just bring me soup and rice at mealtimes, and I could read and keep up with my studies from here. I could learn to write code and work for an Internet start-up without ever leaving home.

At eleven o'clock, Mom finally peeks in. "Sana?" I pull the

covers off my head. I'm not ready to get out of bed, but I figure she deserves some thanks for letting me sleep in. It must be killing her that I'm not up and doing something useful.

"How are you doing?"

"Mmf."

Mom comes over and sits on the bed next to me.

"Dad wanted to talk to you, but he had to leave."

Figures. "He's a coward."

Mom stiffens. "I told him to go," she says.

"Why do you let him do that to you?"

"There are things you do not know. It's my choice to live this way."

"You could get a divorce. You could go to marriage counseling."

"That's the American way. I am not American." Here we go again. She continues, "Americans think that the divorce will solve all kind of problem. But divorce will not make me happier. I don't think it will make you happier. It only disappoints everyone. Think of my parents—they will have two divorced daughters."

"Mom. Who cares who you disappoint?"

"I care."

"Well, what about counseling?"

But she won't budge. "It's a same thing. Americans think that talking about the problems will solve them, but it doesn't. Not always. Some things cannot be changed with talking."

"Like what? What are you talking about?"

She looks at me carefully. "You are still so young," she says. "But maybe you can understand. Let me tell you a story of how your father and I got married."

"I know it," I say. "Baba told me the whole thing once. And Dad's told me, too."

"That is why I sent him away this morning. I'm going to tell it differently." She puts her hand on my head and strokes my hair gently, like she used to do when I was a little girl. "Love marriages are normal in Japan now, but sometimes they are still difficult, especially in the countryside, where your father and I grew up," she begins in Japanese. "Your father's family is an old one, and proud. They have been samurai, farmers, scholars, and priests in the same area for many generations. My family, too, is old. My great-great-grandfather was a tea farmer, and he became very wealthy that way."

I nod. I've heard this part before. When we visited her in Japan, Dad's mom, Baba, showed me the family's collection of netsuke, button-like charms that samurai once used to fasten their purses to their sashes. There's even an ancient sword resting in a place of honor in the two-hundred-year-old farmhouse where Dad grew up. And I've seen and smelled the boxes and jars that my mother's family used to store and transport the tea they sold. Baba told me how Mom and Dad were good friends since toddlerhood because their families had known each other for generations. For generations, both families had only sons; the women were all daughters-in-law from other families. Mom was the first girl in four generations in both families, and everyone wanted her and Dad to get married one day. But neither of them wanted to. Both of them had relationships with people they met in college—in fact, Mom was even engaged. But then Dad's girlfriend broke up with him and he got all depressed and sick, and Mom basically whipped him back into shape. Here, Baba chuckled and said, "You are her daughter. You can imagine how she was." In the process, they fell in love, Mom broke off her engagement with the other guy, and now they're living happily ever after.

"But you had a love marriage, right? You and Dad were lucky because you loved each other."

"That's the story that Baba and Dad have told you. Baba has told it so many times, she probably believes it's true. But it's only partly true. Your father and I were each in love with other people. My fiancé was a medical student from Tokyo. I met him at college. That much is the same as Baba's story. The woman your father loved, though, was different.

"Her name was Yūko-san, and she was a college student, too, at the same school as your father. She was from the city of Kobe. She was smart and pretty, a good girl. But her family was dōwa, the class of people who used to handle dead things in the old days of Japan, hundreds of years ago. Butchers and undertakers. Leatherworkers. They are the lowest class, the untouchables, and many of them hide their backgrounds out of shame. But there are practical reasons, too. It can be difficult to get hired or promoted if you are dōwa—many companies do background checks before they hire their workers. And it is difficult to get married, especially into old families like your father's and mine. Yūko-san did not tell anyone about her family background, not even your father.

"When your father and Yūko-san's relationship became serious, his family hired a private investigator to research her family background—yes, people still do that. If you marry into the wrong kind of family, it can hurt everyone: you, your children, the rest of your own family. It's important to protect your children, especially. If we lived in Japan, I would hire someone to investigate anyone who wanted to marry you—ah! Don't interrupt. And don't look so shocked. I know you think it's old-fashioned and wrong, and maybe you're right. But that is the way things are. Stop complaining, and listen.

"Your father did not want to break things off with Yūko-san. He loved her, no matter what. He had a terrible fight with Jiji and Baba, your grandparents. Eventually, though, it was Yūko-san who left, so that she wouldn't cause any more pain. She knew that your father would cut himself off from his family for her, and she didn't want to be the reason for such an old family to fall apart. She didn't want your father's children to suffer discrimination like she did—it would have been even worse for them, since he would have lost his family connections. Can you imagine having no family at all? It was the honorable thing to do, and I admired her for it.

"The next part of the story, the one that Baba has told so many times that she thinks it's true, really did happen. I helped your father get better from his sadness. I called him every day and bothered him until he got out of bed. I brought him his favorite foods. I made him study for his graduate school classes. But I didn't leave my fiancé, like Baba says. He grew tired of waiting for me to give him my attention. He left me, which broke my heart. Your father helped me through that time, and eventually we decided to marry each other."

"So you fell in love with each other?"

Mom frowns. "We were not in love. But we loved each other. We had suffered together, and survived together, and we knew that we could make a good marriage."

"But—"

"Would you prefer that we had not married? Would you prefer not to have been born?" I don't have an answer for that. "Yūko-san was an English major, and she eventually moved to America. We moved to Wisconsin, and after a few years, your father found her. She was here, in California. He visited her over and over."

"Did you know about her? Did you know what he was doing?"

"He told me soon after he found her. At first, I was angry. Of course I was. I was sad. I didn't want my husband to go with another woman, after I had worked so hard to make him happy, to make a good home for him in this country. But after a long time, after I thought and thought about it . . ." She shrugs. "I knew, when we moved to California, that he wanted to be closer to her."

"And you let him?!"

"She suffered, and your father suffered. For years, Sana. He was in love with her. It was easier than having him gone on so many trips to California."

"But what about you?"

For a moment, a ghost of something—grief? pain?—flits across her face. But I blink and her face is set back in its usual no-nonsense expression, her mouth pressed into a hard, straight line, and I wonder if I just imagined it.

"I am not in love with your father," she says firmly. "Yūko-san, who loves him, never complained. She suffered and endured heartbreak."

Gaman. "But so did you."

She twists her wedding ring, remembering. "Before I married your father, yes, I suffered. But the man I was engaged to did not have gaman. He had no patience for suffering. He had no patience for enduring. And I have no use for a man like that." Mom looks at me. "Your father works hard, he makes money for us to be comfortable, and he is kind. He loves you. He cares for me. I care for him. That is a good family. That is all I need."

"But it's not a good family! It's not fair! You can't just accept stuff like that. You don't have to have gaman."

"And if I don't have gaman, then what? Your father leaves Yūko-san and we are all sad together for the rest of our lives?

Or I divorce your father and become a single mother, and make my family in Japan sad, as well? No matter what, we suffer. This arrangement is the best way. This way, we all get what we need."

"No, we don't. *They* get everything. You only get—"

"I have what I need," she says again. "And Yūko-san does not have everything. She does not have a family. She does not have a daughter." Mom looks straight at me and takes my hand, and I feel my heart soften and my throat tighten. But I'm not done fighting yet.

"But what about me? I get a dad who's never home. I get a dad who cheats on my mom, and who knows how long he'll stick around, and my mom just sits by and lets it happen."

She sighs, and strokes my hair. "It's hard for you, I know. I'm sorry. Your father is very, very sorry. But he's an honorable man—"

"He's a cheater."

"No. I told you already, he loves you. He will not abandon us. I've known him since we were children, and I know this about him." It still doesn't seem fair. She takes my face in her hands and looks me in the eye. "Don't be angry at your father or Yūko-san. Don't feel sorry for me. I've thought about it many times, and many times again, and no matter how I look at it, this is the best way. I am content. I could have left your father and gone back to Japan with you—some Japanese wives do. But I stayed here because I want to have a strong, independent daughter who can grow up to be whatever she wants, and who can love whoever she wants. You can live the life that your father and Yūko-san could not.

"Your father didn't want you to know. I tried to tell him that you were ready when we moved here, but he wasn't ready to tell you. And then you figured it out on your own—it was only a matter of time for a smart girl like you. You are stronger and more independent than I was prepared for. I suppose that's what happens when you grow up in America. Perhaps I need to give you more room to grow." She smiles ruefully. "Sometimes the parents have to run to catch up with their children, instead of the other way around."

37

MOM STROKES MY HAIR ONE MORE TIME, LETS her hand linger on my shoulder for a moment, and then withdraws it and resettles herself next to me on the bed.

My head is spinning. Nothing is what I thought it was. It's like my life was a sinking ship, and Mom has just plunked me into a lifeboat, but I can't figure out how to work the oars. The villains are the long-suffering and lovelorn victims; the long-suffering victim is the gallant heroine. I still want to be angry with Dad and That Woman—I mean, Yūko—but how can I be when they're just two people in love? It's the story of Yama-sachi and Toyo-tama-himé. No wonder Dad loved it so much. I want to feel sorry for Mom, and mad at her for letting all of this happen to her, because no matter what she says about being content, she got a raw deal. But how can I when she helped make it happen? She and Dad stayed married for me—so that I could grow up here. Would she have been happier with a divorce? Would I?

Then there's all that stuff she said about me. She wants to let me be stronger and more independent. She's going to give me more space. She wants me to be able to love whoever I want. Is she dropping a hint here? Does she know more than I gave her credit for?

I realize that Mom is waiting for me to say something. And I realize that now, after she's let me in on the Secret of Dad and Yūko, this would be a good time to tell her the Secret of Sana and Jamie. Though I guess it's just the Secret of Sana now.

"So you know how you said that you wanted me to grow up and love whoever I want to love?" She eyes me warily. Not good. "Well, um." I clear my throat. There's still time. I can still back out. I could just ask her something innocuous, like if she'd be okay with it if one day I married a white American. But I feel the weight of my secret again, dragging me down, like the secret of the phone number and the earrings. Like Mom and Dad's secret. And I remember that hiding the truth doesn't stop things from being true. Not talking about things doesn't stop them from happening. Pretending that a thing is something else doesn't change its true nature.

And I don't need to pretend to be something else. I don't want to be anything but what I am. And I don't want to hide my true self anymore, like Toyo-tama-himé did. So I close my eyes, brace myself, and plunge ahead. "I'm gay."

She blinks. "Gay?"

"Lesbian. I like girls. Like, romantically. Instead of boys."

Her mouth makes a little "o," but no sound comes out. Then she closes her mouth and nods her head once. I wait. And wait. Finally, I can't wait anymore. I have no gaman left. "Are you okay?"

"Hn." She nods again. "Sōka." So that's the way it is.

More waiting. "What? What are you saying? You're okay with it?"

"Hnnn." Then silence. Then, "You are so young. Are you sure? How do you know?"

"I'm sure. I just know, that's all."

"For how long?"

"Since it started mattering, I guess. But it's not like I woke up one day and I was gay. I sort of . . . figured it out. It's just the way I am."

She stares at her fingers as she twists them in her lap. I can't tell how she feels, but she seems to be taking it well. She looks up at me. "I read in the magazine that the gay can't change to normal."

"I *am* normal, Mom."

Mom shakes her head. "No. Gay is not normal. If gay is normal, then everybody is gay."

"It's normal for *me*."

She scoffs, as if she's never heard anything more ridiculous. My heart contracts as my hopes for this conversation, which had been rising, begin to sink.

Then she asks, "Do you have . . . girlfriend?"

And now my hopes are in free fall. "I did. Jamie." She takes a quick breath and looks away as this sinks in.

"She is not your girlfriend anymore?"

"No."

I expect to see her nod her head, satisfied, but instead she says, "Nandé?"

"Um. She broke up with me because I—I lied to her."

"Sana," she says reproachfully.

"I thought she liked someone else, and I wanted to be with someone who only liked me, so I—I kissed someone else. I know it doesn't make sense. And I didn't tell her. And she found out and broke up with me." My voice shakes a little and tears threaten to well up. I fight them back.

"You shouldn't kiss so many people! And you shouldn't lie. Of course she broke up with you. Kissing the person who isn't your—your girlfriend—is bad. You will get a bad reputation."

And then I give up fighting and let the tears come, because I hate who I've been and what I've done lately, and Mom clearly does, too. And yet it seems unfair for her to criticize, because who else has been kissing people they shouldn't, and then lying about it to me? And worst of all, what if she's disappointed not only in what I've done lately but who I've always been? The person I'll always be? What will I do then?

"Sana." Her voice is gentle.

"What?" I croak.

"Gomen-nasia. Warui koto iū-temōta ne." Huh? "You suffered, too. And your father and I were the cause. Our lies to you. It was wrong of me to scold you, when we did wrong, too. I'm sorry."

"Oh." Well, this is a first. "Okay." I sniffle, and she hands me a tissue. "Though I think Dad owes me an apology, too."

She nods.

But there's still that other thing. "Aren't you upset about me . . . having a girlfriend?"

"You are too young for girlfriend or boyfriend. And you don't have girlfriend anymore."

Okay, not what I meant, but whatever. I try again. "What about me being gay?"

Her shoulders rise, then fall. "I am surprised. I am sad. Your life will be more difficult. People will discriminate." She looks at me, and I wait for her to go on, to tell me that I should work hard to act like everyone else. But she doesn't.

"That's it? Nothing else?"

Her forehead wrinkles, then she shakes her head. "No."

"But . . . you just said that gay people aren't normal. You even said once that we were freaks. You said we shouldn't be out because it makes people uncomfortable."

"Hn." She nods her head in assent.

"But that's . . . awful. You can't call people freaks if you're okay with them."

"Freak is bad?"

"Freak is bad."

She frowns, then waves her hand dismissively. "I meant that the gay are different—they are! You are!" I open my mouth to protest, but she cuts me off. "Chotto! Be quiet and listen to me. In Japan, be gay is not a sin like in America. Just different—you cannot deny that gay is different from most people. But in Japan, too different is uncomfortable for the other people. It's disrespectful to make the other people uncomfortable. Even if you can't help being different, it's your duty to become like others. It's your duty to fit in. So in Japan, the gay can't be out of the cabinet. They can't get married. They can't have children." She puts her hand on my back, gently. "But different is okay in America, even though I forget sometimes. You are okay, even though you are different."

I'm floored. In the movie version of my life, I would now say softly, "I love you, Mom," and she'd reply, "I love you, too, Sana." And we'd hug each other and smile and weep and she'd kiss my hair and wipe away my tears and the scene would fade out.

In my real life, I can't help thinking that there are still plenty of people in America who need reminding that different is okay: Glen Lake Country Club, and the cop outside the 7-Eleven, and Mrs. Lowell, for starters. But I decide to let it go for now and just be happy that my mother doesn't think I'm bad—just different. And she's okay with that. And that's okay with me. She puts her arm around me and gives me an awkward squeeze. "It was good to talk," she says. "I feel free." Me, too. I close my eyes and soak it in.

Then I can't help it. I say gently, "Mom, it's out of the *closet*. Not the cabinet."

"Erasō." But she smiles, so I know she doesn't really think I'm being a disrespectful smart aleck. "Futari de gamba-rō ne." Let's work hard and do our best together. In America, in English, "work hard" just means hard work. In Japan, it also means, "I'm rooting for you. I want you to succeed." Maybe there's no guarantee, like when American moms say, "It's going to be great." Because the reality is that life can be hard, and awful, and sometimes all you can do is keep working at it. But there's hope. There's a future together. I can work hard for that.

While I'm in the shower, Mom calls Dad to tell him to come home. He must not have been far, because I'm still combing my hair when he arrives.

"Tadaima," he calls.

"Okairi," Mom answers. I'm not quite ready to welcome him home, but I drift around the living room until he sits down on the couch and motions me over.

I sit gingerly on the edge of the couch and twist my fingers. I don't know if I want to have this conversation with him. Hearing the story from Mom was weird enough. But to have to look my father the adulterer—or is it tragic hero?—in the eye and hear it from him is something else. We sit in silence for a moment before he speaks.

"Sana, gomen-nā," he says. "I was selfish, chasing my own

happiness and allowing you to worry. Your mother told you about Yūko-san and me. . . ."

"Yeah."

"You must be very upset?"

"Yeah. No. Mostly confused, I guess."

Dad looks at his feet, which are tapping nervously. He nods a couple of times, still looking at his feet, and then looks up at me and says, "Sana, I will never leave you and Mom, even for Yūko-san. But if you want me to stop seeing Yūko-san, I will."

Whoa. I did not see that one coming. Do I really want to be the one to break up Dad and the woman he loves? Even if that woman isn't Mom? Mom seems to be okay with it. Is it still cheating if your wife is okay with it? I think of everything that Mom has decided to accept because she wants me to be happy and to love who I love. If she can do it, maybe I can, too. "It's okay," I hear myself saying, "I still have to think about it, but I think it'll be okay." I say those words again inside my head, hold them in my heart, and wait to see how they feel.

They feel okay.

Dad's face breaks into a smile. He nods once, claps me on the knee, and nods again, his eyes shining with—tears? Wow. After lunch, Dad takes off again, presumably to celebrate with Yūko-san, and I feel a stab of regret about telling him it's okay to keep seeing her. And he hasn't mentioned *my* secret. I wonder if Mom even told him. But he's not gone for very long. In fact, it hasn't even been an hour when I hear his voice again, calling, "Tadaima!"

"Okairi." This time, I can answer him. I watch him as he takes his shoes off, which he does with some difficulty because of the white paper bag he's holding in his hand.

"Sana-chan," he says. "Oidé."

I go over to him, and he holds out the bag. "This is for you."

I take it and unroll the top. Inside is a white Styrofoam cup full of chocolate ice cream.

No, wait. It looks denser, softer than ice cream.

"Chocolate frozen custard."

"Sea dragons' favorite food," he says.

I look up. His mouth is curved in a cautious smile, his eyes a little anxious. "Do you remember?" he asks. I do. He rests his hands on my shoulders, looks me in the eye, and says gruffly, "You're a good girl, Sana," before tousling my hair and stepping back. Which is the closest he'll probably ever get to hugging me and saying, "I love you, no matter what," so I'll take it.

Poetry Journal, Honors American Literature
Monday, November 30

"Wild Geese"
by Mary Oliver

I love this poem for lots of reasons. First of all, the first line: "You do not have to be good." We are who we are, and we shouldn't have to suffer for it, or prove anything to anyone. We just have to "let the soft animal of your body / love what it loves" and share our pain with each other. Nature loves us and is beautiful no matter what, just like us.

Seeing wild geese flying is always exciting for me, because it's like they're on this big journey, and I feel like I'm part of their journey somehow. Oliver talks about how their "harsh and exciting" calls announce our place "in the family of things," like they're reminding us that in the big picture, on our journeys, we can all find a place where we can be accepted for who we are, no matter what.

38

THE WEATHER HAS FINALLY TURNED. WHEN I woke up this morning, it was raining. It's just a long, steady downpour, but the news is calling it "the first winter storm." I don't know if that's because the news likes to make a big deal out of nothing, or if people in California are just that clueless about weather.

It's time for a new season in my life, too. I text Reggie, who texts Thom, who texts Caleb to check to see that he's home alone. He is.

By the time I pull up in front of Caleb's house, the rain is coming down in sheets. I park on the street, and as I get out of the car, I step right into a puddle. Excellent start. I sprint up the driveway to the front door and ring the doorbell. It's probably a good thing that it's raining so hard, because despite dreading a face-to-face with Caleb, I can't wait for him to answer the—

There he is. "Hi," I say, squinting through the rivulets of water streaming down my face.

"Hey." He doesn't budge.

"Um, can I come in?" He steps aside to let me in. I wonder if he'd have closed the door on me if the sun were shining. I stand dripping in the foyer. Caleb just stands next to me, watching.

"I need to talk to you. To, um, apologize."

"Okay."

"Is there somewhere we can sit down?"

Silently, Caleb leads the way into the kitchen, where, from the looks of it, he's been eating a piece of toast. He sits down and looks at me like, *So?* I sit. I fidget. I wish this conversation was already over. "So . . . I'm gay."

"Yeah, I got that news flash."

"Oh. Right. Sorry." Ugh, why am I so bad at this? I start over. "Okay, so first of all, I'm really— I'm sorry. I'm sorry about what I did and how I acted and what I said. I should have been honest with you. I shouldn't have kissed you. I shouldn't have led you on. It was thoughtless and selfish."

"And mean."

Okay, fine. "And mean."

"And fucked up."

"And . . . fucked up."

Caleb looks out the window at the rain, which is coming down so hard, it's hard to see anything else.

I wait. I look at my hands. I twist my fingers. Finally I can't take it any longer.

"Well, are you going to say something, or—"

"I felt like a total idiot."

"I know. I'm sorry."

"I mean, I liked you, you know? And you just . . . used me. I mean, you *kissed* me. *You* kissed *me*. What the fuck was that about? Why did you do it?"

"I know. I—I don't know, I guess I was afraid that Jamie was going to leave me. Like I was afraid my dad was going to leave me and my mom. And I didn't want to be like her—like my mom, I mean. I thought my mom was just letting it happen to her and I thought I was going to be different, and *do* something. . . . It was just the wrong thing."

"No shit."

"I didn't think it through, I guess. I just—I wanted to be with someone who really wanted to be with me."

"Well, I did want to be with you."

"I mean . . . maybe I wanted to be with you, too, for a moment, because I could tell that you wanted to be with me, and I did—I *do*—like you."

"But not the way that I liked you."

"No, I guess not."

"And you wanted to be with Jamie more."

"Well, I . . . yeah. And I should have told you right away. I should've worked it out with her instead of messing with you and then lying to you both. I was just so afraid she'd leave me.

I panicked. And then I thought—I knew—you'd be mad at me. So I was afraid to tell you. I'm just a loser, I guess."

"You can say that again."

"I know."

"No. Seriously. Say it again."

But the corner of his mouth is twitching.

"I'm a loser."

"And you're sorry."

"And I'm sorry. I'm a loser and I'm sorry."

"You can say that again."

"Shut up."

"Okay, fine. Apology accepted."

"Okay. So . . . we're good?"

He shrugs. "Yeah. We're good."

"Good." I try a smile. "I was worried you would hate me forever."

"I thought about it." He points his finger at me. "Don't get complacent, though. I could change my mind."

"Got it." I just need to make sure he knows how great I think he is. "You'd be a fantastic boyfriend. Just not for me."

He heaves an enormous sigh. "I know."

"Because I'm—I mean—"

"I *know*. I get it. Thank you. But you don't have to rub it in. Fuck."

"Oh, right. Sorry. I was just trying to be honest."

"It's all right. Just . . . work on your timing."

"Okay."

"Want some toast?"

"Sure."

Caleb gets up and drops two slices of bread into the toaster, and soon we're munching on buttered toast in companionable silence, looking out at the rain together.

39

IT'S NICE NOT TO BE A BOULDER ANYMORE, not to have to sit still while the whole world whirls past in flashes of color and light, and the wind and tides rush in and out around me. Things with Caleb are still a little fragile, but now that we're talking again, the dull gray ache inside has eased a bit. My smiles aren't painted on. Laughing feels less like heaving bricks and more like tossing confetti.

Sometimes, anyway.

Other times, the fog condenses around me again. Because there's still Jamie. Jamie, who I only see from afar, but who I can't stop thinking about. Just like it was in the very beginning. Except then she didn't know I existed, and now she hates me. I don't know which is worse. Actually, I do. It was better when she didn't know I existed, because at least then there was hope. And even though my heart hurts every time I see her, I go out of my way to be where I know she'll be just so I can torture myself with a glimpse of her crossing the quad or walking down the breezeway.

I've written countless texts and emails, some in my head and some on my devices, but I haven't had the guts to send anything. I have imaginary conversations with her multiple times a day. I walk past her classrooms, past her locker, past her table at lunch, just to be where she's been. I haven't looked at her long enough for her to catch me looking, so I have no idea if she knows I'm stalking her—I mean, that I'm not over her. She's surrounded by a force field that I just can't break through.

One afternoon, Mom gives me a book of poetry written by Japanese courtiers, way back in the year 1000. She says that nobles back then used to have poetry-writing contests to see who could best express a certain feeling, or describe a certain scene, and they would send poems called tanka to each other instead of letters—or even instead of talking. But they had to be short, just a few lines. Thirty-one syllables. The idea was to capture and communicate the essence of what you felt.

"Like text," she says. "Or twittering."

"Tweets."

"Yes. But not so many every day. That's not challenge.

Only two or three. Or maybe only one in a week, if the other person was far away."

"Instead of letters? But that leaves so much to misunderstand."

"Japanese people can understand. Each person spent time to think about the best words so the reader can understand. The careless person throws the lots of words—talking is so easy to throw out the wrong words. Tanka makes you think. Now you know why the Japanese people don't talk so much about the feelings."

I imagine noblewomen writing tanka-letters to someone, just one or two a day, taking time over each one to get it just right. Kind of like the poetry notebook I had with Jamie.

That's when I get my idea.

I spend a week trying to write a poem like the ones in my new book, but after a while I realize that loving poetry and being a good poet are two very different things. Everything I think of is cheesy, or it doesn't say what I want it to say, or it's too long and boring. You'd think, since it's so short, that poetry would be easy. Not so much.

But I'm not giving up.

I go through my journal with a pack of post-it notes. I spend an entire weekend on poetry websites, chasing poets and poems down rabbit holes and through a maze of related poems, related poets, biographies, and analyses. Talk about a time suck—there's a ton of cool stuff out there, but only a tiny bit of it says exactly what I want. By Sunday night, I have what I need. I hope.

I have to dig deep for the courage to do it, but on Sunday, I tell Reggie, Elaine, and Hanh that I'm still head over heels for Jamie and that I want to get back together with her.

"Duh," says Elaine.

"Finally," says Reggie.

"Why are you always so late with your own news?" asks Hanh.

"Whatever. So I need your help." And I tell them my plan. I need one more person, so I ask Caleb, but he turns me down.

"You want me to help you win back the girl you left me for? Uh, too soon. Timing, remember? Work on it," he says. But not unkindly.

So I text Janet and recruit her to help. I text Caleb later and tell him I'm sorry about my terrible timing. He texts back:

Shut up already. Know when to stop talking

. . .

Don't worry

Still friends

I've chosen six poems to deliver to Jamie on Monday: one before school, one for each of the four block periods, and one for lunch. I know that a thousand years ago this process of sending poems to your beloved would have taken a week instead of a school day, but I'm too excited to drag it out that long.

I'll start with "Missing you" by Izumi Shikibu, a court lady who was born in 976:

> Missing you,
> my soul escapes my body
> and wanders, glowing
> like the fireflies in the marsh.

I write it as neatly as I can on rice-paper stationery that I found in Japantown, and tuck it into an envelope.

"When You See Water" by Alice Walker is next, for how indefinable Jamie is, how unrestricted by categories, and how no one else could be anything like her.

After that, "Poem" by Lucy Ives. It's about how you can tell yourself to stop loving someone who doesn't love you back, but you still can't help loving them.

Then "Elliptical" by Harryette Mullen. For all those things left unsaid, all those things I could have done, thought, and tried differently, all those questions about intentions and how things could have been.

"Scientists Find Universe Awash in Tiny Diamonds" by Mayne Ellis because of how precious Jamie is to me, and how valuable and unique and connected by beauty we all are.

Finally, "I Ask the Impossible" by Ana Castillo. Because that's what I'm about to do.

40

I ARRIVE AT SCHOOL WELL BEFORE THE FIRST
bell with the poems in my backpack. I go to Jamie's locker and
tape the "Missing you" to the door, to make sure she doesn't
overlook it if she's in a hurry. Feeling like I'm committing a
crime ("a crime of loooove," I can hear Hanh croon), I steal
away, heart racing. There's nowhere I can hide to see if Jamie
gets her poem, and I'm so full of nervous energy, I can't even
pull together enough focus to sustain a walk around the quad,
so I pace back and forth in front of the trig classroom until class
starts.

Elaine, Reggie, Hanh, and Janet arrive, and I distribute the
poems among them. Five minutes before the bell, I send Hanh
off with "When You See Water" to AP Spanish, Jamie's first-
period class. She returns just as the bell rings, and gives me a

thumbs-up across the classroom. I'm pretty much useless for the entire period. The hands on the clock cannot move fast enough, and my body and brain feel like those wind-up teeth that chatter and clatter all over the table. I'm dying to talk to Hanh and find out what Jamie's reaction was, and whether it seemed like she'd read the first poem that I left on her locker door.

Finally, the bell rings. I rush over to Hanh. "Well? Did she say anything? What was she like?"

Hanh shrugs. "She looked surprised, I guess."

"Good surprised or bad surprised?"

"I dunno. Neutral? I mean, she didn't smile or anything. But she didn't look mad, either."

"Did she read it?"

"Sorry. I didn't stick around to see. I had to get back here, remember?"

Elaine has already rushed off to Jamie's physics class with "Poem," and my Spanish class is basically a repeat experience of trig: Elaine scoots in just before the bell rings and gives me a thumbs-up; I tap my feet and pencil for eighty minutes; I give her the third degree at the end of the period. Elaine's answers are as unsatisfactory as Hanh's.

Reggie takes "Elliptical" over to Jamie during lunch. "Christina wanted to know what the heck was going on," she reports.

"Did Jamie say anything? Did she read it? What did she look like?"

"What—do you think I'm going to just hang around and watch? Like that wouldn't be totally obnoxious?"

Janet leaves early from lunch to deliver "Scientists Find Universe Awash in Tiny Diamonds" to Jamie's next class, but Janet's not in my English class, so I don't even get a thumbs-up. Anguish. Finally, the bell rings and English is over. Time for the last poem. The one I'm going to give to her in person, while I look her in the eye and say, "I'm sorry, Jamie. I screwed up. Please, can we talk?"

I'm about to head out the door to deliver "I Ask the Impossible" when Ms. Owen stops me. She wants to talk to me about my poetry journal. She *loved* my reaction to Adrienne Rich's "Cartographies of Silence." What a fabulous choice! What inspired me to choose it? She wants to thank me for my honesty, she can see why I would be drawn to the poem, it's one of her favorites, *blah*, blah, *blah*, blah, *blah*.

Any other day, I'd be stoked about a teacher taking this much interest in my opinions and my life. But Jamie has trig with the legendary Mrs. Byrd, the meanest, bitchiest, most old-school schoolmarm ever to set foot on a high school campus. I have to give this poem to Jamie before the bell rings, or she'll never get it. With a minute to go, I extricate myself from my conversation with Ms. Owen. I tear down the breezeway, turn left, then right, then cut diagonally across the quad toward the math building. I still have to pass the science labs and go around another corner when the bell rings. Please, please, please let Mrs. Byrd be late. Please let her be sick and have a sub. Please let her be talking to another teacher. Please—

I turn the corner. It's too late. There's no one outside the classroom and the door is closed. Damn.

I could turn around. Jamie's already got five poems. That's plenty.

But the whole point of this plan was for me to face her and hand her the last poem myself and break the silence between us. The whole day has been leading up to this very moment— well, the very moment that was supposed to happen two minutes ago. I can't back out now.

I'm going in.

I knock on the door and open it. Mrs. Byrd is already at the whiteboard going over a homework problem. The whole class turns around to stare at me as she stops mid-sentence, peers over her glasses, clearly annoyed at the interruption, and says icily, "May I help you?"

Her gaze is pure, unadulterated evil. Every cell of my body is screaming at me to mumble an apology and run away. Instead, I croak, "Yes, um, I have something for Jamie Ramirez." I hold up the envelope and start toward Jamie's desk—which is, as luck would have it, at the opposite end of the room. She starts getting out of her seat to meet me halfway.

"Jamie, sit down."

Jamie sits.

Mrs. Byrd turns to address me.

"Is it a message from the office?"

"No."

"Is it a medical emergency?"

"No."

"Is it a family emergency?"

"No."

"Then it can wait until after school."

"Oh. Um, I'd rather just give it to her now, if that's okay."

"No, it is *not* okay. You just interrupted my class to give your friend a personal message. If it's important to deliver it this minute, you can read it to her from where you are."

"It's kind of private."

"Then you have a decision to make. Deliver the message out loud right now, or wait until after school." I stare at her. "Well? You're wasting valuable class time." Wasting time? Who's the one making a big production out of this? No wonder everyone hates her.

Jamie is watching me intently. She's not shaking her head. She's not smiling. Nothing about her body language is telling me it's okay to wait until after school. She's waiting for me to step up and read the poem. I look back at Mrs. Byrd, who is frowning at me with her arms folded, actually tapping her foot. Waiting for me to back down and leave. All around us, I can see the class's gaze shifting from Jamie, to me, to Mrs. Byrd: Who's going to crack?

It's the thought that counts, isn't it? Jamie knows I was here, she knows I tried. She knows I have a poem for her. She has to know, after all the other poems, how I feel. She knows how uncomfortable I am with public displays of affection, how hard it is for me to reveal personal stuff to anyone (*forget* about Mrs. Byrd's entire trig class).

Then I think about silence, and truth, and knowing—how Mom says that Japanese people don't need to say a lot of words to know things that are true and deep, like feelings. And yet how the truth about my feelings for Jamie lies in the words I hold in my hand.

I think about gaman, how Yūko-san, Dad, and Mom all had to do it. Gaman isn't just about enduring hardship in silence—and it's not about backing down. It's about stepping up and choosing which hardship you endure. And enduring it with grace because of something important, like honor, or family. Or some*one* important. Like Jamie.

"Make up your mind, please. Read or leave," says Mrs. Byrd.

My mind is made up. With trembling hands, I open the envelope, and with trembling fingers I unfold the paper inside. I take a deep breath, and with a trembling voice, I begin.

"'I Ask the Impossible,' by Ana Castillo."

It's kind of a bold poem, because the impossible thing the speaker asks is to be loved forever, no matter what. No matter how isolated, no matter how tired, or bored, or old anyone gets, she asks to be loved with tenderness, without judgment. And at the end, she basically says, "because *I* love *you* no matter what."

I'd like to be able to say that as I read, my trembling voice steadies and grows stronger, and finally rings clear and true on the last lines. But no, it's shaky all the way through. And even though I know the poem by heart, I have to read it, all the way to the last line, after which I finally manage to lift my gaze from the paper and meet Jamie's eyes.

But she looks down at her desk almost immediately, so I can't tell what she's thinking. I think I see the ghost of a smile playing on her lips, but I can't be sure if it's real or polite or if I just imagined it. Some of the boys are snickering. Some of the girls are putting hands over their hearts and going, "Ohhh."

"Well," says Mrs. Byrd. "That was . . . interesting. Are you finished?"

"Yes."

"Then please excuse yourself so that I can teach my class." I put the poem back in the envelope and hand it to someone to pass to Jamie. I'm dying to exchange one last look with her, but she's watching the progress of the envelope as it makes its way from hand to hand across the classroom.

"Good-*bye*," says Mrs. Byrd, nodding toward the door.

"Bye."

Psychology, my last class, is agonizing. I keep my phone on my desk, hidden under part of a notebook page so I can see if Jamie happens to text me during class. I have it on mute with the vibrate function off, obviously, so this necessitates me constantly flipping the page over to check for texts. So class goes something like this:

Mr. Albrecht: Jungian dream theory, blah, blah, blah . . .

Me: (*flip*) no

Mr. Albrecht: blah, animus, blah, blah, anima . . .

Me: (*flip*) no

Finally, the bell rings. I check my phone (no) and head to my locker, taking a detour past Jamie's locker.

No Jamie.

Maybe she'll be waiting at my locker.

No.

Maybe we missed each other, somehow. Maybe if I take a long time here, she'll show up. But the only people who show up are Elaine and Hanh. "How'd fourth period go?"

"I don't know." I tell them the story, and they look appropriately horrified, and then encouragingly exhilarated.

"Oh, that's so romantic!" Elaine exclaims. "It's like something that happens in the movies—she's totally going to take you back. I would."

"Right? You totally stepped up for her," says Hanh.

I'm not so sure. I mean, that she'll take me back. "But what if she was embarrassed, or what if she thinks I was trying to manipulate her? You know, so she'd look bad rejecting me in front of all those people."

"She did that once already, didn't she? Anyway, you didn't *plan* to read out loud, and you did it anyway. That's the important thing. You totally killed it!"

"Yeah, I guess I did." I'm starting to feel better now. Reggie, Thom, and Caleb appear and Hanh retells the story for them.

Caleb grimaces. "You must really like her a lot."

"I do."

"Lucky her." And he smiles.

"The ball's in her court now," says Reggie sagely. "All you have to do is wait."

Right. No problem. Just wait. That's all I have to do.

On my way home, I finally get a text:

Thank you

But that's it. What do I text back? You're welcome? That seems a bit entitled. I love you? When can we talk? Heart? Smiley face? I send her a heart. And a hopeful-looking smiley face.

She sends nothing.

41

IT'S TUESDAY, AND I'M A WRECK. EVERYONE kept texting me last night to check to see if Jamie had texted me yet. Every time I replied "no" my heart sank a little further.

I stalk Jamie between classes, but it doesn't help. I walk by her table at lunch, but she's not there. She's avoiding me, I know it. The bell rings and I leave history, my last class of the day. I'm sure by now that it's over. Jamie's grateful to me for trying, she appreciates my effort, here's a certificate, thanks for participating. I open my locker to trade my history textbook for my trig.

There's the notebook.

I drop my bags and pick it up. I flip the pages, my heart pounding, past "Loose Woman," past "In the Morning in Morocco," past "Missing you."

A poem. By Emily Dickinson. It begins, "Her breast is fit for pearls."

With each line, my heart lifts a little. The fog clears. By the time I get to, "Her heart is fit for home— / I—a Sparrow—build there / . . . My perennial nest," I am flying—above the trees, above the clouds—I'm practically in orbit. My heart is her home.

Someone clears their throat behind me.

Jamie.

"Hey," she says.

"Hey." I look down at the notebook in my hand, still open to the poem. "This is—do you mean it?"

"Yeah. I'm sorry it took so long—I wanted to get it perfect, you know? I wanted to surprise you. Like you surprised me. Holy shit, I did *not* think you were going to read that poem in front of everyone."

"I hope it was okay."

"It was . . . amazing. You were amazing."

"I was terrified."

Jamie laughs. "I could tell." Then she takes a step forward. "But you did it anyway. You spoke up."

Oh, right—speaking of speaking up. "I'm sorry I screwed up. I should have trusted you, I should have waited, I should have talked to you again instead of just rushing off with someone else. I should have—"

"Shhh." Jamie puts a finger on my lips. "Later."

She leans just the tiniest bit toward me, and my heart jumps.

"So like, I really want to kiss you right now," she whispers. "But I know it's not your thing . . . in public—"

I don't even have to think about it. I step forward and kiss her. Because I want everyone to know the truth about how I feel.

POETRY JOURNAL, HONORS AMERICAN LITERATURE
FRIDAY, DECEMBER 18

"Cartographies of Silence"
by Adrienne Rich

From the very first line, I felt like Adrienne Rich was talking about my life in the past few weeks: "A conversation begins / with a lie." She describes how even if you share a common language, it can split you apart. You can't take stuff back—stuff you said but didn't mean, stuff you meant but didn't say.

I have trouble saying what I mean, especially if it's personal. Sometimes I say things I don't mean, just so I don't have to say the things I do mean. Or sometimes I say exactly what I mean, and it still comes out all wrong. So sometimes I don't say anything at all.

But I've realized that not saying anything at all can be the same as lying, or worse. Other people in my life have done this, too. Like the speaker says, "Silence can be a plan / rigorously executed." She says more about silence, and I didn't get most of it at first. She mentions a silent film called The Passion of

Joan of Arc and the actress who starred in it, Renée Jeanne Falconetti. (Don't be impressed, Ms. Owen. I had to Google all of this.) When I saw the images of Falconetti in the film, it helped me understand. Her face is haunting. It expresses pure emotion. So I think Rich is asking this question: What if we could have silence that was really, truly pure, where it didn't mean lying or hiding yourself or whatever? What if we could communicate the truth without all the words to screw it up?

Sometimes I wish that we could always do things that way. It would make life a lot easier.

Except it doesn't work that way in real life. In real life, silence often is just lying, hiding, and dying.

In the end, even though language can mess us up, Rich ends up choosing "these words, these whispers, these conversations / from which time to time, the truth breaks moist and green." I love that image of the truth, like some small, fragile thing that you have to take care of, but maybe it will grow into something strong and beautiful. It comes as a result of all the words, even the bad ones. It makes everything worth it.

42

"SANA, COME ON!"

I look up from the patch of beach that I've been examining to see Jamie waving her arms and hollering. She runs a few steps toward me and beckons me over to where she and the others are making their way through the narrow corridor that separates the ragged cliffside from a huge rock arch the size of an office building. At low tide, the corridor is a damp strip of sand. At high tide, it becomes a channel of frigid seawater so cold it makes your teeth hurt. Through this channel and beyond the cliff is the rest of the beach, where we've left our stuff.

"The tide's coming in! If you wait too long, you'll have to *swim* back to the other side!"

* * *

This morning, we had salt-pickled kombu seaweed and tiny sardines cooked in soy sauce for breakfast, and I imagined that I was in the undersea palace of the Dragon King, having a royal feast. Mom went crazy for our New Year's breakfast. She spent a week preparing all the traditional good-luck foods: the sardines for abundance, the kombu for joy, black azuki beans for health, salty yellow fish eggs for many descendants, and prawns cooked in their shells for long life. Plus about a hundred other things. She doesn't always go to such lengths. When we lived in Wisconsin, if she wanted to do a full-on New Year's breakfast, she had to drive all the way to a special store in Illinois to get all the ingredients.

But this year, Yūko was invited to have New Year's breakfast with us. Sorry—that's Yūko-*san*. Mom insists that I speak of her with respect. I was setting the table when the doorbell rang. Mom answered it and called me over to introduce me. Yūko-*san* bowed deeply to me, apologized for all the suffering she'd caused, thanked me for understanding, and said she hoped we could become friends in the new year. Then she went into the kitchen to help Mom with her gazillion New Year's dishes. Awk-ward.

I mean, Yūko-san is beautiful and nice and—as Mom has repeatedly pointed out to me—honorable. But to be honest, I'm still working to wrap my head around the idea of her and Dad being in love, of her and Dad being something permanent. I still don't know how she's supposed to fit into my life.

Or how I'm supposed to fit into hers. And I still want Mom to find a life and a love of her own.

Yūko-san and Dad looked so happy together, though, and Mom seemed totally fine with the whole thing, laughing with Yūko-san about Dad's bad habits and idiosyncrasies, and reminiscing about old times. Maybe it's easier if you have history together. Yūko-san was wearing the pearl earrings that Dad gave her, and I thought about what he'd said so long ago about everyone having something powerful and precious inside them—especially Mom. Now I think I understand what he meant.

Jamie, JJ, Christina, and Arturo came to pick me up after breakfast, and off we went to the beach. I've invited the others to meet us here later: Reggie and Thom, Elaine and Jimmy, Janet, Hanh, Caleb, and a couple of others. Hopefully they'll show up.

During winter break, the week after my epic performance in Mrs. Byrd's classroom, Jamie and I met Christina, JJ, and Arturo at Psycho Donuts downtown. They were already sitting at a table when I arrived, holding hands with Jamie.

"So, props for standing up to The Bird."

"Thanks."

"And I liked that poem. 'Elliptical.' About how whites and Asians see Mexicans and Blacks—like we're always 'they.' Like, people think they know about us, but they're really just guessing and making stuff up and judging . . . so . . . yeah . . . that was pretty cool."

"Oh," I said, "yeah. I'm glad you liked the poem. I hoped you would. And I'm sorry about all the things I said."

So that was good. The thing is, I'd thought the poem was actually about uncertainty, about how we can all look back at our lives and wonder what we could have done, thought, and said differently. But the instant I heard Christina's interpretation, I saw that she was right. It made much more sense her way—white (and some Asian) people saying about Blacks and Latinos, "They just can't seem to . . . They should try harder to . . . We all wish they were more . . ." Thinking we're trying to understand, but actually just sitting in judgment.

Duh. How could I have missed it? And here I was, thinking that I was smarter than her, even though Jamie told me she was smart. That I was nice and she was mean. Which, okay, yeah, Christina was no sweetheart. But I saw her through a veil of mistrust and—I'll just say it—racism, and it colored the way I saw everything she did.

Maybe people get tired of trying to be nice to folks who keep saying, "They just can't seem to . . . They should try harder to . . . We all wish they were more . . ." Maybe it feels useless to keep explaining when no one listens. Maybe Christina is like the woman in Sandra Cisneros's poem. The one who makes me uncomfortable but whom I admire. She just is who she is, and she shouldn't have to apologize for it or explain it to anyone. Christina and I are still not a hundred percent comfortable with each other. We still tread on each other's toes every once in a while. But it's getting easier. We're learning to trust and listen to each other enough to dig for the truth together.

The strange thing about this beach is that there is no sea glass. Smooth gray stones and pebbles, yes. Bits of creamy white seashell, sanded and polished until only the ghosts of their ridges and spines remain—yes. But no emerald green, no amber, no startling sapphire blue. Nothing that was tossed, sharp-edged and broken, into a world where it didn't belong, and survived to become a rare and unexpected gift on an endless stretch of sand.

But this beach teems with life in a way that I never saw on the shores of Lake Michigan. Sea stars and sea anemones cling to rocks in the tide pools, which they share with scuttling hermit crabs and darting sculpins. Huge colonies of mussels cover stretches of exposed rock, and limpets and periwinkles cleave to cracks and crags exposed by the receding tide. The hidden ocean kingdom I used to long for is much closer than I'd ever imagined.

So much of what lives here makes it through life by closing itself off from intruders—poke a sea anemone and it tightens like a fist; reach for a hermit crab and it scoots behind a rock and tucks itself into its borrowed shell. Sea stars protect their tender bellies with brightly colored hides as hard and gravelly as asphalt. Sit and wait a few minutes, though, and the anemones bloom green and pink and blue, the crabs venture out, and even the sea stars stir occasionally.

I don't know which I like better—the serene and startling beauty of the sea glass on the sand, or the tenacious survivors I've found here, who reveal their secret, dreamlike lives to anyone who cares enough to wait for them.

"Sana! Hurry *up!*"

I take another look at the surf—the waves are surging around the arch and lapping at the bottom of the cliff on the other side of the channel. Yeah, better get moving. I stand up and jog to catch up to everyone, and we make our way back up the beach together.

A NOTE FROM THE AUTHOR

what in fact I keep choosing
are these words, these whispers, these conversations
from which the truth breaks moist and green.
—Adrienne Rich, "Cartographies of Silence"

When I began writing *It's Not Like It's a Secret*, I had in mind a book about two girls in love that reflected the reality of the high school where I used to teach. That high school is roughly one third Asian/Pacific Islander, one third Latinx, one third white, and pretty LGBTQ+ friendly. My students and I didn't talk about race, ethnicity, and sexuality every day, but those issues were with us in the classroom every day. When I wrote the book, they automatically wove themselves into the narrative.

Please remember, however, that there is no one Asian American story, no one Latinx story, and no one LGBTQ+ story. There is no one love story. No one family story. Many kind and generous people trusted me with their stories and their wisdom, and I hope that I was able to convey the truth of their experiences. But I am still growing and learning. The characters in this book cannot speak for populations. They can only speak for themselves—the same as any real person—and through my imperfect words.

To me, this book is about open secrets: things that everyone knows are in the room with us, but that no one wants to talk about, like race and sexuality; ethnic pride and assimilation; and jealousy and infidelity. We avoid having conversations about these things because they're awkward and emotionally risky. We're afraid of saying the wrong thing and hurting someone, and of being judged or hurt ourselves. But if we want to move forward, if we want to make real connections, we must keep having these awkward conversations and taking these emotional risks. We have to keep opening ourselves to one another.

It's not easy. So much prevents Sana from trusting people enough to reveal her true, secret self. So much prevents her from looking and listening hard enough to recognize the true selves of others. All those open secrets, all those things that no one knows how to talk about cause Sana to make mistake after mistake after painful mistake. But she keeps learning. She keeps trying to stand up and speak out, keeps seeking connection. She never gives up. And neither should we.

xoxo,

Misa

A WORD ABOUT POETRY

I've been a poetry nerd pretty much from birth, and I just couldn't pass up the opportunity to spread the love. Here are six reasons why I think poetry is one of humanity's greatest inventions:

1. Poetry feeds the soul. Sometimes I read something so beautiful—or terrifying, or true, or sad, or glorious—that it makes my heart ache.

2. Poetry is multilayered. You can love poems for the first lightning-strike impressions they leave with you, and you can read them again and again and love them for their complexity and depth. And both ways are right.

3. Poetry is diverse. Because it's so connected to individual experience and emotion, because there are no hard-and-fast rules about form, grammar, and all of that, there's a lot of it out there, by all different kinds of people, *for* all different kinds of people. It can be about a flea, or it can be about the fate of humanity. It can be casual, formal, funny, tragic, epically long, or blink-of-an-eye short. Speaking of short,

4. Poetry is (often) short. I *love* novels, but they take hours to read. They're like five-course gourmet meals. Sometimes you want something light and crispy— or rich and juicy—that you can consume in a few minutes.

5. Poetry lifts the veil. Sometimes I find a poem that expresses something deep inside me that I never knew existed. Or it challenges me to examine, maybe from a new angle or through a new lens, the things I thought I knew.

6. Poetry connects us to each other. Just as it does with the characters in this book, poetry creates bridges between people who might not otherwise understand each other, and between people who already understand each other perfectly. It opens doors. It opens eyes. It opens hearts.

There is a poem out there for every person in the world. There is a poem waiting to make you think, to touch your heart, to show you the heart of another human being. There is a poem out there for you. Go. Find your poem.

xoxo,
Misa

POEMS IN ORDER OF APPEARANCE

A FEW ONLINE RESOURCES

www.poetryfoundation.org

www.writersalmanac.org

www.poetryarchive.org

www.favoritepoem.org

www.poets.org

www.poemhunter.com

www.loc.gov/poetry/180

www.poetryslam.com

www.theliterarylink.com/yapoetry.html

SOURCES

I've listed collections in which the poems appear, but you can find any of them online.

Elizabeth Bishop. "One Art." *The Complete Poems 1926–1979.*
(Farrar, Straus and Giroux, 1983)

Ana Castillo. "I Ask the Impossible." *I Ask the Impossible.*
(Anchor Books, 2001)

Sandra Cisneros. "Loose Woman." *Loose Woman.* (Alfred A.
Knopf, 1994)

Emily Dickinson. "I'm Nobody! Who are you?" *The Poems
of Emily Dickinson,* Ralph W. Franklin ed. (The Belknap
Press of Harvard University Press, 1998). "My Garden—
like the Beach—." *The Poems of Emily Dickinson,* Martha
Dickinson Bianchi, Alfred Leete Hampson, eds. (Little,
Brown, and Co., 1932). "Wild Nights—Wild Nights!"
The Poems of Emily Dickinson, Ralph W. Franklin ed. (The
Belknap Press of Harvard University Press, 1998). Tell
all the Truth but tell it slant." *ibid.* "Her breast is fit for
pearls." *The Complete Poems of Emily Dickinson,* Thomas
Johnson, ed. (Little, Brown, and Co., 1961)

Mayne Ellis. "Scientists Find Universe Awash in Tiny Diamonds." *Cries of the Spirit*, Marilyn Sewell, ed. (Beacon Press, 2000)

Kimiko Hahn. "Wellfleet, Midsummer." *The Narrow Road to the Interior*. (W.W. Norton, 2006)

Kay Ryan. "Still Start." (*Poetry*, May 2013)

Lucy Ives. "Poem." (*PoetryNow*, 2015)

Harryette Mullen. "Elliptical." *Sleeping With the Dictionary*. (University of California Press, 2002)

Mary Oliver. "Wild Geese." *Dream Work*. (The Atlantic Monthly Press, 1986)

Adrienne Rich. "Cartographies of Silence." *The Dream of a Common Language*. (W.W. Norton & Co., 2013)

Izumi Shikibu. "Missing you." Misa Sugiura, trans. *The Ink Dark Moon: Love Poems by Ono no Komachi and Izumi Shikibu*. (Vintage, 1990) Mariko Aratani and Jane Hirshfield, trans.

Mary K. Stillwell. "In the Morning in Morocco." *Maps and Destinations*. (Stephen F. Austin University Press, 2014)

Alice Walker. "When You See Water." *The World Will Follow Joy*. (The New Press, 2013)

ACKNOWLEDGMENTS

They say that writing a novel is a solitary occupation, but as I wrote mine, I was blessed with a supremely talented, dedicated, and loving support crew. Here they are:

My stalwart editor, Jen Klonsky, captained my book expertly and patiently through the process of making it into the best version of itself. Her unflagging enthusiasm kept my spirits up during my neurotic author moments, and when the waters got rough, she was right there at my side. These exclamation marks are for her: !!!!!!

Leigh Feldman, agent par excellence, literally flew in and offered to champion this book for me, and then did exactly that like a boss. Leigh is forthright, unafraid, and utterly amazing, and I couldn't ask for a better advocate and advisor. Working with her has been a dream come true.

Leigh's intrepid assistant, Ilana Masad, plucked me out of the slush, keeps me company on Twitter, and makes me feel like a rock star.

Catherine Wallace provided additional editorial support, and Christina MacDonald weaned me from my tendency to over-hyphenate, among other copyediting feats. I owe my beautiful cover to designers Sarah Creech and Michelle

Taormina, and to artist Grace Lee. Elizabeth Ward, Sabrina Abballe, Molly Motch, and Stephanie Hoover gave this book its final push into the wide world.

Sandra Feder, Prudence Breitrose, Louise Henricksen, Viji Chary, and Alicia Grunow gave me crucial input on plot ideas, and asked all the right questions to help me develop Sana's character. Andrea Ellickson, Vicky Guyon, Ashley Walker, and Denise Stanford pushed for more information about Sana's childhood relationship with her father, which led me to the myth at the center of this book.

Treasured friends and gifted educators Kim Vinh and Kristin Kapasi generously opened up their classrooms and recruited some amazing students to answer my questions, review a couple of key scenes, and generally keep me honest. Deepest gratitude to Benicia Chang, Denisse Velasquez, Amelia Wheaton, Abby Wheaton, Eddie Barrera, Sabrina Villanueva Avalos, Samantha Ayala, and Lily Moncayo.

A few wise and witty young women from Mountain View High School's Queer Straight Alliance gave up their lunch periods to sit with me and tell me about their lives and their perspectives on being lesbian teenagers in Silicon Valley.

Meredith Dodd, Chau Ho, Carrie Holmberg, and Roseann Rasul, my beloved and brilliant friends, took time out of their very busy lives to read and give me feedback on the manuscript before I sent it out to strangers.

My brother-from-another, Ophny Escalante, and my kid-mom BFF, Dina Barrios, were my Spanish language gurus.

Math teacher extraordinaire Jeff Muralt designed the trigonometry problems. My niece Ellie Alberg fine-tuned my texting grammar and a few key plot details. Kumiko Morimoto and Kazuko Eames helped me dial in Sana's parents' Kansai dialect. Jennifer Torres and Claudia Guadalupe Martinez offered me gracious, honest feedback about Jamie and her friends; I can't imagine this book in the world without their work. Any mistakes or culturally insensitive passages that remain are mine and mine alone.

The aforementioned reader friends were joined on the sidelines by my Princeton dad, legendary real estate investor Larry Owen (I love you more); and my Princeton uncle, the ever-gracious Michael Hudnall, and his lovely wife, Mamm.

My mother taught me how to chop vegetables and peel apples, and she poured herself into raising a stubborn American daughter; my father followed a dream to the United States, worked tirelessly to achieve it, and modeled the importance of hard work and a principled life. I owe them everything.

My brother and sister have been enthusiastic cheerleaders of my writing, but more important, they were my companions in the trenches when we were Asian kids growing up in an Anglo suburb and my role models as they each pursued atypical career paths.

My two sons endured missed exits, late pickups, and burned meals on days when the book hijacked my brain. They would have preferred stories about animals, or about gun-toting steampunk renegades, but they let me write this one.

Thank you, boys. I love you.

And Tad, my sounding board, proofreader, and partner; picker-upper of my messes and shutter of my half-open drawers; finder and folder of lost loads of laundry; love of my life, thank you most of all.